Nashville Grizzlies
Book 1

# CARLY MARIE

Editing Services: Jennifer Smith

Cover: Tall Story Designs

Copyright © 2022 by Carly Marie

All rights reserved.

This book or any portion thereof may not be reproduced or used in any manner whatsoever without the express written permission of the author except for the use of brief quotations in a book review.

This is a work of fiction. Names, characters, businesses, places, events, locales, and incidents are either the products of the author's imagination or used in a fictitious manner. Any resemblance to actual persons, living or dead, or actual events is purely coincidental.

CONTENTS

| | |
|---|---|
| Chapter 1 | 1 |
| Chapter 2 | 13 |
| Chapter 3 | 27 |
| Chapter 4 | 41 |
| Chapter 5 | 51 |
| Chapter 6 | 65 |
| Chapter 7 | 77 |
| Chapter 8 | 89 |
| Chapter 9 | 101 |
| Chapter 10 | 115 |
| Chapter 11 | 129 |
| Chapter 12 | 143 |
| Chapter 13 | 155 |
| Chapter 14 | 165 |
| Chapter 15 | 175 |
| Chapter 16 | 187 |
| Chapter 17 | 199 |
| Chapter 18 | 211 |
| Chapter 19 | 223 |
| Chapter 20 | 235 |
| Chapter 21 | 249 |
| Chapter 22 | 261 |
| Chapter 23 | 275 |
| Chapter 24 | 285 |
| Chapter 25 | 299 |
| Chapter 26 | 313 |
| Chapter 27 | 325 |
| Chapter 28 | 339 |
| Chapter 29 | 355 |
| Chapter 30 | 367 |
| Chapter 31 | 381 |
| Chapter 32 | 393 |

| Chapter 33 | 407 |
| Epilogue | 421 |
| *A Note From Carly* | 431 |
| *About the Author* | 433 |

# CHAPTER 1

## BRAX

"I'M SORRY, did you say Nashville?"

"You got your wish. You've been traded. I wouldn't be picky if I were you."

*Fuck you, asshole.* My brain at least had the common sense to not say that, but it was difficult not to. Vincent Drysdale was a ruthless general manager and all-around douchebag. He swore there was only one hockey team that mattered in the NHL and that was Boston.

Boston was a great team, but it wasn't the right fit for me or my style of play. I was stuck as second best on a team of old hats who had been groomed specifically for his club and the way he wanted to see hockey played. I hadn't been the only player to ask for a trade in the last handful of years, and the team was gaining quite a reputation around the league.

My problems had started well before I'd asked for the trade, but Drysdale had made my life as miserable as he could since then.

"Not being picky, sir." Not being picky at all. Quite the opposite actually. I wanted to make sure I'd heard him correctly before my heart got ahead of me. Not that he would understand my excitement at being traded to Nashville. Knowing the old goat like I did, he wouldn't be able to imagine why anyone would be excited to go to Nashville.

A dry scoff sounded in my ear. "They agreed to send us Castile for you. Expect a call from them shortly with flight details. Start packing."

"Thank you." Those two words had never been so hard to say to a person in all my life. I did appreciate the trade, though, and was excited to finally be leaving Boston after two stagnant years stuck on a third or fourth line that never jived while the first and second lines were filled with players who had been in Boston for years. There were no indications of things changing.

I wasn't bitter about the lines as much as I had been about the style of play. As the years progressed, Boston had become known for dirty hits and dirtier plays. After two years on a team that appeared happy with the way things were, I started worrying about my future options. I'd requested the trade before the end of the previous season, but until that day, there hadn't been any interest in it. I'd have welcomed the trade to Nashville even if they were the worst team in the league.

Thankfully, Nashville wasn't the worst team. Far from it. The last four seasons had seen a major turnaround in the Grizzlies. After a coaching and front office shake-up, the Grizzlies had gone from one of the worst teams in the league to a powerhouse that had continued to improve year after year. They'd even made it to the Stanley Cup playoffs the season before.

Not only were they an amazing team, they had also become a magnet for queer players.

Their current alternate captain, Seth Johnson, had come out as gay before his draft day, becoming the first openly gay player in the NHL. Seth had shaken the hockey world at the end of the season when he had kissed the breath out of Mazdon Grabowski, one of their star defensemen. The team had been nothing but supportive in every single press conference or interview since.

Those things were enough to make me know I didn't need to fear coming out to my teammates but it was the captain, Trevor Cane, that had my heart thundering just a little harder than it should have and my dick thickening at the thought of being near him day after day. Playing against him six times in the last two seasons had kept my dick struggling to behave and my mind way too focused on the way his tiny yet strong frame so effortlessly covered the length of the ice and thought little of colliding with someone against the boards when need be.

Drysdale's scoff reminded me that I was still on the phone, and I forced myself to clear my throat. "I'll look forward to the call. It has been a pleasure to play for Boston. Thank you for the opportunity."

He grunted out a reply that I was going to take as a pleasantry, or as close as Vincent Drysdale would come to one, and the phone went dead.

My thoughts swirled through my head and giddy butterflies danced in my stomach that I hadn't felt since I was thirteen years old. Being a second-round draft pick to Chicago at eighteen hadn't made me feel like this, and being traded to Boston's farm team two years later had been more frustrating than exciting. The call-up to Boston had been exciting, but not in the same way thinking about Trevor was. It was turning my insides to goo.

I really needed to call my dad to tell him the news, but I wanted to bask in the moment for just a minute longer. He was way too perceptive and I knew he'd be able to tell something was different about me if I called him when my dick was fully erect and my thoughts were focused way more on Trevor Cane than the trade to Nashville.

There was no reason to go to afternoon skate now that I wasn't officially a member of Boston's team, but I'd been dressed to head out the door when Vincent's call had come in. My favorite sweatpants had been worn so many times that they were stretched in the ass and thighs, the extra room doing nothing to prevent a noticeable tenting in the front.

"Brax! It's time to go!" My roommate's voice broke through my thoughts and reminded me that I was still lying on my bed and Easton had no idea I'd just been traded.

I forced myself to get up and adjust my dick. It wasn't perfect but hopefully the dark blue would hide enough that my bulky sweatshirt would be able to keep the situation in my pants unnoticeable. "Not me."

Easton stopped at my bedroom door. "What? Are you okay? What happened?"

A slow grin spread on my face as the news really began to sink in. "Finally got traded."

Easton's eyes got big as saucers. "Seriously? For real?"

All I could do was nod. Easton's friendship was going to be the one thing I missed about Boston. We'd both been new to the team at the same time. He'd been traded from the West Coast, a few years older than me with more miles under his skates. The two of us had clicked immediately, sharing many of the same interests and both general homebodies. When he'd offered his extra room, I'd jumped on the opportunity and we'd been sharing his condo ever since.

As my best friend, he'd been the first person I'd told that I'd requested the trade. We'd also spent many nights commiserating over the lack of progress and trying to figure out when it would be my time.

"Holy shit! Dude, where are you going?"

I lifted a shoulder, trying not to let on just how excited I was, though I could feel a telltale smile breaking on my face as I answered. "Nashville."

"Hell yes! It's like your every dream come true." He rushed me, wrapping his arms around me and enveloping me in a bear hug. "Gah, I can't wait to visit you. And that's closer to your dad and Leo, right?"

"They're in North Carolina, so it's only a few hours' drive."

Easton's watch beeped and he cursed. "Fuck. If I don't get out of here now, I'm going to be late. Will you be here when I get back?"

"Don't have a clue. Waiting for a call from Nashville to tell me the game plan."

"Wonder who we're getting?" My phone ringing with a 615 number interrupted him. "Shit, take that. Go. Good luck. If you're gone by the time I get back, I'm gonna miss you, Brax." He gave me another hug then ran for the door, waving over his shoulder at me.

I turned my focus to the phone ringing in my hand. "Hello?"

"B-Braxlyn? Brax? Um, Braxlyn Cernak?"

The voice on the other end of the line held unmistakable nerves that I instantly wanted to calm. Taking a breath, I lowered my voice to the same tone I used with nervous subs at the club Easton and I went to on nights we were free and had the energy. Unfortunately, those nights were few and far between during the season. "Brax, yes."

He let out an uncomfortable chuckle, though it held a bit less nervousness than when I'd first answered. "Oh, hi. I'm Blaise Emory, Assistant Director of Hockey Operations with the Nashville Grizzlies."

I returned to my bed and got comfortable. "Good to hear from you, Blaise."

"Coach Cunningham asked me to call you. He's on a plane and won't be back until later tonight." He paused to gather his thoughts and I could hear something bouncing, likely a pen against his desk. "He asked me to schedule you a flight for this evening. He'd like you here by tomorrow morning. I-I know it's last minute, but there's a skate tomorrow midmorning and he thinks that it would be good if you were there. It will give you two full practices before the next game."

I appreciated Blaise's worry about my schedule but I was a hockey player, and we were six weeks into a season that would span nearly six months. I was used to not having a predictable, set schedule. "Great. I like that plan," I said, hoping to calm his worries. "Have you managed to get flight details yet?"

Blaise let out a sigh that was clearly relieved, his words coming more easily from there. "I do have a flight. It's late; it leaves at nine. I tried to make sure you had enough time to get stuff organized there, but not so much that you were going to be dragging ass tomorrow. Transfers are never easy but there's no reason to make them more miserable than they absolutely have to be."

His thoughtfulness made me smile and I knew then that Nashville was going to be the right place for me. "Thank you." Unlike the *thank you* I'd said to Vincent ten minutes earlier that had been forced and awkward, the one given to Blaise was genuine and flowed easily. "I really appreciate your thinking about timing. Nine is good."

That gave me plenty of time to pack up enough that I wouldn't risk leaving important things behind, and I'd get to see Easton again before I left. With Nashville being an hour behind us, it would give me a little more time to sleep the next morning, given that I *could* sleep.

"Awesome. We're excited to see you. I'm going to send you the details in an email now. They're also going to your agent too. Please let me know if you have any questions. This is my cell number and you're welcome to call me at any time. I know the entire team is looking forward to meeting you tomorrow."

The conversation with Blaise had reality smacking into me, my erection from a few minutes earlier totally forgotten. I was about to pack up and head to a brand-new team in a new state, to effectively start over again. I needed to pack and call my dad. He and Leo would be able to calm the case of jitters I'd suddenly come down with.

I knew better than to continue to dwell on the move without talking to my dad and forced myself to stand up to find a suitcase as I tapped on his number.

"Hey, kiddo!" His voice was warm and inviting, unlike the ruthless defenseman he had been when he'd played hockey as I was growing up.

My pounding heart slowed slightly. "Hey, Dad."

"Shouldn't you be at practice right now? Is everything okay?"

Not only was he my dad, he was also my closest confidant when it came to life. "Well, if I were still a Bulldog, I would be."

Dad sounded more relieved than surprised. "Did Drysdale finally get off his ass and find you a deserving team?"

"He did. Well, at least he found me a team that had something or someone that he wanted. I'm heading to Nashville tonight."

"A Grizzly now? That suits you. That team is amazing. I have mad respect for Cunningham and Bouchard. Hell,

Huber is a bit of an airhead at times but he's a good man too. Helluva lot better than Drysdale and his crew of minions."

"Yeah. I've heard nothing but good about the entire team." *Captain included.*

Dad went silent for a moment. It was late enough in the morning that I could see him standing in the kitchen with Leo as they worked on lunch. I couldn't remember a time that Leo hadn't lived with us. There were pictures of my mom, dad, and me as a baby and toddler that hadn't included Leo, but by the time I was three or four, he had become a constant in our photos. I'd introduced him as my uncle for years.

I'd been glad Leo was there when my mom died of breast cancer when I was fifteen. At sixteen, I'd finally had my aha moment and told the two to cut the shit and stop pretending they weren't together.

The only thing surprising about the entire revelation was that I hadn't put it together sooner. Since then, they hadn't been shy with their affections toward one another and I was happy for them.

"They are good people. Their style fits you much better than Boston's. When do you leave?"

I folded a shirt and placed it in my bag. "Nine tonight. I'll head to the airport around seven or so."

Dad hummed and Leo sounded over the line. "Where are you staying?"

"Waiting for the email from the team's assistant now." My phone pinged, alerting me to a notification that could very well be the email I was waiting for.

"Wait, that kid that lived here with us for a few years, Trevor, doesn't he play for the Grizzlies now?" Leo asked. He tried so hard to keep up with the hockey world but was woefully clueless about most of it. He knew a few names but was more likely to remember wives, girlfriends, and kids than anything to do with the teams or who played where.

The only reason he likely knew Trevor Cane played for the Grizzlies was because he knew him a bit. I mostly remembered Trevor staying to himself if it wasn't dinner or team related, but those times had given me plenty of chances to realize I was very not straight.

I'd come out as gay to my parents shortly after Trevor left, convinced my heart was broken and would never be whole again.

Dad's warm chuckle made me smile as I emptied my underwear drawer into the suitcase. "He's the captain now. Actually, I just talked to him a few weeks ago. We still keep in touch. I'll give him a call, see if you can stay with him. It would be nice to not be alone in a brand-new city. He lives a few miles from the arena near a few other players."

"What?" I'd been heading to my sock drawer when he'd said it but my feet were now rooted to the floor. "No! No, don't do that. I'm sure the hotel the team has will be fine until I figure out where I want to stay."

Dad and Leo both cackled—their twin noises couldn't even be considered laughter. "Wow," Dad said as he pulled himself together but was still chuckling lightly. "It's been ten or more years since he lived here. You can't tell me you're still crushing on him, Brax?"

Leo took the chance to add his two cents in. "They say you'll always have a place for your first love."

His tone had gotten too sappy as he spoke and I groaned. "Eww, you guys are gross. Go finish your lunch."

I hadn't had enough time to talk about my nerves but I knew it was pointless trying to talk to them once they got like that. Instead of a long goodbye, I ended the call by telling my dad that he didn't need to call Trevor.

I should have known he wasn't going to listen to me.

## CHAPTER 2

TREVOR

"Cane!" Coach Cunningham's voice stopped me before I could make it to my car. We'd traveled from Seattle that morning after the first long road trip of the season and had just made it back to the arena where we could finally leave. I really wanted to get to my car and get home to sleep but Coach had the power to prevent that.

Seth and his boyfriend, Maz, were parked next to me, so we'd been walking with each other. Seth held out his hand. "Give me your bag. I'll take it to your car."

"Johnson, you too."

Maz laughed. "Give me the bags and I'll get them to the cars." He held out his open hand for my bag. He and Seth had been sharing luggage all season; it didn't make sense to pack two bags when they shared a room and traveled together. I handed my bag over and Seth leaned in to give Maz a kiss. "Sorry you've got to wait on me."

His boyfriend just gave an easy shrug. "I'm always waiting on you. It's nothing new. But go see what Coach wants so that we can get home."

"Yick, you two are sickeningly in love."

Seth grinned. "When are you going to let me find you someone? I bet I could find the perfect man for you."

*I bet he couldn't.* Before I could say that, Coach's voice called out again. "Is Wojtek still here?"

Seth rolled his eyes but was smiling as he responded. "He hightailed it home to his wife, Coach. She's nine months pregnant and he's been a nervous wreck all trip."

Cunningham shook his head. "Right. I forgot about that. It will just be a few minutes. Follow me for a moment."

Calling the captain and both alternate captains into an unexpected meeting only meant one thing. "Who got traded? It's so early in the season!" Trades usually happened over the summer, before training camp. Not at the very beginning of the season.

"And who'd we get?" Seth followed up with his question before we'd made it down the hallway of the arena.

"You two are like bloodhounds."

Seth crossed his arms, managing to look a lot more intimidating than I ever did without pads on. At five four, I had a tendency to look more like some of the players' kids than an NHL player. "Coach, come on. Don't beat around the bush here. We're not dumb."

Cunningham unlocked his office door and tripped over a brightly colored ball, then began to curse. "Fucking. Ouch. Dammit, I swear, this place is like a nursery school!" He shot me a look that was meant to be stern but failed miserably.

"You told me that they were okay." We'd played lacrosse in the hallway after practice before we left. A ball must have rolled into Cunningham's office at some point.

He narrowed his eyes at me. "*Outside*. They were fine outside, not in my office."

Seth covered his laugh behind a cough, then tried to get the conversation back on track. "You wanted to see us?"

"Oh right. Yeah. Have a seat, guys."

Once we were all seated, the mood in the room sobered and we were all business. "Seriously, who's going and who's coming?" Seth asked when Cunningham didn't speak immediately.

"Castile's going to Boston. It's been in the works for a long time, but the trade had gotten held up in red tape."

I groaned. Not just because I really liked Antonio Castile, but because that likely meant we were getting someone from Boston. Not only were they a brutal team to play against but I couldn't think of many people on the team that I'd want to play with. We'd worked so hard to turn this team around, but one bad trade could do us in.

Seth elbowed me, reminding me to hear Coach out but keeping his words cautious. "Who'd we get?"

Even Seth held his breath when Coach opened his mouth. "Braxlyn Cernak."

"*Brax*?" The way my jaw dropped open and my voice rose a few octaves, it was impossible for me to hide my shock.

Coach narrowed his eyes. "Is that a problem?"

Shaking my head, I tried to get my thoughts in order. "I know it's a small world, but I lived with Tom Cernak my first two years with the Mustangs."

Coach visibly relaxed. "Well, that's better than what I'd conjured from your reaction."

"Cernak stayed in Carolina after he retired. He's got family there. I think his wife was from there too. I still keep in touch with him." I didn't mention Leo, despite knowing the two were still together. They'd kept their relationship under the radar while Tom was playing. The three had never come out and said that they were together, but it hadn't been hard to see that when I lived with them. When LeAnn died, Leo hadn't left. They'd come out to a few people over the years, but their relationship still wasn't front-page news.

If I had to guess, it was probably because they didn't want to detract from Brax or bring extra scrutiny to him. They were happy together and didn't need the world to know they were anything more than good friends.

"Oh right! I forgot about that. Guess we can expect to see Tom around here, being so close and having his boys on the same team."

I hoped the flush I felt was mostly made up. "He's definitely close to Brax, so it wouldn't shock me." I intentionally ignored the plural, focusing my statement on Tom's *real* son. "Though I guess I should expect a call from him soon."

On cue, my phone rang and I reached for it. "Speak of the devil."

Cunningham waved us off. "Get out of here, guys. Just be ready for the shake-up tomorrow."

"Thanks," we said in unison and stood to leave the office.

I made it as far as the doorway before swiping up to answer Tom's call. "Hello?"

Seth slowed to wait for me, getting a front-row seat to the shock Tom leveled me with. The conversation started off innocently enough, catching up, telling me he'd watched the games, then telling me that Brax had been traded to the Grizzlies.

"Yeah. We just got out of a meeting with Irvin Cunningham. He'll officially be a Grizzly by practice tomorrow."

I heard Tom hum and began to prepare myself for whatever it was he was going to say next. I'd expected him to tell me that I needed to look after him, watch out for him, and make sure he was doing all right. What came out of his mouth was far from expected. "Would you mind if he stayed with you until he figures out the area?"

"With me?"

Seth and I had been walking slowly toward the door. He hadn't been openly eavesdropping on the conversation until my voice rose in shock just before we reached the doors to the garage.

The sigh I heard was definitely Leo's and his voice, while farther away, was still near enough that I knew he had heard our conversation. "Thomas Julius Cernak! I know Braxlyn told you not to call Trevor. The boy does not need you butting into his life like that!"

"But it makes no sense for Brax to be in a hotel all alone when Trevor lives right there!"

"What if Trevor has a boyfriend or girlfriend? What if he's happy living alone? What if he doesn't want a houseguest for an indeterminate length of time? Just because you have less than zero problems opening the house to people doesn't mean that Trevor will feel the same."

The two were funny and I found myself smiling. I also knew that, no matter my list of reservations about having Brax in my house, I was going to agree. "Guys, guys, guys!" Raising my voice was the best shot I had at getting their attention when they got into it like this. The fact that both their voices had gotten more distant told me that Tom likely wasn't holding the phone to his ear anymore.

I looked up at Seth. "This is one of those times I miss landline phones, when you could bang it on a counter and get someone's attention."

Seth grinned. "You, Trev, are clearly not from a massive family." He put his fingers in his mouth and let out a piercing whistle that made me wince but served to get Tom's attention.

"Sorry, Trev. When'd ya learn to whistle like that?"

"I didn't. That was Seth. He's been standing next to me. Anyway, now that I have your attention again, fine, he can stay with me for a bit. At least until he has time to go out and find a place."

"Awesome! Thanks, Trev. We'll see you before long, I'm sure."

"Bye, guys."

When the line went dead, I sank against the wall by the door, the reality of the situation fully sinking in. Seth crowded my space. "Hey, what's up? You look like you're going to be sick."

"Brax is moving in with me tonight?" I ran my hands down my face as my thoughts started to collide in my brain, everything I needed to do quickly overwhelming me. "I need to figure out when he's going to be here so I can get him from the airport, get the spare room ready, and clean my house."

It wasn't like my house was a mess, but it was that last part that had me wanting to puke. My house was clean, but I also wasn't used to having people over, so I wasn't always as careful as I should be. I thought about the fun divided plates and plastic cups in my dishwasher and cabinet. I'd been coloring the night before heading on the road trip. Had I cleaned up my crayons and coloring books? Things I hid from almost everyone in the world I left out at home because my house was my safe space.

Seth gripped my shoulders and gave me a little shake. "Hey, I need you to focus on me, Trev. You're panicking. One thing at a time. Let's figure out when he's going to get here."

Seth pulled out his phone and pressed a button. "Hey, can you bring Huck in?"

There was a brief pause in which I stared dumbly at Seth. "Just inside the door. Hold on." Seth looked over at me. "Where's Huck? Still in your backpack?"

I nodded, too surprised, possibly mortified, to find a word. I should have known that Seth would have picked up on

Huck being more than just my team bear. Huck had been my constant companion since I'd bought the original twenty-three bears four years earlier, when Coach had first announced me as captain.

Then I remembered what else was in my bag. "Wait! Just, uh, no. Don't worry about it. I'm fine."

Seth gave me a look like I was nuts, not that I didn't feel just a little insane at the moment. "Huck makes you feel better. Let Mazdon bring him in."

I shook my head again, this time fear causing my voice to fail me. Any zipper he opened, Maz would find out more about me than he should. It could be my cartoon pajamas, my blanket, my pacifier, or my sippy cup that I took when we traveled. With one phone call, I was finding my carefully constructed bubble crumbling.

"Hold on, Mazdon." Seth pressed a button and dropped his voice to a whisper. "Do you really think that he's going to find anything that we haven't figured out already?"

"Seth, please. Just…" My words trailed off and my face heated with unmistakable embarrassment. I'd gone over ten years with no one finding out more than I wanted them to, and now I didn't know what to say or do. I wanted Huck, but I couldn't ask for him. I needed to get home to clean up, and I really needed a nap. What I needed most of all was space to melt down. Maybe I could call my friend Derek and freak out to him. He'd get it.

"Change of plans. I'll be out in a minute. Love ya." He clicked off the phone and crouched down to stare at me. "Trev, listen to me. Whatever's in your bag isn't going to freak me out. I'm a gay man. My dad owns a BDSM club. Do you really think that there is *anything* you could say or do, shy of committing a crime, that would surprise me?"

My hand rose to my mouth, an instinctive move when I got overwhelmed, but Seth caught it first. "Ick, not here. You haven't washed your hands since the plane. Come on, you need to wash your hands first, then I'll take you home and help you clean up. Mazdon will figure out flight times and such. He can help too."

"No!" My yelp was louder than the space warranted and I froze as I waited for someone to come into the hallway to see why I was freaking out.

Seth sighed and shook his head at me. "Trevor, this is not the place to have this conversation. Come on. Hands first, then home." He gripped my elbow and guided me toward the bathroom down the hall and waited while I washed my hands. "Where are your keys?"

I patted down my pockets. "Wait, I gave them to Maz when he took my bags."

"Perfect. I'll need to stop at some point today to get Brax a bear, but I can pick your brain on what to get him after you tell me what's up."

Seth had turned into a dog with a bone and wasn't going to let it go. As he talked with Maz for a minute, I shot a text to the only person I thought might understand.

**Me**: *I'm going to have to out myself to Seth.*

The text came back in seconds.

**Derek**: *Seth's good people. Daddy works with his brother. He's safe, his entire family is. You'll be fine. But I'm going to need to know deets soon.*

I'd forgotten for a moment that Derek's Daddy—and husband—worked with Seth's oldest brother. The reassurance and reminder helped to relax me in time for me to see Seth heading toward me and my Denali, my key fob in his hand. "Okay, Mazdon's going to follow us to your place. He's already on the phone with Blaise to get the details of Brax's arrival. In. You can melt down on the way."

My climb into the car was always comical and I had to rely on the running board, but I hauled enough stuff that I needed the space the large vehicle allowed. Seth's grunts and muttered curses as he tried to fold himself into my seat and then adjust it so that his long legs could fit behind the wheel said it was more of a challenge for him than it was for me.

He brushed a few wayward strands of hair from his face and sighed. "Next time, we take my car."

Seth's smile and dramatic sigh took some of my anxiety away, at least until he dropped my backpack on my lap. "Find Huck. He'll help."

I had my bag halfway unzipped before my brain caught up to me. Seth had taken everything I'd ever shown him with far too much ease. Nothing surprised him. He'd known for years that my thumb would gravitate toward my mouth if I got too anxious or tired. He didn't know that it was because my pacifier wasn't readily available, but it had never bothered him. If we were in a place that was totally private, he wouldn't say a thing. If we were somewhere people would see, he'd grab my hand or whisper to put my hand in my pocket. Or, like he had in the hallway, tell me to go wash my hands first.

The way he'd rolled his eyes at me when I told him that Maz shouldn't open my bag was too knowing. Too much was changing in my world. I really needed time to decompress in my playroom, but that wasn't in the cards for today, possibly not for the foreseeable future.

With private time out of the question, I gripped Huck and angled my body toward Seth, asking what I had never wanted to broach with anyone, especially a teammate. "How much do you know?"

He navigated out of the garage, looked in the mirror to see that Maz was behind us, and waited until we were on the road before he glanced over at me. "Do you want me to answer that honestly? Just rip the bandage off? Or do you want me to dance around it until you finally decide to tell me?"

On ice and with the team, I was a leader. I was confident and take-charge. I led by example and had found ways to still bring my little side out in safe ways. The silly games we played and our bears had become synonymous with the Grizzlies. It gave the team a way to bond and have fun together, but it gave my inner little a sense of peace when it wasn't safe to actually *be* little. No one knew, or at least I hadn't thought anyone had. I got the impression that had changed at some point and all I could do was wonder how many others knew.

Faced with the question that Seth had posed, my submissive side had no idea how to answer. I needed someone to make that decision and Seth seemed to pick up on it.

"My dad owns DASH. My entire family is kinky. If you think your being a little is going to surprise me, you're wrong. Littles are nearly vanilla compared to some of the things my family is involved in."

My mouth hung open. He'd just confirmed my worst fear, yet had made it sound so commonplace that I was struggling to be upset.

"When you aren't so overwhelmed, I'll tell you about me." He winked and I didn't know if I should be excited or nervous, but I knew that some of my fears had begun to fade when Seth just told me that he knew and was perfectly accepting of it.

The anxieties returned when he finally asked the question I'd been expecting but hoping to avoid. "What has you so freaked out about Brax staying at your place?"

I had to remind myself that Seth was safe to talk to. Hiding was ingrained in me and it was going to take my brain longer than a few seconds to accept this change. I squeezed Huck and let out a long sigh. "Because, while I try to keep my stuff in my room, there are things all over the house."

Understanding showed on Seth's face and a smile grew. "Oh, I get it. Mazdon and I will get you and your house as good as possible. We've got your back."

My anxiety decreased again, though not because they were going to help me. My anxiety had only decreased because I got distracted by the fact that the entire world called Seth's boyfriend Maz, but Seth always called him Mazdon and it was cute. At least the distraction helped keep my mind off of why Seth and Maz were taking me to my house.

## CHAPTER 3

### BRAX

"You did what? Dad!" I knew Leo was nearby, probably right next to my dad, so I pleaded to him. "Leo! Come on. Seriously?"

Leo chuckled. "I'm sorry, kiddo. He did it while I was getting a shower. I have thoroughly scolded him, but what's done is done. For what it's worth, Trevor didn't seem that upset. Surprised but not against it."

I flopped back on my bed, mortified that my dad had called Trevor to ask for me to have a place to stay. My flight was in five hours, Easton was due home at any minute, and I was still packing. Until my dad had decided to be helpful, I had been more excited than nervous about the move.

The front door opening drew my attention and a sigh from me. "Easton's home. Gotta go."

"It will be fine, kiddo. Let us know when you get into Nashville. Love you."

"Love you too." I might have groaned the words, but it couldn't be helped.

Easton found me a few seconds later, still flat on my bed but with a pillow over my head. "Looks like things are going well here."

I growled into the pillow and felt the bed dip.

The pillow was pulled from my face and Easton's face was way too close to mine as he spoke. "Doms do not pout."

"They do when their parents get involved in their lives."

Easton flopped down beside me. "Tell me, what did Tom do this time?"

I angled my head backward so I could see Easton, though from this position he was upside down. "He called Trevor Cane and asked him if I could stay at his place until I got my feet under me."

"Seriously?" Easton got too much pleasure out of my admission and he was grinning broadly. "Your dad called Trevor?" He had the decency to bite his cheek to try not to laugh, but I could see the amusement dancing in his eyes.

"Shut up. Do not say it!"

"This is perfect!"

I flung my pillow at his stomach and part of me hoped that they'd done core workouts at practice. When he only laughed, I knew the pillow hadn't done anything but amuse him more. "This is not perfect. First off, the man has never been linked to anyone. Ever. Ten years, and he's been single! He came out as bisexual in solidarity with Seth and Maz last season and he still hasn't dated. What makes you think that he's going to change his mind for me? Hell, I'm probably not on his radar. I was—" I did some quick math, trying to remember just how old I was when Trevor had lived with us. "Twelve or thirteen when he moved out. You know a twenty-year-old who is just taking off in the NHL isn't going to even notice a twelve-year-old kid is in the house. Hell, I don't know that he remembers me."

Easton blew out a raspberry that made him sound like an exasperated sub, not the leather-clad Dom I knew he was when he had the chance. "But *you* noticed him. And he's stuck with you all these years."

"Stop talking, Easton."

"Hell no, you need to hear me out." He flipped onto his stomach and hovered over me, close enough that our noses nearly touched and my eyes started to cross when I tried to focus on him. "It's like fate stepping in."

I pushed his head back as I shook mine. "No, it's my well-intentioned dad overstepping. Besides, I'm not looking for a boyfriend."

"You're looking for a boy. Yada yada yada. I know, I know, I know. Gah, how many times do I have to hear that?"

"As many as it takes for it to sink into your thick skull."

Easton collapsed beside me, our cheeks nearly touching, and gave a dramatic huff. "I did some research on our break this afternoon. There's a gay kink club in Nashville. Everything I've read says they take discretion seriously. There's an extensive confidentiality clause and vetting process before you can be accepted as a member, but they have intro nights that are easier to access. I dug a little deeper and found something interesting."

The last sentence had been delivered with more excitement than caution, drawing my full attention to what he was going to say. I rolled so I could look at him without seeing double. "Go on."

He flipped around so he was facing me. "It's built a name for itself on its population of boys. Well, littles specifically, but boys too. People all over Kentucky, Tennessee, Alabama, and the Carolinas who are in the lifestyle know about it."

"Littles?" I knew about littles but I didn't know any myself. In all my trips to the kink club here in Boston, I'd never come across one. Hell, I hadn't come across a boy who would take me seriously. I wasn't a hairy, muscled-up Dom who wore leather and boots. I was a lean, tall guy who wore comfortable jeans, button-downs, and tennis shoes. I was more often than not mistaken for a sub than a Daddy, despite my badge clearly spelling out my status. I couldn't count on one hand the number of times I'd had someone tell me I'd grabbed the wrong badge.

If a boy couldn't believe I was a Daddy and didn't take a younger Daddy seriously, I couldn't imagine a little wanting anything to do with someone who was likely younger than them.

Easton shrugged. "Yeah. Don't know much about them, but the pictures are certainly cute. I could see you with a little. You're such a teddy bear."

Regardless of how true it was, I was beginning to think there wasn't a boy in the world looking for a teddy bear Daddy who would rather spoil their boy than punish them. It felt like every time I went to a club, the only boys who noticed me were brats who wanted to be spanked. I spent months of my life on blades a third of an inch thick, careening down the ice at speeds approaching twenty miles per hour, chasing pucks and slamming into other men, and sometimes sacrificing my body in order to stop a puck sailing toward the goal at eighty-plus miles per hour.

As a hockey player, I worked hard and played harder. When I had the chance to relax, the last thing I wanted to do was punish a bratty sub whose goal was a spanking or paddling. I wanted quiet nights making dinner for my boy, helping him sort out problems at work, and being his rock. That would be the closest thing to perfection I could have.

At least talking about boys and littles had steered Easton away from trying to hook me up with Trevor Cane and I was willing to indulge him to keep the conversation away from Trevor.

"I like sweet boys, but you've seen how they don't take me seriously."

"So maybe you need a little. Look how cute this one is." He flipped his phone around to show me a picture of a boy in a thick diaper and a T-shirt with little lions on it. He was holding a small lion in one hand and a chunky building block in the other. A pacifier was clipped to his shirt by a ribbon and I was pretty sure the thing out of focus beside him was a bottle.

I was still studying the picture when Easton started talking again. "Isn't he cute? I could totally see you falling for someone like that!"

"East, dude, can I focus on the move more than finding a boyfriend, or a boy, or a little? One thing at a time."

Easton stuck his tongue out at me. "Are you packed up?"

I shrugged. "As much as I can be. I'd just gotten my car shipment squared away when my dad called. I can live without everything else until we have a break and I can come back and clean out my room. Unless you're planning on getting another roommate?"

"No more roommates. I love you, I'm going to miss you, but you've been the only roommate I've been able to stand for more than two weeks."

"That's because you're a pain in the ass and can't clean up after yourself. I just happen to like cleaning. It's relaxing. You've called your cleaning service, right? This place will be a disaster within the week without it."

Easton stood and headed toward the door. "So much faith in me! Give me ten. I'll help you load stuff into the car and then we can go to dinner before you leave." He stopped in the doorway and winked. "I called the cleaners on the way to the arena this afternoon." He then ran for his room, cackling the entire way. The man was a menace, but I was going to miss him.

"Do you think the rumors are true?"

Easton had bounced topics at least twelve times since we'd placed our orders, so I wasn't going to pretend to follow his train of thought. "What rumors?"

"About all the crazy traditions the Grizzlies have. Oh, I want to see a picture of the bear you get!"

Ever since the restructuring that the Grizzlies had gone through, rumors had swirled around the league about weird things they did as a team. Their teddy bears were things of legend. Every single player had one. They showed up in team photos all the time. I wouldn't be surprised if they ended up with trading cards of their own at some point. Grizzlies, teddy bears, it made sense if I turned my head to the side and really squinted. It was hard to believe the rumors that games of kickball and tag actually happened at practice, though.

When was the last time I'd played something other than hockey on ice? Maybe when I'd helped out with a summer camp a few years earlier.

"I'll send you a picture of the bear. I highly doubt that the rest is true. At a certain point, you have to believe that there would be more evidence than rumors. Look at how many pictures get taken of our practices."

Easton was quiet while the server delivered food, putting more thought into my words than I had thought necessary. "Maybe," he said eventually, grabbing his fork to stab a piece of broccoli. "I mean, you're right about the photos, but the rumors aren't going away."

"People like to gossip." I picked up my burger and took a bite. "Damn, I'm going to miss this place."

Easton was poking at his phone before I took another bite. "You'll be here in a few months. We'll come here after the game."

"Perfect." I pushed another bite in my mouth and enjoyed my dinner while I thought about the traditions and what I was getting myself into.

I thought about it all the way through dinner, through the ride to the airport, and until I took a seat at the gate, when the reality of the day finally hit me and I forgot all about the oddities and rumors surrounding the Grizzlies.

Just as the flight attendant started to make announcements, a message pinged my phone. I was expecting it to be Easton or my dad but was surprised to see that it was the Grizzlies' assistant.

***Blaise***: *Sounds like there was a shakeup in your housing plans. Here's Trevor's address and number. He told me to pass them along to you. I also passed your flight information on to him, he volunteered to pick you up tonight. Let me know if you need anything. Have a safe flight.*

There wasn't time to respond before turning my phone to silent. I lamented in my thoughts about the trade, the move, and now moving in with the man I'd had a crush on for a decade until I eventually fell asleep, only waking up when I heard the landing announcement. I looked out the window to see the lights of Nashville come into view. I'd been here a number of times before but always as a visitor. Taking in the lights of downtown, I tried to imagine flying into here over and over again.

I'd gotten so used to the lights of Boston over the last two years that it felt wrong to think of Nashville as home. I knew it would change with time. I fired up my phone and was greeted with a number of texts.

**Dad**: *Hope you had a good flight. We're heading to bed, but please let me know when you get into Tennessee.*

**Leo**: *He claims he's going to bed, you and I both know that he's going to lie in bed and stare at the ceiling until you text. Safe travels, Brax.*

**Easton**: *You need a boy like this. He's so cute. If I was a Daddy, I'd be totally looking for a little.*

The last one caught my eye, making me ignore the rest for now.

**Unknown**: *Your flight says it's still on time. I figure you'll have bags and whatnot, so I'll be there around 11:30. White Denali. See you soon.*

I checked the time. My phone had updated to Central Time and was reading just past eleven. I took the time that the plane was taxiing to the gate to update my contacts with Trevor's number, then shoot him a quick text letting him know that the timing would be fine.

With that complete, I sent a text to my dad and Leo letting them know I'd arrived safely and would be heading home with Trevor shortly, then flipped over to Easton's text.

The link took me to the Instagram account of a little. To my surprise, the account was tagged local to Nashville. Easton had said that the littles scene in the area was huge, but I hadn't expected it to be that easy for him to find the social media account of one. I had to give Easton that the boy was cute, but I still didn't think it was worth getting my hopes up that I'd find a boy or a little at this point in my life.

The last I thought of the boy was as I pocketed my phone to say thank you to the pilot and flight crew as I stepped off the plane and headed toward baggage claim. It took some maneuvering to gather my three suitcases and the two boxes I'd checked, but with a little creativity, I managed to get everything onto a cart and pushed out to the arrivals line by eleven twenty-five.

***Me***: *Made it. I'm the one with the cart.*

I propped myself up against a pillar to wait for Trevor's arrival.

Three minutes later, a horn alerted me to a sparkling white Denali about thirty feet away. I made my way over and glanced at the driver to make sure I recognized Trevor's brown hair and light blue eyes.

Wearing an oversized hoodie, he looked like any other person picking someone up at the airport at a ridiculously late hour. But his smile and the sparkle in his eyes was just like I remembered from when he lived with us.

"Hey. Let me help you load up." The tailgate opened at the same time as his door and he all but disappeared on the other side of the car. He had a larger-than-life presence on the ice, making it easy to forget that he was as tiny as he was. I was already putting my stuff in the back when he made his way around to help.

The hoodie swallowed his top half and the sweatpants he was wearing were no better. They each had to be at least two sizes bigger than he was, but he looked like he was ready to curl up with a blanket and a story for bedtime. *And I was officially going to kill Easton when I met him on ice the next time.* I wasn't going to give him a warning either. He'd planted the idea of littles in my head and now I was thinking about Trevor as a little.

Easton deserved a friendly check into the boards.

We had everything loaded in short order and Trevor motioned toward the front of the car. "Get in. We've been lucky. I don't think anyone noticed us yet."

Conversation was nonexistent until he pulled out of the lot and into the flow of traffic, where he finally pushed the hood of his sweatshirt back and shook his head, letting his thick, wavy crew cut fall back into place. "Sorry, tried to go under the radar. Maz let me borrow his sweats. I kinda feel like I'm playing dress-up."

And that hadn't helped my mind get out of the gutter. Just how hard could I check Easton? And did I need to wait weeks to do so? The asshole, best friend or not, was the reason I was thinking of very different things than I should have been.

"It's all good. I'm sorry my dad put you in such an awkward place."

Trevor ran a hand through his hair and gave me a smile that I could tell didn't fully meet his eyes. "It's okay. He's right, new teams and new cities, when you don't know anyone, are rough." The highway lights illuminated the car just enough that I could see Trevor's light blue eyes that had always sent my stomach swooping as a kid. I hadn't seen them up close in nearly ten years, but they still did funny things to my insides, and now my dick was reacting as well.

We hadn't made it to his house yet and I was already having a hard time reminding myself that we really didn't know one another. My dick desperately needed to get the memo before things got awkward.

*A two-minute minor for fighting wouldn't be so bad.*

## CHAPTER 4

### TREVOR

No one not from Nashville understood the hell of Nashville traffic during rush hour. I thanked the small miracle that we were navigating the highway back to my place at nearly midnight and not five in the evening. Getting out of the car sooner rather than later would be better anyway. Then again, that meant getting to my house. Seth and Maz had spent hours cleaning my place with me.

I'd even opened my playroom up for them to put things in. Derek had been the only one to ever see my playroom before, and my anxiety had been sky-high when I'd turned the knob to the room for them. Neither had blinked an eye. Seth had murmured something about it being cool and perfect. Maz had mentioned that the animal decorations were cute, then asked where I wanted to put my bottles and sippy cups.

Most. Surreal. Conversation. Ever.

After hours of cleaning, I was confident we'd found anything easily able to be found, but I wasn't so confident that we'd gotten everything. Living alone, I didn't always worry about putting pacifiers away or think hard when something came up missing.

Who was going to find it?

*Braxlyn Cernak, that was who.*

Unfortunately, I hadn't realized that was a possibility until late that morning, jet-lagged and sore from an exhausting week away from home.

"Thanks so much for picking me up. I could have taken a ride service."

For a moment I was struck by how different Brax's voice was from the kid that I'd lived with so many years before. It was a ridiculous thought. He'd been twelve or thirteen, awkward and just beginning puberty. Of course his voice had changed. I'd hardly known him then, but the memories I had were of him turning fire-engine red every time I tried to talk with him and many stammered conversations around the dinner table.

It was hard to believe that the nervous kid with a squeaky voice had turned into the confident man sitting beside me who was now not only my teammate but roommate as well. To make matters worse, his smile in the pickup lane had gone straight to my heart. That was something I was going to need to have a conversation with myself about later that night. There was no way anything was going to happen between us.

He was at least eight or nine years younger than me, his dad was my mentor, I was his captain, and I wasn't looking for more than a hookup. There was no way in hell I was going to get involved with Brax Cernak, and the sooner my heart figured that out, the better for everyone.

"Tell me a little about Nashville. I've never been past the arena. We did hit one of the honky-tonks one night after a game. That was a good way to shake off the whupping you all gave us."

That had been the season before, and a whupping was a nice term for it. We'd had the game of our lives right after New Year's. Our chemistry had been on fire and Boston had come in cocky and overconfident. Seth had scored in the first minute of play and it had been downhill for Boston from there.

I couldn't help smirking and teasing him a little. "That was a good game for us. From all the talk Anders did before the game, you should have beat us handily."

"Yeah, well, if Coach doesn't have a big mouth, he doesn't have anything."

*Ouch.* Those weren't the words I'd expected to hear from a player leaving Boston, one of the most prestigious teams in the league. They had built a name and reputation on being one of the original clubs, and they reminded everyone of that frequently.

I did chuckle a bit, though, because his assessment was absolutely spot on. "He likes to hear himself talk."

Brax gave a rich laugh that filled the entire car and pulled my lips into a smile. "So, Nashville?"

"Oh yeah. Nashville. I mean, I live outside of downtown. There's a lot of touristy spots, but there's a lot of nice, quiet areas too. I live close to Seth and Maz, same neighborhood, actually. As for the team, we like to have fun, but we're pretty tame compared to what you've been around the last few years."

"Truthfully? That sounds nice. I'm not huge into parties and drinking every night. I mean, don't get me wrong, East and I love to have a few beers after a game, but that's usually at home, when we can just walk thirty feet to our beds."

Easton Lafferty was a defenseman in Boston, closer to my age than Brax's. "Lafferty?" I asked for clarification.

"We both got traded to Boston at the same time. Since neither of us knew the city for shit, we shared the condo the team set us up in. We both liked the area. A unit came available a few months later and East jumped on it then offered me a room. I'd have been a fool to turn it down, so I've been living in his condo since."

We'd arrived at my house and I was feeling a little more comfortable just from the conversation flowing easily. I hadn't been able to put my finger on it before, but I knew I'd been worried that we would have nothing in common and the entire living arrangement would be not only stressful but awkward too. Brax didn't sound like so many of the Boston players, and everything I'd learned so far told me that he was serious about his job and would fit in well with the team. He'd have his age in common with our younger players but would also be able to easily talk to the veterans as well.

At least I only had to worry about the stressful part for the time being. And that was enough for me.

"Honestly, it sounds like you're going to fit in well with us. We're more likely to fall asleep at one another's houses watching movies than hitting up the bars. And the bars we go to are never the local tourist spots. I can't remember the last time one of us hit up a bar on Broadway." I shuddered at the thought of the crowds and hype that came with an outing in one of Nashville's busiest streets.

From what he'd said, it shouldn't have surprised me when he let out a relieved hum. "That sounds perfect! East keeps telling me I'm too old for my own good."

I parked the car in the garage and turned off the engine. "Good, because I *am* old. I'm practically ancient in hockey terms."

In the light of the garage, it was impossible to miss the way Brax ran over my body with appraising eyes. It did nothing to remind my heart that something between the two of us was the worst idea in the history of hockey and would lead to nothing but drama.

The heat of his gaze made me need to clear my throat to speak. "Come on, I'll show you to your room and let you get settled in. I'm sure you're tired. It's been a chaotic day for you."

With both of us, it only took one trip and we had everything into one of the rooms upstairs. Seth and Maz had debated for twenty minutes about which room to give him before Maz finally relented and agreed with Seth on the far room.

It had good natural light, it had its own bathroom, was spacious, and was away from my playroom. I hadn't seen how that last part was important, since my playroom was just off the steps on the first floor in the room that should have been the office. Seth had confidently said that it would give me additional peace of mind, especially if I needed some time to wind down while he was in the house. His reasoning had made a lot more sense then and we'd both agreed quickly that the far room was the best.

"Your house is really nice. Thanks for letting me stay here. I do appreciate it, even if it was only because my dad butted in."

The light blush that covered his cheeks at the mention of his dad reminded me a lot of him as a kid, though now I had to look way up at him to see that blush. I'd had to look up at him when he was a kid as well, just not that far up. Seeing that he wasn't quite as confident as he'd appeared the last twenty minutes had me relaxing some. At home, I was never as confident and in charge as I was with the team and having someone who was as confident as he'd been to this point but not a Dom or a Daddy made my brain confused.

That little blush might not have been much, but it was enough that I felt more equal and sure-footed as I gestured toward the steps. "Let me show you around downstairs before I head to bed. My body is all sorts of confused about what time it is and we've got a skate tomorrow. Thankfully, Cunningham will go easy on us."

I'd already begun to turn to head down the steps, but I caught a glimpse of surprise on his face. "Easy?"

I shrugged but didn't turn around as I held the handrail and focused on what was in front of me. Last time Derek and his Daddy had come over for the afternoon, I'd ended up in time-out for running down the steps and not holding onto the handrail. Colt wasn't my Daddy, but he took the job of watching after me seriously and he had been convinced that little boys needed to be careful on the steps. In my little headspace, the time-out had been pure torture. Three weeks later, I was still holding onto the handrail when I walked up or down the steps so that it became a habit for the next time they came over to play.

"He knows we're all exhausted by the time we're done with a road trip. The first practice after is usually just some basic conditioning. Though I think he and the trainers are looking for injuries we're trying to hide more than anything else." But it also allowed for plenty of time for games at the end of practice. "He gets unhappy when he realizes we've been playing through injuries and haven't told anyone."

We'd made it to the kitchen and I turned to find Brax staring at me. "Seriously?"

"Um, about what?"

He scrubbed at his face. "Sorry, it's been a long day, must not have schooled my reaction well enough. I just can't imagine a light practice."

I shrugged. The games were usually more physically demanding than our after-travel practices, but he'd find that out the next day. That reminded me that I needed to remember to bring the dodgeballs in the morning. It had been weeks since we'd played. We'd spent the last two weeks playing every variation of tag we could think of. Not only had it been fun, but the coaches also noticed that we were getting faster on ice. But after two weeks, I was tired of finding new ways to play tag.

"Cunningham is really good about knowing when to push us and when to give us a break. After long road trips, I think he needs a break just as much as we do." Changing the subject, I gestured around the kitchen. "Pantry and fridge are full. Help yourself to whatever. I'm not one of those people who is going to get overprotective over food. Living room's over there. Feel free to watch TV and relax."

The next words out of my mouth were harder to say, but I knew I needed to say them. "Make yourself at home."

As difficult as the words had been to say, his smile made me glad I had said them. His parents had opened their house to me for two years and had never made me feel like I was a burden or unwanted. Just because I was struggling with sharing a house didn't mean I needed to be rude or make him feel unwelcome.

I yawned, exhaustion catching up with me quickly. I knew it was time to get to my room when my thumb started gravitating toward my mouth. "I'm going to call it a night. You've got to be exhausted too. I'm sure your clock is just as messed up right now."

"Thanks. I think I'm going to try to get some sleep myself. I'll see you in the morning."

"Night."

I double-checked my door was shut before stripping my clothes off and digging through my dresser drawer to find a pair of pajamas. I settled on the cobalt blue pair with different-colored stars all over them. They looked cuter with a pair of training pants under them but I didn't want to risk accidentally walking out into the kitchen the next morning with noticeable training pants under the snug pajamas.

Enough of the guys on the team had ridiculous pajamas. Our goalie Yuri had come to breakfast at the hotel earlier in the week wearing a footed onesie, bitching that it was too cold in the hotel. My slim-fit, vibrant pajamas might be surprising, but I didn't think they'd raise Brax's eyebrows too much if he saw me in them.

I just needed to make sure to leave my blanket and pacifier in my bed when I left my room in the morning. Snuggle time on the couch with a sippy cup of juice or a bottle of milk while I ate breakfast had become a morning ritual that trumped coffee. I fell asleep wondering if there was enough space for a small couch and coffee table in my unused reading nook. With a little reorganization, I would probably be able to fit both in there and still be able to enjoy my morning routine.

## CHAPTER 5

### BRAX

As I watched Trevor walk to his room, I really, really hated my best friend. He had to pull the ridiculously oversized pants up as he walked, and the sweatshirt might as well have swallowed him whole. And thanks to Easton's texts, all I could think about as he headed to bed was that he was such a cute boy.

I dragged my hands down my face and shook my head in frustration at myself, at my dad, at Easton, at this entire thing. Now my brain was going so fast that trying to sleep would be futile. Instead of bothering, I grabbed a bottle of water from the fridge and headed to the living room to find something to watch. I knew I was going to be dead on my feet in the morning, but my brain didn't care about that.

I'd been surprised by how much warmer Nashville was than Boston in October, but at this time of night, there was a chill I couldn't deny and was happy to find the light quilt on the back of the couch. Covered up, I spent a minute looking around the room. For a single guy who spent a lot of time traveling, his house was homey. It felt like a family lived here, from the pictures on the wall to the throw pillows and blankets scattered on the couches and chairs.

From what I'd seen so far, the house was far from small. The exterior alone had been large and sprawling, but it didn't feel big or cold inside. Little figurines and knickknacks filled the bookshelves, and the basket by the fireplace was filled with more blankets. It felt a lot like my dad and Leo's house in North Carolina, filled with love and memories.

The late hour allowed me plenty of time alone to do some more research on the club Easton had told me about. Of course, I had to scroll past the numerous links he'd sent me from social media accounts of littles he'd found in the area.

How was it that the man had found so many accounts in such a short period of time? And why the fuck had the last one come in not thirty minutes earlier? He was proving to be a pain in my ass from over a thousand miles away.

While I was curious about the club, I'd definitely gotten sidetracked with the other links for a bit before finally settling in to research the club. It was past one in the morning, I really should have been in bed, but now that I'd found the website, there was no way I was going to rest before checking it out.

Easton hadn't exaggerated any of the good points of Dom And Sub Haven, a gay BDSM club known more commonly as DASH. I had no idea where he'd found the time to do that much research while at the Bulldogs arena, but he'd been thorough. There were a few pictures of the inside of the club, and the ones there had all been taken while the club was empty. I understood the logic behind it and was glad to see they took privacy as seriously as they did.

The spaces dedicated to medical or pain play didn't interest me that much. There were some roleplay rooms that looked interesting and the aftercare rooms were all warmly lit and welcoming. When I clicked on the link to the playroom, I didn't know what to expect. It was a kink club, so *playroom* could mean anything. From the information Easton had given me earlier, it shouldn't have surprised me to find a room that amounted to a nursery for littles.

Judging by the numerous pictures that had populated on the site, I knew this room was just as popular as Easton had made it out to be. It had to be a draw for their clientele, or there wouldn't have been so many pictures. I tried to imagine boys and their Daddies in the space and I found myself wishing that DASH wasn't so focused on privacy. I wanted actual photos to go with my imagination.

There were so many things to take in from the pictures that I wanted to see how the boys interacted with the toys— blocks, fire trucks, cars, stuffed animals, books, and toys of every kind. There was a table with coloring books and crayons along one wall.

My brain kept circling back to Easton being right. This definitely felt right to me, not so much the toys but having a boy who loved those things. I already knew that I preferred cuddles and quiet nights to punishments and chaotic clubs. Being a Daddy to a little would take that need to care for my partner in a different direction, but I was pretty sure it would be the perfect fit for me.

Without much thought, I filled out the form to join the next intro night and hoped like hell it didn't conflict with a game. As I clicked off my phone, I was cursing my best friend for putting the idea of being a Daddy to a little in my head. I doubted I'd find a little who wanted a Daddy with a crazy schedule, one who ate, breathed, and slept hockey for eight or more months a year, and one that should have just graduated college had I gone that route. I was young and my life was chaotic at the best of times. It wouldn't be suitable for a little who wanted a predictable Daddy with normal hours who could be around to care for them.

It was time for bed. I was getting depressed over something I didn't know anything about except a few pictures and social media sites. My foot slipped between the couch cushions as I hoisted myself up, and my toe landed on something cold and hard. If Trevor was anything like Easton, he'd probably been looking for his TV remote for days.

I stuck my hand between the cushions, fully expecting to pull out a rectangular chunk of plastic, not a pacifier. Trevor didn't have kids, but that didn't mean he didn't have a niece or nephew and I knew a handful of guys on the team had kids. As I tossed it onto the coffee table for him to figure out what to do with it in the morning, I thought that the nipple looked bigger than pacifiers I'd seen in the past. Not that I knew much about them.

It had been a long day and I needed to sleep, not contemplate the size of a pacifier.

After far too little sleep, I found myself loading bags of balls into the back of Trevor's SUV as he tossed a bear and a gym bag into the back seat of his car. I understood the bear, in an abstract way at least. After the third mesh bag filled with kickballs, I couldn't help asking why I'd just loaded a playground's worth of balls into his SUV. "Um, what are you doing with all those?"

Trevor climbed into the driver's seat and waited until I was in and buckled before responding. "They're for practice."

I blinked. He'd spoken a complete sentence with words I fully understood the meanings of. What I couldn't wrap my head around was how the playground balls related to hockey. "I'm sorry?" My brain was stubbornly refusing to believe that these would be used for hockey practice, no matter what the rumors around the league were. The Grizzlies had numerous trades a year. There was no way that the games had never been confirmed by someone.

He focused on backing the vehicle out of the garage, then glanced over to me. "I'm so tired of tag. We've been playing it for two weeks now."

Leo would slap me upside the head if he saw me staring like I was. "Tag?"

A light blush stained Trevor's cheeks and he averted his blue eyes, focusing way more intently on the road than the neighborhood warranted. "Um, yeah. It's a tradition."

"You mean... you mean it's real?"

The question had his eyebrows creeping up his forehead. "Real?"

My hands waved about of their own accord. "Yeah. The rumors about silly games."

He winced like I'd slapped him. I hadn't meant to offend, but I could see how the description could be offensive. "Sorry." I apologized quickly. "Poor choice of words. It's just surprising."

Trevor's defenses were higher than I thought they should have been, but I could tell it was a touchy subject for him. I was guessing some negative things had been said in the past.

To his credit, he kept his tone casual, but tension was evident in his shoulders and a muscle ticked in his jaw. "It's a team-building thing. It gives us a chance to spend time together doing something other than hockey. When I first joined the team, we were a mess. No one spoke off the ice. We had no connection and it showed on ice. When Coach announced I'd be captain, I knew I wanted to help us find something that would bring us together but knew that we weren't at the point that players would want to hang out outside of the rink. This was the best way I could think of. Coach agreed. Four seasons later, it's become a part of the Grizzlies."

*Good job, Brax.*

"Oh. That makes sense. I really didn't mean that they were silly. Sorry again."

Trevor shrugged like he wasn't bothered, but I could tell my words had offended him. Unfortunately, I had no idea how to make things better and stayed silent until we reached the arena. Thankfully, he didn't live far from the practice arena, making the awkward silence last only a few minutes.

As soon as the car was off, it was like Trevor became a different person. He swung his door open and nearly jumped from the driver's seat, calling to a guy in a sports car who had just pulled up. "Yuri! Get over here. Meet Brax and help me out."

Yuri Yurievich was the Russian netminder who had played backup to Igor Ozols for the two previous seasons. He'd become the starter more often than not this season and was having an impressive early season, letting in an average of just over two goals per game. The rumor mill was that Igor was getting ready to retire. My dad and Igor had been in the NHL for a number of seasons together, though never on the same team, and my dad had a lot of respect for Igor. He still joked that Igor was the one goalie he dreaded playing.

I slid out of the SUV and came around the hood just as Yuri walked up. He was an impressive height, at least two or three inches taller than my six-foot-one frame and the small bear in his arm was comical, though after putting my foot in my mouth about dodgeball, I wasn't about to say anything about the bear.

"You beat Seth?"

Trevor looked around, though I wasn't sure how much he could see over the towering front ends of the vehicles around us. "Appears so. He had to stop at the mall first."

A large black SUV came around the corner and Trevor laughed. "Speak of the devil."

"He is happy. Mall, yes." While Yuri's Russian accent was still thick, the sarcasm and innuendo had been clear and the three of us were still snickering as Seth Johnson and Mazdon Grabowski parked and stepped out of the SUV.

Seth was full of energy and his boyfriend kept giving him fond smiles every time Seth looked away.

Seth was holding two bears in one arm and a box from the fill-your-own teddy bear store in the other, leaving his boyfriend to heft both of their practice bags. "You must be Brax?" Seth tried to hold out a hand but struggled with everything he was holding. "Sorry, well, this is for you anyway." He thrust the box into my hand and kept his hand out. "Nice to meet you."

In less than two minutes' time, I'd met three players and could already tell the team was closer than Boston had ever been. Hell, they were closer than Boston's farm team had been. These guys were open and friendly and I immediately felt at ease around them.

"Hi. Nice to meet you."

Yuri pointed to the bear in my hand. "Name quickly."

Seth and Trevor both broke out into cackles and Mazdon smirked but took pity on me and filled me in. "Yuri didn't name his bear, so they took it upon themselves to name it Puck Bunny. Well, Puck Bunny got lost on a bus one time. The story is told—repeatedly—that the entire building thought he'd lost a girl, not a bear, because he kept going around muttering that he'd lost his Puck Bunny and asking if anyone had seen it."

Imagining Yuri, with his thick accent, asking if someone had seen his Puck Bunny was enough to have me laughing as well.

Mazdon was still grinning as he nodded. "Yeah. Pretty much. I'm Mazdon, by the way, but everyone calls me Maz. Well, everyone aside from Seth. I'd shake your hand but…" He trailed off as he lifted the bags he was carrying.

"Nice to meet you."

Trevor opened the back hatch, gesturing to the bags in the back. "Grab a bag and let's get going. I'd rather play dodgeball than do bag skates."

I slung my bag over my shoulder and grabbed a bag of dodgeballs, watching as Trevor and Yuri each grabbed one as well, and we headed into the building. I still didn't know what to make of the dodgeballs or meeting the rest of the team, but I was getting the feeling this wasn't going to be as strange or awkward as I'd feared a trade would be.

The commotion in the locker room, mostly centered around the new guy, died down as soon as the coaches came in. They weren't much older than some of the players. In stark contrast to the coaching staff I'd become familiar with, these guys were full of smiles and laughter and appeared to have a great relationship with the team. Coach Irvin Cunningham had come over to introduce himself and the assistant coaches and welcomed me to the team. The assistant coach, Imil Bouchard, took time to find Blaise and make sure I'd met him.

Blaise looked like he wanted to crawl out of his skin in a locker room filled with hockey players. He was tall and lanky with big eyes that showed just how uncomfortable he was, though Bouchard wasn't willing to let him go until we'd been "properly introduced."

"Brax, this is Blaise Emory. Technically, he's the Assistant Director of Hockey Operations, but more than just the front office would be lost without him."

The color Blaise's cheeks turned at the praise couldn't be called a blush. Blazing inferno was closer to accurate. Whatever color it was, I knew it wasn't a healthy color for a human to turn, so I tried to make the meeting as sweet and painless as possible for him. "Nice to meet you. I really appreciate your consideration yesterday. It made the day much less stressful."

In my attempt to make it better, Blaise somehow turned redder, the tips of his ears turning the same color as his cheeks. His attempt at a nod came out more as a twitch and I could see him picking furiously at his thumbnails. Bouchard whispered something quietly into his ear and Blaise's color cooled considerably as he turned and headed out of the locker room.

Bouchard's features softened as Blaise left the room, and then he turned to me. "He's amazing at his job, but he gets really overwhelmed. These guys, as loud and crazy as they all are, wouldn't hurt a fly off ice. He'll warm up to you." He clapped me on the shoulder. "Let's see what you're made of, shall we?"

I nodded and followed the team out to the ice for a series of drills. Cunningham and Bouchard pushed us but not so hard that the team wasn't joking around. I didn't know why I was still shocked to find that Trevor had been right about day-after-road-trip practices, but the light skate and basic conditioning drills were a welcome reprieve after the last twenty-four hours.

When three bags of balls got dumped onto the ice, I knew I needed to get used to being surprised. I also needed to take Trevor more seriously. Coach split us up by jersey color and suddenly the light practice turned into utter pandemonium. Balls were flying through the air, laughter and screams filled the rink, and the coaches started jeering and taunting us. While their pokes were oddly kind and gentle, they picked apart everything they saw wrong. Our form, the way we cut back and forth on the ice, and footwork were all picked apart for twenty minutes, though laughter and camaraderie were the most prominent takeaways of the game.

On our way to the locker room, I jogged up to Trevor and put my hand on his shoulder. "Hey, I owe you a sincere apology. I'd been surprised and taken a little off guard when you mentioned playing games at the end of practice and I definitely spoke without any knowledge of what I was talking about. That"—I motioned behind us—"was amazing. I see why it's so important to the team."

Trevor glanced up at me, actually looking at me for the first time since the car ride, and I watched as a smile spread on his face. "Thanks. It's really important to us. Thank you for giving it a try."

We made it to the locker room and each went our separate ways to change. As I pocketed my phone, I noticed a voice mail from an unknown number and took a minute to listen to it.

"Hi, Braxlyn, this is Alice Johnson from DASH. I got the application that you submitted last night and would like to discuss the next steps with you. Please give me a call back." She left a number, and all I could do was question why a woman who sounded well past middle age had called me about the application I'd filled out for the BDSM club.

If I'd learned one thing that day, it was to expect the unexpected, and I wasn't going to figure anything out by not calling her back. I just needed to find some time alone first.

## CHAPTER 6

TREVOR

Two days wasn't enough time for me to get used to having Brax in my house, but it was enough time for my dick to take a very keen interest in his naked torso. I'd quickly discovered that Brax didn't like shirts. He'd joked at dinner the night before that he would rather be naked but knew that wouldn't go over well with most people. No matter what societal norms or my brain said, my dick hadn't gotten the message and I'd had to adjust myself under the table.

Even the horror of finding one of my pacifiers on the coffee table the morning before hadn't been enough to make my dick behave for more than a few seconds. And he hadn't said a thing about it anyway, so maybe he hadn't been the one to find it. I was going to pretend that he hadn't seen it and Seth, Maz, and I had managed to overlook it in our whirlwind clean.

When I walked out of my room, I knew Brax would already be up. He'd been up with the birds the first two days, and judging by the smell of coffee wafting into my room, today was no different. I also knew he wouldn't be wearing a shirt, meaning I needed to put jeans on instead of the lightweight cotton pajamas I'd put on before bed. Pursing my lips, I searched for a pair of underwear and jeans that were going to keep everything in place until I could get my dick to behave itself. At that point, I'd get my running shorts on and head out for a jog before coming in to do my normal routine before a game.

Except my normal routine was going to be all sorts of messed up because I couldn't take my cup to the living room and watch cartoons while I colored. I really needed to prioritize that remodel of my seating area in my room. It wouldn't take much. There was always my playroom that I could go to, but that was way too risky with Brax in the house.

I was back to square one with how to get my normal decompression time before a game. At least my musing had gotten my dick to stand down. Actually, it had left me grumpy enough that I didn't think the jeans would be necessary at all. I pulled my running shorts on, grabbed one of my T-shirts, and headed toward the kitchen for a snack before my run.

"Hey." Brax was smiling at me as soon as my door opened, but to my surprise, he was wearing a T-shirt and joggers.

"You've got a shirt on." I slapped my forehead at my reaction. "Sorry, I'm just so used to seeing you without a shirt now."

Brax let out a warm laugh that settled happily in my stomach. "Yuri's on his way to pick me up so we can play video games before the game. Easton and I used to do the same thing." He took a sip of his coffee, his eyes going wide. "I never asked, what's your thing?"

I gestured toward my outfit. "I take a long run through the woods. Sometimes Seth and Maz join. Then I come home and chill for a bit."

"Oh, do you want me to stay at Yuri's until game time? I can ask him to drive me to the arena."

His concern was touching and I found myself relaxing as I shook my head. "No, you're fine. It's really just a chill day for me. I always sleep better in my own bed. Not that your bed is really your own bed, but you know what I mean."

Brax hummed and nodded slowly. "Then I'll probably head back after a few hours."

We both went our separate ways a few minutes later, my way taking me out the back door and to the trail that led through the wooded park behind my neighborhood as I found a good pace to loosen my pregame tension. I'd managed to clear my mind and lose myself in the rhythm until Seth and Maz fell into step with me. If it hadn't been for Seth's distinct navy-and-bright-pink shoes, I'd probably have been more surprised.

"How's the new roommate situation?" Seth asked when we'd run in silence for a few hundred yards.

"Honestly? Not as bad as it could be. He stays pretty much to himself, but it is nice to have someone to chat with after practices." Seth didn't need to know that I'd worn more jeans in the house the last couple of days than I'd worn in the last year. At home, I was definitely a shorts or sweatpants guy, not jeans.

Maz's snort from beside Seth made me look over to find him grinning. "Care to share what has you blushing with the class?"

I stuck my middle finger up and shook my head. I'd have sprinted ahead, but their legs were both longer than mine and I'd have run out of steam way before them. That would have also defeated the purpose of a relaxing jog.

Thankfully, Seth pushed at Maz's arm. "Behave yourself." Then he focused back on me. "Ignore my boyfriend. He's been taking lessons from Austin."

Seth's twin brother, Austin, was a force of nature and no one ever knew what would come out of his mouth next. "Heaven help us all."

When Seth stopped laughing, I caught him studying me from the corner of my eye. "Are you having enough time for yourself?"

I almost tripped over a tree root. He'd spoken vaguely but I wasn't used to my little side being spoken about at all, much less by a teammate. I kept reminding myself that he was a safe person to talk to and he already knew, but it was going to take some time for my brain to believe that as well.

We turned the corner that would lead us back to our neighborhood and jogged past an older couple out for a walk. I didn't bother pretending that Seth or Maz had forgotten the question. Seth was related to Austin and just as persistent as his twin. "We haven't had much time at home the last few days. I'm planning to rework my bedroom a bit to find some space for a few things. Today's going to be the real challenge. I usually get some little time in before I take my time getting ready. It's going to be harder with Brax around."

To my surprise, Maz was the one who responded. "You're always welcome to come to our place. We have a nice spare room that we could easily convert to a quiet space for you."

"Oh! That's a great idea! Yes. Do you like blue? It's already a light blue color and the carpet in there is super soft!"

Momentarily too touched to speak, my pace slowed to a walk before my feet finally stopped and I stared at the two. "You two are serious?"

They both stopped and studied me. "Mazdon's right. It's just the two of us. We know about it and can give you plenty of privacy and space. Just say the word."

I doubted that I'd take them up on the generous offer, but I wasn't going to turn them down outright. At least not until I had time to think about it more. "That's a really sweet offer. Let me think about it for a few days."

We jogged the rest of the way in comfortable silence before I snaked off the trail toward my house, waving goodbye and telling them I'd see them later that afternoon. Arriving home, my mind was ready to shut off totally for a bit and I showered quickly before changing into a pair of cotton shorts and a shirt covered in cartoons.

Armed with my blanket in one hand, Huck in the other, I made a quick stop in my playroom to grab a sippy cup and a few coloring books and a box of crayons, then headed toward the kitchen. When I settled onto the floor in front of the coffee table, the adult world was already slipping away. I set the alarm on my phone so I didn't lose track of time, then let myself forget the rest of the world. Coloring, cartoons, and my snack were a lot more interesting than Brax, the game that night, or Seth and Maz's offer.

I must have been more stressed than I'd led myself to believe because I barely made it through one show before my eyes got too heavy to fight any longer. My bed felt very far away, so I tidied my coloring supplies, placed the snack plate on top of them, turned the TV off, and climbed onto the couch with my blanket, cup, and Huck. There was enough of a chill in the air that I pulled the big blanket from the back of the couch over me, stuck my cup in my mouth, and let my eyes close.

My alarm startled me awake sometime later, leaving me disoriented for a few seconds. I'd burrowed completely under the blanket, leaving me in total darkness and making it harder to figure out what was going on. Unsurprisingly, my thumb had replaced my cup while I'd slept and I used my free hand to grope around for the ringing device, desperate to make it shut up.

Closing my fingers around my phone, I suddenly remembered why I'd set the alarm in the first place. My thumb came out of my mouth so fast that it made a popping sound as the suction broke and I sat up to survey my surroundings. My cup had been tucked under the big blanket, as had my blanket and Huck. I'd turned off the TV and straightened my coloring supplies before falling asleep. The house was quiet, meaning there was a good chance that Brax hadn't returned yet. I wasn't going to take any chances and rushed to gather everything and head to my room to change and get my head into a better space.

In the safety of my room, my heart rate finally began to return to normal. As I rinsed my plate in my bathroom sink, I seriously contemplated Seth's offer. A text pulled me from my thoughts.

**Derek**: *How's the new housemate?*

***Me****: I mean, aside from him making me feel ancient, not so bad.*

The phone rang, Derek's name appearing on the screen.

"Hey."

Derek didn't bother with pleasantries, jumping right in with his thoughts. "You played with his dad, right?"

"I did. Tom was at the end of his career when I joined the team and Brax was already very involved in hockey, so it isn't like he was a baby and is now playing in the NHL. *That* would make me feel really old, but I can honestly tell you that I am feeling older than I did at the beginning of the week."

My friend's warm chuckle filled my ear and helped soothe the last of my frazzled thoughts. "So, what are you up to?"

"Daddy and I were looking at the schedule and the kids are going to my parents' for fall break next week. We thought it would be a good time to meet up if you have some free time."

And just like that, my worries about Brax disappeared in plans to have Derek and his husband over one evening. "I'll look at the schedule and talk with Brax to see if he's going to be out at any point. I'm sure we can make something work."

Derek hummed thoughtfully. "If we can't make it work at your house, you can come here sometime."

I didn't often go to Derek and Colt's house. They had three kids and it was sometimes difficult to make time and space to have little time at their house. Since I lived alone, playdates happened here, but knowing that I had at least a few options available had the last of my anxieties easing. "Awesome. I like that idea. We'll definitely figure something out." My phone buzzed and I looked at the time. "Shit, I need to get dressed. I've got to get out of here soon."

"Okay. Good luck tonight!" The phone went dead and I set to work getting ready for the game.

Thirty minutes later, after another shower to tame my wild hair, I headed to the kitchen. I hadn't heard Brax come home and had been planning to text to see if he was coming back before the game, only to find him sitting at the island in the kitchen, scrolling through his phone.

The bright blue suit he'd put on should have been tacky, but he'd somehow made it look good. Not just good, sexy. It fit him like a glove, hugging the firm muscles of his legs and ass. A bright orange pocket square had been perfectly folded into the upper pocket. I'd have never pulled it off, but Brax made it look effortless. He was gorgeous. From his perfectly styled hair to his expensive leather shoes, he was perfection.

I really needed to stop thinking about him that way. The light gray suit pants I'd put on were not going to hide an erection, and I wasn't ready to deal with the awkwardness if he saw.

Brax looked up and I watched as his mouth hung open in surprise. He didn't leave me wondering what was so shocking when he pointed to my chest. "You Tennessee people are weird."

"What?"

"It's nearly sixty and you're wearing a sweater under your coat like it's fifteen! Snow's forecast next week in Boston."

"And that's why I don't live in Boston." I went to the fridge to grab a bottle of water. "What time did you get back? I never heard you come in."

"Not surprising. When I got home there was a Trevor-shaped mound of blankets on the couch. Well, I'm hoping it was you. If it wasn't, we should probably call someone, because there was something sleeping under the blankets."

The anxiety that I'd pushed to the side in my room came back with a vengeance, logic and his words about my being totally covered be damned. My brain was whirling with what he might have seen.

He chuckled to himself. "I was halfway to the stairs before I noticed the pile of blankets on the couch. It took me until I was almost to my room to realize there had to be a person under there. I seriously don't know how you were able to breathe like that! I came down after my shower to grab a bite to eat and you were gone, so I figured you hadn't suffocated."

I hoped like hell that my chuckle didn't sound as manic as it did in my head. "It's cold today! I don't like being cold."

Brax shook his head and stood to throw his empty water bottle away. "Hate to tell you this, but you chose the wrong sport."

Watching him heading across the kitchen had my brain thinking about very different things than my temperature preferences, unless of course those preferences were for a certain hot man in a suit that might as well have been a second skin.

Fuck, I was in trouble.

"We better get going." My voice cracked and I winced at myself, thankful Brax still had his back toward me.

## CHAPTER 7

### BRAX

Something I'd said had frazzled Trevor. He'd been on edge since he'd seen me sitting in the kitchen, but he'd gotten substantially more nervous as we'd talked. On ice, Trevor was cocky and confident but I'd learned quickly that his off-ice personality was not the same. For being the captain of an NHL hockey team, he was quick to blush and easy to frazzle.

I'd stuck to safe topics, like hockey and things to do around Nashville. It seemed like every time I veered from them, Trevor found a new shade of red to turn and I didn't understand why. There were a lot of things I'd wanted to ask him about, like the pacifier I'd seen and the pile of coloring books that had been on the coffee table when I'd arrived home that afternoon.

While Trevor busied himself getting ready to leave, I pulled my phone out and pretended to scroll through it, when in reality I was watching him move around the kitchen. Not for the first time that week, I cursed my dad and Easton.

Trevor was gorgeous in his light gray suit with a dark blue sweater and red tie. It wasn't flashy by any stretch. He could have been going to teach a college class or heading out on a date, but the way the material hugged his body, the slight stretch of it over his shoulders, the way it hugged around his hips and thighs just so, accentuating his dick, all had me needing to bite my lip so I didn't moan.

This was not in my plans, nor was it my fault.

My dad had foisted me upon Trevor, giving him no choice but to say yes. Easton had been on me to find a little, still sending me social media posts and texts multiple times a day, and between the pacifier and the coloring book and his tiny frame, I couldn't shake the idea of being Trevor's Daddy.

Trevor cursed under his breath and left the room to look for something. I might have heard something about his keys, but I'd been pretty lost in my thoughts. With him out of the room, I looked down at my phone and the last picture Easton had sent me. The guy was cute, but damn he was young. Maybe he was looking for a Daddy, but I wasn't looking for a barely legal guy who would want more than I could offer.

*Me*: *Dude, stop. He's cute, but I don't want a 19 or 20yo who hardly knows himself.*

***Easton***: *You're barely 23. How much more do you know about yourself?*

***Me***: *I had already been drafted by the time I was 19. I wasn't living in a college dorm, I was busting my ass to make it here. At 20, I was moving from the AHL to Boston. You know damn well I'm not a typical 23yo. I'm willing to admit I want a boy, but I'm realistic enough to know it ain't happening any time in the near future. Hell, maybe not in the distant future.*

"Aha! Found 'em! Get your bear and let's go. Traffic's gonna be a nightmare if we don't leave now." Trevor's voice echoed through the house and I only just made out Easton's next text as I turned off my phone. My bear was already in the small bag I was taking to the arena, though I hadn't come up with a name for it yet, despite Yuri's warning.

***Easton***: *Fine, I'll drop it for now. Good luck tonight. I'm watching!*

Trevor rounded the corner just as I pocketed my phone. "You good?"

After two days at the rink, it already felt strange to just get into his car and leave. I was already used to adding weird things—yesterday had been lacrosse sticks—into his car before heading to the arena.

"Dammit, Nashville traffic is going to be a bitch already." He shook his head then glanced over at me. "How are you feeling about the game tonight?"

I looked out the window, watching as the dense neighborhood turned to a small business district before we made it to the highway. "I'm excited. I'm nervous. I'm concerned that I haven't heard from Dad or Leo today."

Trevor's eyes narrowed in thought. "You haven't heard from them today?"

Shaking my head, I realized just how odd that was. "Fuck, they're coming, aren't they?"

Trevor shrugged casually, but I could hear the barely masked amusement in his voice as he spoke. "How far away do they live now? Four, five hours? It's a seven o'clock game. They've had plenty of time to get here if they wanted to."

My head fell against the window. "You've got to save me!"

Trevor didn't bother hiding his laughter. "Oh, hell no. I lived with them, remember? You're on your own."

I loved my dad and Leo to the ends of the earth, but Leo was clueless about hockey. He was the guy that constantly asked what happened and what was going on. My dad was loud and proud. He'd been the one screaming in the stands with all the hockey moms throughout middle and high school hockey. He could be heard over the crowd in the AHL games, and every NHL game he'd been to he always ended up on the Jumbotron, hooting and hollering.

We merged onto the highway before Trevor looked over at me again. "You look like a petulant child."

He sounded so much like Easton that I forgot who I was talking to for a second. "Right now, I *am* a petulant child! A Dom can be petulant too."

The squeak that came from Trevor reminded me that I was definitely not talking to Easton, and a glance to the side showed he'd gone unnervingly pale.

"Fuck. Sorry. I didn't mean to say that." I scrubbed my hands down my face. *Good job making things awkward.*

Trevor pulled himself together quickly, shaking his head like it would make things make sense. "It's okay. If that's the biggest bombshell you drop on me, you've got a long way to go. Seth could probably give you a manual on how to shock the shit out of people. His family knows no boundaries. He'd probably have a manual for your parents too."

I didn't need to have a manual. I'd succeeded in embarrassing myself enough already. Dad and Leo really didn't need a manual either, and I loved them for it. They were my parents, so of course I loved them regardless, but I hadn't planned on them jumping into the car and driving to Tennessee to see my first Grizzlies game.

In the awkward silence that followed the exchange, I tried to figure out what to say to get us on the right track. I wanted to ask about the bear and if I really needed to name it, but each time I tried to broach the subject, my mind jumped track and I started thinking about the littles that

Easton kept linking me to. Logical or not, my brain kept trying to put Trevor's face on each of them.

I hadn't realized I'd growled my frustration until Trevor glanced over at me again. "You okay?"

"Yeah, why?"

Trevor kept his eyes on the traffic in front of us. "Because you've growled at least four times in the last thirty seconds."

Great. Just fucking great. I wasn't able to keep my frustration to myself either. "Got lost in thought. Mostly annoyed with Easton."

Trevor's lips pursed and his eyebrows drew down into a line as he thought. "He hasn't been giving you shit since you came here, has he? I thought you two were friends?"

He was clearly trying to keep his tone friendly but I had a feeling that if I said anything remotely suggesting that he was giving me a hard time, Easton would have a target on his back the first time we met again. "Nothing like that. He's just being a pain-in-the-butt friend."

The response made Trevor's lips twitch into a smile. "I know a thing or two about pain-in-the-butt friends. I can name about twenty-one of them that we're going to see in the next fifteen minutes."

I found myself smiling at the response, some of the awkwardness lifting from the car. "Anything I should know about game days?"

He thought for a moment before shaking his head slowly. "No. Nothing weird or surprising."

When we fell silent again, it wasn't awkward and I managed to keep my thoughts away from littles, my dad, and Leo, and more on the game I should have been mentally preparing myself for in the first place. Coach had sent a text earlier in the day that had me on the third line with a group of guys I had jelled with in practices. Igor was starting goalie that game, a slight shake-up in the roster but not completely unexpected.

The ping of an incoming text as we exited Trevor's SUV had me biting back a groan, at least until I looked at my phone. It had been a text from the car hauler, telling me that my car would be arriving on Tuesday, a day earlier than expected. There was an intro night at DASH on Wednesday and I'd hoped to be able to go but wasn't about to ask Trevor to borrow a car and didn't want to use a ride service to get to or from the club.

With a car in Tennessee, I would be free to go without anyone questioning me.

The new information gave me a little spring to my step as the two of us made our way down to the tunnel and the inevitable cameras. Dressing for a game had become somewhat of a challenge for me. I never wanted to be the eccentric player that made the social media rounds for their crazy outfits. I'd always been happy leaving that to Easton. That didn't mean that I didn't like to look good and maybe a bit flashy.

I preferred outfits with color, usually bright or with a bold pattern. I also tried to add some of the team's colors somewhere in my outfit. That night, I'd chosen the bright blue with pops of orange not only because they looked great together but because the Grizzlies official colors were blue and white, but the logo had orange in it. It was a hell of a lot better than the original brown and orange from a handful of years earlier. Back then, their uniforms reminded me of a farm, not a professional hockey team, but I liked the way they'd kept the orange in the logo after the change.

Trevor had rushed us out of the house so early that I hadn't thought that the locker room would be busy. Hell, once we'd made it off the highway, downtown hadn't been all that busy yet. Nothing compared to what I remembered it looking like on game days when we'd played Nashville. Instead of a quiet locker room like I'd expected, it was filled with players and their families milling about, chatting and laughing.

"Oh, right. Um, this is sort of a thing. When I said we didn't really have anything special for game days, I kind of forgot about the home game gathering. At least that's what I call it. I don't know if this has an official name."

I looked around the room in awe. A large group stood around Seth and Maz, both of them shaking their heads but grinning at something someone in the group had said.

Wives chatted while kids ran around playing tag, and a few of the older ones played knee hockey in the hallway. It was an absolute zoo, yet fitting for this team. I found myself sucked into conversations and introductions, allowing me to forget any nerves I had about my first game with the Grizzlies.

I'd even forgotten about my parents' possible arrival until I came face-to-face with the two. I'd known it was a good possibility they'd be there. I had bitched and moaned that they were going to be embarrassing, but having their arms around me again made all of the impending shenanigans small potatoes.

"Hey, kid." Leo kissed one temple and Dad kissed the other.

"Hey." I had to blink back tears and swallow a few times before I could say anything else. "I had a lightning bolt moment on the way here when I realized I hadn't talked to either of you today. Dammit, I'm glad you're here."

They both laughed at me, though it was kind. Dad pulled me in tighter for a moment before finally releasing me. "Did you really think we'd miss it?"

It was my turn to laugh. "Think? I guess, had I thought about it, probably not. Did I wish? Well, part of me had."

Leo rolled his eyes and opened his mouth to say something before cutting himself off to greet Trevor. "Trevor! Jesus, it's been forever since I've seen you!"

The spotlight was off me and I found myself trying to slink away from the commotion of the two, my heart full enough in the knowledge that they were there that I didn't need to stick around longer. I managed to get about ten feet from them when I noticed the red tint on Trevor's cheeks and stepped back, ready to forcibly separate them if I had to.

Once I got close enough to hear them, I knew Trevor's pink cheeks were probably more from heat than from embarrassment. My dad's voice was warm and he was poking fun at me more than Trevor. "Is Brax behaving himself? He can be a bit intense when he decides to be."

Trevor's head ducked slightly and I watched as he licked his lips, making them shimmer from the overhead lighting. I'd been doing a decent enough job keeping my long-standing crush on the man at bay, but the bashful blushes and the moisture on his lips was making it really hard to continue to ignore it. With my dad and Leo towering over him, my desire to step in and save him from the imposing men was stronger than it should have been.

It was ridiculous and I could logically understand that, but I was quickly discovering that my need to protect—both as a defenseman and as a Dom—was strong with Trevor. It didn't matter if he wasn't my boyfriend; his discomfort made me uncomfortable and I wanted to fix it, social norms be damned.

The familiar taste of copper in my mouth drew my thoughts from Trevor and my parents. I'd been biting the inside of my cheek so hard while I warred with my thoughts that I was now bleeding. *What a way to start the day.*

"Money for thoughts?" Yuri's thick Russian accent was difficult to miss, but the absurdity of what he'd said was what really pulled me away from the conversation happening a few feet away from me.

"What?"

He waved his hand around. "You look like you need to poop."

My blank stare made Yuri huff and call over to Seth, who quickly excused himself and jogged toward us. When he was near, Yuri pointed to me. "Brax does not understand. I ask, money for thoughts."

Seth snorted a laugh. "Yuri, bud, that isn't Brax, that's your butchering of American sayings. It's *a penny for your thoughts.*"

Yuri pursed his lips. "That saying is stupid. Penny is cheap. Thoughts worth more."

The man had a point but he'd also managed to get my mind off Trevor. "I'm good. I'd just gotten lost in thought for a bit. Promise, I'm good."

Seth patted us both on the back. "Yuri's translations need translators. Thankfully, I've become a master at them. And, since you're fine, come meet my family."

## CHAPTER 8

TREVOR

I'D NEVER BEEN SO happy to have the family time end as I had been that evening. I'd understood but hadn't shared Brax's hesitations about Tom and Leo showing up to the game. I respected Tom, and Leo had always been an open ear when I'd lived with them. The two were wonderful men who loved Brax with every breath in their bodies.

My parents lived in Canada and didn't come to very many games, even when we were playing in Montreal. When they did, we'd meet for dinner if time allowed. I always made sure they had tickets waiting at the arena and I knew they were there, but it wasn't like anyone else knew they were in the stands.

Things were different with Tom and Leo. Tom was famous in his own right and always the doting dad. Leo was loud and proud and downright clueless. I'd never understand how a man who had lived with a hockey player for twenty or more years didn't know the game backward and forward. He either hadn't figured it out, or he played clueless very well.

For the first few minutes they were there, I was happy to see that Brax had relaxed considerably. It was when he'd stepped away and I was left alone with the two that things had gone sideways. There had been something in the way he'd asked if Brax was behaving himself that hadn't sounded like a dad just asking if his son was a decent houseguest. Hell, the implied *hint-hint, wink-wink* when he'd tried to tease that Brax could be intense had made my hands clammy.

It had felt like time stood still as I'd tried to find a way to tell him that Brax had been nothing but kind and polite. All I could think was that he'd somehow known that I was submissive and Brax was a Dom. Which was stupid. There was no way he would have known either of those things. Parents and kids didn't talk about that stuff, unless of course they were Seth's family. I was sure that Tom and Leo didn't own a kink club, so there was no way they'd talk about things like that. At least I hoped not.

I was saved by the conversation between Yuri, Seth, and Brax, and had never been so thankful for a distraction in all my life. But I had wanted to curse the slip-up from Brax in the car. Not only was my new roommate sexy, he was kinky to boot. That left questions about what type of Dom he was, which were very dangerous thoughts in a locker room before a game, surrounded by friends and family.

Seth sidestepped toward me during the singing of the national anthem. "You okay? You looked off in the locker room."

What happened in the locker room stayed in the locker room. On ice, I was the captain of the Grizzlies. I was a leader. It didn't matter what crazy shit was going on in my personal life, I needed to be a leader. As soon as my skates had been laced up, I had pushed the conversation out of my head. "I'm good."

*Now, ask me the same question after the game, when I'd had enough time to process everything.*

Seth didn't sound wholly convinced by my response but nodded once and remained silent the rest of the song.

If there had been any question where my head was at, I hoped it was answered halfway through the first period when I managed to net a one timer from the blue line.

As the second shortest player to ever play professional hockey, I'd learned to not only play hockey, but play aggressive hockey. It meant I had a lot of penalty minutes and got into more fights than most centers did, but it also kept me out of trouble more often than not. I'd earned the respect of players on my team and others and they knew that I wouldn't hesitate to retaliate.

I was not only nearly a foot shorter than most other players, I was also between twenty-five and thirty-five pounds lighter as well. My lower weight made me fast, but I had to work twice as hard to get down the ice because it took me a lot more strides. I could move the puck and change course more easily than taller players, but I wasn't the one to be able to reach out and stop a puck going wide. There were benefits and disadvantages to my height, and I just had to take full advantage of the things that I was good at.

It was more difficult than normal to keep my head in the game when I slid off ice and had to watch Brax fling himself over the boards. His bulky hockey gear did not hide enough of his body for me to not think of what he'd looked like in his suit as we'd arrived at the arena. Thankfully, the distraction was mere seconds at most. My attention was usually drawn to Bouchard or Cunningham to discuss strategy.

The game went according to plan until well into the third period when we were behind by one and in the midst of what was beginning to feel like the longest penalty kill in history. I'd tried to skate off three separate times in fifty-three seconds, only to have the puck careen toward me or a player get in my way. My legs felt like lead and I knew I was starting to slow down to the point that I wasn't going to do anyone any good on ice.

Brax came over the boards with fresh legs, making a beeline toward me. "Go!" he barked. "Go, go, go." I'd just sent the puck flying deep in the offensive zone and powered my way to the bench, thankful another player would finally be taking my place. I was already slowing down to take a step off ice when I was suddenly airborne, my skates lifting completely off the ice as I was sent into the bench area, landing half on the floor, half on Yuri's lap.

The whistle had blown before I'd landed and I recoiled to protect my face from skate blades as the entire bench was up, screaming and yelling at whoever had knocked into me. The screaming of the team could only be shouted down by the fans booing. It quickly turned into a cheer, which let me know someone had gone after the offender.

I tapped at Yuri's leg, screaming for him to help me up instead of holding me so I didn't fall on my head.

"Sorry. Sorry, Trevor. Sorry." His big hands grabbed me and pushed me upright, my face contorting in pain when a very unhappy rib let itself be known.

"Shit. You okay?"

There was no way I was answering that because he'd know immediately that I was far from okay. I was going to be out at least the next few days, if not longer, but I was willing to muscle through it for a few more seconds if I got a chance to take a swing at whoever it was that had sent me ass over head into the bench.

It couldn't have been more than five or ten seconds that I'd been down, but when I got up ready to get back out there and finish the fight, the sight before me drew me up short.

Utter chaos had broken out on ice and on the bench. Brax was locked up with someone along the boards nearest us, a ref trying to pull them apart. Bouchard had Toby and Mazdon by the collars, screaming at them to sit their asses down. Cunningham wasn't just on the bench screaming at Morti Knight, Tampa's head coach, he was standing on top of the boards, leaning over the divider between the benches and ripping Knight and anyone else in earshot a new one.

On ice, only Tampa's goalie hadn't gotten into a fight. Igor was in the middle of his own brawl with Tampa's center in front of our net, the refs not paying a bit of attention to them.

"Who the fuck hit me?" Between my panting, sore ribs, and the pain of my exhausted legs, the words hadn't come easily, but I'd gotten them out.

Yuri pointed to the guy Brax was still locked up with. The refs were holding them back enough that it had effectively turned into a fierce hug while each of them roughly nudged at the other's face with a fist. Part of me was happy that it had been Brax to be the first at him; another part of me wanted to level the asshole on Tampa for the cheap shot.

I wriggled free from Yuri's grip and made a half step forward before Bouchard's voice stopped me in my tracks. "Cane, you take one fucking step toward that ice, I will personally *glue* your ass to the bench for the next week!"

Pursing my lips, I crossed my hands over my chest and winced again. Yuri and Bouchard both saw it. "Get back to the trainers, now." Our normally easygoing assistant coach was all business and the tone of his no-nonsense command had my submissive side deciding to surface at the most inopportune time.

Whether I wanted to go or not, I knew myself well enough to know that I'd do something ridiculous like pout or whine if I stayed, so my exhausted, sore, and already stiff self hobbled down the tunnel and toward the trainers and team doctor.

From inside the medical room, I could hear the play-by-play from the announcers. It sounded like they were finally getting the fights broken up. It would be a few more minutes before they figured out the penalties, but I couldn't find the mental capacity to think about that as the team doctor worked to get my jersey off me and my chest pad unfastened.

Between the doctor, the trainer, and me, we managed to get me freed from my uniform, though the doctor insisted on cutting my jersey off me to minimize discomfort. Away from the melee on ice and with the adrenaline beginning to crash, the pain was increasing steadily and not being helped by the poking and prodding the doctor was doing to my side.

"Good news is nothing feels broken. I'm guessing you're going to have a pretty nasty bruise for the next few days, but

I want to get some imaging first." That didn't help a hell of a lot, especially not as angry voices could be heard coming down the tunnel.

Igor's cursing was loudest, his broken English clearer than Yuri's, and when he was fired up, he could hold his own with a New Yorker fighting for a cab. "Cheap fucking shot. Asshole Gatzenburg! Where is Trevor?"

A scoff tried to escape me, but all it managed to do was make my ribs hurt worse.

"That replay. Jesusfuckingchrist, I'm glad Yuri was there!" That was definitely Seth's voice. I couldn't remember if he'd been on the ice at the time or not, but given that the game wasn't over, I had to assume he had been. It sounded like everyone on ice at the time had been booted from the remainder of the game.

"Trevor!" The voice wasn't as familiar as the others, but I knew it well already.

While I wanted to call out and let everyone know I was fine, I knew that wasn't going to be a good idea. Instead, I looked up at the doctor and tried to speak calmly. "Will you please tell those idiots that I'm in here? They'll scream my name until they find me."

The doctor shook her head. "Triage room. Why is this so hard? Every time one of you gets hurt, the rest of you act like you've never seen this room before."

I'd been guilty of the same thing in the past and knew well enough to keep my mouth shut.

Sighing to herself, she called out, "Triage. He needs—"

Before she could finish the sentence, four heads popped around the corner: Igor, Seth, Jean-Luc, and Brax.

"An X-ray." The doctor shook her head. "Go, get out of that gear." She looked up at them and sighed. "And then get back here so I can put you all back together and see just how much damage you did to yourselves."

"Jean-Luc got ejected from a game?" I asked the room. Jean-Luc didn't fight. He had the fewest penalty minutes on our team, one of the lowest in the entire league. The only players with lower penalty times were those who had just moved up from the AHL.

The doc ignored me as she set up the X-ray. "Let's get this done. You know they're going to be in here again as soon as they get changed." She might have been rolling her eyes, but she was smiling just the same.

"Let's hope they at least shower first."

She barked out a startled laugh. "Like you have room to talk."

"I'm injured. I get a reprieve. Even if something is broken, you're still going to send me to the shower next."

She was still laughing as she took the X-rays of my ribs.

Five minutes later I could hear the announcers, the game drawing to an end. We were now one ahead, and there was an empty net but only five seconds left in the game. "Nothing broken. There might be a hairline crack. I want to repeat the X-rays in a few days when some of the inflammation has gone down. For now, rest, ice. I'll get you some painkillers because it's going to hurt like hell to breathe for a few days. Day-to-day."

I groaned. At least day-to-day was better than four-to-six weeks, but I was going to miss a game for sure. We'd see if they'd let me be with the team for the game on Sunday, though I wasn't holding my breath. There was no way I'd be ready to play that game.

Brax's head popped around the corner just as the buzzer sounded and the tunnel erupted in noise.

The doctor ignored the chaos in the tunnel and beckoned Brax closer to study his jaw. "Any significant pain?"

"Just a bruise. He's got a hell of a hook."

The two didn't have a chance to say anything else because Cunningham walked in. He must have hightailed it from the bench, through the players, and to the triage room because he was the first one through the door. "How is he?"

"Fine," I said as the doc spoke over me.

"Bruising. Potential hairline fracture, but I need to give it a few days and repeat the imaging."

Cunningham cursed, looked me over a few times, then shook his head sadly. "Go get showered up. Let Cernak drive you home tonight."

I ran my hand through my sweaty hair instead of pushing my thumb in my mouth like I wanted to. The pain was getting intense now, making the need to find comfort in my thumb nearly too much to resist. "Couldn't drive anyway. Doc says painkillers for a few days."

"Oh! Right!" She handed over a pill with a sympathetic smile on her face. "I know you hate these, but you're going to hate the world a lot less if you take one now and give it a few minutes before you try to get showered."

A bottle of Gatorade materialized in front of me, handed over by none other than Brax. "Drink up and go rest for a few."

I grumbled but did as I was told, going to find the nearest bench to sit on for a few minutes. I had thirty minutes before the pill leveled me and I wasn't going to be able to do more than sleep. I needed to time things perfectly to make sure I was in the car by then.

Five minutes later, I was pushing myself up, still in pain but knowing time was ticking. I left the room to Cunningham and Brax, who were talking about postgame interviews.

## CHAPTER 9

### BRAX

NOTHING LIKE STARTING my career with the Grizzlies off with a bang, or an effective ejection after being handed a five-minute fighting major with less than five minutes left in regulation play. It was definitely worth it for the cheap cross-check that Gatzenburg laid on Trevor. We'd all known that his legs had turned to rubber. He'd been skating hard for over a minute on a penalty kill and had already racked up an impressive amount of ice time for the game.

When it became apparent that Tampa was blocking him from getting off ice, Coach sent me out to forcibly get him off. I'd done my job clearing the path, and Seth's skates had already hit the ice. Trevor had slowed, his foot already over the threshold of the bench area, when Gatzenburg had leveled him with an illegal check that had sent him flying.

That need to protect Trevor had reared its head and I was halfway across the ice before he'd landed on Yuri. Gatzenburg had had his gloves off before I'd reached him. The play whistle had blown, and the fans were on their feet booing the play before my fist made contact with his jaw. My attention was focused solely on the man in front of me as I avoided as many hits as possible. Gatzenburg and I had tangled before and he had a hell of a hook. I'd found that out the hard way in the past and had been reminded of it when his left fist made contact with my jaw. I would be feeling it the next day, but I made sure he would be too.

It wasn't until the two of us hit the ground that another ref joined in to pull us apart. As I got to my feet, I noticed for the first time that Igor's helmet, jersey, and both his gloves were off as he fought with one of Tampa's forwards. Gatzenburg and I were escorted to our benches by the refs, squabbling the entire way. Trevor was already down the tunnel by then. I wanted to know how badly he'd been hurt, but the scene in front of me was a lot like a train wreck.

Coach Cunningham and Tampa's coach were standing on the boards, leaning over and screaming at one another. Coach Bouchard was screaming at a ref but had death grips on the backs of Maz's and Toby's jerseys. Yuri was already getting his helmet and gloves on but was screaming at Igor in Russian. From the look on his face, I guessed he was cheering him on, but it wasn't like I could make out enough of his native language to figure out anything he said.

It took another thirty seconds before all the fights were broken up. More than one lip had been split open, and I was pretty sure Igor was going to need the gash above his eye glued together. Yuri looked over at me as he stepped onto the ice. "YouTube, ESPN, that fight gold."

YouTube and ESPN were barely going to scratch the surface of all the coverage; the last few minutes were going to be Twitter fodder for days to come. I could already hear a review board groaning at the scuffle. The ref gave us all five-minute penalties and sent us to our dressing rooms. The penalties were going to be small compared to the fines Cunningham and the other coach were going to be facing for their current verbal war.

*Welcome to Nashville.*

Just as I turned to head down the tunnel, the camera panned to my dad and Leo. Dad was giving a satisfied grin and Leo's cheeks were flushed red, probably from screaming at me and everyone else on the ice. I loved those two, but now I needed to focus on finding Trevor to make sure he was okay.

Igor was already bellowing his name. I jogged to catch up to him, Seth, and Jean-Luc just as they turned into a small room I hadn't known was there but really should have. I could see the doctor and nurse ready to scold us for barging in, but then her eyes widened at the sight of us.

"Go, get out of that gear." After giving us all a once-over, she sighed in resignation. "And then get back here so I can put you all back together and see just how much damage you did to yourselves."

A nurse chased after Igor with butterfly bandages to keep his head together long enough that he could strip his gear off without bleeding all over the locker room.

"How much do you think Coach's screaming match is going to cost him?" Jean-Luc asked as he peeled his jersey over his head.

Seth laughed. "Not as much as it will cost Gatzenfuck. That was a suspendible hit, and he's been in trouble for shit like that in the past. Last season he got a four-game suspension for a near-identical hit. The guy's a loose cannon."

Igor blotted at a stream of blood that was pushing through the bandages on his eyebrow. He looked at Jean-Luc. "How are you?"

Jean-Luc managed to free himself from his pants, an angry purple bruise already making itself known on his jaw. His knuckle needed some attention, but I doubted it would need more than a little super glue. "Toby's gonna be worried about me, but I'm fine."

He was so young, I doubted he had to shave often. No-Shave-November was always an interesting month for some of the younger players who could barely grow scruff on their chins, much less a full beard.

Starting with Boston before my twenty-first birthday had been a shock to the system. I couldn't imagine playing in the NHL at barely nineteen, but Jean-Luc and Toby were both in their second season. After growing up playing together, the two were still best friends and shared a house.

I finished stripping my gear off as a whistle could be heard coming from the ice. The play-by-play piping through the sound system called a slashing penalty against Tampa. The cheers from the stands quickly turned more frantic and the announcer mentioned another fight.

"Is it always like this with Tampa?"

Igor lifted a shoulder. "Usually. We play, we fight."

Seth nodded. "Bad blood. Don't really know why, though. It's been there since I started playing here. Definitely no better when we go there. Dammit, Mazdon's gonna be grumpy with me too. He hates when I get in fights, especially when he isn't on the ice with me."

This group of men was the most unique I'd ever been around and for the first time since I'd been picked up by Boston, I felt like I fit in. There were no cliques or impossible bars to cross to be considered a member of the team. We played together, we fought together, we laughed together. It was refreshing after the last few years of feeling like I was on the outside of an organization that had, in theory, wanted me.

I finished getting my gear off and headed toward the door. "I'm going to go see the doc."

I didn't need the doc, but she'd said to come back when we had ourselves out of our gear. Besides, Trevor was there and there was something gnawing in my brain that wasn't going to settle until I could make sure he was okay.

The buzzer sounded as I walked through the doorway and both the doc and Trevor looked up at me, though Trevor was looking worse for the wear at that point. His face was pinched and slightly pale, like he wanted to puke but wasn't about to let himself.

The doc glanced over at me, then came to study my jawline. "Any significant pain?"

I shook my head. "Just a bruise. He's got a hell of a hook."

She opened her mouth, but Cunningham's appearance in the doorway cut her words off. "How is he?" His voice was quiet, but there were lines of concern etched in his eyes and forehead. The inquiry hadn't sounded self-serving and I found it touching.

Coach Anders had only shown worry when one of the top performers was injured, and even at that it was mostly about how long they would be out. He'd left any feelings to trainers and directors. A coach caring about a player's health was novel.

I zoned back into the conversation in time to hear Trevor saying the doc had said he was going to need painkillers for a few days. Judging by the look on his face and the quick apology she offered, I could tell Trevor was not a fan of them. All I could do was hand Trevor the unopened bottle of Gatorade I'd walked in with. "Drink up and go rest for a few."

He grumbled but took the pill and slowly made his way to a bench.

Igor came in. The doc took one look at him and sighed. "Come on, let's get you put back together."

Trevor's head was leaned back against the wall, his eyes closed, and his breathing measured. I knew he had to be in pain—the replay of not only the hit but the way he'd landed on Yuri looked painful. Had Yuri's lap not been there, though, the damage would have been directly to his head and face. Yuri's knees might have bruised his ribs, but they had probably saved him from a nasty concussion and numerous stitches.

"You're still living with Cane, right?"

Coach's question had my head back to the present in a hurry and I was nodding before my mouth formed words. "Yeah. Haven't had much time to find a place yet."

I was pretty sure that the look that crossed his face was relief. "Good. Great, actually. Trev doesn't do well with painkillers. They knock him out. The few times he's taken them, we've had to send him home with someone else because he can't function on them."

*Fun.*

"Well, I'm still there, so that's fine."

"Great. Now we need to figure out postgame interviews."

Trevor grunted and we both glanced over to see him pushing himself up. He walked out of the room and across the hall to the locker room, probably to shower. Cunningham waited for him to disappear into the locker room before turning back to me. "I'm going to have to make some sort of excuse for you. What a shit show." He scrubbed his hands down his face. "Good first game, by the way."

I couldn't help but laugh. "It was memorable, that's for sure."

He heaved a sigh. "Go hit the showers. I need to check on Iggy and the rest of the guys. That was one massive brawl. You all left blood from the ice to here."

"Not me." I rubbed at my jaw. "Just a good bruise. Didn't even lose a tooth."

I left the room to Coach Cunningham's laughter and hurried through a shower and changed, slipping into my suit as fast as I could, but it looked like it hadn't been fast enough when I got back to the locker room to a group of guys crowded around Trevor.

"Foot up, Cap. Let me get your shoe on." Yuri had gotten out of his goalie gear and had managed to get his undershirt off as well, leaving him in just a pair of undershorts and his socks. That was when we all wanted into the shower the most, but he was standing there holding Trevor's shoe out and trying to get him dressed.

When I got to them, Trevor was barely functioning, his eyes half-closed, and Maz had crouched down to grab his leg so that Yuri could slide the shoe on him. All I could think was that they hadn't been kidding that Trevor didn't handle painkillers well. I definitely understood why he'd groaned when the doc had told him to take one, and now I had to find a way to get the guy home.

Seth spotted me and was suddenly very close. He'd showered before I had, but his hair was still wet and dripping onto the collar of his dress shirt. "You sure you can handle him tonight? He's going to be out of it, so it won't be so bad. Unless he forgets where he is. Last time he got hurt, he fell asleep on the bus to the airport, slept through Iggy carrying him to the plane, and woke up in Nashville panicked because he had no idea where we were."

"Fun."

"Doc promised not to give him that particular one again, but given how he is right now, I don't think this one is going to be much better. He gets loopy. He doesn't remember anything. He must be feeling like shit if he didn't argue about taking painkillers."

This was sounding better and better as the guys talked. The more Seth spoke, the more my need to protect Trevor made itself known.

"He's welcome to come back to our place if it's too much. You barely know him. You just finished your first game with us after a hectic week. I know you must be exhausted. If taking care of a guy who might as well be drunk off his ass is too much, I don't blame you one bit. Trev can come home with us."

Seth had barely started speaking and I'd known where he was going. That didn't change the sour feeling I got in my stomach at the thought of not being the one to take care of Trevor. Even knowing that Seth had spoken from a place of genuine concern and kindness, it took effort for me to not snap at him. "No. I appreciate it, but I've got him." There was no way I was letting him out of my sight until I knew he was okay.

Seth looked like he wanted to argue, but Maz came up and put a hand on his shoulder as he leaned over to talk with me. "You ready to get him home? He's going to be a zombie in about two minutes, whether we get him out of here or not."

Once again, Seth tried to argue, but I cut him off with a decisive nod. "Yeah, I'm ready, just need to grab my phone and we need to find Trevor's keys."

"Got 'em." Toby dangled a set of keys from his finger and I swiped them out of his hand before turning to grab my phone from my locker.

Igor's voice echoed from the doorway, the cut on his eyebrow cleaned and bandaged together. "Coast is clear. Get Trevor."

Maz headed back to the seat where Trevor was. "Come on, buddy, get up for me. Let's get you to the car."

Trevor got to his feet, his eyes heavy and his feet unsteady. Instinctively, I stepped closer to Trevor and Maz, but Igor beat me to him, chuckling as he steadied him by the shoulders. "Seth, grab Huck. Brax, go get the car." People scattered at Igor's commands, me included.

Jogging toward the players' entrance, I noticed Toby and Jean-Luc heading the other way with a ball and a few sticks, both grinning like they were up to something.

"Diversion," Seth said to me as we exited the building.

"Excuse me?"

"Toby and Luc, they're going to create a diversion to keep the media and anyone else from seeing Trev so out of it."

These guys were a well-oiled machine. I loved how they had each other's backs, everyone willing to help, jumping in to figure out where they were most needed.

"Shit, my dad and Leo are here."

"I saw them on the screen a few times. They were hysterical. I'm pretty sure your dad was yelling for you to hit him harder next time."

"Knowing my dad, he probably was." I pulled my phone from my pocket, unlocked it, then handed it to him. "Can you please message him and tell him I'm not going to be at the arena because I need to get Trevor home? He'll understand."

I didn't know what I'd been expecting from Seth, but an approving smile hadn't been it. "Got it." He took the phone and began to tap out a message as I adjusted the seat so that I could get into his car.

"It's moments like these that I miss the manual adjusters."

Seth turned my phone off and tossed it in the center console. "Hit the number two on the door. It's programmed for me. I drove him home a few days ago and nearly squashed myself when I got in."

I stood up and pressed the button on the door and watched with satisfaction as the seat quickly positioned itself to a spot I was much more likely to be able to use. "Brilliant."

"I try." He winked. "Oh, here comes Igs." He jumped back and let Igor help Trevor into the front seat then stepped back for Seth to give him both our bears. He stopped just long enough to hand Trevor's buckle to me to latch into place. "Drive safe."

"Yeah, thanks." The door shut and Trevor curled toward the window. He was out and I was left to hope that the GPS would get me home without trouble.

## CHAPTER 10

### TREVOR

A STABBING PAIN shot through my chest when I gasped. The sun on my face felt familiar but unwelcome. The night before came back to me in small fuzzy pieces. The fall explained the throbbing pain in my ribs that had gotten worse when I'd startled awake. The X-rays said it was only bruising but then the doc had handed me a painkiller.

That was why everything was so hazy between the shower and now.

*I still hated painkillers.*

At least I had Huck tucked in my arm and my thumb pushed in my mouth to ground me as I came back to my senses. Pain meds gave me nightmares and made me feel like I had a hangover from hell. If I took them for more than a few days, I would end up itchy and miserable.

I burrowed into the blankets, only to have them pull me closer. The stabbing pain from a few seconds earlier was nothing compared to what I felt when I jolted back. It was too intense for me to keep my mouth shut. "Fuck!" I gripped my sides, trying to get the pain to subside.

My exclamation made the blanket jump.

Ribs still throbbing and my eyes watering from the jolt of pain, I could only just make out the figure staring at me. "Brax?"

He shot up quicker than I had, his sleepy eyes panicked as he tried to blink me into focus. "Are you okay?"

I ignored his question to put voice to a far more pressing one. "What are you doing in my bed?" *When had we gotten home? What time was it? Shouldn't he be at practice? Why had we been snuggling?* There were so many questions, but the pain in my ribs made me unable to ask anything else.

Brax chuckled uncomfortably. "Well, Seth warned me that you get really confused when you take pain meds. When we got home, you kept trying to go to the room by the steps, but the door's locked and you were getting frustrated."

Embarrassment heated my face and I could feel the heat spreading down my chest. There was no way I was going to ask if I'd said *why* I wanted in that room. Telling my teammate that the locked room was my playroom was *not* on my list of things I wanted to do that morning, or ever.

"You couldn't remember where the key was and were really upset. I finally got you in here and into bed, then headed upstairs to get ready for bed. I only managed to get changed before I heard you yelling. I thought you were in pain and I came running down here."

All I could think was that I was thankful the drugs made me loopy enough that I couldn't remember the key was in my nightstand drawer. Not only would he have seen my dildos, but he'd have also seen my playroom.

"Turns out you were having a nightmare or something. You kept screaming that there was something in the closet. No amount of assuring you that there was nothing in there was working and you just kept getting more upset, so I finally offered to stay here in case something came out. That did the trick and as soon as I sat down on the bed, you rolled closer and settled."

Lifting my arms hurt, but it didn't stop me from hiding my face in my hands. "I am so sorry." Unfortunately, I could totally see my medicated brain deciding there were monsters in the closet or under the bed. Or bugs.

*Bugs were the worst.*

Brax never missed a beat as he shook his head. "Don't be. You were out of it. I'd been warned that you and pain meds don't mix and you barely made it to the car last night. I was expecting something crazy to happen and I guess of everything that could have happened, thinking there were monsters in your room was pretty tame.

"I broke my arm one summer in middle school. The doctors gave me a drug that was supposed to make me not feel anything. Except I had an adverse reaction to it and screamed that they were trying to murder me until it finally wore out of my system."

I winced in sympathy. It wasn't hard to imagine me having much the same reaction. "That sucks. But I'm still sorry you had to ride the painkiller-induced insanity with me."

The first sign of uncertainty crossed his face and I watched as color filled the apples of his cheeks. "As long as Huck didn't fall, you slept fine."

Had it not been for the pain in my ribs, I would have fallen over dramatically and buried my head under the pillows. He knew Huck was my favorite bear, but he'd been sleeping in my bed all night, and there was no way he hadn't noticed my thumb in my mouth. Now I was left questioning if I mentioned it and got the big—real—monster out in the open now, or if we were going to be okay pretending it didn't exist.

"How's your stomach feeling?"

*Apparently we were ignoring it.* "Fine."

"How about your ribs?"

*They hurt like a bitch.* "Sore."

Brax hummed. "Well, let's get breakfast, then maybe see how some Advil does?"

"Good plan. Let me hit the bathroom first. Don't you have practice today?" I made to stand and my ribs pinched, pulling the breath from my lungs.

"Stay there, I'll come help." He was out of bed and jogging over to help me. "Take it easy. Cunningham was worried about you last night. The last thing I want is to have to tell him that you hurt yourself more by being a stubborn ass."

I was still marveling at Brax's well-defined arms and torso as he was reaching under my arms and lifting me to a standing position. Logically, I knew it had been over eight hours since I'd taken painkillers, and I wasn't still loopy from them—the pain in my ribs could attest to that. All that bare skin on display was making me feel off-kilter. I wanted to wrap my arms around him and bury my face in his chest and inhale.

Instead of making things more awkward than they already were, I offered a smile. "Thanks. I'm going to go shower." As I turned away, I could have sworn I saw Brax checking me out. In a T-shirt that hung halfway to my knees, I knew I wasn't particularly attractive, but having him looking at me was nice. Impossible relationship or not, my cock liked the attention and I was thankful for the baggy shirt as I entered my bathroom.

Thoughts of Brax were washed away with the pelting water on my chest and back. A gnarly purple-red bruise had popped up overnight, spreading for inches from just below my nipple to the base of my rib cage. Looking at the bruise, I knew just how lucky I was that nothing was broken. The hit and fall had happened so fast that I hadn't had time to think about it. I'd been on my feet, then across Yuri's lap.

Bruised ribs was far from the worst injury I'd sustained playing hockey; however, this was one of the most pointless, targeted attacks I'd been part of. Time ceased to exist as I stood in the pelting spray, rinsing my body and letting my mind drift.

It would have been so easy to roll closer to Brax that morning. It had been longer than I could remember since I'd woken up with anyone in my bed. I'd known I was attracted to guys in middle school. It hadn't been until much later that I'd discovered that I was also attracted to women, though much less often. There had been a few short-term girlfriends in my past, our sex lives good, but the emotional connection had always been lacking. While I was open about being bisexual with the team, I knew I was most likely to end up with a man one day.

When Seth and Maz had come out toward the end of the last season, I'd come out as bi. Open about my sexuality or not, being a hockey player didn't give me the ability or the reassurance I needed to have hookups whenever I wanted.

My security items and my thumb aside, I was the team captain, and I needed to set a good example for my team.

Hookups weren't satisfying when I knew what I was looking for wasn't someone adding a notch to their bedpost, but a person who could accept all of me. That wasn't going to happen at a bar, on an app, or with a sexy teammate. Seth and Maz had lucked out by finding love in the locker room, and I knew better than to think that lightning could strike twice.

An image of Brax, all smooth chested with a perfectly muscled back and legs for days, came to mind as I thought about finding love with a teammate. The gnawing thought that there could possibly be something between us wasn't letting up, but I knew better than to believe fantasies or medication-induced lust.

A shudder ran through my body as I thought of the mess that would be caused if anything happened between us, a logistical and ethical spiderweb of complications before ever scratching the surface of my needs and desires.

*Hey, Brax, you're really hot and I think I'm attracted to you. Yeah, I know you're the newest player on the team and I'm the captain. And yeah, I know that I've technically known you since you were a kid and not only do I know your dad but played on the same team with him. Oh, and did I mention that I'm a little looking for a Daddy?*

Nope. Wasn't happening. I was locking that shit up in a box and throwing away the key.

I was halfway through drying my body before I noticed that my back and side had loosened up considerably as I'd showered. There was a little pulling and stiffness in my ribs but nothing unbearable. I'd see how I was feeling after breakfast and maybe head to the rink with Brax. This level of soreness was easily able to be played through.

After a lifetime of playing hockey and ten years in the NHL, I wasn't good at sitting home doing nothing, so I dressed with the intent to go to practice. Hopefully the doc and trainers would let me skate with the team, but if not, I could at least do a light workout in the training room.

With my thoughts on our practice, I'd nearly forgotten all about Brax being in the house. I had totally forgotten what he'd said as we were getting out of bed, so finding him in the kitchen, still in his pajamas and with his hair sticking up at odd angles, was a total surprise to me.

He'd put earbuds in and was dancing as he worked at the stove, his hips and ass moving in a hypnotic rhythm as he worked at flipping pancakes. Thank fuck for small miracles—having his back turned toward me allowed me plenty of time to hide the growing problem in my pants behind the island while still watching him work.

*Perving*, I was totally perving on Brax as he made us breakfast.

When he dropped the empty batter bowl into the sink, I knew I couldn't keep watching him without his knowledge. If I were in his shoes, I'd probably have a heart attack if I turned around to find someone staring at me. While I didn't want to have to stop watching Brax move, I also didn't want to have to do CPR on him because I gave him a heart attack. Coach wasn't going to love that I was out for a few games as it was; he really wouldn't be happy if I killed the new trade.

"Smells good in here."

Brax jumped and yanked one of his earbuds out as he swung around to look at me. "Jesus, I didn't hear you come up. Sorry. Got lost in what I was doing."

I gave him a smile that I hoped was apologetic. "I didn't want to scare you, but I knew no matter what I said, it was going to startle you. But it does smell good in here."

The smile that spread across Brax's lips lit his entire face up. "I made pancakes. Leo still makes them for me when I feel like crap or I'm injured."

Leo had always been the cook in their house, and his love language was food. He knew everyone's favorite dish and exactly what would make them feel better. "Leo's a good cook."

Brax turned back to the stove but hummed in acknowledgement. "He really is." When he turned back around, he had two plates in his hands and slid one across to me. It took a moment for me to process what I was seeing, and I finally had to admit that I was looking at pancakes that looked like a bear's face.

"Teddy bear pancakes?" I asked, an eyebrow raised in question.

"With blueberries. I remember they were your favorite when you lived with us." He glanced away, embarrassment staining his cheeks and turning the tops of his shoulders red as well. "When I found the basket in the fridge, I figured you must still like them."

I couldn't figure out how he'd have remembered that I liked blueberries in my pancakes. We'd barely spoken when I was living there, our worlds so far apart that they might as well have been different universes. There had been a few times that I'd seen him playing video games or drawing, but most of the time, he'd kept to himself or had been at his own hockey practices. The only time we'd ever spent time together had been if he'd come to a game or during dinner.

"Thank you. They are still my favorite." I glanced down at the adorable bear faces he'd made and felt warmth pool in my stomach. It couldn't be described as lust or attraction, like I'd been dealing with earlier. It was something softer, an emotion I couldn't quite put my finger on. "These are adorable."

"I'm glad you like them. Leo taught me how to make designs a few years ago."

I used the side of my fork to cut off an ear and had it nearly at my mouth before I remembered that Tom and Leo had been at the game the night before. "Shit, did you get to spend time with your dad and Leo last night?"

Brax took a swig of coffee before answering me. "No. I texted them that I was getting you home because you weren't in any shape to drive. They saw the hit; they knew you weren't going to be feeling well. They understood, though they've both texted this morning to ask if you need anything. I wouldn't be surprised if they showed up while I'm at practice."

My eyes widened. "Here?"

"Oh, I actually meant at the arena. They stayed in town last night. Knowing them, I'm going to be sightseeing all day. Be thankful you're stuck here."

I stabbed another bite of my waffle with my fork. "I was going to try to come to the arena with you today. I'm actually feeling a ton better after my shower."

Brax's light laughter filled the kitchen as he shook his head. "Nope. Cunningham texted this morning and said you're not allowed at the rink until tomorrow. Apparently, you make it a habit of pushing through injuries." He slid his phone across the counter and pointed to the screen where Coach Cunningham's text was displayed.

**CC**: *I'm telling you this because I know Cane well enough to know that he's going to avoid his phone this morning. He* *needs to rest. I don't care how much he begs and pleads, I don't want to see him until tomorrow, unless he needs to see the doc sooner.*

I pushed the phone back toward Brax. "Dammit. That's just not fair."

"You get a day off before Halloween. That's nearly unheard of in this world."

I muttered a protest, but it was half-hearted at best. I knew Coach was right, and I really could use some sleep. Maybe I could catch a nap in my bed in the playroom while Brax was gone. Knowing that he'd be gone for hours would give me plenty of time to relax and rejuvenate before he returned.

"I'll keep my dads away from here so that you can rest in peace."

The urge to protest needing to sleep was strong, but I knew it wasn't going to do me any good. Instead, I focused on something Brax had said a few times now. "You've been calling them your dads. That's new." Leo had always treated Brax like his own. There had been a conversation that had come up while I'd lived with them that had always stuck with me.

Tom and LeAnn had been annoyed that Leo was still as adamant as he was that they not tell Brax they were together. He'd been worried about confusing Brax but had also been concerned about what would happen if the news of their relationship spread. The entire time I'd lived there,

Brax called Leo his uncle. Leo might have been fine with it, but I knew that Tom and LeAnn weren't. The two just refused to go against Leo's wishes.

Tom and I had stayed friendly, but we weren't close enough that I was privy to the information about when they'd finally told Brax, or when he'd finally figured it out.

"Yeah, I guess. The two are together. They've been together as long as I can remember. In public, I still say he's my uncle, but that doesn't feel right anymore. He's been just as much a part of my upbringing as Dad was, hell, even Mom. There were years there that it was basically Mom and Leo raising me while Dad was working. I definitely knew Leo better than Dad for a number of years."

His eyes went unfocused as he thought, finally letting out a long breath and shaking his head slightly. "It took me a long time, but a few years back, I realized that Leo is a lot more than an uncle to me. In my head and around people I'm comfortable with, they are my dads. But since they aren't out to the world, I'm careful who I say that to."

"That makes sense. I'm glad you're comfortable with me." I meant the words sincerely. I liked that he considered me comfortable company. As awkward as my feelings were, I didn't want to be someone that my teammates didn't trust or didn't think they could talk to.

Brax shoved the last bite of his pancake into his mouth and placed his plate in the sink. "Yeah. I'm comfortable with you. And Dad told me that you've known they were together longer than I have. They trusted you and that says a lot."

The compliment, as roundabout as it was, left me speechless. Brax took the moment of silence to duck out of the kitchen. "I better get ready. Enjoy your day of peace and quiet. Oh! Can I borrow your car for practice? Mine won't be here until early next week."

I answered by pointing to the hook by the door where I usually hung my key fob before I remembered I hadn't drove home. "You have my keys."

I was going to be home alone for hours when he left, possibly the entire day. My playroom had all my art supplies and it had been way too long since I'd had a chance to do more than color. The possibilities in my room were endless, from coloring, to my chalk wall, to all my Play-Doh.

My toes curled around the rung of the chair, the excitement of getting a few hours alone already making the adult world begin to fade away. I needed to keep myself focused until Brax left, and then it would be fine to sneak away to my room.

## CHAPTER 11

### BRAX

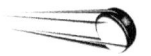

It was time to admit that my head was a mess.

The last ten hours had been a blur of emotions, from anger when I saw Gatzenburg hit Trevor, to fear as I watched Trevor disappear below the boards. There had been worry as we'd waited for the doctor to read the results, and humor as we'd worked to get the loopy man to the car.

None of those emotions compared to the terror I'd felt when I heard him screaming in his room. I might have brushed it off that morning, but the scream he'd let out was bloodcurdling and I'd made it from my bedroom to his faster than an Olympic sprinter. I'd had no idea what I'd be walking into, but Trevor curled into a ball pointing at the closet like someone or something had been in there had not been it. Despite doing what amounted to a monster check in the closet, bathroom, and under the bed, there was no amount of reassurances that would ease his mind.

Seth's reminder that painkillers fucked with Trevor had been the only thing keeping me from taking him to the hospital for hallucinations. The only thing I'd been able to think to do was sit down next to him and hope that my presence would calm him.

My ass had barely hit the mattress and Trevor had been nearly on top of me. He'd dragged an old blanket and Huck with him and had curled as close as he could get without actually climbing into my lap. My arm had instinctively wrapped around his shoulders to rub at his arm. Burrowed into my side, Trevor's breathing had evened out and the tension had left his body. Within minutes of sitting down, I had been left with a sleeping man attached to my side while trying to place the rhythmic sucking sound.

It had taken way too long to figure out the noise had been coming from my chest, but when I did, I'd quickly realized it had been the sound of Trevor's thumb in his mouth as he'd worked it while he slept.

I'd been left questioning if it was a byproduct of the meds or something different. The blanket he'd been clutching was clearly not something he'd grabbed just because of the meds. The thing was well loved and well past its prime. The way he'd been clutching both it and Huck had explained why his bear looked so much older than most everyone else's.

With Trevor finally asleep and me not willing to risk another meltdown, I'd settled in for the night. When I'd run to his room, the thought of spending the night with the man of my childhood dreams curled around me had never crossed my mind. I had also never thought that I'd spend the night with his teddy bear and a blanket resting on my chest as I listened to him sucking his thumb.

Somewhere in the list of things I was struggling to wrap my head around but maybe shouldn't have been was that I had been hard as a rock over half the night. I was back to blaming Easton for putting insane thoughts in my head. I'd spent my life around some of the toughest men in sports. I'd seen it all, including more than a few guys with security items or who were scared of the dark. Logically, I knew that Trevor's blanket, Huck, and his thumb-sucking didn't mean he was the boy Easton was so convinced I needed, but I was having a really hard time convincing my brain and dick that it wasn't the case.

Those thoughts had carried me through the morning and straight through breakfast when Trevor's eyes had lit up at the blueberries in his pancakes and the little bear heads I'd tried to make out of the batter. They weren't anywhere near as good as Leo's but if Trevor's smile could be believed, he hadn't minded.

After breakfast, I changed as quickly as I could and hurried down the steps to find Trevor still at the island, focused on his phone. "Hey, if you don't need anything else, I'm going to get out of here."

Trevor glanced up from his phone, his eyes soft and his smile warm. "I'm good. Thanks. Don't forget your bear."

I couldn't put my finger on it, but I swore even his voice sounded softer.

I held my bear up and reached for the keys. "Got it. I'll see you later." As I opened the door, I called over my shoulder, "Take it easy today."

Trevor waved me goodbye and I was out the door. Finally breathing a sigh of relief, I started the engine and hit the remote to the garage door. I was going to be nearly forty minutes early to practice, but I was out of the house and giving myself some space from Trevor and the ridiculous ideas that Easton had put in my head.

I was in line at the coffee shop when I realized that in my haste to leave the house, I'd left my gym bag in my room. There was every chance my dads really would force me to go out after practice, and no one was going to want to smell me in my workout clothes. Hell, I wasn't going to want to be in the car with myself if I didn't have a change of clothes. There was no choice but to go back.

The week had been such a blur of events that I still had Boston's schedule on my phone and it only took a quick search to see that they had the morning off. I grabbed my coffee from the barista and headed back to the car, pressing Easton's contact on the way.

"That was one hell of a way to start your career with Nashville," Easton said by way of greeting.

"I hate you."

Easton laughed at me. "That's nothing new. What did I do this time?"

The car connected to Bluetooth and I pulled out of my spot to head back to Trevor's. "You've got insane things in my head. Why can't you lay off the fact that I need a little?"

"Hold on a second, let me finish getting my coffee. I feel like this is a conversation that actually needs more attention from me."

Mugs clanked in the background, then the sound of the fridge opening and shutting before Easton came back on the phone.

"What have I done now?"

I wanted to throw my head back against the headrest, but I was in the middle of traffic and had to focus on the road. "I can't get the idea out of my head. And Trevor's so fucking cute—"

"Ha! You do have a crush on him!"

"But that doesn't mean he's a boy!"

Easton went silent, and an eerie, almost ominous moment stretched over the line. "Doesn't change that you want him to be."

"Doesn't change that he's not. But after spending the night holding him so that he could actually sleep, I'm having a hard fucking time convincing my brain of that!"

"Whoa! What? You slept with him last night?"

The fierce growl that came from my chest surprised even me. "Not like that, asshole! The doc gave him a painkiller and it fucked with his head. He was hallucinating things in his closet. I went to figure out why he was flipping out and ended up sitting down on his bed. He fell asleep attached to me like a barnacle and stayed that way until this morning. But all fucking night I had those damn posts you kept sending me dancing through my head. This is all your fault."

Easton had the nerve to laugh. "Sorry, not sorry. Maybe Cane isn't a boy, but hopefully this gets you to finally step out of your comfort zone and go to that club I told you about to find one. If anything, this will get you over your childhood crush."

I pulled the car into Trevor's garage and killed the engine, picking the phone back up and putting it to my ear as I headed toward the house. "But I'm *living* here, East."

I dropped my voice to a hiss as I walked through the quiet house. Trevor was nowhere to be seen, so I hoped that he'd fallen back asleep. "I had to put a fucking cup on to make breakfast so he didn't see how goddamned hard I was!"

At the bottom of the steps, I noticed the door to the room Trevor had been trying to get into the night before was open and a soft light was spilling into the hallway. Curiosity got the better of me and I stepped forward, Easton's laughter at my earlier predicament barely registering in my brain.

The soft music coming from the room wasn't anything I'd have expected to hear in the house. It was upbeat and bouncy, but not pop, more like something I'd hear on a children's show or one of the soundtracks I'd heard teammates playing to get their kids to go to sleep.

"Hey, listen, I just got back to the house. I need to grab my bag and get to practice. I'll talk with you later." I hung up and pocketed my phone before Easton could respond. I didn't really care what he thought or had to say.

Even if I hadn't wanted to look in, the door was directly off the steps. It would be impossible to miss as I headed to my room. I'd never thought anything of the closed door before the previous night. Hell, I hadn't thought anything of it that morning either. The memory of Trevor trying to get into the room had been blocked out by the countless other things that had happened afterward.

I told myself I wasn't going to look. I told myself I was just going to get to my room, grab my bag, and get out of there. If Trevor was trying to sleep, I was going to let him. I didn't need to bother him.

My resolve lasted exactly long enough for my foot to hit the first step and my peripheral vision to take over. A rocking movement caught my attention and I turned automatically, my feet rooting where I stood like I was a tree planted in place.

Trevor was lying on his stomach in the middle of the room, a pile of pillows below him to cushion his ribs. His feet were swaying back and forth as he focused on the giant mat in front of him. I could see scribbles and coloring on it and somewhere in my brain, I wondered what it was that he was coloring on as I'd never seen anything like it before.

That thought wasn't as important as everything else I was seeing. The room was light blue with a twin-sized bed along one wall covered with a bedspread that looked like someone had thrown paint all over it. There were pillows that looked like crayons strewn across the bed and floor. A small table sat in one corner, and in the center a basket held a huge stack of coloring books and another held crayons and markers. The shelves around the room were filled with books, stuffed animals, and more art supplies—including more Play-Doh—than I'd ever seen before. One wall was black, and it took me a moment to figure out it was a giant chalkboard.

Everything was soft and warm, including the pajamas that Trevor had changed into after I'd left. The one-piece pajamas accentuated his bubble butt that I couldn't help noticing looked softer than normal. A sippy cup sat in easy reach next to his blanket and Huck, but Trevor was oblivious to everything, me included, as he colored.

My nails digging into my palms finally brought me back to the present and reminded me that I wasn't supposed to be seeing what I was. This was Trevor's time to relax and the last thing he needed was to see me staring at him. Besides, I had a practice to get to. The extra minutes I'd had when I left had been eaten up by coffee and the trip back to the house. If I didn't get my bag and leave now, I was going to be late.

That was what finally had my feet moving from the spot I'd become affixed to. I hurried up the steps, thanking the plush carpet for muffling my footsteps. I could figure out what to do after practice. For now, my head needed to get in the game, literally.

I somehow made it to my room, grabbed my bag, left again without disturbing Trevor, and made it to the arena before practice started. Players often said there were two sides to them: the off-ice side and the on-ice side. It didn't matter what was going on in their off-ice life—when their skates hit ice, their on-ice side took over. I'd never been more thankful to be one of the players that could turn off the off-ice shit. As soon as my skates were on my feet and I walked to the rink, what I'd seen at Trevor's left my head until the final whistle blew after a game of sharks and minnows.

But once our skates were off, we were due in the workout room and I didn't have the same capability to shut off my brain on the treadmill as I did on the rink. I went through the motions as we went through our circuit, but my mind was precisely eleven-point-six-five miles away in the light blue room that held the team captain, my long-time crush, and apparent little, Trevor Cane.

I wanted to call Easton but I knew I couldn't because I'd be outing Trevor. I needed to talk to someone but I had no one to talk to until the intro night at DASH. Was I going to make it to then without exploding? Maybe it was time to follow some of those links Easton had been sending me and see if I could find a way to talk to—

"Earth to Brax. Come in, Brax." A hand waving in front of my face startled me and my foot slipped off the peddle of the bike I was on.

The peddle hit my shin and I hissed. "Fuck, ouch." Then I looked up to see who was looking at me. Seth and Maz were standing in front of the bike, but no one else was in the room. "Shit, I zoned out."

Seth chuckled softly. "Yeah, you did. You were a million miles away. Want to talk about it?"

I worried that the laugh that bubbled out of me sounded deranged. "Want and can are two very different things." Shaking my head, I sighed. "Fuck, you're going to have me committed at this rate. Sorry, ignore me. My friend has been driving me insane. It's gone to my head, and I got lost in thought."

"Well, if you stay on that machine any longer, your legs are going to be dead for tomorrow's game."

A glance down at the tracking display told me I'd been here for thirty-five minutes. Well longer than I should have been. "Shit."

Seth handed over a bottle of blue sports drink. "Rehydrate. Then you can tell us how Trevor did last night."

Maz's lips formed a straight line as he nodded. "Seth's been worried sick. I had to stop him from coming over at midnight."

I downed half the bottle, then looked over at them. "Probably better that you hadn't. If he wasn't still flipping out with hallucinations at that point, I'd just got him to sleep. Don't care who you are, I wasn't going to risk moving and waking him up, and had you woken him up, I might have strangled you."

Seth stared at me with huge brown eyes and eyebrows moving in rapid succession as he processed my words. Words that, admittedly, had been spoken out of sheer exhaustion and the racing thoughts that my brain had been dealing with since I'd spotted Trevor in his... I didn't know what to call the room he'd been coloring in. Was it a nursery? A playroom? A toy room? There was only one person who could answer that question, and he didn't know I'd seen what I had.

Instead of pushing me, Maz handed over a towel. "Rough night?"

I nodded. "Sorry, I'm exhausted. It's been a long few hours."

Maz directed both of us toward the locker room that was, blessedly, empty. "You should have just told Coach that Trev had a rough night and you wouldn't be in."

The thought had never crossed my mind until then. The truth was, once I'd seen what I had, I knew that there was no way Trevor would have relaxed like that if he'd known I was in the house. I was glad I'd been able to leave to give him that space, even if I couldn't get space from my thoughts.

"Hopefully, he's feeling better tonight and you can get some decent sleep," Maz said sympathetically. "I know I don't sleep well when Seth is hurt."

Seth nodded, though I wasn't sure if it was to Maz or something else entirely. He looked genuinely lost in thought. I understood the feeling.

I grabbed my phone to make sure Trevor hadn't texted. The only message was from my dad.

**Dad**: *Hey, kiddo. Leo and I are heading home. We both know what it's like to deal with injuries and want to let you get back in case Trev needs something.*

The text was a relief, but that also meant I was heading back a lot earlier than I'd told him. Hopefully that wouldn't cause a problem.

I looked up from my phone to Maz and Seth. "I should really get going, get a shower, and get back to make some lunch for Trevor. I don't want him overdoing it."

Maz nodded and clapped me on the shoulder. "Good plan. Let us know if you need anything."

## CHAPTER 12

TREVOR

**BRAX**: *Hey, I'm heading home. Have you had lunch yet?*

**Me**: *No. Not yet. Just woke up from a nap.*

**Brax**: *I'll pick something up on the way home.*

A nap that had included all the pillows and stuffed animals in my playroom, a few warm blankets, and cartoons on the TV as I drifted off with a bottle filled with water. In short, it had been perfect. The only way it could have been better would have been if Derek and his Daddy had come over for the afternoon, but playdates between a professional hockey player and a country musician with three kids who was married to the sheriff of Williamson County were not as easy as a *pick up the phone that morning* type of thing. They required planning and timing, and sometimes replanning.

Thinking about Derek reminded me that I hadn't actually talked to him after Brax had told me that he was going out on Wednesday night. And now that I was day-to-day, I would probably be free most of the week. At some point I'd go to no-contact practices, but that probably wouldn't be for a few more days.

I tapped at my contacts and pulled up Derek's name.

***Me***: *Playdate?*

With Derek's schedule, a response could take hours or days, but I'd eventually get one. I just normally didn't get one within seconds of hitting send.

***Derek***: *Oh, when? Daddy's sister has been on us to let her have the kids to give us a break.*

***Me***: *I'm on injured reserve right now. So I'm free until the doc clears me.*

***Derek***: *Let me talk with Daddy.*

I turned my phone off and smiled at the coincidence of meeting Derek on a day I'd happened to wear one of my favorite onesies to the rink. I didn't normally wear a onesie, but I'd been feeling exceptionally little that afternoon, so I'd slid it on under my sweatshirt before heading to the rink. It had been a family night for most of the players and their kids, and a good night to just relax and have fun. Seth had brought his brother, who had invited his boss—Sheriff Colt Westfield—and his family, thinking their kids would enjoy skating.

At some point during the evening, my sweatshirt had ridden up and Derek had caught a glimpse of the pattern on my shirt. I'd been shocked when Derek had gone out of his way to find me alone, and more than a little confused when he'd blushed as he gestured toward my sweatshirt. "I have the same shirt at home."

I'd looked down in confusion. The Grizzlies sweatshirt wasn't anything special and hardly unheard of at a team event.

"Not that one, the one with puppies on it."

The statement had left me speechless, my head reeling with thoughts. I would have thought he'd been mistaken, but the red his cheeks had turned told me he was admitting something big to me. "You do?"

He nodded and pointed over to his husband. "My Daddy bought it for me."

That had been the beginning of a close friendship and plenty of playdates over the years. Since neither of us were comfortable going to the BDSM club in Nashville, we'd started having playdates at my house whenever we could. Being public figures, we both understood the need for discretion and privacy, and without kids or a family, we had plenty of both at my house.

**Derek**: *What about Wednesday? Daddy's got stuff going on at work this week, and we're going out on Thursday night.*

I looked at the calendar, trying to decide how long I'd be out with this injury. Even if I was practicing with the team again, workouts would probably still be light, and Brax had already told me he was planning on going out that night.

*Me: That works. Block the late afternoon to evening out. I'll let you know if I have more time closer to then.*

Feeling lighter than I had all day, I pocketed my phone just in time to hear the garage door open. I did a once-over of the house to make sure I hadn't left the door open or my bottle or sippy cup out. Nothing looked out of place and I took a breath as the door opened.

Brax's head came around the corner first, looking around like he was afraid he'd startle me. When he spotted me at the island, he smiled. "Hey. You look better than you did this morning."

"I'm feeling better. Still sore, but I crashed hard for about an hour and I think I finally slept the medicine fog away."

He set two bags on the counter in front of us from a local takeout place. "How are your ribs?"

"Sore, but not enough so that I'm going to take another painkiller." I definitely wasn't willing to put myself through another meltdown. Waking up wrapped around Brax with my thumb in my mouth and my blanket and Huck on his chest was embarrassing enough for a lifetime. He hadn't mentioned it to me, but with a little bit of space, I had to assume it was intentional avoidance more than genuine ignorance. The early morning fog had been nice while it'd lasted.

Brax studied me for an uncomfortable few seconds before finally nodding to himself. "Have you had more Advil since I left?"

"No, it's barely been four hours since then. I was just starting to think about taking a few more."

Without another word, Brax turned and headed to the cabinet where I kept my supplements as well as a stock of anti-inflammatories. He returned with three and set them and a to-go cup in front of me. "Take these now so you don't start hurting too bad."

My hand automatically went to the cup but as my fingers wrapped around it, I noticed it wasn't like the normal drink cups from the restaurant. He'd handed me a short plastic cup with a red lid, the same type used for kids' drinks.

I paused, studying the cup like it might bite me before finally tearing my eyes away to glance up at Braxton. My skin was clammy enough that I didn't know if I was flushed or pale. "What's this?"

"Chocolate milk." The words came out too casual, too matter-of-fact. There was no further explanation or humor to go with the statement.

"Why?" My voice had come out harsh, more suspicious than I'd have liked.

Brax lifted his drink from the holder and took a sip before shrugging a shoulder. "You're injured. Chocolate milk makes everything better." He pointed to the pills. "Take them so you can keep feeling decent. You were missed at practice today."

I took the pills but only because I knew he was right. It wasn't going to be long before the pain got bad and the last thing I wanted was to have to take one of the heavy-duty pills that the doctor had prescribed the night before.

Brax slid a bag of food across the counter toward me, my stomach's rumble reminding me that it had been hours since I'd eaten, and I eagerly reached into the bag to grab my lunch. The fries were going to be enough to have the team's nutritionist shitting a brick before I ever got to the chicken strips and ranch dressing.

This was a cheat meal if I'd ever seen one, and it looked and smelled amazing. Besides, I was injured. I was allowed to cheat a bit.

A tiny bowl filled with ketchup appeared in front of me. I'd eaten half the fries before I looked at the meal for what it was: an adult-sized kid's meal. The only thing missing was a toy. I glanced over to Brax to find him eating a burger over the sink, his meal looking nothing like mine.

Swallowing hard, my brain began to work in double time. *He knew.* He knew, or he suspected a lot more than he was letting on. But what did this mean?

I pulled my phone out of my pocket and opened a text with Seth.

**Me**: *Brax knows. He knows. He has to know.*

It was read immediately and I'd never been so happy to see the dancing bubbles below a name.

**Seth**: *Whoa. What does he know? I need you to spell this one out for me.*

**Me**: *He made pancakes this morning shaped like little bear heads and filled with blueberries.*

**Me**: *And he just came home with lunch for us. He got me chocolate milk in a kid's cup.*

**Me**: *And chicken fingers and fries!*

Seth was typing out a response that I swore took way longer than it should have.

**Seth**: *You like all those. Blueberry pancakes are your favorite. And you love chocolate milk and chicken fingers. I think you might be reading too much into this.*

**Me**: *But he has a burger! This looks more like a kid's meal without a toy!*

I wanted to be able to talk to Seth on the phone, but I couldn't with Brax standing right there, so I tapped out another text as fast as I could while eating my lunch. It was good and I was hungry. I wasn't going to ignore food just because I was freaking out.

***Me:*** *I had a nightmare or something last night. I don't remember it, but he ended up in my room. When I woke up, I was using him as a pillow. My thumb was in my mouth and I had Blankie and Huck on his chest! His CHEST! Seth, he* has *to know!*

I could feel how flushed my body was, and the way my heart was pounding felt like it was knocking against my bruised ribs. I must have made a sound because Brax looked over and concern instantly showed in his face.

"Jesus. You look like shit. What's wrong?"

I shook my head, trying to tell him nothing was wrong, but my ribs were not going to let their protestations go.

"Yeah, that's not nothing. I'm guessing you waited too long to take Advil. Come on, let's get you set up in bed where you can rest until it kicks in. We'll give it fifteen or twenty minutes. If you're not feeling better then, I'll grab one of the pills the doc prescribed."

No matter how badly I wanted to protest, I knew he was right. I needed to get away from the kitchen and lie down for a bit, if for no other reason than to give me space.

That was until we walked into my room and he made it a point to help me into bed and find Blankie and Huck. He left a moment later, but I was too busy being mortified to hear what he said as he exited. When I heard him leave, I pulled my blanket over my head and stuffed my thumb in my mouth to try to calm down.

The only decent thing about the entire situation was that I was alone in my room and able to let my guard down just a bit. My thumb had been my first line of defense in stress relief since I was born. It hadn't stopped through school, juniors, or my NHL career. I'd gotten better at hiding it as I'd gotten older, though Seth's sixth sense as to when my stress level was rising had kept me from being seen on a number of occasions. To my knowledge, he, Maz, Derek, Colt, and more than likely Brax were the only ones that knew.

At least tucked away in my room, my panic was starting to ease and with it the pain in my ribs was subsiding. It took a few more minutes of shallow breathing before the tightness in my chest eased completely.

Finally convinced I was overthinking everything, I sat up and pulled my phone out of my hoodie pocket to text Seth. I gave my thumb a cursory wipe and pulled up Seth's contact. I'd gotten all of four words in when Brax appeared by my bed with my remaining lunch in his hands.

He gave me an uneasy smile. "Glad to see your color back to normal."

"Sorry to scare you like that. I'm feeling a lot better right now."

Brax relaxed noticeably and held the plate out to me. "Great. Figured you'd still be hungry since you only ate half your fries. I was going to leave them on your nightstand if you were asleep."

"Thanks, I appreciate it. I am still hungry."

Instead of leaving after he handed me the plate, Brax sat down next to me and grabbed the remote sitting on my nightstand. "I hear you're only halfway through season two of *The Crown*."

The TV clicked on while I deleted the text I'd started to Seth and tapped out a new one.

**Me**: *I'm going to kill you.*

I got an angel emoji in response and scoffed.

"Everything okay?"

"Fine. Just going to kill Seth when I see him next."

Brax laughed, the warm sound making me smile through my embarrassment. "He's a good guy. A little scary, though. Definitely wouldn't want to get on his bad side."

"And you don't know his siblings well. One of his brothers is the deputy sheriff just south of here. Another is an attorney and one is a retired firefighter who looks like he could bench-press the entire team. Surprisingly enough, not all of them were there last night."

The look Brax gave me, like he had no clue how to take my words, had me chuckling. Of course, the movement hurt like hell, but I couldn't help it. "They're a trip. I don't know if you should be more afraid of Seth, or his siblings, or upsetting Seth and having his siblings come after you."

"Johnson family is scary, got it."

They weren't scary. They just loved fiercely and had more passion than any other family I'd ever met. Brax would figure that out eventually but for now I was okay with letting him worry a bit, especially after the heart attack I'd nearly had at lunch.

He propped his feet up on the bed and hit play. "I can't believe you're only on season two."

I struggled to come up with something to say in response, so I decided on just eating the rest of my lunch while we settled in for a *The Crown* marathon.

## CHAPTER 13

### BRAX

I KNEW I wasn't making up the stiffness in Trevor's manner, and it wasn't from the bruised ribs. He had been distant all evening, even as we watched TV together. I might have pushed him a little far with lunch, and there had been a few minutes there that I'd worried I'd sent him into a full-blown panic attack. Thankfully he'd recovered from that relatively quickly, but I'd been left trying to navigate a minefield.

It wasn't how I'd wanted to spend the evening. When I'd finally gone to make dinner, Trevor had followed me to the kitchen, trying to force a casualness he clearly hadn't felt. I'd actually been relieved when he'd called it a night shortly after ten. I'd gone upstairs to my room around eleven but had only made it fifteen minutes before I'd begun to worry that he'd have a nightmare and headed back downstairs.

Without a reason to climb into his bed and hold him tight like I had the night before, I'd settled for the couch and kept an ear out for him. At 7:00 a.m., I was cursing myself for the decision. I hadn't slept well on the couch but I'd been too stubborn to go to my bed. I needed to get up and moving, I needed breakfast, and my phone was already vibrating beside me.

A quick stop in the bathroom to pee and brush my teeth, and I was back in the kitchen, looking through the pantry to see what I could make for breakfast while trying to process the text that Seth had sent me.

**Seth**: *Do you like him?*

I had no idea where the question had come from. I thought I'd been hiding my attraction to Trevor fairly well. Trevor hadn't given any indication that he reciprocated my feelings, and after the last eighteen hours, I kind of thought any hope of that happening was gone.

So why was Seth asking me if I liked Trevor at seven in the morning? Maybe I was missing something.

**Me**: *Like who?*

Maybe he thought I was crushing on someone else. While I waited for a response, I found some oats and knew there were berries and yogurt in the fridge. It was looking like a fruit parfait breakfast kind of morning.

I'd just gotten everything on the counter when my phone pinged.

**Seth**: *Santa Claus. Who do you think I'm talking about?*

**Me**: *I woke up ten minutes ago and I haven't had coffee yet. You need to spell this out.*

Speaking of coffee, I needed to start a pot.

**Seth**: *I don't want to hear about it being early. I am not a morning person.*

**Me**: *Yet you're texting me riddles at 7am?*

My phone rang a few seconds later and I fumbled it in an attempt to answer it fast enough that it didn't wake Trevor up. I caught it just before it hit the floor and swiped to answer the call.

"Hello?"

"Why are you being stubborn?"

The noise that came out of me was half sigh, half groan. I barely knew Seth Johnson, I hardly knew anyone on the team, yet he was calling me at seven in the morning ready to pepper me with questions that I didn't know how to answer.

"I'm not being stubborn. I honestly don't know who you're talking about. Until you tell me, I can't tell you if I like him or not."

"Gah!"

In the background, I could hear Maz talking quietly to Seth. There was a rustling noise, and then Maz's voice sounded in my ear. "Sorry, Seth doesn't function in the mornings. When he says he's not a morning person, that's really an understatement."

I had no idea how to respond and there was still no caffeine in my system. "Good to know?"

When he responded, I could hear the smile in Maz's voice. "It really is early. I think you've missed a few key exchanges. Want to come over for breakfast?"

This day was only getting weirder the longer I was awake and I'd only been awake all of fifteen minutes.

Before I had a chance to say anything, Maz spoke. "I'll be there in five to pick you up."

The line went silent and I pulled the phone from my ear to see the call had disconnected. "Yeah, awesome. I'd love to have breakfast with you two, just give me fifteen minutes so that I can look somewhat decent." Rolling my eyes, I put everything away, scrawled a quick note to Trevor in case he woke up, then went to find a shirt and shoes. Pajamas were just going to have to suffice.

I'd barely made it to the front porch and a large black SUV pulled up, dark windows rolled down so that I could see Maz behind the wheel and no passenger beside him.

"This morning is definitely up there with the weirdest I've ever had," I said as I climbed into the seat beside him and shut the door.

Maz just laughed. "It's a Johnson thing. I've gotten used to it. I also know that Seth isn't going to chill the fuck out until he has a chance to talk with you and none of us needs his anxiety bubbling over onto the ice."

"That sounds ominous."

He pulled out of the driveway, made a turn at the end of the road, and drove three houses before pulling into a gated driveway. "I don't think it's going to be that bad. Come on, let's go have breakfast."

At least I could agree to breakfast. My stomach was beginning to growl.

The best part of the morning so far was the smell of coffee that hit my nose as we entered the house. Maz led me into the kitchen and I watched as he casually wrapped an arm around Seth's waist and pulled him in for a kiss and a whispered exchange. I was pretty certain I heard a warning for him to behave as Maz stepped back.

Their casual embrace and the way they showed affection so easily had my chest tightening. It was something I'd wanted for a long time but still didn't know that I'd find, especially not as an active player. The casual touch was especially painful now that I'd discovered Trevor's secret. He was struggling to look me in the eye, so I had no idea how I'd talk to him about anything, much less my decade-long crush or the fact that I was pretty sure our needs and interests aligned perfectly.

Maz swatted Seth's ass and I watched in perplexed awe as Seth wiggled his butt, nearly challenging him to smack it again. I wasn't going there. I didn't need to know, didn't need to *think* about what my teammates got up to in their homes, and my socks—one with a hole in the toe—became very interesting.

A mug of coffee was thrust under my nose, forcing me to look up to find Seth staring at me. "I should probably apologize for the call this morning." He hesitated a beat before adding quickly, "But not quite yet."

"Seeeeeetttth," Maz all but growled out, elongating Seth's name to an impressive length.

He rolled his eyes before huffing. "Fine. I'll behave."

Maz was the one to roll his eyes that time, and he opened his mouth to say something else when the oven timer went off. "*Behave* has never been in a single Johnson family member's vocabulary."

Seth looked oddly proud of the declaration, and for whatever reason it made him look less like he was going to yell at me. "Take a seat. Maz made a quiche this morning. He can function that early."

Once seated at the table, I had no idea what to expect, but it wasn't the thoughtful look that Seth gave me, his head turning side to side as he studied me. Maz came over with three plates and set them on the table before taking a seat next to Seth.

"How's Trevor? Honestly?" Seth sounded genuinely concerned, and I was back to feeling like I was missing something.

"He slept through the night and hasn't had any of the heavy-duty pills since Doc gave them to him right after he got hurt. He was moving pretty slow last night, though."

Despite my stomach's growls and the breakfast that looked amazing, I wasn't in a hurry to eat, still trying to figure out what was going on.

"Oh, good lord," Maz said, rolling his eyes at his boyfriend. "Listen, this isn't an interrogation. Trev sent Seth a text yesterday that has him too damn nosy for his own good, but he's going about this in all the wrong ways. And really, all he wants to know is how you feel about Trevor."

Seth gasped, I blinked, and Maz stabbed his quiche. "I might function better in the morning, but I've had enough drama for the day. I just want this conversation done before the game."

There were a lot of thoughts that flitted through my head as I sat staring at the two men across the table from me. My gut instinct was to deny everything, but there was something about the look in Seth's eyes that told me a lie was not going to be the right answer. The simple fact was, if I lied now, the truth would come out at some point. A lie would just complicate things in the future.

I didn't have to tell them everything, but I could at least tell them enough of the truth that it wouldn't get me in trouble later.

"He lived with my parents for a few years when he was first drafted. I was young, like thirteen or so when he moved out." Looking back on it, the story was kind of funny. "He was how I knew I was gay. I'd known girls weren't for me before then, but Trevor was the nail in the straight slash bisexual coffin for me. I spent the year that he lived with us avoiding him at all costs because every time I saw him I got hard. And all he thought about was hockey, which is understandable. Two years ago, that was all I was thinking about too."

Maz was smirking now and Seth's face had softened considerably. "Maybe there's a bit of a crush going on on my end. But I'm absolutely positive it's one-sided, and I'm not about to do anything to push him into a relationship he doesn't want."

Seth's lips pressed into a line as he listened to me. When I was done, he looked over at Maz and the two had a silent conversation consisting of head shakes, nods, and a few lifted eyebrows. It looked as though they'd both followed the other's train of thought and when Seth looked back at me, he was actually smiling. "Even after the last few days? After caring for him and looking after him?"

The question was strange enough to draw me up short and I pondered how to answer it. "He can hardly be held responsible for a bad reaction to meds. There are far worse things than a hot guy trying to smother you with a stuffed animal in his sleep or getting excited over chicken fingers and chocolate milk for lunch." He didn't need to know that Trevor had freaked out in the middle of lunch, but I'd seen the way his eyes had widened when he'd seen what was in the bag. It had been a look of happiness, not shock, at least at first.

Seth grinned at my response. "After the game today, there's somewhere I want to take you."

The tables had turned and I was now the one looking at him skeptically. "Does it happen to be a six-foot-deep hole in the middle of a forest somewhere?"

Maz choked on the drink of coffee he'd just taken, though Seth gave a genuine laugh. "No. That would be too messy. With brothers who are lawyers and another who's a sheriff's deputy, I'd find a much better way to hide a body. I actually want to take you to the club my dad owns. I think you might find it interesting."

I nodded slowly. "As long as Trevor's still feeling okay when he gets up, I think that's fine. If he feels like shit, I'd rather get back to the house in case he needs me."

My words had Seth beaming. "Deal. Now eat so Mazdon can get you home before the game. Oh, you should take some breakfast to Trevor!"

Maz placed a kiss on Seth's temple, a simple gesture that held love and compassion but didn't hide the flicker of amusement in his eyes.

At least the tension had been broken and we spent the next ten minutes talking about my first week with the team and how I was liking Tennessee so far. The conversation gave me whiplash, but I was happy to get to know both of them a little better.

When Maz dropped me back off at Trevor's, I had a full belly, a plate with a large slice of quiche on it, and a smile on my face that only grew when I walked in the house to find Trevor standing in the kitchen with unruly bedhead and his bear tucked in his arm.

## CHAPTER 14

TREVOR

I'D SOMEHOW FORGOTTEN that Brax lived here now. My normal, up-with-the-sun routine had been thrown on its head with this injury. When my eyes popped open at nearly eight, I was instantly ready to go and anxious to get breakfast. Opening my door to a completely quiet house hadn't raised alarms because after five days I still wasn't used to Brax living there.

My ribs hadn't screamed in agony as soon as I'd rolled over and I wanted to get moving. Coffee, breakfast, and maybe a light workout before heading to the arena to check in with the doc and Coach and see what the plan moving forward would be had been the only things on my mind. Huck had come with me, like always, and I hadn't bothered to change my pajamas into something more suitable. I was still wearing the oversized T-shirt that looked like my jersey and fit more like a long nightshirt when I heard the door shut.

The two of us stared at each other in shock for a few seconds before Brax shook his head, a small smile spreading across his face. "Sit down. I have breakfast for you. You don't need to be digging through the fridge half-asleep."

"I'm not half-asleep. I've slept more in the last two days than I have in the last two months!" *Why was I choosing that to argue about?*

He crossed the kitchen, plate in hand, and pointed to the seat across the island. "Sit. Let me get the pot of coffee actually made this time. I didn't have time before Maz showed up earlier." He unwrapped the plate and slid a large slice of quiche over to me.

"Maz?"

Depositing a fork onto the plate, Brax turned toward the coffee maker. "Long, weird story. But in the end it resulted in my having breakfast with Seth and him. Seth insisted that I bring some back to you, so now you've got breakfast too. How are you feeling?"

I heard the coffee maker hiss to life and Brax turned around, propping a hip on the counter to study me. Those hazel eyes were going to be the death of me. They were warm and caring, yet stern and knowing at once. It felt like, with a single look, he knew everything I was thinking without my saying it but would still wait until I told him exactly what he wanted to know.

Those damned eyes had a habit of making my cock stir to life and my brain conjured up images of how he'd look on top of me, behind me, or more dangerously, watching over me.

"Trevor." The command in his voice had the fantasy fog clearing from my brain and me shaking my head.

"Sorry, what? Still waking up, my brain isn't functioning yet." It was a lie. I was wide awake in way too many ways, and my brain was also very awake and very functional.

He narrowed his eyes, leaving me worried that he was going to call me out on the blatant lie. Just when I nearly cracked and told him that he was too damn distracting, he repeated the question that had sent my mind into the gutter. "How are you feeling?"

Thankfully, I stayed focused on the question. "A lot better."

When his eyebrow quirked upward in question, I quickly clarified. "I am. I woke up this morning and it's a little tender, but not pulling or pinching, even as I rolled out of bed. I'm not going to be playing today, obviously, but I think I'll be good enough to do some cardio during the game. Compared to Friday night, I'm nearly back to normal, but I know it would bring me to my knees if I got hit again. I need a few more days until I'm ready to rejoin the team for a game."

My answer appeared to satisfy Brax. "Good. Glad to hear it. I'm supposed to be going out with Seth and Maz after the game for a bit. Will you be okay to get home on your own?"

Part of me really wanted to know why he'd been at their house that morning, but another part of my brain was convinced I probably didn't want to know. If I pressed to know, there was a good chance that I'd spill about the panicked texts I'd sent Seth the night before and letting Brax into that part of my life was something I wasn't ready to do.

"Yeah. I think I'll be fine. Let me drive to the rink just to make sure, but I'm pretty sure it will be fine."

Brax's expression softened considerably, his eyes going warm and the corners of his lips turning upward. "That sounds like a good plan. If you're in too much pain, I'll just drive you home and then head over to their place. Now that I know they are just around the corner, it isn't like it's going to be an inconvenience."

"You know Yuri lives next door to Igor?" Their places are just a few blocks the other direction from Seth's. We'd teased them mercilessly when Yuri bought the house next to Igor. They'd pissed the HOA off when they modified the fence between the two properties to make one giant backyard that housed a massive ice rink in the winter months. Since there had been no restrictions on backyard rinks at the time, and they had found a way to put the fence up again each night, there was nothing the HOA president had been able to do.

Thank fuck the neighbors on either side of them loved the rink, and in exchange for not giving them a hard time about it, Yuri and Igor had let them skate whenever they wanted. I still didn't want to know what the electric bill was to keep that thing cold enough to be skateable, but that didn't mean we weren't there frequently.

"And that apartment complex on the other side of the development is where Toby, Luc, Blaise, and a few of the other younger unattached players live. Coach Cunningham and Bouchard both have houses in a subdivision about five minutes from here. If you cut through the park behind the house, it's only a four-minute jog."

We'd seemingly made a home base of sorts for the team without ever trying to. I'd found this place shortly after being traded to the Grizzlies. Cunningham was the one who had alerted me to the house going on the market. I fell in love with it at first sight. Then when Seth arrived a few months after me, he'd bought his place almost immediately.

With his family from the area, he already knew where he wanted to live and this neighborhood fit the bill perfectly. From there, it felt like everyone who joined the team found a place nearby. It made staying close in the off-season a lot easier and there was always someone to hang out with when the mood struck.

"So what you're really saying is that I'm not going to be able to take a piss without someone knowing."

The giggle that escaped my throat surprised me. "Pretty much."

Brax rolled his eyes, though I could see that he didn't mind. "Finish your breakfast. I know you're going to want to be at the arena early, and I'm positive you aren't going to want to show up in your pajamas."

I ducked my head, heat filling my cheeks and the tips of my ears. I'd somehow forgotten I was still in my pajamas. At least my shirt was long enough to cover the training pants I'd fallen asleep in the night before. I would have died on the spot if he'd seen those.

Either he didn't notice or chose to ignore my embarrassment, but Brax headed out of the kitchen and to the steps as he finished his thought. "Ugh, I stink. I need a shower. See you in a few. Take Advil before we leave. You don't need to overdo it today. The team needs a captain, not a hero."

With him gone, I managed to breathe a little easier and not worry so much at the fact that my dick was still more than half-hard in my underwear. Cursing my bad luck—because what else would it be to end up living with a gorgeous, take-charge, and totally off-limits Dom—I headed to the cabinet to grab a few tablets and swallow them down with my coffee before going to get ready.

Getting ready to head to the arena reminded me that I wasn't back to playing form yet, but at least I hadn't had tears in my eyes while I'd gotten dressed. Ten-and-two was out as a driving position, but if I kept my arm relaxed on the wheel, it wasn't uncomfortable and I was confident I'd make it home.

I still really wanted to know where Seth and Maz were taking Brax, except when I opened my mouth to ask, my brain kept reminding me that I might not want to know. If Brax wanted me to know, he'd tell me and at the end of the day, it wasn't my business.

Once I parked the car in the players' lot, we both slid out and Brax came to walk next to me. "Still feeling okay? I noticed you weren't using your arm much."

I had to look way up at him, the bright sun causing me to squint. "Yeah. I'm good. I'm glad to be back, honestly. I hate feeling like a bump on a log. Being home yesterday while you were at practice was rough. I kept feeling like I wasn't doing enough and letting people down."

Brax's hand landed on my shoulder and he gave it a gentle squeeze. "You were taking care of yourself. Sometimes, the best thing you can do for the team is take care of your own needs."

Something in that statement sounded off, like he was trying to say something without saying it. I wasn't willing to put too much thought into it, because the way I'd been taking care of myself was spending hours in my playroom and taking a nap with my favorite blankets and stuffies.

Icy dread ran down my spine. Could he have known? There was no way. I'd waited nearly twenty minutes after he'd left to go into my room just in case he came back. He hadn't come back in that time and he should have been at the arena by then. I'd been cleaned up with my room locked well before he returned home. There was no way he'd seen it.

My voice cracked as I nodded my head and tried to answer casually. "Yeah, yeah, you're right. I know that."

He dropped his hand from my shoulder and a different type of cold washed over me, that one feeling more like a warm blanket being pulled from me on a cold day. I didn't have time to process the feeling fully because we were walking into the players' entrance, media cameras already poised to snap pictures.

While growing up and dreaming of hockey, having my wardrobe critiqued on a near-daily basis had never crossed my mind as being part of that.

Brax stepped in front of me, almost blocking me from the photographers and definitely keeping anyone from even casually enquiring about my status for the day. I was sure Coach had already posted the lines, so everyone knew that I wasn't playing and there was no reason to ask anyway. The unfortunate part of Brax's move was that it left me with a great view of his ass being hugged by the most perfect light gray slacks, his coat only grazing over his waist and leaving his miles of legs and perfect bubble butt right there for me to stare at and enjoy.

Damn his timing and damn his good looks. I was going to die of lust and no one was going to know why.

I'd never been so thankful to enter a locker room in all my life. It was already busy, though not with players so much as with equipment managers, coaches, trainers, and staff making last-minute preparations for the day.

"Cane!" Coach Cunningham's voice called to me before I'd seen him, thanks to Brax blocking my view. "Come on into my office. Let's chat."

If that had been any other coach I'd played under, I'd have worried I was about to be sent packing or was going to be riding a bench for the next week. With Irvin Cunningham, I knew he was simply worried about me and wanted to touch base to make sure I wasn't pushing my return to workouts too soon.

By the time I left his office to head over to see the team doctor, Brax was already dressing while he chatted with Luc and Toby. I made my escape unnoticed and breathed a sigh of relief as the doc began peppering me with questions.

## CHAPTER 15

### BRAX

SOMETHING FELT VAGUELY familiar about the street we were on as Maz drove us to the club after the game. It was nearly five in the afternoon and I'd only seen Trevor for a brief moment before the game when he came in to wish us all luck. He'd been going to do some light cardio and lower body work with the trainer while we played and was gone by the time the game was over.

He had at least sent me a text to let me know he'd made it home and I couldn't help but be thankful he'd done that. I'd spent an unreasonable amount of brain power worrying about him driving while I should have been paying attention to the game.

I watched the buildings pass from the window while Seth and Maz chatted. We hadn't been driving long, only about five minutes from the arena, and the landscape had already turned from skyscrapers to something that resembled a warehouse district filled with a random assortment of bars, manufacturing companies that were deserted on Sunday, and... a drag show?

"*Drag Dinner?*" I hadn't expected to see that in downtown Nashville. We were in conservative Middle America, in an even more conservative state, and I was reading a chalk sign on the sidewalk announcing a Drag Dinner with UK's favorite, Bitch Fit. "*International* drag show?"

Seth spun in his seat, an excited look in his eyes. "Oh! Bitch Fit is amazing! She's here for some promotional stuff. We'll have to take you to a show sometime. Or maybe the Drag Bus tour! Oh, that was fun!"

Maz snorted. "We will not be taking Nathan again. I thought his head was going to explode. We still can't talk about that afternoon without him turning red."

Seth grinned at me. "It's the best. We'll introduce you sometime. But for now, we're here."

Maz had pulled off the main road and behind a building that I'd mistaken for another manufacturing company. The windows at the front of the building were blacked out with heavy curtains. The only signage on the entire building was a single vinyl sign on the front door that I could only make out when we got right up to it.

Red letters spelled out DASH, and a collar wrapped around the *A*. I already knew where we were before I read the smaller print on the bottom, *Dom And Sub Haven*.

My mouth moved without my brain's permission. "Your dad owns DASH?" There was a good chance my eyebrows had flown straight off my forehead when they'd shot upward in surprise.

Seth turned the key in the door lock before turning back to me, a pleased smirk on his face. "You've heard of it."

It wasn't a question, he almost sounded relieved if I was being honest with myself, but I still nodded. "I'm signed up for the intro night on Wednesday."

Seth bounced slightly and poked at Maz. "I knew it! I'm gonna have to give Gram a hard time when I see her next." Before I could ask who Gram was, Seth called out, "Dad! Maz and I are here. We have a friend from the team with us!"

This was one of those times that truth was stranger than fiction and I found myself pinching the bridge of my nose. I was at a BDSM club with a teammate and his dad owned it. A BDSM club that catered to the LGBTQ+ community, from what I'd read. Tennessee was full of surprises.

An older man in a pair of jeans and a sweater came around the corner. His gray hair was combed casually to the side, a few stray strands sticking out of place like he'd run his hands through it a few times. His big smile and warm eyes reminded me of Leo, a hard image for my brain to shake but one that needed to be banished quickly.

He wrapped Seth and Maz up in giant hugs, then shook my hand and introduced himself as Zachary.

Logically I'd known the owner's name was Zachary from the research I'd done, but the shocked part of my brain that was struggling to process everything being thrown at me was appreciative of the confirmation. "Brax," I said, still too stunned to add anything else.

Zachary didn't mention my deer-in-the-headlights look as he turned to speak to his son. "If you're looking for Nathan and Elliot, they just left."

Seth screwed up his face. "Eww. No. I didn't know they were going to be here, and I'm really glad we missed them. There's something weird about knowing what those two get up to here. Part of me still thinks of him as my grouchy big brother with a stick up his ass."

Zachary laughed. "Elliot's been good for him. None of you all keep anything from one another, so I don't know why it still weirds you out so much."

Sounding much more like a kid than a professional hockey player, Seth nearly whined to his dad. "Because it's *Nathan*! And Elliot was so quiet and reserved when they first met—and dammit, you've got me off track. I'm not here for any of you nut cases. I'm here to show Brax around. Turns out, he was already signed up for Wednesday night, but I think there are some things that might interest him that I'd like to give him a chance to see without a bunch of people around."

That sounded shady as fuck, but Zachary just hummed. "Ah, got it. Okay, I'll leave you boys alone. Let me know when you leave so I can reset the alarm." With that, he was gone and Seth started walking me through the club, giving me a tour much like what I'd gotten at the club in Boston when I had first joined with Easton.

Thinking of my best friend, I knew he was going to get a kick out of this when I told him about it.

We moved through the main play space quickly, everything much like what I'd been used to in Boston. The one thing I noticed was that the space was brightly lit and the vibe was far less dungeon and much more welcoming. I must have looked at the walls too long because Seth stopped and pointed to the ceiling.

"LED lights. They change colors depending on what's going on in here." He jogged over to what looked like a meeting room and returned with a complex remote. Pushing a few buttons, he turned the overhead lights off and a dim red and warm yellow spilled from what I'd originally mistaken as molding. With a few more presses, the red was replaced with a bright blue and then again with the bright white.

"Dad has a lot of different events in here, and the puppies and littles don't usually like the dark as much as the Doms and subs who are looking for a more moody vibe. It's a lot easier to change the lighting to cater to the event this way."

I'd been listening to everything he said, but my mind had caught on the littles that he'd mentioned. He'd said it so casually that I knew I needed to buck up and ask the question that had been plaguing me since Easton had brought it up and that had not been far from my thoughts since I'd seen Trevor coloring the previous morning.

"Littles? Is it true that the club has a huge little community?"

Seth and Maz shared a knowing look before Seth nodded. "Huge. It's actually kind of legendary. I'm really proud of my dad for creating this. My older brother too. He was basically the driving factor in creating a welcoming space for littles, middles, and boys of all varieties and, of course, their Daddies."

There was a chance my mouth was hanging open. I knew my eyes were so wide they were drying out. I forced myself to blink a few times, trying to come up with the next question to ask, but Seth was way ahead of me as he began to explain how the space transformed for both mosh and little gatherings. He went into great detail about how everything was made to be moved and stored easily, though he focused a lot more on the little nights than the moshes, despite having never asked me why I was coming to the intro night.

I couldn't help but wonder if he thought I was a little. I didn't think I'd given off any indication that I was submissive, but maybe I'd said or done something to give him that impression.

Seth started walking again, this time stopping at a number of different rooms, each one a different space I'd seen online while doing research and none of them speaking to me in any real sense. When he turned to head down a hallway toward the back of the building, I swore there was a skip to his step. When he swung the door at the end of the hall open, an unsaid *ta-da* hung in the air.

It was the nursery room I'd seen in the pictures, and I could honestly say the pictures hadn't done the space justice. The entire room was warm and welcoming, even the temperature a few degrees warmer than in the rest of the club. Soft furniture and plush rugs filled the center of the room while the walls held shelves of books and toys. An overflowing toy box of stuffed animals was in one corner, another had a few gaming chairs and a TV and game systems. One wall had a chalkboard like Trevor's room.

Of course, Trevor's chalkboard had been colored with little animals and small trees while this one was covered in random scribbles clearly designed by various artists. It didn't change the fact that I could easily see Trevor lying on one of the rugs playing or standing at the chalkboard coloring.

And fuck my life, standing there with two of my teammates watching me, I had to accept that Easton had been right. "I'm going to kill him," I said, not realizing I'd voiced the words until Seth and Maz began staring at me with concern in their eyes.

I found myself apologizing and clarifying before I could worry them more. "Easton. I'm going to kill him. He's been pushing me to find a little since I got traded. He's the one who found this place and told me to get a membership. He's been on me to find a boy for a year and now he's got it in his head that I need a little, but he won't listen to me when I tell him that no little is going to want a younger Daddy, and I'm not looking for a boy that's not going to understand that I'm basically married to hockey three-quarters of my life."

That wasn't even going into the fact that I'd found a boy who might be perfect for me but had no idea I was a Daddy and I had no idea how to tell him that. Hell, he'd looked like he wanted to crawl in a hole and die when I'd walked into the house that morning, and I swore he'd given an uncomfortable shiver when I'd placed my hand on his shoulder. At the very least, he'd gone uncomfortably stiff. If he didn't want to be around me, there was no way he'd ever want to knowingly show me his little side.

The hum that Seth let out sounded almost like a squeak, and when I looked at him, he was nearly vibrating beside his boyfriend. "I told you! I knew it!" He was poking a finger in Maz's chest as he spoke.

Maz shook his head. "Mm-hmm, and what do you plan to do with that information now?"

Seth stopped bouncing, a look of confusion crossing his face. "I don't know." He scratched his head and leaned against the doorway as he thought. "Shit, this is complicated. It would be so much easier if we were dealing with my family."

"That's because your family doesn't know boundaries," Maz said, a smile tugging at his lips despite the eye roll he gave his boyfriend.

Seth stood rooted to the floor, but I let him think while I looked around the room again. *Trevor would love this*, my brain kept telling me. Then again, Trevor had this already. He had it in the little room in his house that was decorated just for him, with all his favorite toys.

"What if I had a boy I thought you might like to meet?"

Seth's question surprised me. It sounded nice, but I found myself being more honest with him than I had been with Easton—at least as honest as I could be without outing Trevor. "I'd tell you thanks, but no thanks. I already found myself a boy who wants nothing to do with me."

There went that knowing look again, Seth and Maz sharing a silent conversation that I didn't understand the meaning of. Maz clasped my shoulder and directed me from the playroom and toward the front of the building.

Seth joined us a few seconds later. "I highly doubt that he wants nothing to do with you."

I heard myself give a disbelieving snort. "And how would you know that?"

Seth chewed his lip while he thought. "Because submission, especially when it takes the form of something outside of the box, is scary as hell to talk about. Sometimes *life* and *lifestyle* don't match. It's like, the way you want to express yourself doesn't match how everyone sees you, and you know it can have huge implications for your life. Trusting the wrong person with that part of you could end everything you've worked your entire life for."

I knew he was speaking from a place of deep understanding. He wasn't telling me anything superficial or generic. Seth was talking from personal experience, and I appreciated his candor with me, but I was more focused on how his words related to Trevor.

"So, maybe I don't make him as uncomfortable as I think I do?"

Maz pushed the front door open. "He's catching on."

"Exactly. Maybe you're the person he's scared to believe exists." Seth patted my chest. "But you're the Dom. You're going to have to figure this one out."

I groaned as we climbed into the car. "I really, really hate Easton right now."

"Let's get you home. I think we've overwhelmed you enough for one night."

With a rare day off the next day, my brain had fixated on how to talk with Trevor. I still didn't have a good idea of how to bring any of this up to him, but I knew I needed to. And now that I was thinking about it, I wished I knew more about Trevor's needs.

The house was quiet when I arrived, giving me a chance to head upstairs, strip out of my suit, and grab my phone.

*Me: So, let's pretend for a moment that I found a little I'm interested in, but he doesn't know I know he's a little. What would you suggest I do to let him know I'm interested in being his Daddy?*

I hit send and pulled up one of the accounts Easton had sent me, looking for anything that might help me make sense of my life.

## CHAPTER 16

### TREVOR

Monday morning rolled around and the house was still quiet. After the morning before, there was no way I was going to let myself make the same mistake. I changed into a pair of sweatpants and a T-shirt before ever leaving my room, my focus entirely on a light jog.

Truthfully, my thoughts were more focused on my ribs. They felt good enough that I was hopeful I'd be cleared for practice the next morning and back in the game come Thursday. The first step in making that happen was getting out and pushing myself through a light run.

I went through my normal morning routine on rote memory, the steps falling effortlessly into place as I moved through my bedroom, then through the kitchen. It wasn't until I began tying my shoes that I realized I hadn't heard, much less seen, Brax. Given the smell of coffee hadn't permeated the house, I figured he was sleeping in.

Part of me felt relieved to know that he was in bed and I was free to move around the house. Part of me missed him. Despite being horrified that Brax had seen me in my pajamas the morning before and spending most of the last day avoiding him at all costs, a large part of me had liked the way he'd looked at me. It hadn't been in disgust. I was certain heat had shown in his eyes a number of times throughout the morning.

My brain was not going to figure anything out by standing in the kitchen obsessing over my teammate slash housemate slash crush. Because that was what I had, a crush on Brax that wasn't going away, and it was only getting bigger each time he was nice to me instead of recoiling at whatever I did or wore around him.

*Dammit.*

The only solution to my current problem was to run, so that was what I did. I shoved my shoes on my feet and headed out the back door toward the running path. There were miles of trails I could run and if I kept my guard up, I could avoid any of the other guys out for a run. Most of the time I loved running with a teammate, but I needed to focus on me and my thoughts. Mostly the running from them.

Once my shoes hit the dirt, things inside me began to settle. My feelings didn't feel like a giant precarious boulder teetering on a ledge above me. I passed the one-mile mark with no pain in my ribs and barely out of breath. The light jog I'd planned had been forgotten—what I needed was a long run to clear my head, and I was going to give myself just that.

I'd made it the last ten years in the NHL without a serious relationship. I'd made it fifteen years since figuring out that I was a little without a caregiver. I'd come up through juniors and broken into the NHL knowing I was a little and that one day, way in the future when my career was over, I'd finally get to find a Daddy.

Derek was my friend and that was more than I'd ever thought I'd have while playing professional hockey. The fact that we both understood how important privacy was and understood that we couldn't talk about our playdates with anyone had eased my fears about someone else seeing me vulnerable like that.

*Derek got it.*

And he was safe. At least safer than a teammate.

Seth's familiar voice drew me from my thoughts, the sound of feet padding toward me. "Have you had a chance to figure shit out yet?"

I turned right, knowing he and Maz would go straight.

Seth was a different issue entirely. I'd been so panicked, I'd let my guard down and let him and Maz see my playroom. They'd taken it well. Hell, he'd already had it figured out. But there was something different between suspecting and knowing. Now I had two people on the team that knew my deepest secret.

Being out in professional sports wasn't anywhere near as difficult as being a kinky submissive who liked regressing. The fallout for being gay was almost nothing, at least within our team. No amount of support would get me through if someone found out I had a playroom filled with toys and coloring supplies. I'd have to retire and go into hiding.

The thought alone was enough to turn my stomach and make my steps falter.

The voice that answered Seth's question didn't belong to Maz. "No. Not really. I thought a lot, but nothing concrete." The voice faded as they passed on the main trail, but I didn't need to see the person to know it was Brax.

Fucking hell, I couldn't get away from him.

I jogged ahead, paying more attention to my surroundings than my thoughts and at some point, I lost myself in the rhythmic sound of my feet hitting the leaves on the path and my beating heart. My watch vibrated, letting me know I'd put in three miles and I looked around to see that I was nearly directly behind my house.

Slowing my pace to a walk, I focused on stretching and the way my muscles felt after days of very little movement. My thighs were a little stiff, but they'd loosen with a hot shower. My neck was tight, but nothing I wasn't used to. My ribs, well, they were still sore when I took a deep breath in, but

I'd played through far worse over the years. As long as I could make it through practice the next morning, I fully suspected that I would be cleared for the game on Thursday.

The thought of being back on the ice was what got me home and through a quick shower. I wished I knew how long Brax would be out because I'd have taken a bubble bath instead, but I knew I'd be too tense to enjoy it if I heard him moving around in the house.

Once dried, I slipped on a pair of loose cotton shorts and headed to the kitchen. With a water bottle in hand, I slid onto the island and pulled my phone out of my pocket to see if Derek and I could hammer out some playdate details.

*Me*: *Still good for Wednesday?*

The message wasn't read immediately, but that wasn't surprising. I flipped over to social media. It was a guilty pleasure of mine and I had a nice following on some of the different sites. I kept everything fairly boring, pictures of meals, holiday decorations, and sometimes game day outfits, but my followers always enjoyed the content. It was also the only way I was able to keep up with some friends from other teams during the season. Throwing a heart on a post or two was as good as a call in many cases.

I'd made it four posts through Instagram when the door to the garage opened and a very sexy... err, sweaty Brax walked in, using his shirt to mop sweat from his face and chest. Before

I'd even seen his eyes, my cock had already taken notice. This was not a normal reaction for me. At least he usually had to *look* at me for my cock to decide it liked what we saw.

Perched on the counter, there was no way I could easily exit without being noticed. Dropping down would make a noise and with my dick getting harder by the second, there was no way Brax wouldn't notice it. I wasn't huge, but I was bigger than my short stature led one to believe. And I'd foolishly chosen light gray cotton shorts. There was no hiding my body's reaction to his bare chest and glistening skin.

Derek, or someone, chose that moment to text, the sound drawing Brax's attention from drying off, and he looked up. That was definitely a smile that crossed his face when he saw me sitting on the counter.

"Hey."

When I went to respond, I realized my lips had been parted as I stared at him. Heat spread up my neck and through my cheeks and I had to wet my lips before I could say anything. "H-hi."

He tucked the spent T-shirt into the waistband of his black pants—smart color choice, I should have thought of that—and headed toward the fridge, a glint in his eye that I'd never seen before. "I wondered where you went this morning. You weren't anywhere when I got up and your door was open."

Brax's eyes flitted over toward the hallway. For a brief moment, I could have sworn they fell on the door to my playroom, my heart rate ratcheting up at the thought. Just before the moment stretched too long for comfort, he focused back on me, his eyes twinkling with an emotion I couldn't read clearly. "Have a good morning?"

I nodded, trying to swallow the anxiety and nerves that had lodged in my throat through the pause in the conversation. Once convinced I could speak, I swallowed. "Went for a run. Wanted to see how my ribs were doing."

Whatever he'd been thinking about vanished and his eyes suddenly turned studious, the concern in them crystal clear. "How are they doing? Did you overdo it?"

My hand went up to stop him, but that meant it was no longer hiding the erection tenting my shorts. "I'm fine. They feel good. I ended up running longer than I thought I would and I still feel good."

Those damned eyes strayed from mine and I dropped my hand quickly, trying to place it back in my lap before he saw what his presence was doing to me. The sudden movement drew his attention faster than I could move my hand, and I saw the brief flash of surprise when he saw what I was trying to hide.

His lower lip got pulled between his teeth like he was trying to hide amusement at my situation, but when he looked up at me, his rich eyes had turned molten, undeniable lust reflecting through them as he studied my face.

"Is there a reason for that?"

*And fuck my life, he wasn't going to leave it alone.*

I blushed so hard my eyes burned like I was fevered, my mind struggling to come up with something to say that might be somewhat believable. There was nothing. Not a single thought, much less a word, came to dismiss the current situation. We were both men, so it wasn't like either of us weren't accustomed to the random, inconvenient erection when our dicks took interest in something totally outside of our control. It should have been easy to say it had been a sexy thought, or that I didn't have a clue why I was hard as a fucking rock, but nothing came out of my mouth.

*And why the hell was my erection not going down?*

It had to have something to do with the way he was looking at me. When I hadn't immediately come up with a flippant excuse, his gaze had turned knowing and my insides had responded, turning hot and liquid the longer his eyes stayed on me.

Then Brax moved, stepping forward, his lower stomach pressing against my knees, his hands bracing himself on either side of my thighs. He leaned in, the smell of sweat and earth and hard work not the turnoff it should have been, and brushed his lips against the shell of my ear as he whispered. "Were you being naughty? Did you get hard when you saw me walk in? Or were you already hard thinking about me?"

I gulped, the sound of my Adam's apple bobbing in my throat deafening in the quiet of the house. "I-I-I..."

My stutter trailed off. I had no idea how to respond. I was pretty sure the answer was yes to all of the above, but I didn't know how to tell him that.

"That's a yes then." He gave a deep, throaty chuckle that promised wicked things if I didn't refute that.

It was a bad idea. I knew it was a bad idea, but I had no idea how to tell him what a bad idea it was because I didn't want it to be bad. "I'm going to kiss you, Trevor Cane."

My eyes shot open, but my head bobbed slightly, a barely there acknowledgement and consent. It was all Brax needed, his lips brushing against mine in a feather-soft touch before he pulled back slightly. One of us hummed just before his lips met mine again, no more urgent but still so soft that I could feel the smile that turned the corners of his lips up.

Gentle kisses were pressed to the seam of my lips, my lower lip, and again to my chin before he finally pulled back, my body instinctively chasing his. "Holy fuck." His words came out on a breathy exhale. The smile on his lips reminded me of postorgasmic bliss, where everything feels distant and far away but the waves of pleasure are still strumming through your body and making you loopy from the sensory overload. "It's better than I ever imagined."

The lust in my brain cleared long enough for his words to fully settle in. "Wait, what?"

He pushed back, the cocky hockey star momentarily replaced by an awkward twenty-three-year-old as he blushed and struggled to meet my eyes. "I might have a crush on you." His chuckle was uncomfortable and I knew he couldn't believe he was putting voice to his thoughts.

"You what?" How could this man have a crush on me? That just complicated my already complicated feelings. He was supposed to be my teammate. Lines weren't supposed to get crossed, not like this. If my crush was reciprocated, the odds were that I'd end up telling him things I didn't want to tell him.

He rested his forehead against mine, for a moment making me think I'd ruined the mood between us. That should have been a good thing, but I couldn't help but feel disappointment in my chest. Then he adjusted and I could feel how hard he was against my leg.

*Fuck me.* Literally and figuratively.

"I've had a crush on you for years. But please don't mistake right now as an ill-advised opportunity. I had a crush on you before I really knew you. Now I know you better and that crush has turned from a farfetched fantasy to very real feelings."

He'd once again rendered me speechless. My brain stuck on his words, my dick stuck on everything else about him, and my insides told me that if we didn't do something about this quickly, I was literally going to explode or come in my pants just from the proximity of him.

"Let me make you feel good. Please."

How long had I waited to hear those words from someone? Longer than I cared to imagine. He might not have been saying those things as my Daddy, but he'd said them earnestly. Bad idea or not, I already knew I was going to say yes. There was no way I was going to turn down an offer like that. We could figure out the messy bits later.

I nodded. "Okay." The single word wasn't enough, but I risked exposing too much of myself if I said more.

Thankfully, Brax didn't need more words from me. He found my mouth and kissed me again. There was nothing slow, sweet, or exploratory about it. He kissed me breathless and claimed my mouth, tongue, and thoughts in the process.

He only pulled back when his fingers found my waistband and he realized there was no way to get my shorts down with our mouths attached. His mouth was red and swollen, and I was sure I looked the same, just with a beard burn where his beard had rubbed against my smooth jaw and chin.

"Lean back for me. I want to get these off you."

I did as I was told, putting my weight on my elbows. I hissed out when the cold granite of the counter made contact with my heated skin, the feeling like an ice bath after a grueling workout, but my pants sliding down my legs provided an instant distraction.

"Fuck, you're gorgeous." He ran his hand down my smooth chest and abs, tracing where my treasure trail should have been. The few stray hairs that grew on my chest and stomach had been so few that it had made sense to have them permanently removed instead of shaving or waxing them off.

Strong fingers wrapped around the base of my erection and I didn't bother trying to stifle the moan that escaped.

A possessive, hungry grin spread across his lips. "Oh, I'm going to make you feel so good."

## CHAPTER 17

### BRAX

AFTER A QUICK GROPE of his balls, I adjusted so that I could press a kiss to his nipple. A very real portion of my brain was telling me this was too good to be true. Hell, if it weren't for the cold stone beneath my hands, I'd have believed I was dreaming this entire thing. If he let me, I was willing to take Trevor apart, inch by agonizingly slow inch. I had ten years of fantasies built up in my brain. Everything from the rushed kisses and groping my brain had conjured up as a young teen, to the more sensual yet still improbable ones of my early adult years, to the explicit ones that I'd been playing on repeat since Easton had brought up the idea of me finding a little.

Not a single one had ever been as perfect as the real thing, and I wanted to catalog every square inch of Trevor's body. I wanted to know what made him gasp, what made him shiver, and what made him beg. I wanted to hear him begging Daddy to let him come and I wanted to know what he sounded like when he finally got the permission to do so.

My tongue circled around his nipple and he let out a whimper that made my cock ache to be touched. Repeating the same on his other side, I had a silent lecture with my brain and dick that this wasn't about us. We'd have time later but for now, this was all about our boy. Whether he knew it or not, I had every intention of getting there with him.

The run with Seth that morning had been just what I'd needed to get my thoughts together and formulate a plan. Granted, the plan hadn't involved Trevor spread out on the kitchen counter like a buffet to be devoured, but that was where we were and I was fully prepared to roll with the punches.

Seth had assured me that things would work out—I just had to show Trevor I was serious. It had come with a number of warnings about his inevitable freak-out and insight into the pressures Trevor always put upon himself. Seth had promised to be there for both of us if and when we needed him. I hoped it didn't come to that, but knowing he could be a voice of reason if things went tits up had been the boost of confidence I'd needed.

My tongue circling his nipple had Trevor's hips thrusting upward into my stomach as a stream of babbles fell from his lips. "Ah, ah, ah. Have I told you that you can grind against me?"

He stilled, his body going tense, and I half expected to feel cum pooling between us. When I felt nothing, I pressed upward to look him in the eyes. He was shaking his head no, his pupils wide and unfocused.

"Words, Trevor."

"N-no. You didn't?"

I grinned. At least he was still with me. "Right. I'm making you feel good; you're not making yourself feel good."

He swallowed, emotions playing across his face in rapid succession. Fear, pleasure, excitement, and uncertainty, but above all else his submission outshone every other emotion. He wanted to obey, he wanted to make me happy.

I smiled, softening my voice and trying to pour everything I knew I couldn't say into my next words. "Good boy."

I'd almost expected him to freak out when I said the words but he relaxed, every ounce of tension he'd been holding leaving his body as he watched me. I'd intended to take this slowly, wanted to take him apart and tease him and drag this out until he didn't know which end was up. That all changed when I saw the way he was looking at me.

All I wanted to do now was make him feel good, give him the reward he hadn't known he'd been waiting for.

I kissed my way down his stomach, my new target coming closer by the second, stopping only for a few moments to lick and kiss around his belly button a few times after he squirmed and laughed at my initial touch. Before his laughter could break the electricity between us, I moved on, trailing kisses downward.

Trevor slapped at the countertop, a needy groan slipping from his parted lips when I bypassed his cock to kiss his balls. They were already pulled tight against his body, and sucking one into my mouth made his cock pulse against my nose.

I released him and looked up. "Good boys do not come without permission."

He gave up holding himself upright and fell backward against the counter, cold stone be damned, and cursed me. "Fuck. Fuck me. Fuck you. Fuck your mouth and your tongue and your lips. You're going to kill me. I can only be expected to last so long! I haven't come in days!"

I got the impression that he'd meant for most of that to stay in his head when he didn't flush or sound the least bit embarrassed by the admission. I still had a lot to learn about Trevor, but judging by how red he turned on the regular, I didn't think there was any way he'd have knowingly said that—lust-drunk or not—without turning unhealthy shades of red.

It took a firm bite to my cheek to not laugh at his curses, but at least my momentary distraction gave him time to breathe. I'd thought it might have brought him back from the brink, but one glance toward his dick and I could see that the tip was wet with precum and had turned an angry shade of burgundy. He wasn't going to last when I finally wrapped my lips around his dick, but I also wanted him to feel like he'd earned his orgasm when he finally came.

I went for the middle ground and licked up his shaft and listened as he babbled nonsense above me. With my hand firmly around the base of his dick, I licked, kissed, and sucked his cock, paying close attention to the ridge of his mushroom head but careful not to touch his slit.

Precum dribbled freely down his shaft, my tongue and lips already coated in it and my hand becoming sticky where I held him.

He groaned, the sound coming out soft and breathy, and I knew I was close to losing him to subspace. I loved sending a man flying, but that wasn't where I wanted him to be. I wanted him blissed-out and sated but still well aware of himself and what was going on.

Releasing his cock, I tapped his stomach and waited for him to look up at me. His eyes were heavy, but he was still with me. I rewarded the action with a smile as I ran my finger down his smooth jaw. "You've been a very good boy. You can come when you need to."

His sharp inhale was further confirmation that he was still very much in the present. With the final confirmation, I ducked my head and took him into my mouth. While his cock was slightly shorter than average, he well made up for it in girth, making my lips stretch to fit around him, though the length allowed me to suck him to the base.

He swelled nearly immediately, a burst of precum coating my tongue before I'd taken him completely into my mouth. I'd be surprised if he made it more than a few minutes if he really hadn't come in days, and I pulled back slightly to prepare for his release. Working my hand and mouth together, I jacked him hard and fast, reaching my free hand below his ass and gently encouraging him to fuck into my mouth.

Trevor didn't need more than a gentle nudge with my hand and his hips began to work with me, pumping up and down as he chased his release. There were no longer bursts of precum, just a steady leaking from his tip that kept his taste on my tongue as I worked him.

"Sh-shit. C-c-coming!" His holler hadn't been necessary. I'd felt the additional swell and pulsation of his cock against my tongue, though the warning had been enough for me to start swallowing his load as soon as he began to empty in my mouth.

He panted and cursed through his release as he alternated between pounding against the counter and gripping my hair in his fist. Thankfully, he didn't pull or tug, and when his cock finally stopped pulsating, he let go and fell back on the counter. I swallowed once more, making sure to clean his dick as much as I could before standing up.

Trevor was gorgeous with sweat beading on his chest and forehead, his heart pounding so hard I could see it in his neck, and his chest heaving for breaths. His mouth was parted as though it had been frozen mid-scream despite no sound coming from him.

My dick ached and I knew the slightest attention would make me come, but that was a problem for me to worry about later, probably once I had a chance to shower because that would have to happen at some point. He might not have said anything yet, but I stunk and I knew it. For the time being, I needed to get Trevor cleaned up and find new pants for him.

I placed a kiss on his forehead. "Stay there. I'll be back to clean you up in just a minute."

He waved a hand in my direction and grunted something that I was going to take as acknowledgement, and I jogged for his room. Thankfully, I'd watched where he'd pulled pajamas from on Friday night and quickly found the softest pair in the drawer. The matching flannel pants and long sleeve cotton shirt had little stars and hearts on them and looked perfect for a lazy little day. Or a day that I hoped would be.

The bathroom was easy to navigate, a stack of washcloths in the closet by the sink, right next to a sippy cup and bottle. I smiled at the discovery, pulling the cup from the shelf before running the cloth under hot water. I made a quick stop by his bed for his blanket and Huck, then headed back to the kitchen.

I couldn't have been gone more than two minutes, yet Trevor's eyes had closed and a sleepy smile was plastered on his face.

"Hey, I'm going to clean you up now."

"Mm-hmm."

"You still with me?"

He didn't open his eyes. "Mm, ask me again in a few hours. Think you sucked my brains from my dick."

He was still with me, snark and all. A conversation could wait until he was cleaned and dressed again. I set to work cleaning him up, starting with his chest and stomach before folding the cloth in half and moving to his balls and dick. He shivered and tried to wiggle away from me as I cleaned his overly sensitive dick.

"Careful. You're still on the counter. I don't want you to get hurt."

He stilled, his eyes opening slowly to study me. "Thank you."

"Of course." Hopefully, he'd still be this calm when we got to what I really wanted to talk about.

With him wiped down, I grabbed the pajama pants. The countertop couldn't be comfortable and I worried that his ribs would start aching if he didn't move soon. "Come on, let's get you dressed again."

Trevor stayed still as I fed the pants onto his legs, not bothering to move at all until I tapped his thigh. "Butt up, let me get these on."

He gave a mighty sigh as he adjusted so that his hips came off the counter to let me pull his pants into place. Given that he wasn't in any rush to move, I left him there for a minute while I filled his sippy cup with water, then turned my attention to getting his shirt on him. "Okay, sleepyhead. Shirt on before you get cold, and then head to the living room. I'm going to need to remember that your brain turns to mush after a good orgasm."

"*Great* orgasm."

I took his hands and tugged him into a seated position. "I'm glad you enjoyed it. Now, arms up."

Trevor lifted his arms without thought, his submission as natural to him as skating was. When the shirt slipped over his torso, his brain came back online. "Wait, I'd just been wearing shorts." He looked down, his face going slightly pale as he took in his pajamas. "Wh-where'd you get these?"

With a finger under his chin, I lifted his head so he was looking in my eyes. "Your drawer. It's cool today and I don't want you to get cold."

Worry lines creased his forehead. Now that his brain had come back online, reservations and hesitations were coming back to him. "Whoa, slow down." I ran my thumb over his forehead, kissing the furrow above his nose. "Let's head to the living room and talk."

The submission that had been tugging so hard against him for the last half hour was hard to see now, but I got a glimpse of it as he picked at his thumbnail. At first glance, Trevor was stoic and firm, ready to shut me and anything between us down, but looking closer, I could see the parts of him that I was beginning to understand were little Trevor. From the way his feet swayed as they dangled above the floor to the way he struggled to meet my eyes to how he almost imperceptibly leaned into my touch. His submission was there, it always was—he was just good at hiding it.

Eventually, Trevor nodded and slid off the island, his feet landing with a soft *thwump* on the rug below him. He headed straight for the living room, never looking back to see me following him with his cup, blanket, and Huck.

I hung back, watching him as he took a seat on the couch and tucked his feet under him before pulling the big throw blanket on the back of the couch over his body. When it looked like he'd made himself comfortable, I headed over and took a seat next to him, purposely crowding his personal space and making it harder for him to dart away.

"You came hard. You need to drink something." I handed over the cup I'd found in his bathroom and knew he wasn't fully back yet because he didn't say anything until the hard spout hit his lips.

The look of terror that crossed his face as he pulled the cup back to study it made my chest ache harder than my dick had been while I'd blown him. "Y-y-wh-whe-wh." He slammed his mouth shut, took a deep breath, and gave me a look begging for an explanation that would make sense.

"When I went to find you pajamas and get a washcloth to clean you up, I found it in the bathroom. I've been trying to find a way to broach the subject with you for days, but I haven't known how."

He was still looking at me, but I got the impression he wanted to be anywhere but on the couch talking about this. Unfortunately for him, I wasn't going to walk away without talking about what was going on. I didn't need to define our relationship right that second, but we did need to clear the air between us. Trevor needed to know that I knew and more importantly was okay with the fact that he wasn't always as in control as he appeared.

I wanted to pull him into my lap, wrap his blanket around him, and hold him while we talked everything out, but I stunk and he was in clean pajamas. I was quickly seeing the holes in my plan. Instead of pulling him into my lap, I placed a hand on his thigh.

"Your desires won't surprise me."

## CHAPTER 18

### TREVOR

YEAH, *right*. Brax's words were enough to have me rolling my eyes and a scoff escaping. I didn't know how much he knew, but I was pretty sure it wasn't enough for him to make that determination with the certainty that he'd delivered it.

At my scoff, Brax actually smiled. "It's going to take a lot more than your pacifier, blanket, Huck, and playroom to scare me off. Though I'm really curious as to what that giant mat was in the middle of the room."

"Wait. How do you know about that? That's *my* space. You told me that I couldn't get in there!"

Logically, I knew I was admitting that Brax knew more about me than he should, but I'd worked so fucking hard to keep my hockey and submissive sides separate, I needed to know how he knew. And if he'd lied to me, there was going to be a much bigger issue at hand than what he'd seen. I would never be able to trust him as a friend or teammate again.

Brax held his hands up in surrender. "You couldn't get in there. You tried really hard, but you were so confused and you kept muttering about a key but not being able to remember where it was. I swear to you, Trevor, I don't know where that key is still. I've never gone to look for it."

I narrowed my eyes. "Then how do you know what's in the room? How do you know about my cups?" I tugged at my hair, frustration and plot holes filling every available space in my brain.

"I left my bag here that morning. I'd made it all the way to the coffee shop before I realized. So I came back to grab it. The door was open. I hadn't meant to look."

*Fuck.* I'd been so damn careful. I'd waited long enough that I was sure he'd be gone and not coming back. I'd listened to the garage. I'd honestly thought I'd kept my guard up, but I'd failed. A crushing disappointment in myself filled my chest, making it hard to breathe.

The last thing I wanted was a visual reminder of what he thought he knew about me. The pajamas, my sippy cup, my blanket, and Huck sitting beside him were all too much and I stood to pace. The space from Brax gave me a chance to sort my thoughts, or at least begin to sort them.

"You have no idea what you saw." I mean, he obviously had seen what he thought, but he couldn't possibly understand why it was so important to me. "You have no idea what that means."

A brief glance in his direction let me know he had questions. A lot of them. He was confused, but so was I. I was more than a little terrified about what I was going to have to admit about myself. I looked at my sippy cup on the couch, nestled in the blankets I'd left piled there when I got up.

He must have done some research over the last day and a half because he was trying to show me he cared and understood. Just like a lie from him would have ruined my trust in him, I knew that a lie from me would ruin his trust in me. As a teammate and team captain, I walked a fine line. There were some things I could play dumb about. There were others I could talk around. This was one of the times that either of those options would just be a flat-out lie, and I refused to lie to a teammate.

As for his sweet but likely misguided attempts to take care of my little side, I really did get the impression Brax *thought* he knew what I needed. The thing was, pajamas, a sippy cup, and my security items were barely touching the surface of my needs.

I was left with just how much I needed to tell him to get him to understand without oversharing. I still had to protect myself, no matter how sweet he was being.

With a frustrated growl, I dragged my hands down my face and stalked over to sit on the coffee table facing him. I didn't want to have this conversation, but there was no avoiding it now. There was a reason Coach had asked me to be captain and I needed to act like a leader, like I had some clue what the fuck I was doing. I needed to show confidence and having a panic attack and burying my head in the sand was not going to do anything productive, no matter how tempting the thought was.

"Brax, I appreciate your trying to understand and trying to show me that you understand. The simple fact is, no matter what you saw, you have no idea what I need or what I'm looking for. You *think* you won't be surprised, but a little Internet research is not reality."

Brax's eyes flashed with a mixture of humor and a smugness I remembered seeing in his dad's eyes a number of times when he was about to lay down hard truths about where I was wrong. The look was a lot sexier and a lot more unsettling on Brax than it had been on Tom. My dick never tried to twitch to life when Tom gave me that look.

"You're making a lot of assumptions. I might be younger than you but I know what I'm looking for. I know what I want. And I can assure you that when I said your needs aren't going to surprise me, that's exactly what I meant."

I opened my mouth to refute that, but he held up a hand to stop me. "No, do not dismiss me as a kid or just Tom's son.

I'm a professional hockey player, just like you. I didn't earn my spot on the Grizzlies or in the NHL because of who my dad is. If anything, it made me have to work harder. I know what I gave up when I decided to make the NHL my life. I gave up any semblance of normalcy. I gave up ever being able to find a boyfriend—a boy—who would understand me and *my* needs."

He smirked when he saw the shock in my eyes. I knew they'd gone wide, but as he'd begun to talk, I knew damn well he was about to throw me for a loop. Just from the confidence in his eyes and the smirk on his lips, I knew he would put me in my place.

"Yeah. I've known for years that I'm a Dom, a Daddy. The boys I've met in the past haven't been interested in a younger Daddy, every single one of them assuming I'm too young to know how to be a Daddy for them. The ones that were interested in me didn't understand that I am married to hockey. Anyone not in professional sports would have a hard time understanding life with an athlete. Nineteen- and twenty-year-olds want nothing to do with a Daddy who's going to be gone over half the year."

He gave a dry scoff. "Not that I can blame them. I look at pictures on social media of some of my high school friends. They're still in college, still out partying. They're trying to figure out how to cram for a final while I'm pushing myself further than I ever thought possible on and off the ice. I spend hours in the gym and even more hours on the ice. I think you can imagine what it's like trying to tell a college freshman who's just learning he's a submissive and looking for a Daddy that I'll be gone six to eight months a year, there's a chance I could be traded at a moment's notice, or that there are times that I hurt too fucking bad to go to the club or a party after a game."

I winced. I'd spent my entire adult life balancing my little side and my professional life. I indulged when I could, but there were times that finding twenty minutes for a bottle and a cartoon was too much energy. My life had been spent avoiding any mention of what I liked outside of hockey, so I didn't bother looking for a Daddy that I knew I couldn't have, but that didn't mean I didn't understand what Brax was going through.

We fell silent, both of us lost in our own thoughts, the moment giving me time to replay his words. In all his explanations, in all his defense, he'd used the word *boy*. He'd never once said *little*. There were two very different types of Daddies. Just because Brax might have been a Daddy Dom did not mean he was looking for a little.

I nearly laughed at myself when I finally took a moment to process my thoughts. Fucking hell, he was a teammate, my friend's son. Yeah, there was no way in hell I was going to be the boy or little for him.

"Brax, I understand that it's a shit position to be in. Believe me, I get it." I pointed toward the couch then gestured down my body to emphasize just that. "No matter how sweet you're trying to be, there is no way that we're right for one another. I'm your teammate—your captain at that. Your dad is not only my former teammate but he's also my friend and has served as a mentor to me for years. And to top it off, I'm not just a boy. I'm not looking for a part-time Daddy. My needs and desires are so much bigger than a Daddy in bed or at the club."

Brax's eyes flashed, a storm brewing behind eyes that had turned nearly emerald staring at me. "So you're just going to dismiss what happened in the kitchen? You're going to dismiss that chemistry because you know my dad and we're teammates?"

*Honestly?* Yes, I was. That should have been obvious, though Brax clearly didn't feel the same.

"Seth and Maz are teammates too! *Your* teammates. It hasn't been a problem for them *or* the team."

He took a deep breath and closed his eyes, rolling his neck while he thought. When he opened his eyes again, they were clear and focused, as though they were taking in not only me but everything in the room all at once. "Do you really think that I don't realize you're a little? Do you really think that I'd bring any of this up if I wasn't confident that I could handle all of you?

"Easton's been teasing me for two years. We used to go to a BDSM club together back in Boston and he was all about finding a sub who wanted to be punished while I was always looking for the shy boy who wanted to cuddle. I was fine for the boy who wanted to escape his head for a night, but I wasn't what they wanted long term. I could see it in their eyes and feel it in their posture. They weren't willing to give me everything. They weren't willing to trust that I would be able to handle them."

And now I felt like an asshole.

He was right. Seth and Maz had been in a relationship for nearly a year. There had never been a fallout involving the team. It didn't mean I was comfortable given our respective positions and seniority with the team, but I wasn't convinced that was the reason I was fighting his advances as hard as I was. The same went for my relationship with his dad.

No matter how you sliced it, it was going to be uncomfortable to tell Tom and Leo, but I knew them well enough to know that if Brax was happy, they'd be happy. It wasn't like we were going to tell them the intricacies of our relationship. I nearly shuddered at the thought of them knowing anything that intimate about me or us.

*Us.* That was a foreign concept and I could admit I was getting ahead of myself. We'd gone about this entire thing backward, so no wonder my head was so messed up. I was struggling to see Brax as more than a teammate or roommate and he was jumping ahead to being my Daddy.

"We need to take a step back. Everything has gone more than a bit sideways. There's a lot more to my little side than childish pajamas and toys. You might know of littles, but you don't know *my* little. You don't know me as a little or what you'd be getting yourself into." I breathed in, wishing I felt comfortable pulling Huck and my blanket into my lap. I needed something grounding that would help me think. The best I could do was stand up to pace again.

"You're saying the right things, but I don't think you truly understand what you're suggesting."

Brax leaned back on the couch, propped one ankle on his other knee, and laced his fingers behind his head. "Then enlighten me. Let *me* make an informed decision about if you're going to be too much for me. I've already told you that you aren't. There is nothing you've said or I've seen so far that freaks me out. And to get ahead of the game, Easton's been convinced I need to find a little since he discovered that Nashville has a huge littles community. I'm pretty sure he's sent me every photo of every little he's found since I moved here."

I didn't know if the information helped or hurt. I was definitely confused, but if he wanted to put this all out there, fine. I'd tell him. I just had to hope that he was as trustworthy as I thought he was. The easiest way to tell him was going to be to show him. "I'll be back." I left him in my living room and went to get the key to my playroom.

I unlocked the door and looked around, trying to take the space in through adult eyes. When I saw this room, I was ready to forget about being an adult. It looked soft and comfortable. Glancing back toward the living room, Brax was watching me, a quizzical eyebrow raised but not coming closer.

With my heart beating harder than it had when he'd blown me earlier, I gestured toward the room with my head. "Come on. Let me show you my room."

Brax sprang from the couch far too fast to be considered casual, his excitement at my offer palpable as he approached. When he reached the door, I flicked on the overhead light, allowing it to cast the room in a warm glow. "This is my playroom."

I didn't want to watch his reaction, yet I couldn't look away as he began to take in the space. He couldn't seem to decide where to look as he glanced around, from the bookshelf next to the plush reading chair to the train table by the door. I didn't much care for trains, but they were Derek's favorite, so I made sure to have plenty here for when he came over to play.

He glanced over at me as he stepped inside. When I didn't say anything, he headed toward the middle of the room, straight to the large water-filled coloring mat on the floor. "What's this? I've been dying to ask. You were focused on it when I saw you. I've never seen anything like it before."

I felt my cheeks flush, but my feet were already taking me to the shelf that had the supplies for the mat. "It's my coloring mat. It's one of my favorite things." I needed to be careful because if I let myself, I'd get lost in coloring. My stress level was high enough that I knew it wouldn't take much to let go completely and lose myself to little space.

With the tiny box in hand, I knelt down and pulled a marker out of it. I'd played with it recently enough that the water in the marker hadn't evaporated. "It's a special pad and marker." I handed Brax an extra marker. "It's filled with water. When you run the sponge marker tip over the pad, it gets wet and turns colors. It dries and the color fades in just a few minutes, so it can be used over and over again."

I made a big swipe across the mat, already imagining a rainbow with clouds on either side. "Oh, wow, that's really cool." He sounded genuinely impressed with my toy and it made me smile inwardly. My happiness only grew when I watched him draw a circle and give it little sun rays and a smiley face. "A sun to make your rainbow shine."

The happy little butterflies working double time in my stomach should have been enough warning that I was dangerously close to letting my worries go in exchange for my toys. Either I wasn't paying enough attention or I was overwhelmed enough I chose to ignore them, because the things I should have been telling Brax were forgotten in exchange for my favorite toy and the soft pillows on the floor.

Well, maybe not totally forgotten. I knew he was there. After he hadn't run screaming the other way, I could admit that it was nice having him near. There would be a lot I—*we*—would have to sort through, but that was a problem for adult Trevor to deal with later.

## CHAPTER 19

### BRAX

I HAD EXPECTED Trevor to continue telling me all the reasons I was not ready to be his Daddy. He'd worked up a head of steam in the living room and by the time he'd ordered me to his room, I had known he was ready to list every single one of them. That all changed when I asked what his toy was.

I'd been curious. It hadn't been a ruse to distract him. He'd been so engrossed in it that I knew he had to like it. When I saw it still on the ground, I'd had to ask about it. Instead of telling me what it was, he'd shown me, but he'd also gotten sidetracked by it.

He'd finished the rainbow and had let it dry while drawing a house and car under it. When the color had evaporated, he filled the space with a tree and birds. The entire time he worked, his feet wiggled happily. I took the time while he was distracted to poke around his room a bit.

Trevor certainly loved art. From Play-Doh, to clay, to markers, to crayons, he had a section for everything. He also seemed to have an affinity for soft things, from blankets, to pillows, to stuffed animals. Everywhere I looked, something soft was tucked on a shelf, on a chair, or along the wall.

By the door, there was a box that was out of place compared to the rest of the organized room. The top was opened and I looked inside, not knowing what to expect. Knowing what I did about Trevor already, it shouldn't have surprised me that there were kids' plates, more sippy cups and bottles, and little forks and spoons. I didn't want to dig around in it and scare him, but I was pretty sure I saw a few pacifiers in there as well.

I wanted to tell Easton that I'd found a boy, but I wasn't sure that Trevor had actually agreed to be my boy. He'd basically agreed to show me why I wasn't prepared to be his Daddy. What he hadn't figured out yet was that I didn't care about what he liked to play with when he was little, or what being little meant to him. I was attracted to him, little side and all.

Once I'd had a chance to fully explore the room, I stood in the doorway for a few minutes watching him color. He'd once again become fully immersed in it. His hand reaching for a blanket reminded me that his blanket and Huck were still in the living room and once I got there, I remembered his cup. He hadn't taken a sip of it before he'd launched into his list of reasons we couldn't work.

There were things we hadn't talked about. I knew he hadn't told me everything before he'd gotten distracted by his toys. Halfway back to Trevor's playroom, I heard a buzzing against something hard. A pat down of my shorts told me I'd left my phone somewhere, likely the kitchen. It didn't take but a quick glance at the counter to find both my phone and the memories of what we'd done there not an hour before.

My dick took immediate interest in the memory despite being unable to do anything about it at the moment. With a groan, I palmed my cock, the momentary relief quickly erased by the growing pressure. Fuck, I'd been ignoring my arousal for so long that I felt like a pressure cooker with a faulty release valve.

I made it to Trevor's playroom on autopilot. I'd been gone less than a minute and Trevor hadn't moved yet. He was still focused on his coloring mat. The tension he'd been carrying that had made all his muscles tense and his jaw tick in the living room had disappeared. His feet were still tucked under him, his toes wiggling back and forth as he colored.

It didn't look like he'd noticed I was gone. It was the perfect opportunity to take just a minute to run up the steps and get changed out of my shorts and into an outfit more suited for hanging out for the afternoon. I had no plans but to spend the rest of the day getting to know Trevor in any way he'd let me.

Not wanting to waste time, I hurried through changing and was back downstairs in less than five minutes, even managing to wipe down my face, neck, armpits, and chest and put on deodorant before leaving my room. I was feeling better despite not having a full shower or washing my hair. At least I was no longer worried about smelling so badly that Trevor wouldn't want to be near me.

In the time I was gone, Trevor had left the middle of the floor and was sitting at the table playing with Play-Doh. He glanced up as I walked in, a moment of surprise showing on his face before he ducked his head and focused on his creation, though I was pretty sure I saw a small smile spread across his face. The smile dimmed slightly when I set his cup in front of him.

"Drink. You haven't drunk anything since I got back."

His cheeks tinted red, a telling sign that he knew exactly what I was referring to. I didn't say anything about the blush and headed for the chair across the room, anxious to see who had been texting me.

**Seth**: *Have you had a chance to talk to him?*

**Seth**: *Is everything okay?*

**Seth**: *Trev's not answering his phone. I'm a little worried about him.*

**Me**: *Sorry, I'd left my phone in the kitchen. It's been an interesting morning. He's currently pretending I don't exist.*

I glanced across the room and saw that Trevor had picked up his cup and was holding it to his mouth with one hand while still rolling the Play-Doh out with the other. A smile tugged at my lips at the sight. This might not have been exactly how I'd always seen myself spending days with a boy, but the peaceful air in the room and the quietness in my head were something I could easily get used to.

**Seth**: *So you talked?*

**Me**: *Kind of? He mostly talked to me about all the reasons we shouldn't try anything.*

**Seth**: *Sounds like Trev.*

**Me**: *But I got to see his playroom. I'm currently sitting in a very comfortable chair watching him ignore me.*

Our run had definitely started off on an awkward note when neither of us were willing to come out and admit we were both talking about Trevor. We'd avoided any mention of his name to the extent that my brain was starting to get confused about who the hypothetical little was and I'd started to confuse myself. I'd finally stopped running and pointedly asked if we'd been talking about the same person.

It had still taken another minute before we were both confident enough that we were talking about Trevor. After that, simply using *he* or *him* had made the rest of the run far easier for both of us.

**Seth**: *I know another little who hid his little side from the world until recently. When I saw that room, I definitely had flashbacks. I'm really fucking glad he has you there.*

Christ, Nashville really was filled with littles if Seth knew more. Then again, his dad owned DASH, and I'd guess that he probably knew a lot of the members.

**Me**: *If he'll even want me. I don't think his plan had been to get lost in playing when he showed me this room. I think he'd wanted to prove to me that his interests were going to scare me away.*

Across the room, I heard a yawn and looked up in time to see Trevor fighting to keep his eyes open.

**Me**: *Hey, I should go. I think this morning was a little much for him. He's falling asleep.*

I ignored the next vibration of my phone and stood to head over to the table. "Hey, put your Play-Doh away for now. We can read a book, then I'll tuck you in. You need a nap."

If I'd been expecting an argument, I didn't get one. He simply put his things away.

"Good job, little bear." I hadn't meant to call him that and for a moment had no idea where it had come from. Then I noticed I'd been looking at a little brown bear on the shelf in front of me that reminded me of Little Bear from a cartoon I'd watched as a kid.

Trevor's ears turned pink but he didn't say anything about the name. I was going to take it as a momentary win and took the silence as an opportunity to direct him to the chair. Now that I didn't smell as bad, I didn't hesitate to pull him into my lap. To my surprise, he didn't pull back or fight it, letting me know that he was absolutely drained. After the morning we'd had, it wasn't surprising to me.

He let out a soft sigh when I placed his blanket and Huck in his lap and cuddled closer to my chest as he let out a big yawn, his thumb slipping into his mouth as the yawn finished. I'd originally planned to read him a book, but I could tell that wasn't going to happen. The odds were he'd be asleep before I had one picked out and I was more than a little afraid that the sound of my voice would pull him out of his sleepy haze.

Instead of going for a book, I pushed gently against the floor and set the chair in a rocking motion. Not three minutes later, Trevor's breathing had evened out and five minutes after that, I realized my mistake. I was trapped in the chair with a very asleep boy on my lap.

The funny thing about professional sports was that everyone's personal stats were readily available. At five feet four inches and 170 pounds, Trevor was nearly ten inches shorter and thirty-five pounds less than me, meaning I could easily lift him... if I wanted to. His bed was only fifteen feet away, but having his solid body curled into my chest on a cool early fall day was too nice to disturb. I was happy to sit in the chair until he woke up, scrolling through my phone and trying to come up with a list of things we needed to work out before practice the next day.

An hour and twenty minutes later, I'd texted more with Seth, touched base with Easton, drained my phone battery, and had dozed off at some point before I felt Trevor move in my lap. My arms instinctively tightened around his body to pull him closer as my eyes fluttered open. When they finally focused on the man in my lap, the patches of skin I could see behind his blanket were flushed red and he was avoiding my eyes.

"Hey, sleepyhead."

He didn't answer, choosing instead to give a long groan.

I stretched my neck, letting it pop and adjust back into place before I pressed a kiss to the top of his head. "Feeling better?"

"I really thought that was a dream." His entire body deflated on a sigh. "Damn, I'd hoped it was a dream."

The chuckle that bubbled out of me was warm and I felt Trevor shake his head, though I was pretty sure that his cheeks had gone up in a smile.

"Not a dream. I hope that bit of playtime and your nap helped you relax some. There are things I really want to talk about."

He finally glanced up, questions written across his furrowed brow. "Uncomfortable things?"

My smile couldn't be helped. "Only as uncomfortable as you make it. You were so certain that your needs would turn me off, but nothing in the last few hours has made me feel differently. I still think you're amazing, sexy, and kind. And I still think that you're adorable."

I booped his nose to prove a point and while he blushed, he let out a small laugh that didn't sound like he wanted to crawl away in embarrassment.

At a certain point, I knew I'd said all I could and the rest was on him. Instead of pushing, I fell silent, allowing him time to work through his thoughts. It took nearly five minutes of the two of us sitting in silence before he let out a sound of pure resignation.

"Fine. This is me." He gestured vaguely around the room. "Well, most of me. This is me when I'm alone. It's not like I'm able to go to the club to play or actively put out into the world that I'm looking for a Daddy. Could you imagine the shit show that would cause?"

His question had been rhetorical, but I shook my head anyway. "I couldn't begin to imagine the disaster that would be."

"Exactly. So this is my safe space. I've known this was part of me since my teen years. I can't turn it off and it's not going anywhere, but I've also always known that I can't look for a partner in the scene. I have a friend and his Daddy that come over sometimes. Actually, they're coming over Wednesday evening. Or at least they were. It kind of depends on schedules and you said you had plans."

I smiled at his rambling. "I was planning on going to DASH for an intro night, but I guess that really depends on if you want me here with you or not."

The way Trevor's eyes widened would have been funny if I couldn't see the sheer disbelief in the expression. "Y-you'd want to *be* here for that?"

A tremor ran through his body and I couldn't decide if it was fear or something else. "If you'd want me here, I'd love to be here."

His thumb rose toward his mouth and I watched as his lips parted without hesitation before it slipped in. Tapping his fist, I gave him what I hoped was a reassuring smile. "How do you hide this out of the house?"

Instead of embarrassment, a giggle escaped Trevor as he pulled his thumb from his mouth. "Seth." He said Seth's name like I should have just assumed as much without asking. "He knows when I'm getting stressed or tired and stays close. He's really perceptive like that."

That didn't surprise me at all. From the things Seth had pieced together without my telling him, I'd known he was perceptive. And with how protective he was of Trevor, I really should have figured that out on my own.

"I'd really like to see where this goes between us. I've been wildly attracted to you for years. That hasn't changed just because my dad backed you into a corner and made you take me in for a bit. If anything, it made it more impossible to ignore that attraction I've always had to you. I managed to keep it mostly to myself because I didn't think that we would be what the other person needed. Now that I know our needs align, I'm going to have a hard time keeping my hands to myself."

His groan came out more playful than exasperated. "At least it hasn't just been me struggling to keep my attraction under wraps."

"Not at all. Now, let's go to the kitchen so I can make us some lunch. You can tell me more about my little bear's interests while I'm working."

He didn't look all that convinced by my enthusiasm and I could see him trying to form an excuse to change the subject, but I really wanted to know what he had kept from me. I was just discovering littles, yet I knew he had more to him than cute pajamas, a sippy cup, bottle, and pacifier. Did he wear diapers? Did he have training pants? What kind of Daddy was he looking for? And how was a relationship between us going to work in public? There were so many questions that needed to be answered, the latter probably the most important.

## CHAPTER 20

### TREVOR

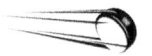

"How'd things go yesterday?" Seth slid up beside me during warmups, nearly bending himself in half as he stretched his back. I was wearing a no-contact jersey for the day but was hopeful to be back to full practice on Wednesday.

I wasn't quite at pretzel state, but most of my mobility had returned and I was able to look over at him with narrowed eyes. "You're too nosy for your own good."

He only grinned wider in response. "Nonsense! I'm nosy enough for *your* own good. Now spill."

There was no way in hell I was going to spill the beans to Seth when everyone was around us. Besides, we were still working things out. "We did a lot of talking last night and went to bed in our own rooms."

Seth's nose scrunched like he'd bitten into a lemon. "That's seriously boring."

It was, but I'd needed the space. I had let him pick out my pajamas and tuck me in, but that was as far as it went. We'd actually tabled any important discussions while he made lunch, and after lunch the conversation had naturally shifted to the logistics of a relationship, not so much my little side. That was on me more than him too. I'd been feeling a little too raw to discuss it after the morning, though he'd made it clear there was nothing I could throw his way that would turn him off.

He'd been so confident and matter-of-fact about things, I didn't think that he'd have been surprised if I'd told him diapers were part of my fantasy. And maybe they were, but I'd never given more than a passing thought to them. They definitely seemed like a thing that should be explored with a Daddy, which I'd never had.

Turning into a side stretch, Seth reached out and jabbed my hip. "You just had an entire conversation without saying a thing. Care to clue me in?"

I shook my head. No, I really, really didn't. "I needed time and space to digest everything. It was a very long, very overwhelming day. I wasn't ready to share a bed with him, at least not in that way."

Seth huffed, his annoyance at me clear. "Did you two figure shit out?"

"Some of it. We're going to take it slow. Work on things as they come."

Stretching the other way didn't deter Seth's inquisition. He'd missed a calling as an interrogator. "What about"—he dropped his voice to a quiet hiss—"your other needs?"

My face flamed red and suddenly Brax's voice cut into our conversation. "You don't have to answer his questions." Even quieter, he spoke to Seth. "Be nice to my boy. You can't go asking him stuff like that when he isn't ready."

Maz chuckled. "Get used to it. Seth hasn't learned about privacy yet. We're still working on it."

I groaned, my embarrassment only overshadowed by the giddy feeling in my stomach at Brax calling me his boy. He'd said it so naturally, he'd obviously been closely tuned into our conversation because he was way closer to us than anyone else and hadn't said a thing until I'd gotten embarrassed.

"We're working on it slowly. Just like he said. I'm willing to give him time."

A whistle blew before we could continue the conversation and I was left with a swirling feeling in my stomach, somewhere between elation and uncertainty. For the last twelve hours, the feeling had been settling closer to elation but moments like these, surrounded by my teammates, reminded me that things weren't always going to be easy.

**DEREK**: *I'm sick. Daddy brought the flu home from work!*

**Me**: *Oh no! Feel better soon. Do either of you need anything? I can drop stuff on the porch if you do.*

Something must have shown on my face because Brax looked over and cocked his head to the side to study me. *Okay?* He mouthed the question from across the locker room, though I suspected my nod wasn't convincing because he stood up to come my way.

**Derek**: *We got everything. But playdate's off tomorrow. I'm sad.*

**Me**: *I get it. But we'll have a few breaks coming up. I'm back to full practices anyway.*

"You sure you're okay?"

I jumped at Brax's voice and turned my phone off quickly. I'd told Brax that I had a playdate with a friend and his Daddy, but I didn't want to out Derek without his permission. If Brax was going to be my Daddy, I'd have to tell him at some point, but the first eighteen hours after deciding to date wasn't the best time to drop a bombshell like "my best friend is a country music sensation and little." That was better third date material.

Then again, how were we going to go on dates if we were living together?

"Trev?" Brax's hand landed on my shoulder, concern clear in his voice.

"Sorry. I started thinking about something else. My friend can't come over tomorrow night. He and his husband have the flu. I'm just a little bummed. We don't get to meet up much because our schedules are really hectic."

Brax gave me an understanding but sad smile. "I'm sorry, LB. That really sucks. We'll try to make tomorrow fun for you. I know you were looking forward to it."

He was trying to be sweet and understanding, but I was caught up on what he'd called me. "LB?"

The bashful grin he gave me sent those confusing emotions I'd been dealing with swirling in double time. Then he leaned in close and whispered into my ear. "I can't quite call you my little bear in the locker room."

I had to be blushing, but I was too busy smiling to care about the color of my face.

The moment was broken by Coach Cunningham calling my name. "Cane, a moment."

Thankfully, I'd already finished dressing and jogged over to the Coach's door. "You rang?"

Cunningham looked me over and gave a satisfied hum. "Good practice today. Feeling better?"

"Much. Didn't even need Advil this morning."

"Awesome. If you get an all clear tomorrow, will you be ready to go on Thursday?"

"Absolutely. I'm itching to get back to games. I thought I was gonna die of boredom on Saturday."

To my surprise, Cunningham snorted. "I'm sure you found something... or maybe some*one* to keep you busy." He raised an inquisitive eyebrow in my direction and I swallowed hard as I felt the color drain from my face.

"I'm sorry?" Somehow, my voice came out stronger than I felt. My brain kept screaming that I had to be reading more into the statement than he'd meant. Hell, Brax and I had barely spoken at practice and we hadn't had anything going on between us until the night before.

He crossed his large arms over his chest and gave me a chuckle. "Do you really think you and Cernak got anything by me? You two have been shooting each other heart-filled glances since he showed up."

My look of shock must have been obvious because he shook his head in amusement. "You had no clue, did you? Please tell me I haven't made that attraction up."

I shook my head to both. "It's... complicated."

An eyebrow got raised in my direction. "Cane, I respect the hell out of you as a person and as a player. The rest of the team respects you as a leader as well. I went to bat for Seth and Maz when their relationship came out last year. I think you know that I'll have your back as well. But if there is something going on between the two of you, I'd like to know now. It's a sticky situation, not for me or the league, but you *are* team captain. As the coach, I need to make sure that you know that what happens off-ice will have an impact here and on the team."

Groaning, I sank into the chair across from his desk. "Believe me. I know. I've been reminding myself of this since I picked him up from the airport. What you're forgetting is that I played on the same team as his *dad* and lived in his house for two years when I was first signed. He was twelve. *Twelve*! I'm feeling ancient and like I'm doing something wrong right now. I'm terrified of this, but... it feels right."

Coach sat down, folding his arms across his desk and leveling me with a concerned stare. "Trevor, are either of you entering into something that you don't agree with?"

I shook my head vehemently. "No, sir."

"Okay. Then there is attraction and you're both happy. Do I need to worry about relationship drama spilling into practice or games?"

"No!" Being questioned by Cunningham was worse than being questioned by my parents while growing up. I lowered my voice. "I mean, no. That isn't going to be a concern. First, we're going to take this one slowly. Second, I'm not about to do something that will negatively impact the team. And third, like I said before, it's so new, there's a chance nothing will come of this."

Cunningham sat staring at me for an uncomfortably long few seconds before shaking his head and giving me a half smile. "Keep telling yourself that, Trevor. From what I've seen the last week, he only has eyes for you, and you've been doing a damn shit job pretending you don't have eyes for him. As long as whatever happens between the two of you doesn't impact the team dynamics, I'm going to support you. Both of you."

"Thank you." I did appreciate the support but was still uncomfortable about how obvious whatever had been going on between Brax and me was to him. Had others noticed as well? Well, Seth and Maz had noticed, so it was likely safe to assume others had as well.

Coach chuckled lightly. "Get out of here, Cane. Get here a bit early tomorrow to be checked out and cleared by the doc before practice."

I nodded and left without another word, returning to the locker room to find it mostly emptied out with the exception of Seth, Maz, Yuri, Igor, and Brax. Brax was tapping on his phone and ignoring the other four, who appeared deep in conversation about where to go eat. Hopefully, they'd learned their lesson and weren't letting Igor decide where to eat. If it was up to him, they'd all have food poisoning by the next day.

"Nothing from any shady fast-food joints," I said as I headed over to where Brax was sitting.

Three of the four shuddered, but Igor just grinned. "No sense of adventure. Food is delicious."

A squabble was inevitably going to break out between them now that I'd said that, but that might have been the reason I'd done it. I sat down on Yawney's bench next to Brax, who had pulled his attention from his phone to study the disagreement in front of us.

"What's that all about?"

I patted his shoulder. "Igs has a knack for cheap food that gives him food poisoning. *Never* let him choose where to eat."

Brax scrunched up his face. "Eww. Gross."

"Yeah. Free porn on your phone?"

"Ha, I wish. It's my dad and Leo. They were worried about you and were wondering how you are doing."

The commotion ended when Igor, Yuri, Seth, and Maz left the locker room without so much as a goodbye. I was pretty sure I heard something about a local—reputable—burger joint and I was confident that the team would all be healthy the next day. "We're going to have to tell Tom and Leo about us at some point." I punctuated the sentence with a yawn. "And your car should be arriving today, so we really should get home."

Brax looked me over. "My dads can wait to find out. It's not like they live here. But you're right, we do need to get home. Not so much for my car but because you're exhausted."

I wanted to argue but knew it was pointless. "First full practice since Friday. It hit me hard."

"Come on, LB. Get Huck and let's get out of here. I'll tuck you in for a nap when we get home."

The nickname he'd bestowed on me the day before should have driven me insane. I'd fought for thirty years to not let my stature define me. There was something in the way he'd called me little bear the day before and how he'd effortlessly started calling me LB that morning that made my heart swell and made me feel taller, not smaller.

With our things gathered, we headed to my SUV. Since Friday, Brax had become the de facto driver. Even now that I was perfectly capable, he was still driving me around. Instead of climbing into the driver's seat, I got into the passenger side and was handed both Huck and his bear before he shut my door and walked around to get in.

Looking down at his bear, a question popped into my head. "Hey, have you named your bear?"

Brax pressed the ignition before shaking his head. "I haven't. Not that I've had a lot of time to put into it. It's been kind of a whirlwind."

"You really don't want to end up with an awful name for your bear. I don't know that I can live with you if I've got to ask you if you've remembered your Backdoor Bo or Five Hole Flow."

Brax barked out a laugh then began to choke on air, managing to half laugh, half cough before tears started pouring from his eyes. When the laughing had turned into mostly wheezes while he tried to catch his breath, I handed him a bottle of water from the stash I kept in the door pocket. "Drink."

I hadn't meant to kill him. I was kind of starting to like the idea of having someone looking after me—not quite ready to call him Daddy, but definitely ready to explore it more.

He uncapped the bottle and took a few long gulps before finally taking a deep breath and sighing. "Oh god. Oh shit. I don't know, those are both epic names. I could totally see him being Backdoor Bo."

"No." I shook my head. "Puck Bunny is bad enough. You need to name him, or *I'm* going to. It's going to be something like Muffin or Shirley Temple."

Brax snorted again but didn't choke that time. "Okay, okay. Let's think of a name on the way home."

We spent the drive throwing names around until he was pulling into the neighborhood. "What about Finn? Huck and Finn."

I looked at the bear in my hands, really studying it closely before nodding. "Finn works. I like it, and no one else has a bear named Finn."

"Great. The name debate is over."

"Welcome to the team, Finn." I was going to need to ask the person who did the jersey customization to put Finn's name on the back of his jerseys. That would need to wait until later since we were pulling into my driveway.

No sooner did the engine turn off than Brax was ushering me out of the car. "Okay, inside and to your room. You need a nap."

"Just me?" I'd needed space the night before, but between the easy banter in the car, Coach's acceptance of our budding relationship, and a little space from the house and my swirling thoughts, I wasn't needing as much space as I had then.

I wasn't looking for just a Daddy. I needed both a boyfriend and a Daddy. Knowing that Brax was not only accepting of my little side but was already familiar with the lifestyle had a lot of my normal concerns with relationships falling away. It left me with a lot more time to think about my attraction to him and less time to worry about how he'd react if I told him I wanted to be Daddy's boy.

Now that we were home, just the two of us in close proximity, I couldn't help but look at the way his arm muscles moved and the way his smile lit up the room at my question. He'd given me an amazing blowjob the day before but I'd never had the chance to touch him. I wanted the chance to change that.

"Well, I might take a nap too."

That wasn't an assurance that he'd be taking a nap with me, so I went for direct. "With me, right?"

My question turned his smile devious. "You want to nap together?"

# CHAPTER 21

## BRAX

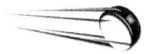

Two hours after climbing into bed, I woke with Trevor's head on my chest, his bear on my side, and his blanket draped over both of us. I could hear more than see his thumb in his mouth, a rhythmic sound that continued for nearly fifteen minutes after I woke up and a solid ten after I began to feel the press of his erection against my thigh.

When he finally sucked in a deep breath and rocked his hips into me, I knew he'd woken up and began trailing my fingers down his back. He'd fallen asleep in just a pair of briefs, leaving his muscular back fully exposed to my wandering movements.

I made it down to his ass, giving it a little squeeze and pulling a breathy moan from him before he froze. His face went warm on my chest and a blush spread across the tops of his shoulders. I'd liked the sleepy, uninhibited movements while he'd been waking up and wanted him back.

Not giving him time to overthink his embarrassment, I kissed the top of his head.

"Someone's awake."

Trevor groaned, trying to bury himself under the blankets. My hand on his back prevented him from being able to fully hide from me.

"None of that. Roll over, let me see you."

He shook his head but when my hand slid beneath his briefs to ghost over his crack, he forgot to be embarrassed and thrust into my hip again. I removed my hand and encouraged him onto his back, rolling so that I was on top of him. His cheeks were still pink and he was trying to pull his thumb from his mouth and dry it on his blanket before I saw it.

Running my finger down his cheek, I smiled at him. "Stop hiding it. I don't mind."

Trevor's blue eyes widened as though he couldn't believe what I'd said, then glanced back at his thumb. It was wrinkled and pale, clearly having been in his mouth for his entire nap. It was something I was already getting used to when he slept or was feeling little. Though I suspected that if he let himself fully relax around me, it would be in his mouth more than just those times. I'd get him to believe that it was fine, but for now I'd focus on making him and his erection feel good.

Moving my hand from his face, I reached between us to grope his dick. "Let's make this better. It can't be comfortable trapped in those undies."

His erection jumped in my grip and I knew he was all in. What I hadn't expected was to have him buck up into my grip or find a coherent string of words. "It's not. But you got to make me feel good yesterday; I want to make you feel good today."

I raised an eyebrow in silent question, wondering where the man who blushed so easily had gone to.

He didn't use words at first, choosing instead to reach his hand up and grope the front of the boxers I'd fallen asleep in, my dick needing no encouragement to fall from the fly of the loose material and begin filling in his grip.

At my response Trevor grinned, gaining confidence by the second. He wasn't my snuggly little bear from the day before or the bashful boy who had woken up embarrassed. He was a hungry, greedy man who wanted to explore my body and I wasn't about to tell him no. Though I decided it was perfectly acceptable to tease him just a bit.

Leaning down, I nipped at his collarbone, sucking just hard enough to leave a mark that would linger for the next few minutes but not hang around long enough to raise eyebrows the following day at morning skate. The contact made Trevor tense, his hand no longer moving on my balls.

When I lifted my head again, Trevor's pupils had widened considerably and he was breathing harder than he had been before. "You have no idea how hard I came last night when I got in bed, thinking about you beneath me, making all those beautiful noises as I blew you on the counter. Holy shit. You were perfect."

The smile that crossed his face was bashful, but a blush never followed.

"I liked taking you apart. I loved watching you relax afterward. And I can't wait for you to explore my body." I leaned down and gently kissed his lips, careful to avoid tongues or anything that would get us carried away. "But you need to ask for permission first."

That last sentence had been harder to get out than I cared to admit. My dick wanted nothing more than the attention Trevor was trying to give it. Needing to stop to establish expectations had been the last thing I'd wanted to do, but I'd known it was necessary.

Trevor's hand fell to his side and peace settled over him, the bashfulness and uncertainty disappearing as the words left my mouth. There were so many emotions that crossed his face, I struggled to keep up with them but in the end, he looked freer and more content. And when he spoke, his voice was confident and assured.

"May I touch you? I want to make you feel as good as you made me feel."

*Jesus,* the man was going to kill me. I already knew there was no other man like him on the face of the earth. I could look for the rest of my life and never find one. He'd needed the expectations and the ability to let go more than I'd known. A single expectation had given him power and confidence.

I understood being a different person on and off the ice. We all had to leave our personal shit at the door when we suited up. Trevor was a rock on ice and around the team. Confident, self-assured, and take-charge. He'd been like that when I was younger too. Even as a young NHL player, he'd never hesitated to step up, he'd never backed down from a fight or disagreement. I couldn't imagine how the two sides of him must have warred internally.

One sentence—one expectation—had physically changed every line in his body.

"You may. How do you want me?"

Trevor studied my eyes, his gaze intense and a furrow of thought creasing his forehead. "Your back, please. I want to be able to see and touch."

*Dead.* I was dead and couldn't decide if Trevor's sweet words were heaven or hell. I'd dreamed of a man like him for years, but now that I had him, I swore my body was going to betray me and I was going to come from his words alone.

I rolled to my back beside him, preparing myself for the sweet torture I knew was coming my way.

He wasted no time in proving just how right I'd been as he climbed over me, a purely devilish grin spreading across his face as he straddled my body. I tried to focus on anything but the way his chest rose and fell with every breath or the way his nostrils flared when he finally got a good look at my cock.

If I'd thought that watching him take in my body was torture, Trevor's hand wrapping around the base of my dick for the first time was in violation of the Geneva Convention. He moved painfully slowly up my erection, as though he needed to catalog every millimeter of my dick. He deserved a medal for how long it took him to reach the top... and then he started back down.

His thumb and pinky had just slid over the tip when he looked up at me and gave a small smirk. The brat knew exactly what he was doing to me and was enjoying it. I was pretty sure this was going to require a punishment at some point, but all my brain cells had been sent to my dick and focusing on not coming like a rocket in ten seconds.

Precum beaded at my tip and Trevor lazily swiped his forefinger over my slit, gathering the liquid and spreading it across my dick.

I bit my lip so hard I tasted blood and I knew I needed him to move his explorations along quickly. "Faster." Hopefully the whispered plea hadn't come out as desperate as I felt. If it did, Trevor didn't mention it, taking the command and moving his hand faster.

Despite the precum I was producing, the friction began to bite at my skin. Trevor moved slightly, adjusting himself while still jacking me, and reached blindly toward the nightstand. My eyes tracked his movements and I watched with a smirk as he slipped his hand into the drawer and produced a bottle of lube. With one hand, he effortlessly flicked the bottle open and poured a liberal amount onto my cock as he continued to jack me. Instantly, the friction eased, and with it the need to come built rapidly.

Trevor used his free hand to roll my balls, humming and murmuring as he did so. "I want this inside of me." It was then that I felt him rock his hips. I forced my eyes open to see him rutting against the bed.

*Fuck,* he was sexy. And yes, I wanted to be inside of him, but I didn't think I would last long enough. However, he hadn't asked if he could be getting himself off while he pleasured me. From the little I'd learned about him since we'd gotten into bed, I already knew he was going to thrive on my control.

I cleared my throat, both in hopes of getting myself to the point that I wasn't going to come in the middle of trying to tell him to not get himself off and to get his attention. Trevor stopped rocking to look up at me, his eyes a smoky blue and lids heavy.

"You never asked to get yourself off."

The look of pure surprise that crossed his face had me fighting a smile of my own. "I-I was?"

"You were."

He ducked his head before quickly looking up again, that time a knowing grin on his lips. "You never told me I couldn't."

Trying to give him a stern look when I really wanted to laugh was difficult, but I somehow managed. "You, little bear, need to ask permission to make your dick feel good."

I hadn't been trying to make him more desperate, yet something in my words had made his pupils dilate and his voice come out husky. "Please, can I make myself feel good while I make you feel good?"

One day that question would include a *Daddy* in it, and I found myself hoping it was sooner rather than later.

"You may this time, but next time you're making yourself feel good without permission, you're not going to get to come at all."

He swallowed hard then nodded his head. "I understand. Thank you."

Without another word, Trevor rocked into the bed again, his dick rubbing against the sheets, and let a long, low sigh escape before he once again began working my cock with his hand. He pumped me harder as he bucked into the bedding until he was begging for me to come and for him to come. His hips and hand moved frantically.

"Please, come for me. I need it. Need to come. Need your cum. Fuck."

He probably would have continued if my balls hadn't begun to tighten as a burning need filled my lower stomach and sent shockwaves around to the base of my spine. "Gonna," I said, the word coming out as both a warning and a sigh of relief.

Trevor tightened his grip a fraction and two strokes later, the first spurt of cum rolled over his hand and landed just above my belly button. He pumped harder and bucked his hips frantically as my dick pulsed in his hand. I knew when he'd finally come because his hand stopped and he ducked his head as his body went rigid and still. The moan he let out as he emptied between himself and the sheets was porn-worthy, but it was his eyes that really got to me.

Storm blue eyes focused on me like he could see into my soul as he rode out his orgasm. His lips stayed parted long after his moan had turned into nothing more than heavy breathing, but he barely blinked until the very end.

"Thank you." The words were barely a whisper, and I would have missed them had I not been staring at him. No sooner had the words escaped than he collapsed beside me.

The words sent my emotions swirling and my head spinning with happiness. "You're welcome."

We lay in silence for nearly ten minutes, Trevor's breathing evening out to a steady, slow pace that made me think he had fallen back asleep. The cum between my legs and on my stomach had cooled and was beginning to get uncomfortable. The sheets needed to be changed regardless but I hoped to keep myself from needing to shower. Much longer, though, and there wasn't going to be an option.

I'd just talked myself into getting up to clean myself off when Trevor's voice broke the silence of the room. "I liked how you did that."

I stilled, my plan forgotten, cold, dried cum be damned. "Did what?"

Trevor tilted his head so he could look at me. "You took control without making it awkward. It was just so matter-of-fact that things came naturally for me."

The corners of my lips twitched upward. "That's how it should be. Easy and comfortable." Another thought crossed my mind that I needed an answer to. "Did you have someone make you uncomfortable in the past?"

Trevor actually laughed. "Not in the way you're thinking. I've had a few vanilla partners who thought they should *be in charge*, or at least liked to pretend like they were in charge. Nothing over the top or even close to touching on real domination, but it has always come across as awkward."

I really wanted to growl in response but he'd sounded more amused than frustrated. He'd delivered the words in a conversational tone that really didn't require a response from me.

"The thing is, it's different when you do it. Maybe it's because I know you mean it? Maybe it's more that I think you're safe. Whatever the reason, it feels easier with you. I feel safe letting you take control, like I can actually let go and not worry about what you'll think when I do."

Words weren't enough, so I pulled him toward me to kiss him firmly. When we finally pulled back, Trevor was flushed, though I didn't get the impression it was from embarrassment. "What was that for?"

"For telling me that you feel safe with me. That's a huge honor. Come on, let's go to the shower and we can talk more."

## CHAPTER 22

### TREVOR

I HAD no idea what we were going to talk about in the shower. It was a unique place to have a conversation; however, we were both covered in cum, the sheets were cold and wet, and my stomach was starting to itch from cum.

Under the spray of the water, I couldn't remember why I'd thought this was a strange suggestion. With his hands scrubbing through my hair, it was hard to feel embarrassed even as he started asking questions I'd never answered for anyone other than Derek.

"I've seen your room, your toys, your pajamas, and I know you have a bottle and sippy cup and some cute plates and a pacifier."

"How do you know all that?" I'd hidden everything well. At least I'd thought so.

"Well, I saw some of it in that box in your room yesterday. But I'd also found a pacifier in the couch the first night I was here. I hadn't given it much thought at the time, but now that I think about it, it had to have been yours. And I saw your plate the day you'd fallen asleep on the couch. It didn't all make sense taken in small parts, but now that I see the whole picture, I understand it much better."

*Oh.* "That makes sense, I guess."

Brax directed me under the water and started rinsing my hair. "So my question is, what else do you have?"

My blank stare told him he hadn't used enough words for me to understand and he smiled softly. "I know littles sometimes wear special undies or pull-ups. Do you have those things?"

Now that I understood, it was easier to process but no easier to talk about. "I have some special undies I wear sometimes, but that's about it." He didn't need to know about everything going on in my head.

A hum came from Brax and he directed me out of the spray to lather my body with soap. He made it all the way down to my dick before he spoke, and his gentle touch moving down my body had my dick taking notice. Then he spoke and killed any and all arousal in one casually delivered question. "What about diapers?"

My mouth hung open as I watched him, my dick flaccid against my balls.

When I didn't answer, Brax looked up. "It's okay if it's something you like. It's okay if it's something you don't. I told you, I've done research. Easton's been sending pictures and links for the last week. I know that littles all have different interests, but you didn't tell me much about yours."

That little he was asking about was coming to the surface quickly, anxious to ignore the current line of questioning. My toe dug into the shower floor, my eyes trying desperately to find something to look at that wasn't him.

"Trev." Brax's voice was stern enough that it pulled my eyes toward him, the submissive in me unable to ignore it. When I looked up at him, all I saw was concern. "I need you to use words. I can't read your mind."

Groaning, I moved a little closer to him, my butt the only thing still in the water, and let him wrap his arms around me. My ear was resting near his nipple, our height difference feeling even greater than normal when standing this close.

"I've never tried them," I said in a rush, though loud enough that he could hear me over the water and the bathroom exhaust fan.

His chest vibrated and his amusement sounded in my ear. "I feel like there's something you're not telling me, little bear."

That nickname was going to be my undoing. I loved how easily he used it. On a sigh, I angled my head upward to look at him, unsure what I'd see when my eyes finally met his. They lacked all judgment, and the only things reflected at me were patience and a desire to know what I wasn't telling him.

"I'm curious, but I don't know if I'll like them or not. I've thought about them a lot over the years but I've always felt like I should have a Daddy with me. So it's never gone past a thought."

Brax hummed as he looked at me, but his expression had turned into pride. "That makes sense. I'm proud of you for telling me that. We can definitely talk about that more later."

I let out a relieved sigh. Talking about diapers and planning on possibly getting them was more than I wanted to discuss in the shower.

"Let's discuss expectations."

Maybe diapers would have been a better topic after all. My expression must have given my thoughts away because Brax grinned. "It's not that bad. I already know you like when I tell you what you should or shouldn't be doing. But I think we should have a more detailed list instead of just flying by the seat of our pants."

He directed us both back under the water to begin rinsing me off and getting himself clean. My brain was working too hard to reach out and help him like he'd been helping me, but I at least got to watch him as he worked and talked like it was the most normal, casual conversation we could be having while showering.

"As a Daddy, I've always seen myself as caring. Probably overprotective to an extent. I like cuddles and making decisions for my partner. Despite not having done much more than play at a club in Boston, I've had plenty of time to think about how I'd like a relationship to look. Being with someone who identifies as a little is a different layer, but not so different that I can't imagine it."

He ran a finger down my cheek, possibly removing some soap or maybe just to touch me. I didn't really care which, since it felt good. "I can already tell you that I'm going to want control over sex. And before you jump to conclusions, I'm vers, so that doesn't mean you've always got to be bending over for me. What that does mean is that I expect you to tell me if you want to touch yourself and you must have permission to come. You didn't have a problem with that in your room, so I'm hoping it's not going to be a problem long term."

Far from a problem, I felt relief. Knowing myself as well as I did, I knew that was what I'd been looking for. One of my favorite fantasies was when I was told I had to wait to come until my Daddy was ready. He'd quickly figured that out and had pushed buttons I'd always dreamed of having pushed. It had been one of the most intense orgasms of my life and thinking about it not thirty minutes later was making me hard again.

He looked down as my dick began to fill and chuckled. "I'm taking that as answer enough."

I couldn't bring myself to care that my cheeks had turned red once again. Not when a man like Brax was taking in every inch of my body like I was a Greek god.

"That's a good sign that we'll be well matched in the bedroom. I know I'm living here right now, but if we're going to different places, I want to know where you are. If you ever need me or need help, I need to know where you're at to get to you."

"Fair enough, but I'm going to say that one goes both ways. I might be submissive, I might be a little, and I might be tiny, but none of that means I can't come if you need something. I'm not helpless, nor do I want to be treated as such. If we're in this, we're equal partners."

The pleased smile that crossed Brax's face was enough to have me smiling. Then he leaned down to capture my lips with his, not pulling back until the water ran over our faces and we had to separate before we drowned. "I would never assume you weren't equal. I can promise you that you'll always know where I am."

"Good. What else?" Now that we'd started talking, it didn't feel as ominous as it had before.

My growing confidence made him smile as he stepped back into the spray to wash himself off. "I'm a stickler for routines."

I scoffed. "We're hockey players. We all are."

The comment had him chuckling. "Point taken. What I really meant was that, especially if you're having a little night, I'm going to want a routine followed."

That didn't sound scary. It wasn't like I was one of the guys who were out all hours of the night partying. I was pretty damn boring for the most part. "I can handle that." With as hectic as our lives were during the season, someone making a routine for me sounded nice.

Brax finished washing off then stuck me under the water again, rubbing his hands over my chest, stomach, and back like he might have missed something the first two times he rinsed me off, then turned off the water. He stepped out of the shower and reached for a towel. Before I could follow him, he held up a finger. "Wait a sec. Let me get you a towel. I don't want you to slip."

I fought to hide my amusement but knew I was smiling when he turned back around with a fluffy towel in his hands. "Come here."

Stepping out, I let him wrap me up, then start drying me off. "You can dry yourself off. You've got to be cold."

Brax angled his head upward so he could continue drying me while he spoke. "I'm fine. Let me do this. I want to know you're warm and dry."

My legs spread automatically as he worked his way up, my heart fluttering faster the longer he spent drying me. I'd never had a guy prioritize my comfort over his after a shower. I knew it was a very Daddy thing to do, yet that didn't stop it from feeling strangely overwhelming.

I'd spent the last week freaking out that he was Tom's kid and my new teammate and I couldn't possibly be attracted to him. Somewhere along the way, I'd lost sight of the fact that we were both adults and there was nothing wrong with the attraction I had toward him. He was just a man who happened to be a knowledgeable Daddy trying to care for me. Care for me while also seeing just how embarrassed he could make me by discussing expectations.

*Spoiler alert*: very.

As it turned out, he'd only touched on the easy questions so far. He stood up to dry my torso, placing a few kisses to my chest and lips before focusing on my arms. "What about interests outside of your little side. Any other kinks, fetishes, fantasies?"

My eyes gave me away when they widened, letting water drip into them.

"Okay, yeah, there's something there. What do you want to tell me?"

I'd obviously shared my little side with Derek and his Daddy, but other fantasies had stayed just in my head so long it felt like they were some big, horrible secret that no one would understand. It didn't matter how many times I'd told myself that my fantasies were mild compared to some others, I still couldn't find the words to put voice to them.

Taking pity on me, Brax started with his. "I'll be honest. I've done a little bit of this and a little bit of that at the club in the past. I played with a few boys who really liked hard impact play. I did a little bit of shibari as well. I enjoy bondage, but I'm not great at rope work. If it's something that you're interested in, maybe we could find someone here to teach us. I never had the patience to learn all the twists and knots, but I'm willing to try."

He finally decided I was dry enough and wrapped the towel around my body before turning to grab his own towel, still talking about his interests. "As I said, I've done some pretty intense impact play, various sensory things—ties, blindfolds, feathers, etcetera. Body fluids are kind of my limit: blood, spit, vomit."

I let out an involuntary shudder. "Definitely no blood play. I hate getting my blood drawn. The others are things I'm not interested in either."

"Well, we have a few good hard limits. Oh, do you have a safeword?"

"Since I haven't had a Daddy, I haven't done much, definitely not enough to need to define a safeword, but I always thought the traffic light system was easiest."

Brax nodded thoughtfully. "I like that one too. It's what I've always used myself. Now you said you haven't done much, but *done* and *thought* are two very different things. I get the impression there's more going on in that brain of yours than what you've said so far. What aren't you telling me, little bear?"

The man was too damn perceptive for my own good. He wasn't letting me hide, no matter how badly I wanted to. Throw in the little bear nickname and I was turning into putty in his hands and knew it was futile to hide my thoughts from him.

My head dipped and I spoke to the floor, but I managed to get the words out. "I've always been drawn to bondage, sort of. Not like tight rope bondage but scarves or something I could get out of easily. And maybe some sensory play. Like when you were talking about feathers and stuff, that sounds like it could be fun."

Brax hummed. "That's all understandable. What else are you thinking about in that head of yours? I already told you that I've done a lot."

"I don't know what I'm going to like. I *haven't* done anything." The statement coming from my mouth took me by surprise. I was glad Brax had experienced these things and knew what he wanted and what he liked, but that didn't mean that I'd had a chance to do that. Living in Tennessee the last handful of years, knowing that I was a little and that my fantasies involved having a Daddy and the ability to have my blanket or still be able to put my thumb in my mouth when I needed it, I had never wanted to expose that part of myself to explore those things.

I was confused and felt lost and unsure of what I really wanted. I had thoughts but no real concrete answers. He was nearly eight years younger than me and had experienced so much more. He was confident and knowledgeable in his wants, needs, and desires while I was thirty and still trying to figure myself out.

And then Brax was there, crowding my space and pulling me close. "Hey now. I didn't ask to upset you. I don't want to trigger you in some way. I'm trying to figure out limits."

I didn't know I'd been crying until I sniffled and tried to wipe the few tears away before Brax noticed. He stilled my hand as he guided me toward the closed toilet and sat me down, quickly wrapping his towel around his waist before crouching down in front of me. "Talk to me. I can't help unless you tell me what's wrong."

Sniffling again, I shook my head. "It hit me that you're confident and know all these things about yourself and what you like and want and need. I only know that I'm a little and want a Daddy. I have thoughts but I've never acted on any of them. I'm scared that they're going to be ridiculous. And what happens if I tell you something and you think that it's stupid or don't like it?" I'd worked up a head of steam and inhaled sharply to stop myself from rambling more.

When I didn't say anything else, Brax took my hands in his. "Trevor, we all have different experiences. Everyone has different experiences. It's okay. I don't have the same experiences as you. I've been living in a huge city, playing on a fourth line of a team with all these huge old-timers that dominate the spotlight. Off the ice, I'd been all but invisible. I had the freedom to do what I wanted, as long as I didn't land myself in the headlines for something stupid. And I didn't.

"You've been in a smaller city. You've been the team captain for years. You've had a career that most of us could only dream of. You haven't been afforded the anonymity that I have. It's okay and I'm not going to hold that against you. We can learn what you like and want together. I'm excited to explore new things with you. You know you're a little. You know you want a Daddy. I'm a Daddy and have known I want a boy. I've been pretty certain that I want a little since before I found out you're one. I think that's enough."

I sniffled again, out of arguments. How was this man so understanding and knowledgeable?

Brax's eyebrows turned downward, a small pout forming on his lips as he thought. "You came out as bi, but you keep saying you haven't tried things because you didn't have a Daddy. Have you ever considered a Mommy?"

The question loosened some of the tension in my chest. "I have, but never seriously. The few relationships I've had with women have been decent sexually, but I've never felt comfortable opening up like that to any of my partners. Calling myself bisexual is probably a bit of a stretch. I have sexual attraction toward women sometimes, but it's not a romantic or even an emotional attraction. It's like we click well enough to have sexual chemistry, but I guess I'd consider myself homoromantic. I've never considered a long-term relationship with a woman."

I gave an uncomfortable shrug, not sure if I was explaining myself well.

To my surprise, Brax's confusion cleared and he nodded an understanding. "That makes sense, actually. I knew a guy in juniors that was straight but aromantic. There's a guy I met at the club in Boston that considered himself asexual but polyromantic."

How did I luck out in finding a teammate who was willing to just roll with the punches and not be upset when things went a little sideways for me? It was going to take a while for me to understand that it was okay to be myself around him. My logical brain, my emotional brain, my adult side, and my little side were all at odds with one another. Except my little side as well as the emotional part of my brain were starting to get in line with the rest of me. Ready to finally let someone else take control and care.

## CHAPTER 23

### BRAX

I SANK into a seat halfway back on the plane. It had been one of the longest weeks of my life and I was still facing a nearly three-hour plane ride and drive home before I could collapse into bed. Preferably Trevor's bed. I wanted to get my little bear home and started on the routine we'd talked about a week earlier.

In some ways, the last week had gone by in the blink of an eye, in others it had felt like it would never end. We'd played a game in Michigan and then flown to Colorado. It was early enough in the evening that I wasn't necessarily tired but the travel had caught up with me. I knew I'd be exhausted by the time we reached Nashville.

For now, Trevor was going to be busy doing his normal captain thing, checking on players, talking with the coaches, and discussing the game with the alternate captains, Seth and Yawney. The first few games had been strange, excluding the very first game since I'd been rushing out of the locker room with a man who was basically high as a kite. Since then, the team bond and rituals had all come to light and I was finally starting to feel like a part of it.

"Bear check!" I could hear Trevor's voice over the din of everyone else's chatter despite only just being able to make out Huck being held above his head, the rest of his body totally hidden behind the last few players boarding.

Twenty-three bears got raised in the air and everyone looked around to make sure no one was missing a key member of the team. Trevor would eventually make his way over to me, though that could be another hour or more. I'd learned on the plane ride from Michigan to Colorado that Trevor did not do well on long plane rides and got bored easily. He'd doodled on every napkin he could find when he finally sat down.

I'd ducked into a corner drugstore after breakfast that morning and picked up a handful of coloring books and two packs of crayons. They were now in my messenger bag waiting for Trevor to sit down. Until then, I was going to busy myself planning some fun ways to explore Trevor's likes. He'd been bummed out about not getting to play with his friend the week before and we'd spent the evening in his playroom, the intro night at DASH well out of my mind.

My thoughts kept circling back to the conversation we'd had about diapers and the things he hadn't tried that he'd wanted to. It was too soon for diapers. He still hadn't called me Daddy, though he'd been open with his affection in the house and even around Seth and Maz to an extent.

"Good game." Maz climbed over my lap and took a seat next to me.

"Thanks. You too."

He glanced around the plane, then behind us and in front of us to see who was around. The nearest people were Igor and Yuri, but they were two rows behind us and already engrossed in a game of cards. "Things going well with Trev? I saw you head to his room last night."

I was going to have to be more careful in the future or the entire team was going to know we were together before long. "Just last night?" I'd actually slept in his room the entire trip, usually arriving well after everyone else had been in their rooms.

Maz waggled his eyebrows. "Sneaky bastard. Things are going well then?"

"So far. Yeah. Not like we've had a lot of time to do much, being on the road. Between press, practice, games, and travel, we're lucky if we have the energy to jack each other off before bed."

"It gets better. But I know the feeling." Maz looked around, ensuring we were still secluded, then leaned in close just as the engines revved to life. "Has he slept okay the last few nights? He doesn't normally sleep well on the road. Seth used to bitch that Trevor heard everything."

I chuckled thinking about what Seth and Maz had been getting up to that Trevor might have caught. "He's a bit restless, but he's slept pretty well." Leaning forward, I whispered the next words. "I was thinking about packing a bottle or sippy cup for the next away game. He seems out of sorts without his stuff. At home, he has a routine. I didn't think about it until this morning."

Maz's eyes widened in understanding. "Why the hell didn't one of us ever think about that? I mean, it's not like he'd talked about that part of his life with us until you got traded here but it's not like Seth didn't figure it out before. That makes so much sense. Dammit. I'm kind of kicking myself in the ass for not thinking about that sooner."

This team was unlike any I'd ever played for. It wasn't just their quirky traditions—they cared deeply about one another. A few years earlier, the Grizzlies had been a disaster of a team. I could clearly remember talk in juniors about it being the team where players' careers died.

After the management and coaching shake-up and the years that followed, the team had made an amazing rebound in a shockingly short time, from bottom of the barrel to one of the top teams in the league every year. Speculation and rumors had swirled about the astounding turnaround, but nothing had ever been confirmed by anyone inside or outside the team. Oddly, even those players traded to other teams didn't talk about what had made the Grizzlies turnaround happen.

Two weeks as a Grizzly and I knew what made this team so special. It really was a family. *Mess with one of them, get the whole team.* I hadn't been part of a team like this one since I played house league hockey when I was nine and ten years old.

A huge driving force to the family was Trevor. He was a man who put a ton of pressure on himself to look after everyone on the team, who wore the captain's *C* with pride, and was currently flitting from person to person making sure they were okay, talking about the games, and asking if they needed anything from him. He was also the person who needed someone to check in on him but had never been able to ask for it. For years, he'd put everyone else and their needs in front of his own, relegating his desires to a room in his house whenever he had time. It was going to be my job to figure out how to prioritize Trevor, every part of him.

"Oh, looks like they're done making the rounds." Maz stood up and climbed back over me, shooting Seth a blinding smile and slipping into the row behind me.

I stood to let Trevor slip into the seat between me and the window, allowing him a little bit of privacy from the rest of the plane. "All done with the rounds?"

Trevor nodded, exhaustion etched in the creases next to his eyes. "Yeah. Ready for a day off."

I could understand that. We all were.

"Few more hours and we'll be home." Leaning forward to rummage in my bag, I found the stack of coloring books and boxes of crayons. "I got you something this morning to keep you from stealing everyone else's napkins."

When I sat up, Trevor's eyes brightened. "You got me coloring books?" He'd hissed the words, an excited smile on his face that I was beginning to associate with my little bear more than the team captain.

"Yeah—"

The rest of my sentence was cut off when Yuri's head popped up. "Coloring books? Where?"

Toby and Jean-Luc's heads were the next to appear over our seats. "You have coloring books? Can we share?" Jean-Luc's puppy dog eyes nearly rivaled Trevor's as he looked at the books.

Trevor's big blue eyes looked between the excited faces, then down to the coloring books I'd bought him. Pink stained his cheeks. "Brax bought them for me?"

His statement came out as a question and I was glad that I'd bought a handful now that news had spread through the plane. "I figured everyone would like to keep their napkins today. Starting to think I should have bought more," I said, making light of the situation. I knew I'd said the right thing when Trevor relaxed noticeably beside me. "Let him pick out what he wants. Then I'm sure we can find some to share."

Trevor picked out a book filled with sea creatures and then looked over to everyone else. And by everyone, I meant at least half the team that had crowded around our seats.

"They're coloring books, not free dirty mags. Good lord, you all are like vultures," I said to the group, a smile on my face and in my voice. I was looking at the group of men around me and back down at the coloring books. "I didn't buy enough for the entire team. You're gonna have to figure out how to share."

Coach Cunningham's voice cut through the noise as everyone tried to pick out a picture or book to color. "What is going on over here?"

"Cernak brought coloring books!" Toby answered for the group.

"And you all are crowding around here, why?"

Patrick, a fourth line brute who was not only muscle at the boards but fast and had a number of points for the season, flipped through the puppy dog coloring book he was holding as he spoke to Coach. "So we can pick out something to color. Playing the same damn games every flight gets boring."

I could just make out Coach's face, but he looked more amused than annoyed, though he did leave us with a warning. "You all need to pick out a picture and head back to your seats quickly."

A smirk crossed my face as I wondered if he realized he sounded more like a primary school teacher than a professional hockey coach. Then again, with this team, the lines were sometimes blurred.

As the group dispersed, we were left with picked-over coloring books. Even the extra box of crayons I'd bought had been taken. Someone toward the back of the plane mentioned they had colored pencils with them and someone else offered a few of their favorite markers. Trevor hadn't appeared to notice much of the chatter once they'd left, his attention focused completely on his coloring book. When his thumb slipped into his mouth, I glanced around to see if anyone was in eyeshot, but everyone had settled down. Aside from Maz and Seth behind us, we were alone, so I didn't disrupt him, though I did keep a closer-than-normal watch for movement around the plane.

As the plane started its descent into Nashville, and noise and movement picked up around the plane, I reached over and gently tapped Trevor's fist. He'd been so lost in his coloring that he jumped slightly at the contact and looked around to see who had tapped him. I gave him a smile and pointed at his thumb, gesturing for him to take it out of his mouth.

His cheeks started to turn pink, but the attempt at a blush faded as he looked around to see that no one was near us. For added assurance, I leaned forward and whispered into his ear. "I kept an eye out for anyone coming this way. No one saw."

"Thank you." The smile he gave me lacked the normal embarrassment or bashfulness. I couldn't help but notice that he looked happier and more relaxed than he had after the trip to Colorado. Despite his easy smile and the lack of embarrassment, I could see that Trevor didn't have the look of confidence and control I normally saw in him. He'd been on every minute of every day since we'd left Nashville four days earlier. Even before then, we'd had an event at the children's hospital and a game as well.

Whether he realized it or not, Trevor was ready to shut his brain off. The hour he'd spent coloring had been enough to relax him, but now it was up to me to make sure he had the time and space to recharge, free of interruptions and distractions.

I took both of our suitcases as we left the plane, leaving him with Huck, Finn, and his carry-on. When he didn't argue about me taking his bag, I knew he was done. I slowed my pace to stay in step with Trevor and noticed that Seth and Maz had done the same, effectively blocking him in and forming a miniature wall around him.

At the car, Trevor climbed into the front seat with the bears, leaving me to walk around to the back and toss our bags into the hatch. Seth walked from around his SUV and stepped next to me as I pressed the latch to drop the hatch.

"Is he doing okay? I mean, with the changes and all. He looks more relaxed than normal."

"He's getting used to things. I'm getting used to things. Definitely new for both of us. My plan for the rest of the day is to get him home and let him relax, see where that gets us. He really hasn't had a chance to shut his brain off in nearly a week."

Seth patted my shoulder. "Good man. Get your boy home and let him relax. I already told the guys that he needs some time off. Everyone's noticed he's a bit spread thin. Everyone's agreed to leave him alone until we go to the arena next time."

That was going to make my life easier. I also needed to touch base with Easton or he'd be on a plane his next day off. He'd been sending me texts every day, but I'd been evasive at best, not sure what or how much to tell him. I was only going to be able to hold him off so long with vague responses that focused more on my being alive and hockey than anything important, like the intro night at DASH that I'd been supposed to go to.

Before I could talk to him, though, I needed to get Trevor home and settled. A snack, bath, and playtime before an early bedtime was definitely in order for my overworked little bear.

## CHAPTER 24

### TREVOR

THERE WAS something different about Brax. Hell, there was something different about me too. After four days on the road, we'd gotten to know one another better. It hadn't been about getting to know Daddy Brax and little Trevor, but more like getting to know each other outside of our common interest.

Brax wasn't like most of the younger hockey players I'd spent time with. He was mature beyond his years, with an eye for the details of the game. He had the flashy skills of the younger generation of hockey players who had spent years watching videos of others while perfecting physics-bending stick and puck handling. But then he also possessed the focused dedication and power of a player with many years on him. He read plays with ease and wasn't afraid to throw his body into the mix, on the boards or open ice.

Growing up around professional hockey players had given him an insight into this life. The notoriety, press, and publicity of professional sports didn't fuck with his head as it had so many young players. It was simply part of life. Tom, Leo, and LeAnn had done a good job preparing him for life as a professional athlete. His natural talents also meant that he'd been accustomed to the grueling demands of the sport well before he hit the professional stage.

For the past four days, the two of us had bonded over our mutual dislike of hotel restaurants and beds. Each night, I'd fallen asleep with his arms wrapped around me as we talked about the day ahead. It had been a blissful few nights, at least as blissful as hotels could be. I always slept like shit on the road, but with Brax in bed with me, I slept just a little bit better.

As we'd stepped off the plane, he'd stood a little closer to me than he normally did, he'd watched me more intently, and once we'd gotten into the car, he'd switched from my teammate to my caregiver—my Daddy. While I hadn't actually called him that, I knew he was sincere when he'd told me it was something he wanted.

There had been a few days there that I'd had a hard time believing he was serious. It had taken longer than it should have for me to convince my brain that Brax hadn't been shocked at my needs. If anything, he'd been eager to show me he both understood and accepted every part of me. It had been me continuing to hold back with him.

Though I'd noticed that he'd done what he thought best today on the plane. Getting me coloring books and crayons had given me a chance to sit down and stop being on. Then again, once I'd shut that in-control part of my brain off, it had been hard to get it to click back on when we'd arrived in Nashville. I'd been happy to have him there to lead the way and I was pretty sure he'd known it too.

Any lingering questions about if he knew that he'd pushed me just far enough to get my little side to the surface were answered when he climbed into the car and connected his phone. Without a word from me, a soundtrack to one of my favorite animated movies turned on. The tenuous grasp I'd had on my adult headspace from the plane to the car left as soon as the *Moana* soundtrack started.

Wiggling in my seat, I fought the urge to sing along to the first song.

"I thought you'd like this one. I noticed you had a few *Moana* coloring books in your room and a Maui pillow."

I'd also memorized all the songs and most of the lines. Derek and I had spent countless afternoons with it on in the background while we played. Colt had even taken us to the theater to watch it on a low-key little day.

My ability to keep the songs in my head lasted precisely two songs, just long enough for me to forget about keeping my little locked inside me. I'd been big for nearly a week, the end of road trips were always difficult, and with the man who was proving to be the Daddy I'd been looking for sitting in the driver's seat, I was ready to shut off for a bit.

"Can I watch *Moana* when we get home?" There was someone next to me willing to make decisions for me. The thought was freeing, letting me let go of another part of the adult world and the stress that came with it.

Brax thought about it, his hum telling me he was giving it serious thought. "Well, it's going to be snack time when we get back. That belly of yours has been growling since before we landed. Then you need a bath. After that, though, we can see how much energy you have left. I think it would be okay to put it on before bed."

I wanted to pout and tell him I didn't need a snack or a bath but before I could protest, my stomach rumbled. "We can skip the bath?" I asked hopefully.

Brax's chuckle made me smile. "You, little bear, need a bath. After a long flight, you definitely need a bath. I'll order dinner while you're in the tub, then maybe dinner and *Moana*."

"Snack and Moana?" I was not above begging.

Brax pulled into the driveway, his eyebrow climbing high on his forehead. "Do you really want to argue with me, little bear?"

*Arguing could be fun.* I had enough sense left to not say that. I didn't think that my idea of fun and *Daddy's* idea of consequences would be in the same chapter, much less on the same page. With a resigned sigh, I shook my head. "Okay, dinner and *Moana*."

With the garage shut, Brax killed the engine. "Good boy. Go inside and wash your hands for me. I'll be right behind you. I need to get the bags."

Adult me would have offered to help with the suitcases, but I'd been given a clear instruction and I intended to follow it. I really wanted to be able to watch a movie later and the only way that was going to happen was if I had good behavior.

I was inside with my coat hung on the hook by the door, my hands washed, and both our bears on the seat beside me at the counter when Brax walked in carrying our bags. He looked over at me and smiled. "Thank you." He rolled the two bags into the laundry room, not bothering to open either, and dropped his messenger bag and my backpack on the seat beside our bears.

"Can you go get me your cup? I bet you'd like some juice with your snack."

A week earlier, I would have rather crawled in a hole than gone to get my sippy cup, but with Brax's clear commands and kind requests, I found it hard to be embarrassed. Juice sounded good anyway, so I hurried toward the playroom to grab a cup.

I was reaching into the box where I'd stashed my cups when two things dawned on me, the first being that my cups and plates really should go back to the kitchen where they belonged. The second being that I was still in my suit pants and dress shirt. If I was going to be little and not let the adult world pull at me, I needed to lose the clothes, but I didn't know what to put on.

As I removed my pants and unbuttoned my shirt, I felt the last of the adult world slipping away and a grin growing on my face. Finding a place for my clothes was far lower on the list of priorities than getting my things to the kitchen for a snack, so I left them on the floor in exchange for the box of kitchen items I'd removed from the cabinets two weeks earlier.

Slipping and sliding in my dress socks as I rushed to the kitchen caused me to giggle and laugh the entire way. "Got 'em!"

The words came out louder than I'd intended and Brax turned from the refrigerator to look at me. "What do you have there?" He automatically reached for the box I was holding before he fully took in my attire. When he had the box in his hands, his eyes widened comically as he looked at me. "And where did your clothes go?"

Standing in the kitchen in just my socks, a pair of briefs, and my white undershirt should have been embarrassing. It should have felt awkward, but it didn't feel anything like that. Instead, it felt like I'd shed a million pounds of weight as I pointed behind me. "In my room."

The shake of his head didn't look annoyed, nor did the way the corner of his mouth quirked upward. "Well, I guess I don't have to worry about you getting your nice clothes dirty with your sandwich. Jump up on the chair. It's almost ready."

"Snack!" I scrambled onto the chair. I was usually conscious of how I climbed onto the tall barstool. It took more effort for my short legs and I hated drawing attention to my size. I would normally avoid the chair altogether or try to hoist myself onto it. Being little allowed me to not think about my size. When I was little, it felt right when I had to make an effort to climb onto something or couldn't touch the ground if I sat back on the couch.

When Brax slid my plate across the counter, I let out an excited squeal. "Moana!"

Daddy nodded—because he was Daddy, whether I'd called him that or not. "Yup, and your Hei Hei cup."

Making grabby hands for my juice was natural. Until that moment, I'd thought I'd known my little side. It had never occurred to me that I hadn't known part of myself, but with a Daddy on the other side of the counter, I was quickly realizing I'd never fully shut my adult brain off. There had always been lingering adult thoughts that had kept me from really experiencing the freedom of age play. With Brax, those feelings were no longer there and I was finding giggles and excitement more natural. The most important things to me were my snack and getting to watch the movie later.

I'd gotten caught up in my thoughts about the movie as I'd eaten my snack and drunk my juice, and a washcloth was in front of my face as Brax tsked and spoke around a warm laugh. "You're a mess. I'm glad you took your shirt off earlier. I think that undershirt's become a play shirt."

I looked down to find two big globs of strawberry jelly on my cotton T-shirt and a smear of peanut butter at the hem. I couldn't remember touching my shirt, but that definitely looked like a fingerprint. There was another spot of blue that I had to assume was from the blueberry yogurt I'd eaten.

"Bath?"

"As soon as I have you cleaned up. I don't want you dropping food all over the house."

He finished with my face, flipped the cloth in half and wiped my hands, then flipped it again to dab at my shirt. "Okay, I'm going to wipe down the counter and get your plate in the sink. Get to the bathroom and go potty. I'll be in to run a bath for you in just a minute."

I caught what he'd done there, thankful for the chance to relieve myself in private. While I had some fantasies about diapers or my Daddy helping me in the bathroom, I wasn't ready to explore either yet. I also hadn't noticed just how full my bladder had gotten while I'd been eating and was rushing a little faster than normal to get to the bathroom before doing a pee dance in the kitchen.

Running toward the bathroom, I heard Brax muttering to himself about the irony of needing to clean me up before a bath.

Just before I reached my bedroom door, I called behind me. "Bring my cup when you come, please!" Good manners had to count for something. After not having more than a bottle of water on the plane, I was thirsty, and my juice had been good. I'd had two cups of it with my snack.

I didn't hear if there was a response because I was running to the toilet and yanking down my underwear before I'd given him a chance to answer. My bladder's screaming need for relief was much more important than my desire to know if I would get my cup when he came back.

With my bladder empty, I gave a sigh of relief, then washed my hands. Impatient for my bath but knowing that I shouldn't start it on my own, I knelt down on the floor in front of the bathroom sink and reached for the little bucket of bath toys I kept stashed there for when I had a chance to take a bath. There weren't many, but I had some bath crayons and foam blocks that stuck to the side of the tub when wet.

"What do you have there?" Brax's voice from the doorway startled me, but my shock quickly turned to excitement when I noticed my cup in his hand.

"Toys." I held the bucket out to him with one hand while reaching for my cup with the other. We traded and I put the spout to my lips.

"Looks like you're all set. Let me get the water running and we can get you undressed."

Without prompting, I reached back into the cabinet for the bubble bath, then got to my feet. Waiting for the bath water to come up to temperature, I rocked on my feet and thought about how much I wanted to tell Derek about my day. It was going to have to wait, as were the intrusive thoughts about telling the team that we were together. We would have to deal with that sometime in the near future but not today. Today was about Daddy and me learning how to be Daddy and little bear.

"Everything okay?"

I blinked in surprise, not sure when Brax had turned from the tub, but he was standing in front of me with concern etched on his face. I didn't want to use words or bring either of us out of whatever space we'd found but knew it was going to be important to tell him how I was feeling.

"I'm fine. Was just thinking about things. Mostly that I'm enjoying right now, a little about the team. But that can wait for later. I think I was promised a bath."

He leaned over and kissed me softly, his lips brushing against my forehead, then nose, and eventually my lips before he stepped backward. I automatically followed, only to be thwarted with a hand to my chest. "There will be time for that later. Right now, I think my little bear needs a bath so he can watch his movie."

Brax didn't give me a chance to protest, reaching for the hem of my shirt and tugging it upward until my arms lifted and he could free me from it. Goosebumps rose on my skin. We'd lowered the heat when we left and the forty or so minutes we'd been home hadn't been enough to warm it fully up.

"I know, I made sure to make the water warm and I have the heat cranked up. It will warm up quickly." He reached for my underwear, pulling the black briefs down until they hit my ankles and I stepped out. The air nipping at my body made me rush to sink into the water, the warmth pulling a sigh from me as my thighs and waist disappeared beneath the bubbles.

I wasn't given much time before Brax sank down beside the tub, my blocks in one hand, cup and washcloth in the other. "I figured you'd want your drink back." He overturned the bucket, letting the blocks tumble into the water. "Play for a bit while the tub finishes filling. Then we'll get you bathed."

The ease with which he'd fallen into the role of my Daddy amazed me. It was like he'd always been there and even when my brain wanted to be embarrassed, it struggled to find the ability. There was a little voice in the back of my head trying desperately to remind me that Brax was a teammate, a teammate eight years younger than me, and I shouldn't be letting him see this part of me. The rest of my brain was telling me that it was okay to be myself around him, that he needed to see all of me. My heart spoke the loudest, reminding me repeatedly that this was what I'd wanted for years and I had it.

Pushing all the conflicting thoughts to the side, I picked up a block and pressed it against the side of the tub, intent on seeing if the blocks stretched the entire length of the tub. I only made it halfway before the water shut off and Daddy was at my side, chasing me with a washcloth.

"Let's get you cleaned up, silly boy," he said as he began to wash my back with a soapy washcloth.

I wriggled and squiggled, trying to continue my line as the washcloth made contact with my underarms and it tickled. "My blocks!"

"You're stinky. I'm trying to get you clean."

I stopped moving and crossed my arms in front of me. "I don't stink! I took a shower earlier!"

He took the opportunity to run the cloth over my chest and stomach, skipping the space where my arms were crossed. "Well, you won't stink when I'm done with you."

Another block floated by, catching my attention and sending me back to the line I was making, forgetting all about the washcloth that Brax was chasing me with. I got three more blocks onto the side of the tub before his hand caught me, the cloth slipping between my cheeks and grazing the underside of my balls.

"Daddy!"

## CHAPTER 25

### BRAX

THE BIG BLUE eyes staring up at me in shock were begging for me to say something. I knew he hadn't intended to call me Daddy but it was out there now and my smile couldn't be hidden for anything. Instead of responding with words, I leaned over the tub and kissed the side of his head.

Coming back to rest with my ass on my heels, I moved the washcloth toward his front and tried to act casual when I felt nothing of the sort. My insides jumped and swooped in a way I'd never thought possible while my skin felt flushed and too tight for my body. Everything was alight and electric yet I didn't want to surprise Trevor with my excitement, so I was trying desperately to not show it.

"Yeah, little bear, Daddy needs to get you clean, all the parts of you. Then we can watch your movie."

Trevor's skin turned pink at my words, but his bashful smile told me he liked them just the same. The little duck of his head and the way he inadvertently batted his eyes at me while trying to avoid full eye contact only served to make him look sweeter.

The real challenge was going to be keeping the next part of his bath as sweetly clinical as possible. My dick had a thing for all things Trevor under normal circumstances. Having him naked and wet in the tub in front of me was every fantasy I'd never known I had. It would be easy to wrap my hand around his dick and watch him fall apart with an incredible orgasm, but that wasn't what he needed.

Trevor needed his Daddy to take care of him and a chance for his brain to shut off. In spite of what his growing erection might be saying, I knew the last thing he needed was an orgasm to bring the real world crashing back in. After a short pep talk, I reached into the water and cleaned his dick and balls, struggling to keep my touch light enough that I wouldn't give him any sexy ideas.

His only reaction was a light gasp as the soft cloth made contact with his balls, but I didn't give him time to react more before pulling my hand away and wringing out the cloth. "That's my good boy. All clean. Pull the plug for me so we can get you dry."

The blocks could wait until later. The sooner I got Trevor into pajamas with his dick safely tucked inside briefs and pajama pants, the better.

As I stood up for a towel, my dick pinched in my suit pants. I had not thought this through and was now paying the price. The only decent thing about the situation was that my dark slacks were loose for comfort during travel and did a decent job hiding the erection that was pressing against my fly. Next time I did this, it would be in soft sweatpants and a T-shirt.

Despite my musings, the reflection of Trevor and me in the mirror was sexy. I could see from his knees, to his hard dick, to his muscular torso, and up to his blue eyes. His thumb was gravitating toward his mouth now that the blocks weren't distracting him. Then there was me, pulling off the Daddy look a little too well in my suit pants and white dress shirt, the top two buttons undone, the sleeves rolled to my elbows, and splashes of water dotting my shirt.

I grabbed the first towel off the stack and turned around to face Trevor. Little goosebumps had begun to rise on his skin, but there was a small smile peeking out from behind his thumb. All the blushes and uncertainty that had been his constant companions the last few weeks had vanished and all that I saw now was a happy blue-eyed boy ready to go watch his movie.

If I didn't move things along, I had a feeling I was going to be chasing a naked boy to the living room. He was getting impatient, if the little wiggles and glances toward the bathroom door were to be believed. He'd been waiting not so patiently to watch the movie and the only thing standing between it and him was a pair of pajamas.

"Okay, okay, wiggle worm. Let's get you dried off and dressed. I think you've earned a movie."

Trevor nearly launched himself from the tub, making me have to brace myself so that he didn't bowl us both over as he rushed into the towel. His dick poked into my thigh as I caught him and wrapped him up. I didn't think it could be comfortable, though Trevor didn't react at all. I wasn't convinced that he realized he was hard and if he did, he was doing a damn good job ignoring it.

With him wrapped in the oversized bath towel that hung from his shoulders to nearly his knees, he looked even smaller than normal. Without much thought, I squatted to wrap my arms under his ass and lifted him off the ground. With his arms wrapped in the towel, all he could do was squeal as his feet left the floor. Sitting at my hip, his legs wrapped around me, Trevor was just tall enough to lean in and place his head on my shoulder, though I did have to lean back slightly to balance us, especially since he was still laughing so hard he kept moving in my arms.

"Stop wiggling or you're going to fall," I said to him, both of us now laughing. He was like one of those ferret ball toys that Yuri's dog had. His entire body moved around as he laughed.

"Down! I can walk!"

I adjusted him in my grip and took a few steps, confident that I could easily make it to the bedroom and deposit him on the bed without dropping him. "Do you really want to get down?"

The question gave him enough pause that I was out of the bathroom and halfway across his room before he responded again. "I feel silly."

"You don't look silly, though you sound silly giggling as hard as you are." My knees hit the bed, so I bent forward, letting Trevor drop slightly. He hadn't been prepared and bounced once before his towel unraveled and fell to the side.

Trevor's giggles turned into full body laughter too hard to control and he rolled to his side, pulling his knees up to his chest. "It hurts." He gasped in a breath and continued to laugh. I might have been able to say or do something to help if I hadn't been laughing so hard that tears were rolling down my face.

I wasn't sure what was so funny, but after the week we'd had, it felt like the laughter was needed. I didn't fully compose myself before standing up and patting his naked ass. "Let me go get you your pajamas."

Trevor's laughter died off as I made my way toward the dresser. As I opened the drawer where he kept his pajamas, he rolled over and stared at me. I could see an unasked question in his eyes and from the way his lips were parted, I knew he was trying to find a way to put voice to it.

"What's up, little bear?"

His thought lines softened at the nickname, though he still wasn't giggling. "Left drawer," he said after a few seconds of hesitation, his words so tiny I struggled to make them out at first.

I reached for the drawer he'd mentioned and pulled it open. At first glance, I couldn't figure out why the underwear had made him hesitate like it had. Upon closer inspection, I noticed that I wasn't looking at regular underwear. They were all brief-style underwear, some of them with childish, bold prints and Y-fronts while others appeared thicker in the center. Admittedly, it took me too long to work out what I was seeing.

He'd told me where to find the underwear he liked to wear when he was little and he was giving me the ability to pick out what he wore for the night. The third pair I looked at were some of the thicker undies covered in little astronauts and spaceships. I smiled as I picked them up, imagining him sitting in the living room wearing them and the pajamas I'd picked out for the night.

The little star-and-moon pajamas I'd found in his pajama drawer must have come from the kids' section of the store, but they looked like they'd fit Trevor perfectly, if just a little snug in the arms and thighs. I suspected that was more of a draw than anything else, though.

The training pants and pajamas were going to be a perfect match.

I slid the drawer closed and turned back around to find my boy blushing a deep red. The last thing I wanted was for his embarrassment to return after having him so carefree for the last hour. The best I could do was grip his legs and pull him toward me, then distract him while I worked on getting him dressed.

"Still want to watch *Moana?*"

The question pulled Trevor's thoughts from the items in my hands enough that the red in his cheeks and down his chest began to fade as he nodded. "And dinner?"

I'd totally forgotten to order dinner. "Dinner too. What do you want to eat? Pizza? Chinese? Macaroni?" As he thought, I took the opportunity to pull his undies up his legs and adjust them around him. The thick material completely hid the half chub he'd been sporting as I pulled them up his legs, and I knew the slight bulk would be visible with the cotton pants stretched around them.

"Chinese?"

I reached for the pants and fed each of his legs into them. "I think that sounds like a good idea. I haven't had that in quite a few weeks."

Not wanting to overwhelm Trevor with questions, I started thinking about what to order for him while I tugged the pants into place and worked the shirt over his head. He was dressed before I'd come up with a solid meal idea, but the look of him in the snug pajamas, his thumb already back in his mouth and his big blue eyes looking at me anxiously, had me pushing dinner thoughts to the side for a few moments.

My body moved of its own accord, my lips making contact with Trevor's forehead. Leaning back, I could feel my smile growing. "You're perfect." And he was. From the bashful smile behind his thumb to his bright blue eyes, down to his feet swinging a few inches from the ground.

In just a couple weeks, this man had gone from my unattainable crush with a slightly prickly exterior to a sweet boy grinning up at me in his pajamas. No matter how much I knew about relationships based on kink or BDSM, no matter how well I knew that they often developed faster, two weeks felt like both the blink of an eye and an eternity. In every one of my past relationships, two weeks hadn't been long enough to even call it more than a repeated hookup. Two weeks with Trevor had been enough time to see us go from reluctant roommates to tentative friends to him calling me Daddy.

If things kept going the way they were, two more weeks was going to be enough for me to give him a lot more than the title of my boy or boyfriend. It was too soon to think like that and I had to shake the thought from my head quickly and get back to the present.

I had a shy boy in front of me waiting for me to make decisions for him and set the pace of the night.

Reaching out my hands, I wiggled my fingers in an invitation for him to grab them. "Come on, let's get to the living room."

Trevor's right hand slipped into mine and his fingers curled around my palm, barely wrapping toward the back of my hand. A glance at Trevor was a constant reminder that he was smaller than me, but at the moment, his hand felt even smaller than usual. His hand fit into mine like a glove, my fingers wrapping nearly all the way around his hand.

We didn't make it but a few steps before he tugged against me. Looking back at the bed, Trevor was staring at his blanket. I had no idea when it had made it to his pillow, but between the car and now, he'd somehow gotten it there and now he wanted it.

In seconds, I had his blanket in my hand and we were heading toward the living room, my mind finally back on dinner and what to order for us. It took a few minutes to get him settled with a new cup—since we left his other one in the bathroom—our bears, and the movie, and another few for me to run upstairs to finally change into more comfortable clothes.

Not that Trevor had missed me. He was still sitting on the pillow in front of the coffee table watching the movie with a big smile behind his thumb. He didn't even acknowledge that I'd returned, leaving me plenty of time to sort through the menu at the local Chinese restaurant.

I knew I wanted the broccoli chicken, but picking a meal out for my little bear was more of a challenge. What would a little want for dinner?

After three minutes of flipping through the menu, I did the only thing I could think of.

**Me**: *What would a little want to eat at a Chinese restaurant?*

I'd finally cleared the Bulldogs' schedule from my calendar, so I had no idea if Easton was traveling, at practice, or if an event had come up between the time I'd left and tonight. I had no idea if or when I'd get a text but could admit that I was happy when bubbles appeared almost immediately.

**Easton**: *I need details.*

**Me**: *I need answers.*

**Easton**: *What aren't you telling me?*

**Me**: *What I can't tell you, not right now. But I've been looking at this menu for nearly five minutes and I'm stumped.*

**Easton**: *Wait, that was a serious question? Like you've got a little you're trying to order for?*

This might have been a mistake. He was going to be like a bloodhound now that I'd given him this tidbit of information, but I had no one else to turn to.

**Me**: *E! Focus. I need to order dinner or we're going to starve.*

**Easton**: *I'm gonna need the story soon, but I'll have mercy on you. Okay. What do kids like?*

**Me**: *Mac & Cheese? Chicken nuggets? I ate a ton of chicken nuggets, pizza, and plain pasta when I was a kid. Just butter and salt, nothing else.*

**Easton**: *Oh! Those fried chicken pieces with the bright red sauce. Fuck, I've forgotten the name. I used to get it when I was a kid, sometimes it has fruit pieces in it. Dammit. What's it called?*

**Me**: *Sweet and Sour Chicken?*

**Easton**: *THAT! Yes, that. And just regular Lo Mein noodles. That is something I bet most littles would like. They could dip the chicken into that sauce stuff. Ack, it's so sweet.*

I tapped out of the text and back to the menu. The idea was brilliant and I figured it would be perfect for Trevor. Though I did order a spicy chicken dish I knew he'd talked about as well, just in case he wasn't feeling as little when it arrived or hated the meal altogether. With the order placed, I finally returned my attention to Easton, who had sent a string of texts while I'd been focused on the menu.

**Easton**: *Is it serious?*

***Easton***: *How'd you meet?*

***Easton***: *Why haven't you told me?*

***Easton***: *Shit, you've only been gone a few weeks. Did you meet this guy at the intro night?*

***Easton***: *Or is he one of the littles I sent you a link to on social?*

***Easton***: *Dammit, B! I NEED DEETS!*

I had to keep my laughter inside. Trevor was humming to the songs and laughing every time the rooster appeared on screen. The last thing I wanted to do was pull him out of his movie or make him think I was laughing at him.

***Me***: *I think it's serious. I can't tell you much more because it's new and I need to talk to him before I talk to you. Tonight is not the time to bring it up though. I'll tell you when I can though, promise.*

***Easton***: *Ohmigod, you have no idea how insane you're driving me right now and how crazy my imagination is going at the moment. I want to know it all. GAH! I'm going to see you in less than two weeks, you better be ready to talk about it by then, or we're going to be working things out ON ice.*

***Me***: *Promises. Bring your worst ;-) I'll talk with you later, E.*

I turned my phone to Do Not Disturb and focused on Trevor. His laughter and happiness were contagious and I found myself enjoying watching him as much as he was enjoying the movie.

The doorbell ringing made him jump and his eyes focused on me. "Dinner?"

Glancing down at my phone, I nodded. "Yup. Dinner. Let me go get the door. How about you go potty and wash your hands while I get your plate ready?"

Trevor was up and hurrying to the bathroom so fast he didn't bother to pause the movie. I did it for him, then headed to the front door to meet the delivery driver and had made my way to the kitchen before Trevor made it out of the bathroom.

From my place at the kitchen counter, I was able to watch Trevor walk back to the living room. The added bulk of the thick underwear wasn't enough to impact his gait, but his pants were rounder than just his ass warranted. The swell and sway of his butt made my cock twitch back to life. I'd spent more time with an erection since I'd moved in here than I had since he moved out of my parents' house a decade earlier and there was no sign of relief.

I put his dinner on one of the divided plates he'd brought out earlier, grabbed a fork for him and chopsticks for me, and headed toward the living room. Trevor was sitting at the coffee table again but the movie was still paused as he watched for me to return. His eyes brightened noticeably when he saw me walk around the couch with our dinners.

I hadn't seen him drinking while he'd been watching the movie, but I checked his cup once I'd put his dinner in front of him. There was still plenty of water left, so I settled onto the couch next to where he was sitting and unpaused the movie. "Eat up and finish your movie." It was later than I normally liked to eat. We'd had a long day, and I knew we would both be getting tired soon.

Trevor nodded and turned to his dinner. His hand hovered over a piece of breaded chicken and he turned to look up at me, his face a mixture of bashfulness and happiness. "Thank you, Daddy." He'd barely whispered the last word, but my heart would have been hard-pressed to believe he hadn't announced it to the world.

"You're welcome, little bear."

He batted his eyes at me a few times and turned to watch his movie, plucking a piece of chicken from the plate with his fingers and dipping it into the well of sticky red sauce while focusing on the TV. He was going to be a mess by the time he finished his dinner, yet I couldn't bring myself to care.

## CHAPTER 26

TREVOR

"What about a relay race?"

I'd taken a seat in Brax's lap when we'd arrived home from the gym. I wasn't necessarily little, but his lap was comfortable and he usually pulled me into it anyway. I'd just eliminated a step.

"What kind of relay race?" It was an intriguing idea. I'd never thought of a relay race before and now I was struggling to figure out how the game would work for practice.

He handed over the sippy cup of water I'd left on the coffee table before we'd left the house. They'd been turning up everywhere recently. One had even made it into my suitcase for the last road trip. Brax had a way of always having one handy when we were alone, to the point that it had felt strange using a glass when we'd had some of the guys over for dinner a few nights earlier.

"Well, we could split into two or three teams, or even by lines, I guess, and each person has to go down the length of the ice doing something... balancing a puck on their stick while doing crossovers, score a goal, then skate back on one foot or something."

The idea was so funny and perfect that I found myself annoyed not to have thought of it before. I pulled the cup from my mouth, the suction breaking loudly as I did, and grinned over at my boyfriend. "I love that idea! We need to come up with a lot of ridiculous things to do, though."

Brax nodded seriously, then put his arms around my body so I was snuggled into him. We hadn't had a lot of time for me to play in my room or for me to really have an extended period of time in little space since that first day, but with being in the middle of the season, that was expected. What we'd had was plenty of time for Brax to show me that he'd taken the job of being not only my boyfriend but my Daddy seriously.

I couldn't remember the last time I'd been up past eleven on a night we didn't have a game, bath time was nearly a sacred time at home, and midday naps had never been so frequent or fun. Well, the naps themselves weren't fun because he took sleep seriously, but the time afterward was almost always enjoyable, even if it was only a handjob or a blowjob before we had to run to the arena or an event.

Speaking of naps, we'd gotten up early to head to the gym and Brax's shoulder was beginning to seem like a very nice pillow. Once I put my head down, I knew he wouldn't bother me until I moved, so I was content to get comfortable, especially when he pulled the heavy throw blanket over us.

Later in the evening, we'd be meeting up for dinner with Easton. Brax had talked a lot about him over the last month and I felt like I knew him already, despite never having met him formally. We'd played games against one another a number of times, so I knew of him before Brax, though we'd never spoken off ice. Heck, I wasn't sure we'd talked *on* ice either.

Daddy's arms wrapped around me and he kissed the top of my head. "Sleep well, little bear. Maybe we'll get you ready to play in your room after you sleep."

I hummed in agreement but only opened my mouth for my thumb to slip in and drifted off while trying to remember everything Daddy had said about Easton. He was the one who had said Brax needed a little, not just a boy. My thoughts got muddled as sleep took me.

Sometime later I awoke with a start, my brain way too awake after a nap. I was still in Daddy's lap, he was still holding me, and the sun shining in the window told me I'd been out for close to an hour.

One arm was wrapped around me, and the other was moving rapidly. It took a few seconds for my brain to process that it was tapping, likely tapping out a text on his phone. Thinking about texts reminded me about why I'd woken up so suddenly.

"Does Easton know you're my Daddy?"

I'd meant to start by asking if Easton had known we were dating, but my brain was still trying to process all my thoughts and given that I'd fallen asleep feeling more little than big, he was still Daddy in my head.

Brax's phone got placed on my thigh and he adjusted me so that he could see my face. "Easton knows I'm dating someone. He doesn't know who, though. I told him I couldn't talk about it because it was still new. The thing with Easton is, he's going to pick up on our relationship quickly."

I blinked up at him, my brain spinning so fast I couldn't figure out which question to ask first. The last month had been a lot to process in terms of people discovering I was submissive. For ten years, I'd hidden my little side from everyone, or so I'd thought.

Since Brax got traded to the Grizzlies, I'd discovered that Seth had known since before Maz came into his life. Maz knew, and Brax had figured it out. Having three teammates, no matter how much I trusted them, knowing about something so private had made me intensely uncomfortable for a number of days. I still found myself more aware of my actions when we were together than I had been before they'd let me know.

Now I was faced with Easton finding out. It wasn't like I could tell Brax not to tell him. I wasn't going to be the asshole that kept him from his best friend because I was insecure about something. I also wasn't going to make Brax lie about who he was dating or pretend that we weren't together. I wasn't willing to put either of us in that position, but that meant I was going to have to let someone else know I was a little.

Seth and Maz had been sweet and caring, and I trusted that they'd never say anything to anyone. Brax had been nothing but supportive and I knew him well enough to know that he'd never out me. I didn't know Easton, though. And I was going to have to trust a huge secret that had the potential to destroy my career to a complete stranger.

"Baby, you're shaking." Brax pulled me closer and rubbed at my shoulder, concern clear in his voice.

I shook my head, trying to push away the fear and uncertainty of the coming hours and days from my brain while finding a way to put voice to my sudden bout of nerves.

Brax adjusted me so that I was straddling his lap and we were chest to chest. He cupped my face and ducked his head so that he could look into my eyes. "Little bear, I need you to tell me what's wrong. I don't care if you tell your boyfriend or your Daddy, but I need to know what has you so worked up."

Opening my mouth, I had no idea who I was talking to. I didn't know if I was little or big, if Brax was my boyfriend or my Daddy, but what I did know was that my worry and fear were real and I needed someone to reassure me that everything was going to be okay. Daddy or boyfriend, Brax needed to be the one to tell me that things were going to work out.

"I don't know Easton. I know he's your best friend, but what if he says something? What if he does something? What if someone finds out that I'm little? What does that do to my life? My career? Us? If the wrong person finds out, I could lose everything, including you."

I had been prepared to keep going because the longer I talked the bigger my worries were becoming, but as I stopped for a breath, I glanced into Brax's eyes and the look in them stopped my words dead in their tracks. His eyes were sparkling with emotion, a tender smile on his face as he listened to me.

When my words stopped, he leaned forward and pressed a kiss to my temple. "I understand your fear. It's valid. Opening up to anyone about something that might be considered outside the box is scary. Opening up to someone you don't know is even harder. I can promise you that Easton's safe. Years back, when he played in Canada, he had a fling with a prince."

My eyes widened. Brax had never said or done anything to make me think he'd lie to me or make something up, but Easton dating a prince sounded far-fetched.

"Cross my heart. I've seen pictures. They still keep in touch and meet up sometimes when they're in the same place at the same time. It's not like the British royal family, but the guy has enough publicity around him that it could cause a major shitstorm if it ever came out. Easton's never breathed a word to anyone."

I'd forgotten about my other worries while my brain spun trying to figure out which pseudo-famous prince it could have been. Brax hadn't forgotten my worries, making sure to address them clearly. "I would never put you in a situation where I think you'd be unsafe or your secret discovered. As your boyfriend, it would be irresponsible and a major violation of your trust in me if I put you in a situation where I thought you could be hurt—emotionally, physically, or otherwise. As your Daddy, it would be reprehensible and unforgivable. From the minute we got together, you became my top priority and you will continue to be so."

*Prince? What prince? Had we been talking about a prince?*

His words had been delivered with such certainty and with so much emotion that my eyes filled with tears I tried to blink back.

He didn't give me a chance to get myself pulled together before he continued. "And if for some reason someone finds out that shouldn't, for any reason, I'm going to be beside you every step of the way. We will figure out how to handle it together."

A devilish grin spread across his lips, the levity in his voice breaking some of the seriousness of the moment. "And if it turns out that Easton says something, I know where he sleeps and I still have a spare key." Then he shrugged. "And I know where he keeps all his toys."

My laugh came out as a choked sob, my emotions a tangled mess I wasn't sure how to sort out. His words had left my heart pounding with something way more than fondness or adoration. It was a new feeling, one I'd never experienced but knew exactly what it was.

I was falling in love with Braxlyn Cernak.

Burying my head against his shoulder, I kissed his neck, letting his happy hum fill me with warmth. "I think I'm starting to fall for you." I'd whispered the words, but by the hitch in Brax's breathing, I knew he'd heard them.

He squeezed me closer. "That's okay. I fell for you when I was twelve and you barely knew I existed. I knew you were it for me way back then and it hasn't changed. Every time I thought about dating someone, I thought of you, and they never compared."

My head came off his shoulder to study his face. He'd sounded so sincere, but I didn't know how it was possible that he'd fallen for me so many years ago. "What?"

Brax leaned forward and placed a kiss on my lips. "I never thought I'd get the chance to be anything more than a teammate to you. For a long time, even that was a far-fetched dream. Then I discovered I was a Daddy and thinking we could be anything more than teammates became an even bigger stretch. And when Easton got it in his head that I needed a little, I knew he was right, but part of my heart crumbled because I couldn't imagine my childhood crush wanting a Daddy, much less wanting to be my little bear."

He booped my nose, his eyes warm and reflecting unmistakable love. "So imagine my surprise when I discovered that you were the boy I'd always wanted and the little I'd only just been figuring out I needed. There will never be another man or boy more perfect for me than you are."

Leaning forward, I let his words and arms wrap around me while keeping my earlier fears at bay. Daddy trusted Easton. He'd never put me in a situation that he didn't know was safe. I'd known as much before he'd said it but hearing that and the sincerity in his voice helped settle my nerves.

We stayed wrapped up on the couch for another few minutes before Brax's phone finally broke the moment. He still held me close, rubbing my head, shoulders, and back with one hand while he answered.

"Hey." The casual answer and the loud laugh on the other end told me it was Easton.

The voice talked fast and I could only make out a few words here or there. *Fuck, miserable, asshole,* and *hot* all sounded like they'd come from the same sentence, but I hadn't been able to figure out the rest of it or how the words were related.

"Yeah, I didn't think you all were supposed to be in until later. Don't worry, though, that coat will come in handy tonight. Once the sun sets, it gets cold."

More fast talking followed and Brax laughed. "That sounds good. I'll call you back in a few minutes and let you know the plan."

Setting the phone down, Brax gave me a wink. "Flight was early. Easton wants to know what to plan for the rest of the day."

That meant no little time in my room that night. It wouldn't be right to make Brax miss time with his friend, but after the conversation we'd had, little space was pulling at me. "We can do lunch, then just take it from there. It's a pretty nice day. I could take you guys to the Parthenon or we could do some touristy stuff."

Brax's eyebrows rose on his forehead, his eyes drifting between me and the door to my playroom. "I know it would be awkward, but would you want to go pick up Easton at the hotel, get lunch, then come back and have some little time?"

I began to nod before my brain caught up with his words and my head stopped suddenly. "You mean little time with Easton here?"

Brax nodded hesitantly. "Alternatively, I can tell Easton to keep himself entertained for a few hours and you can play for a bit, or we can just do lunch with him."

Playing for a bit sounded best in theory, but I knew it wasn't going to work in practice. If I knew Easton was already in Nashville and waiting for Brax to call to tell him we were ready to meet up, I was never going to relax. I also knew that I wouldn't be able to relax if I knew I was cutting their time short. But I hadn't realized how badly I needed time to decompress until I'd taken it off the table as an option.

Making the decision was nowhere near as hard as giving voice to it. My eyes scrunched closed and I could hear the pout in my voice as I spoke. "We can do lunch, then little time with Easton here." Opening my eyes again, I stared at Brax. "He's safe, right?" I'd tried to make my words joking, but I knew I'd sounded more than a little nervous.

Brax gave me a smile that eased my worries. "Very safe. Promise. He's like a living, breathing Fort Knox."

"Okay, then he can come back here."

Brax squeezed me in a hug, peppering my cheek and jaw with kisses. "You're so brave. I'm proud of you. Now, let's get ready to go."

Without warning, he gripped under my ass, moved to the edge of the couch, and hoisted us both upward. I let out a squeal of surprise as I wrapped my arms and legs around his body. Being so much smaller than everyone else, it wasn't uncommon for me to be scooped up in practice or if I fell asleep somewhere I shouldn't. Having my Daddy carrying me around wasn't the same as being thrown over someone's shoulder, though. Despite him having done it a number of times now, it still felt different and made my insides swoop like I was on a roller coaster.

## CHAPTER 27

### BRAX

TREVOR HAD INSISTED on sitting in the back, rationalizing that his legs were shorter and he wouldn't be cramped like Easton would be. I wasn't convinced his reasoning was sound, given how big the back of my SUV was, though catching Trevor smiling or watching out the window each time I looked in my rearview mirror had made me unexpectedly pleased. It had felt right, like he was exactly where he should be. While his outfit didn't look in any way strange, the T-shirt under his flannel shirt had a spaceship and astronaut on it and his underwear was printed with little puppy dogs. I'd found a pair of bright blue socks in his drawer and handed him a pair of tennis shoes with bold blocks of primary colors on the sides.

Safely in the back with a large seat and tinted windows blocking the world from seeing him, Trevor had spent more time with his thumb in his mouth than out as we'd made our way downtown. When I'd noticed he wasn't quite big, I'd put his movie soundtrack on and he'd spent the rest of the trip singing along as he watched the world go by.

His thumb had come out and he'd asked me to turn off the music as we'd driven down the street the hotel was on. By the time we'd made it to the valet parking area where Easton was waiting, all outward signs of my little bear had been safely tucked away and a professional hockey player had taken his place. Looking closely, though, I could see signs of Trevor's little side, from the way his feet wiggled slightly to the way he sank back as Easton entered the car, like he wanted to disappear.

I could understand his worry. He didn't know Easton like I did. He knew Easton as a crushing defenseman on ice. He didn't know that Easton could easily be the strictest Dom or the biggest snuggler. Our favorite place in the condo had been curled up on the couch watching a movie or TV show. I'd gone from a cuddly Dom for a roommate to a cuddly sub for a boyfriend. It was a good thing I was tactile and liked to cuddle.

"Fucking hell. If I had to listen to Dominick bitch about the hotel another minute, I was going to tie him to the bed and leave him," Easton said in lieu of a greeting to me.

"He just likes to hear himself talk."

Trevor moved in his seat, his tennis shoes squeaking on the rubber mat and causing Easton to look behind him. "Oh hey, Trevor. I've heard a lot about you." Easton's voice held a suggestive quality. He was trying to embarrass me but the joke was on him.

I slapped Easton's arm, glancing in the mirror in time to see Trevor give a smile that didn't quite reach his eyes. It wasn't annoying, but I could tell Easton's loud voice was a lot for him to take when he had been more little than big just a few minutes earlier. "Shut up, asshole." I spoke to the mirror as I began to merge into traffic. "Trev, this is Easton. Easton, Trevor, obviously."

Easton at least managed to behave himself as we made our way through downtown, back onto the highway, and eventually off the highway on our way toward the house and a few smaller eateries.

"How's Italian sound?" Easton loved Italian and with Trevor needing some time to shut his brain off, pasta would be easy for him to eat no matter how he was feeling.

Easton's eyes lit up. "Do you know of a good place?"

I glanced back at Trevor. We'd ordered from a place that he said was close to home but I had no idea where it was. In the mirror he nodded to me, some of the tension leaving his body when his eyes met mine. "It's only about a mile away. Straight shot from here. It'll be on the right."

"Thanks." I gave him a smile and a little wink that Easton didn't miss, giving me a curious eyebrow raise that silently demanded more information. Blessedly, the man knew enough or at least suspected enough to not bring it up in the car.

That didn't mean that he didn't watch our interactions closely throughout the rest of the car ride, through the restaurant, and while we decided what to order. It didn't surprise me that Trevor asked my input on his lunch, though I tried hard to not make it obvious by whispering and pointing to things on the menu, well aware that Easton was in earshot.

It didn't matter how covert my conversation with Trevor was—I could tell that Easton picked up on the vibes between us. He was an observant hockey player and a more observant Dom. He had a knack for reading body language that most people could only dream of. With the briefest of glances, Easton was able to take in more of a situation than most people could by studying it for minutes.

The nail in the coffin, so to speak, was when I ordered for Trevor without blinking an eye. It wasn't planned on my part, but he was farther from the waiter and I knew he didn't want to make decisions.

Trevor didn't bat an eye, though Easton gave me a knowing smirk. I could see the cogs turning and the questions burning to be asked. I shot him a warning glare that begged him to keep his mouth shut for just a little longer, until we made it back to the house at least.

With the menus gone, Trevor picked up one of the crayons the server had left on the table and began to doodle on the paper tablecloth while managing to stay mostly involved in the conversation Easton and I were having.

We took a meandering route through how things were going in Boston, teammate drama, and how I was settling into Nashville.

As the waiter placed waters in front of us, Trevor paused his doodling and looked up at Easton with a mischievous spark in his eyes. "Your coaches are idiots for letting him go. But your loss is my—*our*—gain."

Easton's head fell back as his laughter filled the restaurant. "Very, *very* true. On all accounts."

Trevor's cheeks pinked and he dipped his head, and Easton capitalized on the moment, mouthing, *Holy shit*!

The smile that spread across my lips when I looked over at Trevor was a dead giveaway. I couldn't begin to deny it, not that I planned to. Instead I nodded before looking back at my best friend. "Definitely hadn't been expected."

Easton scrubbed his hands down his face. "Fuck, I have so many questions."

Pointing a finger at him, I dropped my voice to a stern growl. "You'll wait until we get back to the house."

He held his hands up in surrender. "Wouldn't think otherwise!" His fond smile widened, though I saw sadness behind his eyes that wasn't normally there. I wanted to prod, but our meals arriving interrupted me and by the time the waiter was gone, Easton changed the subject to the game the following day, ignoring Trevor's ravioli with a plain butter sauce.

Trevor had agonized over the decision, trying numerous times to convince himself that he should get a more "grown-up" meal before I'd told him to get what sounded good. He probably hadn't noticed that he'd been tense until I'd ordered the buttered ravioli for him and his shoulders had sagged in relief.

With Trevor focused more on his lunch than the two of us, Easton leaned toward me, motioning for me to meet him in the middle. When I leaned forward, he spoke both quickly and quietly into my ear. "You know, you could have told me to stay at the hotel."

I rolled my eyes. "I told him that, but he wanted us to have a chance to spend time together."

"Do you want to take me back to the hotel after lunch?"

Just as expected, Easton's observations had been spot on, just like I'd known they would be. He was also saying the exact right things that let me know he understood. There was no question in my mind that he'd make Trevor feel comfortable when we got back to the house, but I had to get us there first.

"We talked about that earlier. If you behave yourself, he's fine with you coming back after lunch." I winked at him as I sat back, knowing I'd said enough so that Easton knew exactly what to expect when we returned home.

*Home.* That word was feeling more natural as the weeks progressed. For the first few weeks, it had felt more like a *place*—temporary and fleeting. Since we'd been honest with one another about our feelings, the house had felt more and more like the place that I wanted to spend a lot more time at.

Easton gave a nod. "And we can chat." He sat back in his seat and focused on his lunch, our conversation turning safe bordering on mundane until we pulled into the garage. The closer we'd gotten to the house, the quieter Trevor had become until he'd fallen silent when we'd pulled into the neighborhood.

I was certain there were fears and concerns running through his head about all the different ways the afternoon could go. It said a lot that he trusted me enough to even consider letting Easton see his little side, whatever form it took that afternoon.

As it turned out, his little side meant a pair of cotton shorts instead of his jeans and playing quietly with a movie on while Easton and I hung out in the living room. As I'd helped Trevor change while Easton conveniently stretched his legs on the deck, I'd pointedly asked how much it was okay to share with Easton. Trevor had blushed and worried his lip before finally telling me that if I trusted Easton, I could tell him. He'd earned kisses to his belly and a sippy cup of chocolate milk for his trust. The kisses had made him smile, but I was pretty sure the chocolate milk had been the biggest reward for him.

Once I'd nodded that it was safe to come in, Easton took a seat out of sight of Trevor but close enough that we didn't have to raise our voices to talk.

I'd just settled myself in the recliner where I could see Trevor easily when Easton leaned forward, hissing in a voice that was almost too quiet to hear and nearly too fast to make out. "Tell me. What the hell? I told you that you needed a boy! You said you found one, but *Trevor Cane?* Fucking hell, Cernak, now I know why you've been so cagey lately. I also need more details! Like every single one of them."

It was hard to stifle my laughter at my normally calm, cool, and collected friend nearly bubbling over with questions and excitement. "It wasn't like I'd planned it like this or had any clue. Then he got hurt and things happened quickly from there. The pain meds fucked with him and made him think there were things in the closet, so I stayed with him that night. Then the next day, I forgot my bag and had to run back to the house and found him playing in his room. Then I had to tell him I knew and things went a little sideways."

Easton stared at me with wide eyes, his mouth slightly parted and a disbelieving smirk on his face. "Damn."

All I could do was nod. "That about sums it up. We talked it out over the course of a few days. Turns out my attraction to him wasn't one-sided. So here we are."

"So here we are." Easton shook his head. "I'm shocked, but not. I always knew you'd be the perfect Daddy for a little."

I chucked a throw pillow at his head. "And I always told you boys didn't take a younger Daddy seriously, nor would they want their Daddy traveling half the year."

"Well, your boy is older than you."

"And he freaked out about me even knowing he was a boy. Discussing a relationship was another ballgame entirely. We still haven't told the team or my dads. He's worried because he played with my dad. He's known them since I was a kid. Not that we're going to be able to hide it much longer."

Easton's eyes narrowed as he tried to figure out why we would have to tell them sooner rather than later, and then they popped open when he put the pieces together. "You all play Carolina that weekend."

I nodded confirmation. "I'm glad we have a break after that. I can't imagine we're going to be able to keep our relationship quiet much longer. At least not from the team. Johnson and Grabowski already know, I'm pretty sure Yuri's figuring it out, and Trevor said that Coach already figured out there's something going on."

"Coach?" If Easton's eyes got any bigger, there was a chance they'd get stuck that way. "How did he handle that?"

"Well. Actually. He reminded Trevor to keep drama off ice and out of the locker room but acknowledged that he was happier and more relaxed, or something along those lines."

"Wow." He let out a low whistle. "I couldn't imagine Anders being as understanding."

*That's because Anders is an asshole.* I didn't have to say the words for Easton to know I was thinking them. Coach Anders had made me nearly forget that decent coaches still existed, while Coach Cunningham was enough to make me *almost* forget there were still a lot of coaches like Anders out there.

"So how are things going with you two?"

I glanced toward the playroom. Trevor had moved from the coloring mat to chalking on the giant chalkboard wall. His right hand was covered in chalk dust, but his left was shoved in his mouth and Huck and Finn were sitting on the floor beside him. "Really well. I'm still scared I'm going to fuck things up and sometimes I want to pinch myself to make sure it's real, but I really think that we're figuring things out. It feels right. God, I'm totally falling for him. Hell, I think I've already fallen for him. Big and little, he's funny and driven and talented, but he cares so damn much about everyone on the team. I've never been around a group of guys that tell each other so much!"

Easton's eyebrows waggled comically and before he opened his mouth, I knew something insane was going to come out. "What about the crazy things we've always heard about the team?"

I mimed zipping my lips. "Nope. That's top secret, classified."

He threw his middle finger up at me and I nearly did the same but stopped myself when Trevor looked over and grinned at me, a smear of chalk on his cheek, and I forgot all about Easton for a minute as I stood up. "Don't touch anything, little bear. You're a mess."

Trevor let out a small giggle and returned to his drawing as I went to get a washcloth to wipe him down. When I returned to the living room a few minutes later, Trevor's hand once again recognizable and his face without a giant smudge of green chalk on it, Easton was grinning at me.

"Oh yeah, you've got it bad. I'm just going to have to live vicariously through you."

I tossed my iPad toward him and he caught it without thought. "Or you could help me pick some things out for him. I've been seriously stumped. He's admitted to being curious about"—I dropped my voice even lower and leaned farther in—"diapers, but he turns bright red every time I bring it up. I thought I'd surprise him but I don't know what to get. And since you seem to be all wise and knowing when it comes to littles, you can help."

"Oh! This should be fun. What are my options?" He tapped in my password by memory, reminding me that I should probably change it, yet knowing if I did I'd spend the next six weeks trying to remember what I'd changed it to.

It wasn't like Easton was going to see anything he hadn't seen before, or at least wasn't expecting. We spent the next thirty minutes picking out things for Trevor, then three hours chatting about anything and everything that came to mind until Trevor walked out of the room patting his stomach.

"What's for dinner?"

I smiled, knowing he'd played himself out. "How about we order in?"

He hummed and took a seat on my lap. "You have my phone—pick a place. I don't really care where. If it's going to take more than forty-five minutes, you might need to get me a snack."

Where I'd expected bashfulness from my normally blushy boyfriend, he looked and felt far more relaxed than I'd seen him in over a week. His playtime had done him a world of good and when Easton hadn't made a big deal out of anything that afternoon, Trevor must have decided that there wasn't a reason to be embarrassed.

Having Trevor sitting on my lap with my arms wrapped around him while the three of us chatted and waited for dinner to arrive was the perfect way to spend an evening.

"By the way," I said to Easton as we drove him to the hotel later that night. "Watch out for me tomorrow."

Easton blinked in confusion. "What? Why?"

"Because I owe you big-time for putting insane ideas in my head about finding a little. I spent many a night lying awake and planning all the ways I could throw you into the boards the next time we met on ice."

Easton shot me a purely devious grin. "From where I'm sitting, I think you should be thanking me."

*Infuriating asshole.* It was a good thing I loved him as much as I did.

## CHAPTER 28

### TREVOR

For all that I'd been dreading the trip to North Carolina and telling Brax's dads about us, I totally forgot about seeing them later that day when Blaise called me. The last person I'd expected to call me was Blaise, so having his contact information displayed on my phone overshadowed the conversation Brax was having with his dad while he started packing.

"Hello?"

Blaise cleared his throat and I could nearly see him fidgeting in his seat. "Hi, Trevor?"

"Yup. Everything okay?"

"Um, yeah. Yeah. Everything's fine. I, I was finalizing hotel reservations and I had a question for you." The words had tumbled from his mouth so fast I had a hard time following them, but there was no way I was going to make him repeat himself.

After giving myself a second to process his words, I finally responded. "Sure, what do you need to know about the reservations?" Honestly, I couldn't imagine why he was asking me. If anything, hotel reservation questions or issues should have gone through the GM, Bill Huber, or someone in the front office, not the team captain.

Something in the background made a rhythmic tapping noise in the silence. I really wished there was a way I could make him less anxious. The one time we'd taken him out after a practice, we'd all had a drink with dinner and he'd relaxed considerably, to the point that he was laughing and joking with us. He'd always been open that he dealt with anxiety and Tourette's syndrome, and talking to people, on the phone especially, was something he didn't enjoy.

It also made the unexpected call much more intriguing. I'd have expected him to text if he had a question.

After a long few seconds, he took a deep breath and let it out slowly. Just when I almost broke and asked him what he needed, his voice filled my ear. It was strong and clear, and I could almost hear his proud smile at managing to ask the question. "Um, does it make sense for me to get Brax and you separate rooms?"

Now it was my turn to fall silent. I knew I had to look like a deer in the headlights, but I had no idea what to say. Then again, it wasn't like we'd been hiding our relationship per se, but we hadn't been overt about it either. "Uh, I..."

When my voice trailed off to nothing and I lacked more words, Blaise took it as a reason to push ahead. Maybe he was simply filling the silence with nervous chatter, or maybe he took my sudden bout of being tongue-tied as confirmation of our relationship. Either way, he sounded a lot more confident than I felt.

"I've noticed you two are really close. He's still living at your house and he seems really aware of your every move. Then again, you're the same with him. I don't mean to be presumptuous, but if you two have been sharing a room, it doesn't make sense to continue to reserve two rooms. And with Brax's dad living in the area, I'm not completely certain that he—or either of you—will be there tonight or tomorrow night."

In the background, I heard Brax wrapping up his phone call with his dad, casually telling him that he'd see him later that day, but the conversation that had felt so all-encompassing not five minutes before was basically white noise, easy to forget.

Scrubbing my hand down my face, I knew I had to say something. I'd been dreading this day, knowing that it would come, but I'd expected it to be from my teammates, not Blaise.

I didn't respond quickly enough and Blaise jumped back in, some of his normal nervousness clear in his rushed speech. "I haven't told anyone. And I won't. I'm really sorry if I overstepped. It's okay either way. Shit, I'll just keep the two rooms. Sorry. I shouldn't have bothered you."

If ever a blush could be heard, I was sure it would sound like Blaise at that moment. Before he could hang up, I found my voice. "Wait! Blaise, don't hang up." I didn't hear anything after that and the call was still showing connected. "Blaise? You there?"

Brax wrapped his arms around me from behind, his hands clasping together at my belly button as he bent low enough to nuzzle my neck. He smelled heavenly and all I could think about was turning in his arms and snuggling into him. Unfortunately, I had to deal with the phone conversation with Blaise first.

Blaise finally answered. "I'm still here." Had he taken any longer, I might have forgotten what the conversation was about. Brax moved us to the chair in the corner of the room and pulled me into his lap.

Taking my own deep breath and letting it escape through my nose, I came clean. "One room is fine. You're right, it's silly to keep getting two rooms when we're only using one."

Behind me, Brax's breath hitched, his hold on me tightening at my admission. This hadn't been in the plans for the day but hell, if we were going to tell his dads, we might as well rip the bandage off and tell the team as well. Though telling Blaise wasn't like telling the team—I knew he wouldn't tell anyone without permission. However, with only one room, it wouldn't take long for the news to spread throughout the team.

A whoosh of air escaped Blaise and I heard him chuckle. "You have no idea how glad I am that I had read you two right. I was really, really worried that I had just put my foot in my mouth because you were just friends."

"You weren't wrong. We just haven't told a lot of people yet. We knew it would come out at some point."

Blaise groaned. "Sorry to put you on the spot then. I didn't mean to make you uncomfortable. I just, well, I thought it was kind of obvious and I didn't know if you'd be as comfortable as Seth had been to tell me to just book one room."

Brax must have overheard Blaise because he started laughing. "That sounds like Seth." Then he placed a kiss on my cheek. "If Trev's okay with one room, I'm good with it. Hell, or at least put us on the same floor. That would be nice."

Blaise gave a warm laugh. "Listen, I can make a lot of things happen, but I'm not the magician of room assignments, just how many rooms to assign. I'll let the coaches know that you two are sharing from here on out. That's going to be okay, right? I kind of have to tell them since they're the ones who hand out room keys and all. They'll know there's one less room than there should be."

"You're fine, Blaise. Coach C already knows."

"Phew. Okay, I'll let you guys pack."

"Bye, Blaise," we both said into the phone just before I clicked off, then turned in Brax's arms so that my legs were draped across his. "Ready for everyone to know?"

Brax rocked the chair lightly and encouraged me to get comfortable. With my head on his shoulder and a blanket wrapped around us, he hummed. "I've been ready. I meant it when I told you that I'd fallen for you."

His breath ghosting past my ear and over my neck had me shivering. "I seem to remember we both said the same thing." We'd admitted that we'd been in various stages of falling for one another, but we'd stopped just short of saying those three magic words that would change everything.

Brax walked his fingers up my stomach, making me squirm and giggle. "Given half the chance, I'd announce to the world that I love my little bear."

I'd been swallowing as he said that and my throat made a funny squeaking noise from the surprise. Hearing that he loved me hadn't been expected, but the words wrapped around me and filled me with confidence and an undeniable happiness that I'd never felt before. I adjusted myself so that I could see him clearly. My smile was so big that my cheeks began to block my vision, but at least I could still see him.

Focusing on his eyes, I could see a cloud of concern swirling within him. I might not have expected a declaration of love before heading to his parents' house, and I might not have ever expected a declaration of love from a teammate, yet I found myself grinning widely, my hands on either side of his face as I studied him closely.

"I am fully on board with that, but I think I'll just tell the world that I love Braxlyn Cernak. I'm good with Daddy and little bear being on a need-to-know basis."

Brax leaned forward and kissed me squarely on the lips. When he finally pulled back, the worry had left his expression, leaving an unmistakable happiness in its place. "That I can handle." He settled us back into the chair, giving us a momentary reprieve from our packing and thoughts of what lay ahead in North Carolina. With a hand on my stomach, he gave a contented hum. "I love you, Trevor."

Heat flooded my cheeks and curled in my stomach. "I love you too, Braxlyn."

He groaned. "That doesn't sound right coming from you. Hell, I'm only Braxlyn when I'm in trouble. But hearing Brax or Braxlyn from you is weird."

I laughed, mostly because not only did it sound weird, it felt weird also. Outside of the house, he was almost always

Cernak, but inside of the house, he was Daddy. I turned my head to kiss his cheek. "I love you, Daddy."

An easy smile spread on his face. "That sounds better. I love you too, little bear."

We sat there for another few seconds before I finally sighed. "We really should get going. We aren't packed and the flight is in two hours."

Brax groaned as he loosened his arms around me. "I guess you're right. As long as we don't forget Huck or Finn and you've got Blankie in your bag, we can get anything we forget while we're in Charlotte. Hell, if we can't get to the store, Dad or Leo will go for us."

The reminder that we were going to tell Tom and Leo we were dating popped my happy little bubble. "This is going to be the most awkward evening ever."

Brax pressed a kiss to the back of my neck, then pushed me to standing. "They'll be excited. Now, go find some pj's and undies for the next two nights."

I hoped Brax was right. We didn't have time to debate the merits of his statement because we really did need to be out of the house in the next few minutes. We rushed about the room, tossing things into bags quickly and double-checking we had the necessities before running toward the garage to throw things in the back of Brax's SUV and head to the airport.

He snagged a bag from the hook by the door on our way out, patting it down quickly and nodding to himself. "What's in the bag you grabbed?" I asked when we were finally pulling out of the driveway.

Brax grinned, though it was a look that I didn't often see on my boyfriend. The soft eyes and gentle upward curve of his lips should have told me that I was looking at my Daddy before he opened his mouth. "Coloring books and crayons. I stopped at the store yesterday and picked up more of both since everyone keeps fighting over them."

When Daddy came out, my little side slipped to the surface effortlessly, so the giggle that escaped me wasn't a surprise. "You found another team bonding thing."

"I wasn't trying to find a team thing. I'd wanted something to keep my little bear occupied so he actually sat down and relaxed." He reached over the center console and squeezed my hand.

"Thank you, Daddy. I like them."

Thirty-five minutes later, we'd made it to the airport, our luggage had been taken to the team's jet, and we'd begun to board the plane. Brax had wedged me between him and the window just over halfway back on the plane. As people passed, they reached into the bag Brax had brought and plucked out coloring books and packs of crayons until the supply was depleted before everyone had boarded.

"Do you have any extra coloring books?" Jean-Luc's puppy dog eyes blinked at me and Brax. He and Toby had been some of the first to board the plane, but Cunningham had caught them and held them up at the front.

Wincing, I glanced up at Jean-Luc. "Pats took the last one." I glanced over to Brax for help, like maybe he'd hidden a coloring book in his bag somewhere.

"Sorry, I don't have any either. I gave Blaise the last extra." I was glad Brax had given a coloring book to Blaise. He didn't normally come on trips with us, so I'd been shocked to see him show up at the airport. I'd overheard him telling Coach Bouchard that his parents lived near Charlotte and he was going to spend some time with them that week.

It was the first time Blaise had been on the plane with us that season and I could tell from the look on his face that he wasn't necessarily comfortable. Brax must have picked up on it too because he'd offered the coloring supplies to Blaise before we'd taken a seat.

"It's okay." Jean-Luc's words said one thing, but his eyes said another.

"You can have one of my pages." I held the book filled with all sorts of sea animals up. I'd only colored a few pages and was happy to let him use a few.

Cunningham walked by on his way to his seat and shook his head. "Come on, Luc. Let me get to my seat. I brought a stack with me. You all have been hounding Trevor and Brax like they're handing out free coffee each flight." He winked at us and kept walking.

Jean-Luc's face lit up and he took off after him. Seconds later, Coach was surrounded by five guys asking for coloring supplies.

"I hope he's got a lot of coloring books and crayons with him."

Brax shook his head. "This team sometimes feels more like a nursery school classroom than a professional hockey team."

I elbowed him lightly. "You love us. Besides, you started this one."

His warm chuckle wrapped around me like a blanket. "And you love it... and me."

Forgetting where we were, I laid my head on his bicep and grinned up at him. "I do."

Brax adjusted slightly to squeeze me to his side. "Tell me what you're coloring this time."

My mouth opened but the sound that came was not my voice. "You two are very close."

"Yuri, leave Trevor and Braxlyn alone. They do not want you to bother them," Igor said, his Eastern European accent thick but his English not as broken as Yuri's.

I looked back at my friends, trying to fight the blush that was threatening. Yuri stuck his tongue out at his best friend. "If they did not want to talk, they would not sit so close and shoot eyes with love."

Igor shook his head. "Yuri, stop with the English sayings. You kill every one of them."

Yuri ignored him and leaned his head between our seats. "You two. Together? No?"

My answering groan told Yuri all he needed to know. A smack came from behind me and Igor yelped. "Ouch. Asshole."

"You owe me a hundred dollars."

"I do not. He never confirmed."

"He did. Pay up." Another smack sounded, that time followed by Yuri's yelp.

Mikael leaned across the aisle. "Why are you hitting your best friend?"

"He owes me money. He lost the bet. I win."

The bickering behind us drowned out my whisper to Brax. "Daddy?"

He turned to face me, a sweet smile on his face. The look told me he knew exactly what I was thinking about. "Sounds like the time has come."

After the call with Blaise earlier, we'd both known it was a matter of when, not if. It turned out that *when* was now, on the Nashville runway, minutes before takeoff.

"At least Blaise is here today. He'll get everything firsthand."

Brax craned his neck around to see where Blaise was. I could just make him out three-quarters of the way back on the plane, sitting on the other side of the aisle from Coach Bouchard, his eye twitching occasionally as he focused on his coloring book. "I hope it's not too much excitement for him."

I poked his side. "I don't think we give him enough credit. I heard him telling Seth about a drag show he goes to regularly."

The bickering between the three behind us was getting louder and drawing the attention of others on the plane. "We should probably say something before the plane gets grounded because these three can't stop fighting," Brax said quietly. "I'm okay coming out to them if you are, but we should either confirm it or deny it quickly."

"We'll tell them. Should I?"

Brax squeezed my leg. "I'm right here, LB. You tell them but I'm here if you need me to take over or if it gets to be too much. I have no problem telling them we're together. I'm not ashamed of you or us and I'm not going to hide us either."

Sighing at how sweet his words were, I ended up with a dopey smile on my face as I turned to get the attention of the guys behind me. "Hey, Yuri, Iggy. Be quiet."

The two fell silent and stared at me. Finding any type of admission hard to put words to, I went for short and to the point. "Igor, pay the man."

The reaction was totally worth it. Igor's mouth fell open and Yuri cheered loudly enough to get the rest of the team's attention. From the back of the plane, Toby's head popped up from the row he was sharing with Jean-Luc. "What's going on up there?"

Yuri never looked at Toby, his eyes focused on Igor's hand as he reached for his wallet, but he spoke loudly enough that everyone from the front to the back of the plane could hear. "Igor lost the bet."

Another voice I couldn't pinpoint spoke from in front of us. "What bet?"

"He said Trevor and Braxlyn are not dating. I say they are. I win."

Yuri's accent was thick, his English pronunciation not exactly accurate, but the point had been made. "The team knows," I said to Brax seconds before the plane erupted in chatter that lasted to cruising altitude, when everyone finally calmed down.

Seth eventually made his way over, slipping into the unoccupied row in front of us and kneeling so that he could hang over the back to see us. "Well, you certainly know how to make an impression. I mean, it's not trending on Twitter and YouTube yet, and you haven't made the For You Page on TikTok, but you certainly found a unique way to come out."

Brax grinned and flipped him off before the two fell into a conversation that took them through the rest of the flight. Knowing it was Seth in front of us, I didn't worry about focusing more on my coloring page than the conversation. I was discovering how freeing it was to let my guard down sometimes, and when Brax was around, I was able to do that.

Whether as my boyfriend or my Daddy, he wasn't going to let anything happen to me.

## CHAPTER 29

### BRAX

DAD AND LEO were waiting at the hotel when we arrived. A few years earlier, I would have been mortified to see my parents standing in the lobby as I arrived with my team. Despite knowing that Trevor was worried about telling them, I still found a weight lifting from me when their faces appeared.

Cunningham had the key cards and a list of names for each room. To his credit, he only paused a brief second as he called Trevor's name, the corner of his mouth twitching upward as Trevor took the room keys. "And last but not least, Swayman." He handed the last key to the second line center, Thatcher.

My dad's eyebrow rose quizzically when my name wasn't called. Questions were in the near future.

Cunningham looked up from the clipboard and people began shuffling around, reaching for their bags and trying to make their way to the elevators. His throat clearing stopped the movement and everyone looked to him for his boilerplate warning. "Do not be late for morning skate tomorrow. I don't care what you all do tonight, but you are expected on the bus at nine."

"Yes, Dad," half the team said in unison, some of them saluting before resuming their move toward the elevators.

"Your room key," Trevor said, pulling a key from the cardboard sleeve and handing it over.

My dad's eyes widened as the handoff was made. *Oh yeah, those questions were happening soon.* "Do you want to go upstairs or just head out with my dads?"

Trevor's eyes widened enough that I knew he hadn't seen them across the lobby. All I had to do was tilt my head in their direction and Trevor's head shot over to where they were standing, then rapidly back to me. His eyes began to ping-pong between us, obviously not sure where to focus.

"They aren't going to bite."

"I've been checked into the boards by your dad before. It's not his bite I'm worried about." He at least managed to give me a smile and waggle his eyebrows so I knew he wasn't too nervous.

My dads didn't wait for us to start walking toward them and were already eating up the distance between us before our feet ever moved from our spots. There was no anger, confusion, or frustration, only genuine happiness in their eyes and on their faces as they wrapped me in a hug.

"Dad." I patted him on the shoulder, pretending to wheeze for breath. "Dad, need to breathe."

I might have been talking to my dad, but Leo's arms around me were just as tight, though they were at least around my shoulders, not my neck.

"We've missed you, kid," Dad said, finally pulling back to hold me at arm's length and study me.

Leo stepped away and pulled Trevor into a crushing hug that left him no choice but to wrap his arms around him and awkwardly pat Leo's lower back.

Dad shot me a knowing look and spoke out of the corner of his mouth. "Do you plan on telling us before you get married?"

I choked on air, which made Leo and Trevor look over at us. "Marriage? Cart before the horse much?"

My dad's head fell back and his laugh echoed across the marble lobby. "But you don't deny you're together, do you?"

I dug the heels of my palms into my eyes. "I am not discussing this here."

"Fine. Spoilsport. Do you guys want to spend the night at the house tonight? You can bring one of the cars to practice in the morning if you want."

Needing to make a decision quickly, I nodded. "We'll bring our stuff. That way if it gets late and we crash there, we've got what we need." Not that I was going to say it, but at least we'd have Trevor's blanket, pajamas, and Huck. With my suitcase at my dads', his sippy cup would be easily accessible also.

"Good plan. Leo will like that." He gave a fond smile in Leo's direction. When my mom had died, there had been a time I'd wondered if either of them would smile again. For years, it had felt like they'd lost the rock that kept them together. Shortly before I'd moved away for juniors, their happiness had come back.

Eight years after her death, we all still missed her, but my dad and Leo were happy together. Every time they looked at one another, unmistakable love and affection shone in their eyes. Sometimes I teased them that it was time they found a third, but that was mostly because they were turning into that couple that dressed alike and finished each other's sentences.

In all truthfulness, I wanted a relationship like theirs. I always had. As contentment settled in my chest as I looked over at Leo chatting with Trevor, his confident smile and relaxed shoulders showing he was at ease, I let myself believe that I'd found the person who completed me. That we could be the kind of couple my dads had turned into.

And maybe Easton was right—I really was a middle-aged man in a twenty-three-year-old's body.

My lips twitched upward in a smile at hearing Trevor's laughter at whatever Leo was saying. When we approached them, he stopped talking and looked up at me with big blue eyes. "Hey."

Aware of being in the middle of a hotel lobby, I resisted the urge to put my arm around his shoulders, settling on stepping just closer than could be considered casual but not so close that it would raise eyebrows. "Ready to get out of here?"

Trevor nodded. "Yeah. Leo's talking about what he's making for dinner and my stomach is rumbling."

"Leo's cooking is legendary." It was one of my favorite parts of coming home. I knew he'd have a huge container of my favorite chicken dish ready, but he'd also have a big salad, tons of vegetables, and balanced carbs that would keep us going between practices and the game.

The ride back to my childhood home was fairly uneventful. We talked a little about the team and our schedule for the coming days, but mostly we caught up on what was going on in Dad's and Leo's lives. They knew well enough that our lives revolved around practice, the gym, games, and travel for the next six months.

Halfway home, Trevor and Leo started talking about a band they both liked. I was pretty sure my dad and I wore matching amused expressions as they chatted the rest of the way home. The two were still debating the best album when Dad parked and we got out to get our bags from the back.

"No way, their last album was so much better," Trevor argued as he grabbed his bag.

Leo shook his head, pulling my backpack from the car and pressing the button to shut the hatch. "Absolutely not."

Dad ignored them both. "You boys can take your bags upstairs. I assume you remember where your room is?"

It hadn't been *that* long since I'd been home, but he'd made his point. "As long as you haven't moved it, I'm sure I'll be able to find it."

Dad laughed and shooed us up the stairs. As we headed up, I could hear my dad and Leo downstairs. "I believe you've been talking about making chicken for dinner tonight."

"Don't be daft. Of course I'm making chicken. I know what our boy likes when he comes home."

*Dammit,* being called a boy shouldn't have sent swoopy feelings through my stomach the way it had, but knowing that Leo considered me his as much as my dad did made those feelings very real. For the first time, I could understand how Trevor must have felt when he knew he was mine. It was safety and security and a sense of belonging that came from being with people who loved you.

I opened my bedroom door and exhaled at the familiarity of my surroundings. Not much had changed since I was a kid. I'd never been one for posters of my favorite teams or bands, though I had a few signed jerseys that had been framed and hung around my room. There was an entire shelf of meaningful pucks that marked important moments in my career. They'd gotten so numerous that they'd spilled over onto my desk and a bookshelf, but I couldn't find it in me to get rid of any of them.

Trevor slipped in the door and looked around. I expected a barb about the pucks or teasing about my Carolina 'Stangs quilt. Instead his eyes fell on a tiny stuffed bear on my nightstand. It couldn't have been more than six inches tall and its butt was filled with little beans, but it had been there since I was twelve.

My cheeks heated with undeniable embarrassment as soon as I saw what he was looking at. "I remember this," he said, walking across the room to point at the little red-and-black bear. When he looked back at me, his lips were turned upward in a knowing smile.

It had been there so long that I had a tendency to forget about it. More accurately, I'd forget about it until my eyes would fall on it, and then I'd remember the little gift bag that a much younger Trevor had left under the tree for me the first Christmas he'd spent with us. He'd only been here a few months, had hardly said three words to me, but my awareness of Trevor Cane's existence in the same space as me had gone from slightly heightened to an impossible-to-ignore crush.

"You do?" I sounded more like the awkward twelve-year-old than an adult talking to his boyfriend. Clearing my throat, I tried again. "Seriously?" At least my voice hadn't cracked that time.

Trevor leaned against me. "You seriously kept it?"

I was pretty sure Leo could have used my cheeks to cook the chicken by the feel of them, and my hand reached behind me and scratched at my neck. "That gift changed... things." I didn't have a better word for it.

Blue eyes gazed up at me as Trevor tried to figure out how to ask all the questions in his head. I saw my little bear in his indecision, but I also saw my very adult boyfriend who was both amused and smug.

"Yes, brat." My embarrassment lessened at Trevor's chuckle. "I'd been low-key interested in you for months, but then you gave me that bear for Christmas and it was like every fantasy a hormonal preteen could have. Very shortly thereafter, I figured out I was very, very gay."

Trevor bowed dramatically, some of the cocky NHL superstar I knew him as on ice coming to the surface. "I'm glad that I was able to help you in your self-discovery. I'm also glad that you didn't think the gift was as awful as I thought it was. I had no idea what to get you. After the fact, my mom told me that you were too old to give a teddy bear to."

His eyes fell to the bag that held Huck, a light pink staining his cheeks. "I hadn't thought of it before she'd said something."

Taking my boy in my arms, I squeezed him tightly. "It was perfect, just like you." When I ducked my head to kiss him, Trevor eagerly stretched to meet my lips. I'd intended for the contact to be nothing more than a brush of our lips but once our lips met, the kiss lingered until Trevor let out a soft gasp. His lips parted with the sigh and my own lips decided to take the opportunity to take control of the moment.

With my hands on his waist, I guided us to the side of my desk where I could lean back and bring us closer to an even height. Trevor moaned into my mouth when my leg slotted between his, my thigh brushing against his dick that was beginning to fill his pants.

Until recently, I'd loved my suit collection. Since moving in with Trevor, I'd begun to curse every pair of suit pants I owned as well as the amount of time I spent in them. We were professional hockey players, not lawyers, and sweatpants would be much more comfortable to get hard in.

Lifting my leg, I rubbed my thigh against his erection, pulling a whimper from Trevor. "Please." He shivered as I dropped my foot to the floor, the contact with his dick disappearing with the movement. "No, no, no." He shook his head, pulling back to look at me.

"Does my boy need more?"

Trevor hissed, his head nodding frantically. "Yes. So much." He paused long enough for a deep breath and to give me plenty of time to take in his blown pupils. "Daddy, please, I need you to make me feel good."

His plea had my dick filling faster, the discomfort from the angle momentarily forgotten in Trevor's need. Leaning forward, I murmured close to his ear. "Such a good boy to say so."

Trevor's breathing came in ragged pants, not slowing any as I tugged his shirt free from his waistband. My hands grazing his stomach and sides made him shiver again, goosebumps rising beneath my hands. His mouth parted on a scream that never came.

I made it as far up as his chest before admitting to myself that the dress shirt wasn't going to come off still buttoned. Releasing the hem, my fingers moved to the top button of his shirt, slowly popping each one open until it fell to his sides. Trevor's well-muscled chest and well-defined abs were on display, his nipples already pebbled.

My mind raced with everything I wanted to do to him. I knew his cues well enough. He was right there—a few strokes and he'd tumble over the edge. Or I could sink to my knees and suck him off in a matter of seconds. Either of those options would be safe, expected. They would get us downstairs quicker, raise fewer questions. I didn't want safe. I didn't want fast. I wanted to give Trevor everything, potential awkward discussions later be damned.

Trevor was in front of me, open and desperate, looking at me with eyes pleading to give him what he needed, ready to take anything I was willing to give him. He sucked his lower lip into his mouth and blinked up at me.

I reached behind him, groping his ass and letting my voice drop low. "I want in here."

His knees buckled at my words and he fell against my chest. "Fuck, yes. Please. Want—need—that."

With my arms wrapped around him for added support, I guided Trevor to my bed. Once he was safely on his back, I popped the buttons of his sleeves before turning my attention to his pants and eventually pulling his socks from his feet. With just a few tugs and a few awkward moves, Trevor was naked, his cock resting against his stomach with a bead of precum glistening at the tip.

It was so easy to lose myself in all things Trevor, I nearly forgot to undress myself. If I'd been hasty with removing Trevor's suit, I was careless with mine. My pants hit the floor at the same time I toed out of my socks. Uncoordinated, fumbling fingers worked at the buttons of my shirt. In my rush, I forgot to unbutton one of the cuffs and my hand became tangled in the fabric. Not caring about the shirt enough to carefully free myself, I tugged hard and the unmistakable *tink* of a button hitting a piece of wood somewhere in my room echoed in the quiet space.

Some of the seriousness of the moment broke and Trevor gave a rough, lusty laugh as the tension inside me eased. Finally pulling in a full breath helped bring me back from my own edge and reminded me that I needed to get into my travel kit for condoms and lube.

Trevor hummed when I bent over to reach into my bag. A glance over my shoulder showed him giving my ass a dreamy look. "Like what you see?"

He grinned at me. "Mmm, of course. I'll never get tired of seeing you naked."

I chuckled, though I had to admit that the appraisal felt nice. My hand brushed against Trevor's pacifier as I pulled my travel kit out. He had never had a problem expressing his pleasure in bed and with my dads downstairs, I knew we needed to keep ourselves quiet. With a smirk growing on my face, I pulled the pacifier out and headed over to my boy.

## CHAPTER 30

TREVOR

Brax returned to the side of the bed, his shave kit in one hand and his other balled in a fist that concealed something. He set the kit down first, then hid the other item behind it. I nearly asked what was there, but Brax's finger teasing my hole made all thoughts of anything else flee as my back arched upward.

"Is this what you want? My dick in this tight hole?"

I moaned. There was no use pretending it was anything else, so I nodded my head. "Y-y-yes."

His chuckle was deep and suggestive, like more dirty, wicked thoughts were running through his head than he knew what to do with. Whatever thought he ended on, I knew it was going to be perfect.

A finger landed over my lips. "You need to be quiet. Can you do that for me?"

He wanted me to be quiet? His other finger was tapping and probing against the tight muscle of my entrance and he was telling me to be quiet? My eyes widened as his words really sank in. "I-I... Try?"

That deep chuckle sounded again, this time more knowing than naughty. "That is not a very convincing assurance." He pressed his finger against my hole, barely breaching me, but the noise that came from my mouth sounded like he'd applied direct pressure to my prostate. "I'm going to take that as a *no*."

Instead of pulling out, he reached behind the bag and produced my pacifier. I didn't remember him packing it but it was there and being guided toward my mouth. "Open for me, baby. This should keep you quiet."

My mouth opened automatically, the familiar silicone nipple filling my mouth and soothing frazzled nerve endings. The rhythmic sucking motion started automatically. My body knew exactly what the nipple was for and like it or not, he was right that I'd be able to stay quiet with it in... or at least quieter than without it.

"That's it." A snick filled the room as he spoke, followed by the squelching of lube being squeezed into his hand. I never heard the bottle shut or felt his body move, but his fingers found my ass again, this time slick and more persistent.

I sucked harder on the nipple as he worked one finger, then the next inside me. My body was ready for anything and everything he was willing to give me, opening quickly to his ministrations. Stars sparkled in my vision, even before he wiggled his fingers. Once he did, scissoring them apart just slightly, I knew the pacifier had been a wise move. Even behind it, my moan was loud enough that it filled the room and there was no chance it wouldn't have been heard if someone had been on the other side of the door.

"That's it, baby. Let Daddy inside."

He crooked his finger again, that time landing directly on my prostate. The noise that escaped me was a desperate whimper, my body ready and willing for anything yet my brain knowing he'd only give me what he wanted, when he wanted.

Whether as Daddy or Brax, he wasn't a man who was going to be swayed by pleas. No matter what my body or my mouth said, he knew that I wasn't ready and sliding into me now would be uncomfortable. While Trevor the adult could handle the burn, the stretch, the slight discomfort of being taken without proper prep, I didn't know that Brax's boy would be able to do the same.

My little side didn't feel anywhere near the surface, but I knew it was still part of me. With Brax, it was always there, in every interaction we had. Just like I couldn't shut that part of me off, Brax couldn't shut off his Daddy side. He would feel guilty if he hurt me, even unintentionally. Likewise, I'd feel the same if I pushed for something that made him feel that way.

Instead of letting my dick do the talking, I took a deep breath and tried to relax every part of my body, including my ass. The more relaxed I was, the quicker I'd get him inside me. In the end, that was what I wanted, what I needed.

"There it is." Brax's voice came out husky and strained, like it had taken everything in him to get the words out. That was okay because it had taken everything in me to relax. There was no doubt in my mind that my voice would sound the same if I had the ability to speak.

With my pacifier in my mouth, all I could do was blink up at the man I'd given my everything to. He'd earned the title of my boyfriend and my Daddy, and he'd earned the place in my heart that he filled so completely. I hoped my eyes portrayed everything I was trying to tell him.

He reached up and brushed a tear from my cheek I hadn't realized I'd shed, his fingers slowing. "Okay?"

I nodded, sharp and decisive. I'd never been so okay, but I didn't have the words to tell him, mouth blocked or not.

Whatever he saw reflected in my eyes must have had him trusting me because he pulled his fingers back, nearly sliding completely from my body before pushing in again. The stretch became intense, the pressure the only thing I could feel as he slid in with three fingers, my vision graying at the edges with the burn.

I understood why he was so insistent on stretching me more. His cock was every bit as big as his fingers and the intrusion had my body forgetting how to breathe for a moment. Once I was able to suck in a full breath, I welcomed the pressure.

Everything about me felt alive and energized, driving my hips to rock into his touch and bringing a satisfied smile to Brax's serious face. "Oh, you're ready now. That's what I've been waiting for." He soothed a hand over my stomach as he slowly removed his fingers and wiped them on the sheets before reaching toward the bag.

It took a few seconds, but a condom appeared. "Fucking finally." He'd spoken the words under his breath, but I couldn't help but agree. It felt like I'd been waiting for this moment my entire life, and to an extent, I had.

Yes, I'd been with other people. Yes, I'd fucked and been fucked, but I'd always known that it would be different with my Daddy. That when I finally found the man that understood every side of me, the sex wouldn't be the same. He hadn't entered me yet and I already knew it was going to be extraordinary.

He finally showed a moment of nervousness when he fumbled the condom and cursed under his breath. Reaching up, I placed a hand on his forearm, his eyes immediately going to mine. The look he gave me really did steal my breath that time and it took me a few heartbeats to be able to remember why I had reached for him.

"It's—" The pacifier I'd forgotten about tumbled from my mouth, but I knew I needed to tell him what was in my head and leave the pacifier on the pillow. "It's okay. I'm not going anywhere."

Brax made a self-deprecating sound. "My hands are still slick."

That was a problem I could handle and sat up, gently taking the condom from his hand and sliding it down his length. Never had putting a condom on felt erotic, but I nearly came just by feeling his cock and veins under my hand as I tugged at the tip. I really hoped he didn't plan on this being a long-drawn-out thing. I was likely to explode if he so much as wrapped his hand around my cock.

His hazel eyes had turned almost brown, lust and desire radiating off of him. "Thank you."

"Any time." And I meant it, especially if it ended up with me below him while he fucked me.

My head had barely found the pillow again and he had pulled me up his thighs, guiding his dick toward my noticeably empty hole. His thick head pushed against my ring, thicker than his fingers, and my body was in an infuriating in-between where I both wanted and was resisting the intrusion.

His hand returned to my stomach, rubbing soothing circles near where my cock was resting. "Relax for me, Trev. Let me in."

I hummed and tried to find that place I'd been at a few minutes earlier when I knew he wouldn't give me more than I was able to take. If my body didn't relax, I knew that Brax would stop, telling me that we could wait a little longer, but it had been nearly a month already. Almost a month of intense blowjobs and handjobs and teasing. I didn't want to wait any longer. I wanted to feel his dick filling me, feel him claim me.

The thoughts were enough to make me relax. My body knowing exactly what it wanted, it finally opened up and allowed him entrance, the stretch the most delicious burn I'd ever experienced. No pain, no discomfort, just fullness that overtook everything and narrowed the world to just us, in this bed.

"Shhh." His chuckle and boyish grin told me I'd made a noise, probably a loud one since the pacifier was once again at my lips. "I don't want to get interrupted."

If Brax sliding into me always felt this good, we had better have a pacifier with us at all times because there was no way I'd be able to stay silent. He held the pacifier in my mouth until I started sucking on it, and he inched his dick farther and farther into me the entire time, not sitting up until his balls touched my ass.

"Oh, fuck. This is perfection."

I would have told him the same, but I couldn't form words at the moment, so I rocked my hips, trying to encourage him to move. Thankfully, he took the not-so-subtle hint and rocked his hips, the movement nailing my prostate and once again sending bursts of light into my vision. My back arched off the bed and my head dug into the pillow. The pacifier in my mouth was doing a good job muffling my noises but even with it, I was managing moans and muffled shouts.

Brax adjusted me again, pushing my thighs apart and back, both opening me wider and giving him a way to brace against me so that he could thrust hard and fast. I knew then that no pacifier would keep the house from knowing exactly what we were doing. Not only were long grunts and moans escaping me, but Brax was grunting and cursing as he fucked me.

There was every chance we'd waited too long to find ourselves in this position, and it was all but certain we'd chosen the second worst place to do this for the first time. Knowing that Tom and Leo were going to know what we'd been up to and have questions we were both going to have to answer was still better than what this would have been like in the hotel with our teammates all around us.

With thoughts running wild in my head, I was still well aware of the movement of Brax's hips and the feel of his cock stretching me and rubbing against my prostate every few thrusts. I was also well aware of the need building in my spine so close but just out of reach. I needed more, needed Brax's hand wrapped around me.

Like he'd read my thoughts, Brax reached in front of me and fisted my cock. My entire body shuddered and I began pushing against each of his movements, my orgasm dangerously close.

"Fuck. Trev." Brax's jaw was tight and his movements shaky, and I knew he was close. I wanted to chase him over the edge, follow him into that abyss, but I couldn't. Not yet. Not until— "Come for me, baby."

My mouth parted as my balls drew up even tighter to my body. My pacifier fell from my lips, the scream that had been building for what felt like hours finally breaking free at the same time the first spurt of cum hit my chest.

Brax's body shuddered, his hips slamming against my ass one last time before he slowed to sharp bucks of his hips as he emptied into the condom. His chest heaved and he grunted through clenched teeth.

We were both panting when he pulled out and tied the condom off, dropping it over the side of the bed and then collapsing next to me in one motion. "Fuck. I could sleep for a year."

I started to chuckle when Tom's voice called up the steps. "Leo's got dinner ready when you're... ready."

"Fuck, that's going to be awkward."

Brax shook his head. "Dad already figured it out. The man doesn't miss a damned thing. We probably could have been quieter, though."

Brax's pillow was comfortable and I found myself burrowing my head into it, seriously debating skipping dinner completely. "Maybe, though I'm pretty sure it would have required a ball gag for me."

My side vibrated with Brax's laughter. "Let me get a washcloth to clean you up, then we can go downstairs."

Sex had made me sleepy and the idea of talking with a man I'd been closer to than my own parents for many years about my relationship with his son was not high on my priority list. I'd managed to doze off before Brax returned, a warm rag running up my crease finally rousing me.

"What?" The word came out muffled around my thumb that had made its way into my mouth in the few minutes I'd been asleep.

A soft smile crossed Brax's face. "Do you want to sleep longer?"

I nodded despite opening my eyes and preparing myself to get up as he finished wiping off my stomach. "I'll never sleep tonight if I don't get up now. Your bed is very cozy, though."

"I've always liked that bed. I'm sure it will be just as cozy tonight with both of us in it." He stepped away and crouched by my suitcase for a moment before returning to the bed. "Arms up, little bear."

I raised my arms automatically only to find that he was pulling one of my play shirts over my head. "Daddy?" It was funny how quickly he'd gone from Brax to Daddy in my head, but this was clearly Daddy getting me dressed.

"I've got a sweatshirt for you too. No one will see, but you're going to be more comfortable for the night."

A small part of me hated that he was right, but the rest of me was thankful he knew that and had already thought about a way to give me that comfort while around people who didn't know. There was no use arguing with him and I let him guide me into an outfit, cute underwear with puppies included, before helping me into a pair of joggers and one of my hoodies.

"There ya go, all set. Let's go have dinner."

*Dinner or a firing squad?*

I managed to keep my thoughts to myself until we made it downstairs. Leo and Tom were in the kitchen with four plates on the long island and both of them struggling to keep a straight face. For once, I was glad for my short stature so that I could hide completely behind Brax and no one could see my embarrassment.

That didn't mean they didn't know, especially Leo, whose knowing chuckle sounded amused and friendly. "I'm guessing you two worked up an appetite?"

The groan I let out was muffled by Brax's sweatshirt but not enough that it didn't echo off the pristine kitchen or pull a hearty laugh from Tom. "I'd say I'm glad our room is downstairs, but I think we might need to build a guest house for you two when you visit."

With my face buried in his shirt, I could hear and feel the laughter Brax was trying to suppress. "Enough. You two are being awful and embarrassing a *guest*."

Tom scoffed. "Trevor hasn't been a guest in this house since he moved in here. He's family. Just not quite the way I'd have expected a few years back."

Brax reached around and began to tug my sleeve, hinting for me to come around and stand next to him, when Leo piped in. "But it's always what Brax wanted."

Brax groaned, his own embarrassment clear in the noise.

"Okay, okay, we're done." Tom's voice sounded definitive, so I let Brax drag me out from behind him.

Leo nodded toward the table. "Grab a plate and take a seat."

Brax grabbed both our plates, so I grabbed the two empty cups and filled them with water before joining them in the dining room. As I came around the corner, Tom leaned close to Brax. "You taking care of him, Braxlyn?"

"Of course." The answer was clear and immediate.

Tom nodded once. "Good. Trevor's a wonderful guy, but he puts too much on himself. He needs someone to take some of that stress away. I'm happy to see it's you."

I didn't know what to make of the statement, but I could admit that it felt good to know that Tom was happy for us. "I'm happy it's him too."

## CHAPTER 31

### BRAX

Trevor had been in his playroom for nearly three hours. He'd been painting the first time I looked in on him and had been building with blocks a little later. By the third time I'd gone in, he'd been snuggled into his little bed, a mountain of blankets and stuffed animals on top of him. The first cold snap of the year had finally gripped Middle Tennessee and Trevor had been in his footed pajamas since we'd gotten out of bed.

Finding him buried in the blankets, I'd known he was still cold. It took less than five minutes to get the heater turned up a few degrees and go to the kitchen to make a bottle of milk for my little bear before hurrying back to the playroom. He'd mostly stuck with sippy cups, but cold and tired, I figured warm milk would warm him from the inside out.

Then it had taken all of five minutes and three pages of a book before he'd fallen asleep. A little over an hour later, I was debating on when to wake him up so that he'd have enough time to transition from little time to big, then get ready to leave for our dinner reservations. We were finally going on our first real date.

I'd decided to give him fifteen more minutes when my phone pinged.

***Easton****: Has the surprise come yet?*

It took me a minute to figure out what he was talking about. When I finally did, I grinned thinking about the box in the closet in my old room. It had definitely become my old room since I spent every night with Trevor in his.

***Me****: Came in last weekend. We've been nonstop since then. We have the next few days off. Trying to figure out the best time to show him.*

I could almost hear Easton's hum when the text went from Sent to Read.

***Easton****: He's going to love them. The lions are adorable.*

***Me****: Are you sure* you're *not the one looking for a little? You have definitely taken a liking to my boy.*

And he had. There was a box of new art supplies and a cute crayon-patterned onesie next to the box of diapers. I'd wondered where it had come from, since it had been addressed to me, for all of five minutes before Easton had texted to let me know that the gift he'd sent Trevor had arrived.

***Easton***: *Not looking for a little, B. Doesn't mean I can't spoil yours.*

***Me***: *Well, he'll appreciate the gift. I'll let him know they're from you.*

"Daddy?" Trevor's voice called from the playroom.

***Me***: *Gotta go.*

"Coming, little bear."

A few seconds later, I was standing in the doorway to his playroom smiling at his rumpled appearance. If I hadn't known better, I'd have thought he'd been asleep all night, not just shy of ninety minutes. His eyes flicked upward as he blinked sleepily in my direction. "Hungry, Daddy."

Of course he was. It was past four and he hadn't had more than a snack since an early lunch. Of course, he'd enjoyed his rainbow fish crackers and grapes while he'd colored, but that wasn't enough to hold him over.

"Can be arranged. Go potty and come on out to the kitchen."

When he joined me five minutes later, my little bear had been replaced with my boyfriend. His cute footed sleeper had been replaced with a team warmup suit and T-shirt. His hair had been tamed into a tenuous submission, though I wasn't convinced it would stand up to a sudden wind.

It still surprised me how easily he switched between his big and little sides, comfortable with it in a way I hadn't expected a month earlier. In minutes, he could go from playing in his room to ready to play a hockey game and vice versa. Tonight it just so happened he was getting ready for a date—our first official one—and I had plans for later.

"Do I get a snack before we go out? I'm still hungry." He winked, playful and mischievous but lacking the innocence of my little bear.

I chuckled as I pushed a plate of fruit and veggies and a few cubes of cheese toward him. "Of course."

He pulled the plate closer and popped a grape in his mouth before sing-songing, "Thank you, Daddy!" His playful mood sobered for a moment, a hesitancy crossing his face I hadn't seen in quite a while before he blew out a frustrated breath. "Can I have a drink?"

"Of course. What do you want?" There was something he wasn't telling me, but I wasn't going to push right away.

"Juice?"

Giving an affirmative nod, I thought about what was in the fridge. "Apple, orange, or grape?" It was always a toss-up which he'd choose.

He thought for a moment before making a decision. "Apple, please."

My hand was already reaching for a glass when something pinged my brain. There had been something innocent about how he'd asked for his juice. He'd been quieter and more hesitant than my boyfriend. I hesitated again, that time wondering if I was making the right decision as I reached for one of his sippy cups. It wasn't unheard of for him to grab one even if he wasn't feeling particularly little, and maybe he was still trying to make that shift in his head.

I wrapped my fingers around his cup and pulled it down, taking it to the counter by the fridge and grabbing the bottle of apple juice from the door. As soon as Trevor saw the cup in my hand, his shoulders dropped and his eyes brightened. "Thank you."

Unable to stop my hand, I ruffled his hair, chuckling as it stuck up again. "Anytime." I leaned against the far counter and watched him eat for a few minutes, gathering my thoughts as his snack disappeared. He'd just popped the last cheese cube in his mouth and reached for his cup when I figured out what I wanted to say to him.

"You know you don't have to be embarrassed to ask for things you want. Big or little." I'd added the last part on a whim, trying to make sure he understood that I was serious.

His face pinked and he sucked his lip between his teeth while he thought. "I know that logically. I'm still figuring it out myself sometimes. Before you moved in, I never thought about what I grabbed. Everything was always right there. Then everything went on its head for a bit. Now I'm trying to figure out what my new normal is. Sometimes, even I'm not sure."

He tried to laugh it off, but I could see he was legitimately confused. It made my plans for later in the evening seem more poignant. "Well, I'm here to talk if you ever need it."

Trevor gave me a smile, more relaxed and genuine. "Thank you. I'll figure it out."

I nodded because I knew he would, and while he was getting ready for our date, I was going to run upstairs and make sure I had easy access to everything for when we got home. And until then, I wouldn't stress him out over it, and I wouldn't push him to choose his adult or little things. Whatever he wanted was fine with me, especially in the house. Though I'd work to get him what he needed outside of the house as well.

"I'm sure you will. While you start thinking, go get ready for tonight. I'm going to get changed and clean up a bit."

Trevor's head was clearly not focused on my words because he didn't react, only nodded and headed toward the bedroom. I chuckled to myself because there was next to nothing out of place. I'd been cleaning most of the afternoon, at least between checking on him and getting him whatever he'd needed.

Without questions from him, I was able to focus on getting dressed quickly, then spent time packing a small duffel with a few diapers, the things Easton had sent, and another surprise I hoped to be able to use on him if his head was in the right space when we returned.

Since he'd mentioned sensory play, I'd been planning on a night to explore some with him, but we'd been so busy with travel, games, and practice, we'd barely had time for him to play in his room, much less find time for anything extra.

I finished as fast as I could and was back downstairs pulling out a pair of briefs from both his little drawer and big drawer—race-car-printed Y-front briefs and a pair of black boxer briefs—when the shower turned off. I stashed the duffel out of sight and made sure everything was set for later in the evening while he dried off and did his hair.

It didn't surprise me to see him walk out of the bathroom with a towel wrapped low on his waist and his thumb in his mouth. Over the last few weeks, he'd gotten more comfortable with me seeing it there. It was so commonplace that I'd actually questioned how he'd kept it a secret from the team as long as he had.

Trevor smiled at me from around his fist, his eyes lighting up with genuine happiness before he noticed the bed. "What's this?" he asked, the words coming out slurred despite his moving his thumb to the side.

"Which undies for tonight?"

He gave the two pairs a long look. "I have the option?"

I hadn't expected the question to give him so much pause. Moving closer, I wrapped my arm around his waist. "You always have the choice. I don't care which you wear under your pants or around the house." Because Trevor hated pants in the house and would go without them whenever he could, usually from the minute we walked in the door until we had to get ready to go again. He'd spent many days running around in just a pair of briefs and a T-shirt, or just his briefs if it was warm enough. Only recently had he begun wearing pants and those were always loose and soft.

A lot of the underwear he considered little undies wouldn't turn a head in the locker room. After Yawney showed up in a pair of briefs with pastel bows on them after his daughter was born, I wasn't sure that a pair of underwear with yellow elastic and piping would raise an eyebrow from anyone.

His thumb finally got pulled from his mouth so he could bite his lip. When he finally pointed at the race car briefs, I couldn't say I was surprised. Not giving him a chance to reach for them, I grabbed them from the bed and knelt down.

It said something about where his head really was that he didn't question me, just placed a hand on my shoulder and stepped in. With his underwear up and his half-hard dick adjusted in the front, I patted his butt. "Go get dressed."

Trevor nodded, hurrying to the closet to find clothes. Three minutes later he walked out looking every bit the sexy, confident man he was on the ice. Slim gray suit pants, a white collared shirt, and a fitted navy sweater made him look like he could own a boardroom, not just the ice. For the first time, I could see Trevor as a manager or a coach when he finally retired as a player. And damn, he would look sexy standing on the bench.

When he caught me sitting on the padded bench by the bathroom, he jumped and let out a squeak that immediately turned into a laugh.

"Trying to kill me?"

Heading over to him, I opened my arms and wrapped him up. "Not at all." I kissed the top of his head. "Just wanted to be here if you needed help. Didn't want to go too far."

He angled his head up for a kiss on the lips, waiting until I gave it to him before he answered. "That's very sweet of you. I like how you always take care of me."

"I like taking care of you. I like being the one who can give you the freedom from all the stress."

"That's what Colt always tells Derek."

Something about the names rang a bell, but I couldn't think of a single person I knew named Derek or Colt. "Who are they?"

The way he hit his face with his hand, I knew he hadn't meant to say what he had. "I'm not trying to be secretive, but I need to make sure it's okay to talk about him. I'll send him a text and then let you know."

His phone was in his hand before I could say anything else and he was quickly tapping out a text. A minute later, he pocketed the phone again. "Okay, now we wait. I'm going to have a lot of questions to answer when he gets that text."

"Well, my curiosity is seriously piqued, so I can't wait to hear about this person. We don't have time to wait for his response, though. We have reservations soon."

Trevor slipped his hand in mine. "I still want to know where we're going."

Maybe I shouldn't have kept it a secret, but I liked the idea of surprising him. I knew his little side loved surprises, and since my little bear was rarely too far out of reach, I had a good guess Trevor would also like the surprise.

"Am I dressed okay?"

"Perfectly." We were just going to a steakhouse that Bouchard had talked up the week before. He'd been raving about their steak and chicken as he'd been ranting about the dinner he and Cunningham had eaten in Charlotte. I'd listened enough to catch the name and after a few Internet searches, had decided it would be the perfect place to take Trevor. As an added bonus, it wasn't near downtown Nashville.

"And I can't wait to *un*dress you afterward."

Trevor actually giggled. "I'm all for that, but first, I've been promised food!"

"That you were."

## CHAPTER 32

TREVOR

I'D BEEN MORE than a little surprised when Brax directed the SUV away from downtown. "Where are we going?" I wasn't above begging if I had to.

The highway this far from downtown was dark, so I couldn't see his face, but the amusement in his voice was clear. "I really don't think you want to know. I think you want it to be a surprise. No matter how curious you are."

"I really don't like when you're right."

"Well, I'm your Daddy. It's my job to be right. Especially about things that have to do with you."

His easy acceptance of being my Daddy had made everything we'd built feel natural. Hearing his sincere words had butterflies swooping in my stomach and a smile growing on my face. I opened my mouth to say as much but was cut off by my phone ringing. Hardly anyone called me, so I figured it was a spam call until I looked at the number.

The swoopy butterflies sank quickly. "This is Derek. He never calls. Do you mind if I take this? There might be something wrong."

"Take it. Make sure your friend is okay."

That was all I needed and I swiped up. "Hello?"

"What the flippity flappity f—"

"Derek, think hard about what's about to come out of your mouth," his Daddy said with a rumbly warning to his tone.

Derek sighed. "What is this about? *Can I tell my Daddy about you and your Daddy?* Since when do you have a Daddy and why am I just hearing about it?"

He'd clearly been loud because Brax laughed at the end of his rant.

"It's kinda new. I mean, it's really new. And we've been busy."

"But *Daddy!* That's a big thing. Like, *something you should be telling me about immediately* big!"

Listening to how animated Derek had gotten, I could feel my little side slipping closer to the surface. He always made me giggle and laugh in person, and the same was true on the phone. "It's new... but he's really special." I looked over at Brax and was pretty sure I caught a giant grin on his face as we passed under a streetlight.

"Special is good. I knew Daddy was the one almost immediately. Is he the one?"

Colt's sigh was audible in my ear. "Buddy, don't push Trevor."

*Was Brax the one*? Had I ever thought about it that way? He was my Daddy and for all my initial reservations about it, I couldn't imagine ever finding a more perfect Daddy for me. I loved him, once again despite my objections to any relationship with him when he'd first moved in. The answer wasn't complicated and it didn't take me long to land on it, and that would have cleared up any hesitations or concerns I'd had, if there'd been any.

"Yeah, I think he is."

Derek squealed. "Tell me!"

My cheeks heated, but my stomach felt giddy at finally being able to tell one of my very best friends. "He's a teammate."

"More info!"

"Cernak."

The word was barely out of my mouth and Derek gasped. "The new guy? Dang, he's cute. Daddy! Can we go to Trevor's house soon?"

Colt chuckled warmly. "We'll work out a time. Sounds like I need to get his Daddy's number."

My cheeks heated. It was such a Daddy thing to do, but I'd never thought I'd have a Daddy like that. Derek didn't give me time to think about it much, pushing forward with his plan. "Oh! Good idea. What's your Daddy's number? Then they can plan a get-together!"

"Is it okay if I give Derek your number so he can give it to his Daddy so that you two can plan a playdate?"

We'd just pulled into a parking lot and I'd managed to totally miss where we were. What I didn't miss was the spark of humor in Brax's eyes. "Only if you tell me who Derek and his Daddy are."

"Oh right! That's what I was supposed to ask." I didn't need to voice the question before Derek started to answer.

"Yes! If he's a teammate, he knows privacy."

I nodded, despite him not being able to see me, then rattled off Brax's number before telling Derek I needed to go because we were at dinner.

"Let me come open the door for you." I didn't know if it was a Brax thing or a Daddy thing, but at the moment, I was a little giddy and it was probably not a bad thing if he wanted to open my door. I had too many thoughts rushing through my head to be bothered with dinner or traffic.

He held my hand the entire way, gripping it tighter as we crossed through the parking lot like he was worried I might walk in front of a car. Then again, I hadn't bothered looking for traffic either, so maybe his concern was warranted.

"So, who are Derek and his Daddy?" Brax asked once we'd been seated at a booth at a quiet steakhouse. The name on the menu seemed vaguely familiar, but I couldn't figure out why. I certainly hadn't been here before, but it looked nice.

I made sure to keep my voice low. "Derek and Colt Westfield."

Brax tried, then shook his head. "The names make me think they should ring a bell, but I'm not coming up with why."

"Derek Scott, lead singer of Hometown."

I wished I had my phone out. Brax's eyes widened farther than I'd thought possible. "Seriously?"

Nodding, I recounted how we'd met at a team event and had become fast friends. I also told him that we'd missed our playdate shortly after he'd moved in and hadn't found a time to reschedule. Before our drink order had been taken, he was thinking about how to make that playdate happen.

"Chicken, steak, or veggie?" Brax asked as we picked up the menus.

The question had come so easily that I answered automatically. "Steak, I think."

He hummed as he continued to peruse the menu, so sneakily asking questions about my preferences—medium, broccoli, baked potato with sour cream only—that I didn't figure out what he was doing until the waiter returned and Brax rattled off two orders before I was able to open my mouth. The waiter didn't blink, just nodded and hurried away to put the order into the system.

"You didn't have to do that."

Brax's eyes twinkled. "I know. But I like doing things for you. It's so easy and your smile makes it even better."

Heat might have spread across my face knowing that I was such an open book, but I couldn't deny his assessment. "I like it too. As long as you like it. I can do things for myself otherwise."

His foot ran up my calf and I gave a noticeable shiver. "I know you can. And you do so much on your own. You work harder than any team captain I've ever had. You know every single person on the team and make everyone feel welcome. You spend time after every single game talking to the guys. You're ready to go early. You spend hours looking up games and figuring out how to modify them for a hockey rink. You figure out how to get a drunk teammate home at one in the morning when he calls you instead of his wife." He lifted an eyebrow in my direction and I ducked my head.

"I hadn't thought you'd noticed that."

Brax's warm laughter let me know he wasn't upset with me, and the foot that had lost a shoe at some point while we talked snaked higher up my leg.

"Hard to miss when your phone rings at one in the morning and suddenly you're out of bed and dashing off to the bathroom."

Words were getting harder to find the higher up his foot trailed. He had already moved it up to my thigh, and his freakishly long legs—or maybe mine were just freakishly short—had reached across the table and snaked nearly to my groin. It probably helped that I kept sliding forward on the bench, trying not to make a scene but also desperate for more contact.

"I'm just glad Val was comfortable calling me. I'd have felt a lot worse if he hadn't made it home okay."

Brax's amused expression told me I'd missed something. "I know that, Trev. And it says a ton about you that they are all so comfortable calling you, even in the middle of the night. They know you're going to answer and not ignore them."

I wasn't good at taking compliments so I didn't know how to respond. Brax didn't need words from me; he simply reached across the table and took my hand. "You take care of everyone, but who takes care of you?"

"You," I answered automatically, then smacked my forehead. "That's what you were trying to get across."

"It was. I like taking care of you. I like taking care of you when you're feeling little, but I also like taking care of you when you're not. I like taking care of my boyfriend. I like letting you know that I've heard you and seen you and that you're special to me."

I really wished we weren't in the middle of a restaurant with our dinners arriving at the table because I wanted to kiss the breath out of Brax and announce to the world how much I loved my boyfriend. I settled on a thank you as I squeezed his foot between my thighs, bringing it into direct contact with my dick.

Brax's eyes shot open and he struggled to get words out, leaving me to blink innocently at the waiter who had appeared out of thin air with our dinners. "Thank you, it looks amazing."

No sooner had the waiter left than Brax found his voice. "Are you being naughty?"

Turning my attention to my steak, I shook my head. "No more than you."

His laughter was rich and filled the dining area as heads turned to stare at us. "You are so going to pay for that when we get home." His eyes flashed hot and I got the distinct impression he was planning something.

THAT FEELING that he'd been planning something had clearly been accurate, but he hadn't shown his hand. He'd joked the entire way home, but his body language shifted subtly as we pulled into the neighborhood. My laughing, joking boyfriend melted away and my Daddy started coming out more as we approached home.

"When we get home, make sure you have Huck and Finn in the bedroom."

My pout was unintentional. It came to me as naturally as Brax had switched from Brax to Daddy. "I'm not tired." And part of me worried that I'd done something wrong and was really going to get punished. It had just been a bit of teasing.

He pulled into the garage and killed the engine. "I hope you're not tired yet. That would put a serious damper on my plans for the evening."

Now I was really confused. "But Huck and Finn usually mean bedtime."

"Or that I want you to have things you're comfortable with." He turned to face me, his finger trailing down my jaw. "Remember your safewords?"

*Oh, this was interesting.*

I nodded slowly. "Green means good, yellow to slow down, and red to stop."

He made a low sound in his throat. "Yes, exactly. You need to remember those tonight. If I ask you what color you are, you're to tell me the first color that comes to mind. Understood?"

I gulped. "Understood."

"Good boy. Head to the bedroom, make sure you have Huck and Finn, and go to the bathroom. Then I want you to wait for me. Do not take anything off."

He was definitely up to something, yet I was more curious than concerned as I hurried into the house and headed to the bedroom. Huck and Finn were on the bed where I'd left them after my nap and I continued into the bathroom. While I peed, I could hear noise outside of the bedroom, though I couldn't make out what Brax was doing. Flushing the toilet and washing my hands blocked the noises, but when I turned the water off, I could tell Brax had moved to the bedroom.

My thumb moving toward my mouth said that I was more nervous than I wanted to believe I was, no matter how curious I was to discover Brax's surprise. It only took three steps into the bedroom to figure it out and my feet stopped dead.

"Oh." My thumb stopped moving when it finally came to rest in my mouth, curiosity being replaced by nerves at what was spread out across the bed.

Brax stopped moving and turned to face me, his confidence faltering slightly when he saw my face. "I got you something I thought we could try together."

My thumb stubbornly refused to move from my mouth, my mind racing at the items laid out before me. The onesie wasn't surprising, nor was my bottle or pacifier. Hell, even the large sheet draped over the comforter and two silk scarves on top didn't surprise me, though they did make my dick twitch with interest.

No, the thing that had my feet rooted to the floor was the item in the middle of the bed. It was the item I'd always been curious about but was too scared to try.

Daddy had remembered the conversation, he'd acted on it, and now I was looking at a perfectly folded diaper with a cute little pastel lion printed in the center. My mouth worked my thumb furiously as I thought about the item I was looking at, questioning if I was ready. It had always felt so huge, so out of reach, that I'd never given it any real thought. Diapers had always been more of a passing maybe-one-day thing that sometimes had come up while I'd been fantasizing about my perfect Daddy.

A pinch in my groin made me look down to see my dick had gone from interested in the silk scarves to rock fucking hard as I'd studied the diaper. So maybe parts of me were more ready than others.

"What color are you?"

"Green." The word was out without thought. Despite sounding more like *geen* with my thumb in my mouth, my Daddy gave me an approving nod.

"What a good boy you are. I'm so proud of you." He walked over to meet me at the bed. "I have a very special night planned for you. You don't even need to think. All you have to do is feel."

That sounded nice in theory, though I didn't know how I was going to not think about a diaper taped around me.

"Let me help you get undressed." He'd made fast work of things while I'd been in the bathroom. He'd already changed into a pair of sweatpants that hung low on his hips. Judging by the bulge in the front, he'd lost his underwear as well. Dammit, I wanted to taste him, but I had a strong suspicion that wasn't in the cards for tonight.

When I didn't make a move to stop him, Brax stepped forward and reached for my sweater, tugging it over my head as my thumb popped out of my mouth so it could come off. He tossed it into the bathroom, I could only assume somewhere near the hamper, and then his hands were back on me, deftly opening the buttons on my shirt before tugging it down my arms.

"You gave me some seriously wicked fantasies when I saw you in this tonight." He popped the button of my pants open. "Seriously, you were so fucking sexy in this. It's almost a shame I'm taking them off you so soon." He paused for a second, hands on my pants, then tugged them to the ground. "Almost. Not completely. Because now I can take care of you."

My thumb found its way back to my mouth as I stepped out of my pants, watching as they got tossed in the same direction my shirt had. I expected my underwear to meet the same fate, yet it didn't. Brax left it on me as he directed me toward the bed and pushed gently against my chest to encourage me backward.

My brain and my dick were having a battle of wills that I was pretty certain my dick was going to win. Since it was pressing insistently against the front of my underwear, it was hard to argue I wasn't interested in this new development.

*Actually, it was just hard.*

Aching and uncomfortably hard and not being helped by the way Brax was looking at my body.

His fingers paused before he reached the yellow waistband of my underwear, his eyes finding mine and giving me a thorough stare. "Still green?"

I nodded, allowing my thumb to slip to the side of my mouth. "Green." So green. There was a little yellow in the recesses of my brain as I really questioned if this was something I was ready for. The little worry was so far from the forefront, it wasn't worth voicing. I knew Daddy would keep checking in on me, but I promised myself I'd keep checking in as well.

I'd wanted this. Wanted this for so long, and now I was going to get it.

Daddy's fingers gripped the waistband of my underwear and removed it slowly, finally pulling it off my feet and tossing it toward the bathroom. It didn't matter where it'd landed; what mattered was that Daddy was looking at me with hungry eyes. Eyes that promised amazing things and stared at me like I was just as amazing.

If he didn't move this along, I was going to get emotional. But then he moved. He reached beside him and unfolded the diaper and for a moment, the world tilted on its axis and time stood still.

## CHAPTER 33

### BRAX

Nervous didn't begin to describe the way Trevor looked. He looked terrified, but there was also excitement in his eyes. He'd fluctuated between emotions a number of times already, and I was pretty sure that his nervousness was likely due to the years he'd spent thinking about this.

I knew exactly how terrifying that first experience could be after spending years thinking about something. I'd had firsthand experience with it when it came to Trevor.

But no matter what his eyes or shoulders said, his cock twitched against his stomach as I unfolded the diaper.

I contemplated leaning down and sucking him off, releasing his pressure valve and bringing him some relief. Then I worried more about him truly falling asleep. Sleep wouldn't necessarily be a bad thing. It would mean he was relaxed, but I really wanted to see how he reacted to what I had planned.

Trevor didn't notice my glance toward the small water bath I'd set up in an old crockpot I'd found in the cabinet. Nestled inside the water were multiple small jars of wax in various colors melting slowly as I distracted him with the diaper. I'd made friends with a kinky wax maker in Boston and when Trevor and I had talked about his interest in sensory play, he'd come to mind.

Dave had spent years perfecting a recipe for a low-melt, all-natural wax that would melt at a low enough temp to pour but not so low that it solidified too fast to be pleasurable. There was just something about wax pooling and dripping off a body that was sensual in ways I couldn't begin to describe.

When I'd sent him the request for wax, Dave had sent a list of colors to choose from. I'd quickly picked a handful of vivid colors that reminded me of Trevor's crayons.

In the past, I'd done intense sensory play that involved layers of wax and knives that carved into it just enough to raise the skin but not cut, and steel pinwheels that sent subs deep into subspace. I had no doubt Trevor would find subspace but I didn't plan on pulling out knives or my Wartenberg pinwheel. The risk of overwhelming him with sensations was a concern as well. Between the silk, the diaper, and the warm wax, we were already going to a place I knew he'd never been. I wanted to make sure he experienced a wonderful floating green to an overwhelmed, overstimulated red.

Trevor was already at risk of overstimulation if his eyes were anything to go by. The normally brilliant blue had turned dull and his pupils had dilated as he'd studied the diaper. He was always tactile, which was why I'd told him to make sure Huck and Finn were on the bed, but sensing his worry, I placed my hand on his stomach and spread my fingers apart.

He drew in a shaky breath and looked up at me. "You have your safewords, but until you use them, I'm going to keep going."

I was fully prepared for him to put a stop to the entire thing as soon as I reminded him of that. Instead of stopping me, Trevor gave me a searching look, then nodded. "Green."

I attempted not to let my surprise show, trying hard to give him a reassuring smile and a wink. "Okay. Please remember you're in control."

The reminder had him relaxing and his thumb moving less frantically in his mouth. We'd said what we needed to, so I moved along, unfolding the diaper and slowly lining it up with his ass. I could at least say that Easton's plethora of links over the past month had given me confidence in the next steps.

Trevor's eyes might have shown hesitancy, but the way he automatically lifted his hips and waited for me to center the diaper under him proved that he'd given the idea plenty of thought over the years. "Down, little bear." My voice came out as a husky whisper, like there was a ball of cotton strangling my vocal cords.

Trevor dropped down immediately, then spread his legs to the side for me to secure the diaper around him. I once again needed to give Easton credit. He'd chosen a diaper with tabs that velcroed, allowing me to adjust it numerous times until I was confident I'd gotten it on him right. Stepping back to examine my work, I glanced up to Trevor's face to find him content in a way I'd never seen before.

Until then, I'd thought he'd been at peace when he was deep in little space, playing, coloring, or watching a movie in his playroom, but that was before I'd seen him like this. He looked complete, like he'd just discovered a long-lost friend or a piece of his soul had been unlocked. The moment was all about my boy, and me giving him what he needed, except I couldn't help but marvel that I'd had a part in it.

Placing my hand against the front of the diaper, I uttered the only word I could come up with. "Perfect."

He pushed his dick into my hand and let out a long, stuttered sigh that accompanied an entire body shudder. If it hadn't been for his dick not pulsating beneath the diaper and my hand, I'd have been certain he'd come. Instead, he fluttered his eyes open and a smile crossed his face. "Thank you."

The two simple words settled in my heart and made my pulse quicken. "You're welcome." Moving to the side of the bed, I picked up the long scarves. "Now, remember, you have your safewords."

He nodded once as his eyes tracked my movements. I held the scarf up so he could see what I had. "I'm going to tie this to your wrist, then your wrist to the headboard." When he didn't respond, I worked at his first wrist, the knot loose enough that he could easily slip out of it. Again, this was about exploration and seeing how it felt, and I wanted him to enjoy the entire experience.

With the first tie secured to him and the headboard, I placed Huck in his hand and looked down at him. He tugged gently at the binding, then nodded. "Green."

His honest answer, without my prompting, made me lean down and kiss his forehead. I'd have kissed his lips, but his thumb was still blocking them. At least he gave a contented hum at the touch.

Standing up, I went to the other side of the bed. "What about this hand?" I asked, tapping his fist. If he didn't want to give it up, I wouldn't force it. To my surprise, he pulled it from his mouth and offered his hand to me. I gave him a reassuring smile and secured the second scarf around his wrist. "If you need it back, just say." That earned me a grin as I secured the other end of the scarf to the headboard.

Trevor didn't struggle or tug against the binding that time, his body going slack on the bed as soon as Finn had been placed in his hand. With the bears' fur to rub, his fingers stayed busy and let the rest of him relax.

My sweet, tactile little bear.

The lid coming off the crockpot drew Trevor's attention and he looked over to see what I was doing. Before I pulled the jar of blue wax from the water bath, I swirled it gently then placed my finger in it, confirming it hadn't gotten too hot while it melted. It was liquid but only warm. Dave had assured me the melting point was so low it wouldn't burn anyone as long as I didn't overheat the water, and he'd been right.

I lifted the jar out and wiped the water on the sheet before showing him what was in my hand. "It's a special sensory play body wax. Have you ever done anything with wax play?"

Trevor shook his head. Even looking for signs of nerves, I didn't see any. "Green." I hadn't asked his color, but I took that to mean he was up for trying it. He'd clearly taken the safewords talk seriously and if that was all he was going to give me, I'd roll with it.

In his line of sight, I poured a little on the inside of my forearm, the wax warm and reminding me of the massage oil some of the trainers used to dig into sore muscles. "It's warm. Like massage oil, but it dries hard." It had already dried on my skin, allowing me to peel it off and place it on his stomach. The muscles quivered under my touch and he giggled.

"I'm going to pour a little on your tummy."

He nodded, excitement in his eyes as he watched the jar rise above his skin and me begin to pour from it slowly. The first contact drew a surprised gasp from his lips and I paused for a second, making sure he wasn't going to tell me it was too hot. He didn't say anything, and when I poured just a bit more out, he let out a contented hum. I focused along the firm lines of his abs, directing the wax into the deep grooves of the muscles and watching his stomach flutter as it rolled down his body. Pouring just a little more heavily toward his chest, the wax began to pool and drip over his sides, some drops drying to his rib cage, others dripping onto the old sheet below him.

Trevor wiggled and bucked his hips each time I stopped or started the wax, sometimes tugging at the scarves that held him. With a good base of blue across his torso, I placed the jar back into the water. The light splash had Trevor's eyes shooting open. "No. More."

Chuckling to myself, I removed the next jar, a vibrant pink, and held it up. "Don't worry, baby, I've got no plans of stopping right now."

He blew out a relieved breath as though my stopping would have truly pained him. He was so responsive, I knew we'd be doing this again. In the future, I'd introduce him to other items, maybe some of the knives or the pinwheel, and see how the various sensations would send him higher and higher.

When the pink hit his chest, he didn't react as strongly as he had with the initial pour of blue wax. The gasp was more of a sharp inhale, the hum that followed longer and more pleasured. He writhed and wriggled below me, each movement accompanied by small grunts or pleas for more.

As I layered wax onto him, I discovered he liked the heat against his nipples, moaning loudly and tugging against his restraints each time I drizzled wax over them. His lower stomach was more ticklish than pleasurable. After the third flinch and giggle, I avoided anything from his belly button down.

By the time I grabbed the red wax, Trevor looked like a canvas. Blue, pink, green, and orange had mixed and pooled across his entire torso and dripped down his sides. The drips on his sides reminded me of the canvases with melted crayons, and the swirls and pools on his stomach looked like an expensive acrylic artwork, both perfectly fitted for Trevor.

He rocked his hips, his cock moving against the material of the diaper with each movement. He'd been consistently grinding, but I'd noticed the movements had become more frantic the longer he lay there. I knew he was getting close, he'd been hard for nearly an hour, and I knew he was skirting the edge of subspace.

He wriggled less as I added the red wax, his moaning turning into heavy breathing, and he stopped tugging against the restraints. The only thing he'd said in the last five minutes had been a whispered "Green" when I'd switched between the orange and red. The only movement was his hips grinding into the padding of the diaper.

When Trevor didn't react to me placing the wax back into the crockpot and turning the machine off, I knew he was on the edge of subspace. If he hadn't been grinding his hips as furiously as he was, I'd have thought he'd already reached it. The wax had hardened already and I hoped the thick coating would help me peel it off his smooth skin more easily. Little trickles and lines were a nightmare and often took a shower with a loofah to remove everything, but that would be a problem later me would have to deal with.

A sudden movement or unexpected touch could ruin the moment for him, so I cautiously touched his stomach. The hardened wax prevented him from feeling the touch, but he clearly felt the pressure of my hand. His eyes fluttered open, a rosy hue on his cheeks and a lust-drunk smile on his face.

"Hey there, Trev. You ready to come?"

He exhaled, the sound coming out more like a groan, and he nodded his head. I didn't need words, the nod was enough, and I moved my hand to the front of his diaper.

The bulk of the material did nothing to hide how hard he was, and even before I touched him, I could see the outline of his erection through the padding. When I placed my hand above his dick, providing pressure to the front of his diaper, he groaned loudly and ground his cock against me.

"That's it, Trev. Make yourself come for me, make yourself feel good." I pressed my hand more firmly against the padding and Trevor rocked again and again, whimpers and pants that made him sound as desperate as he looked.

Pushing my hand against his diaper, I wrapped my fingers around the outline of his erection and moved my hand in time with his thrusts. Trevor's mouth parted, a groan quickly turning to a shout as his entire body tensed. I felt his dick pulse in my hand, a spurt of cum appearing above the waistband of his diaper.

When the spasms stopped, Trevor collapsed onto the bed completely wrung out and his eyes closed almost immediately. We'd been playing for nearly an hour. It was no surprise he'd crashed hard after a powerful release like that one.

My job turned from giving him pleasure the likes of which he hadn't known he'd been missing, to caring for my spent sub. The first order of business was untying his hands, an easy job that only took a light tug to the end of each scarf for the knot to unfurl and his hands to fall free.

He didn't move his arms from where they fell, giving me plenty of time to begin the cleanup process with the wax. Thankfully, it came off in large sheets, the multiple layers making it easier to remove, just as I'd hoped.

Trevor was still out of it, not reacting to much as I used a warm cloth dipped in baby oil to loosen the more persistent pieces of dried wax. I worked quickly, trying to minimize disruptions but also desperate to have my body wrapped around him when he finally stirred.

The last order of business was the diaper. He wasn't quite as asleep as he'd appeared, helping to lift his hips and adjust slightly as I cleaned him with another cloth and ran it over his stomach and sides, removing the oil before wiping his lower belly, dick, and balls. With his skin clean and dry, I secured another diaper around him and helped guide his head and arms into the soft onesie and secured it between his legs. Trevor had helped just enough to make the process successful but hadn't moved more than absolutely needed.

With him finally cleaned and dressed, I slid behind him, my dick frustrated that I hadn't paid it more attention. It could wait. What I really wanted was to snuggle my boyfriend and be there for him when he finally decided to rejoin the world of the living.

Trevor curled into my chest, allowing me to grab the bottle and tease his lips with the water. He opened readily, then clamped his mouth around the nipple to suck vigorously, the water disappearing faster than I thought possible. He'd earned the drink, having expended a ton of energy whether he'd known it or not. Watching him drain the bottle, I was thankful I'd grabbed a sippy cup as well. It would be needed before long.

He sucked air just minutes after he'd started. Before I could pull the nipple away to replace it with his sippy cup, Trevor's eyes fluttered open and he gave me a sleepy smile. "That was intense."

I purposely kept my voice soft as I responded. "It was. And you were perfect."

If he'd had more energy, I was pretty sure a blush would have spread across his cheeks, but he was still a little foggy. "I came," he said, sounding surprised that he had.

My head nodded. "You did. You came hard."

"It feels weird. I wanted to come so much, but I've never been sexual when I'm in my little space. Even if I get hard, I don't want release."

I could understand why the feeling was confusing to him. "I understand that. From what I've read, there are a lot of littles like that. Correct me if I'm wrong, but I didn't get the impression you were feeling very little through that."

Trevor blinked. He was trying to focus on my words, but I knew he was still more fuzzy than functioning. He finally shook his head. "I guess I didn't *feel* all that little. It wasn't like I'd wanted to play, and for the most part, my brain kept thinking you were Brax more than Daddy."

It was interesting to know what he'd been thinking. I hoped one day he'd tell me more, but for now the most important thing was addressing his current hang-up. "That's what I thought. You were my submissive more than my little. Diapers are new for you. It was a new sensation, just like the wax and the scarves. I thought that by introducing you to them this way, it would give you a chance to get some of the uncertainties out of the way without tying them to your little side."

He hummed as I spoke. "That makes sense. I liked that. It was constant contact on my dick, constant stimulation, but so was the wax. The scarves too. They kept pulling my attention from one thing to another, like my body didn't know what to focus on."

I chuckled. "That was the idea. I didn't want you to focus on any one thing. I wanted to give you many sensations."

He adjusted in my arms so that he was looking directly at me and smiled. "Well, thank you. It was perfect. I liked it and you made it perfect."

I leaned forward and kissed him softly. "I mean it. You're perfect," I said against his lips. Pulling back just enough that I could make out his beautiful eyes, I ran a finger down his cheek. "I love you, Trevor. I love you as my boyfriend, as my little, as my friend, as my teammate. I'm so happy you gave me the chance, trusted me enough to give you this."

He burrowed his face against my chest for a moment, then finally pulled back to smile up at me. "Thank you for not giving up on me. Thank you for waiting. I know this isn't where you saw yourself or how you saw me when you first moved in, but you've made me feel more like myself than I ever have before. You make me feel safe. Boston was a bunch of idiots for trading you. They had no idea how amazing you are, but I think it worked out in the end."

Angling his chin upward, he hinted at needing a kiss. I gladly obliged and let it linger until he pulled back to yawn. "And I love you. I love you as my Daddy and my boyfriend." He yawned again, that time his thumb making it to his mouth. "Need sleep."

"Sleep, little bear. I'll be here when you wake up."

He made a contented noise and drifted off against my chest. One thing I could say with certainty—the trade from Boston to Nashville was the best thing that had ever happened to me. Not only did I get a team that valued me, I got a boyfriend who cherished me, and I felt the same about him.

# EPILOGUE

## TREVOR

6 Months Later

"Ozols, you're in net. First line: Cane, Johnson, Wojtek, Hämäläinen, Cernak," Cunningham said, reading off a list of lines for game three of the second round of the playoffs. We were so fucking close we could taste it. We'd been here repeatedly, and we were up two games to one against our friends Tampa.

Brax's head shot over to me, and he pointed to himself in shock. "*Me?* He said *Cernak*, right?"

I chuckled lightly and elbowed him. "Yes, now shut up so we can listen."

Brax stopped talking, but his mouth remained hanging open in shock while Coach listed off the rest of the lines. Brax had been traded to us as a third line forward, capable of hard hits when it counted. Over the months, he'd proven that he was more than muscle as time after time he'd found the net in flashy, fantastic ways.

He was still trying to teach me the lacrosse shot he'd become known for, but I was hopelessly terrible at it.

Over and over again, he'd been called up to the second line, especially when Coach was trying to shake things up. Then, about two months earlier, he'd found himself a regular on the second line, starting a few games here or there when needed. Two nights earlier, he'd had the game of his life with three shots on goal, two assists, and a goal. It wasn't a surprise to me that Coach was looking to bring that level of energy back. Brax had clearly not felt the same and was shocked at the announcement.

I was more surprised that Coach had chosen Igor for the net. He had been mostly a relief goalie for Yuri all season, only starting in a few games. Having Igor start was an interesting choice, one I wasn't sure why Coach had chosen. Not that Igor wasn't a phenomenal goalie, because he was. Maybe it was just the shake-up and a hope to rattle Tampa.

"Okay, guys," Coach said, finished listing off the lines. "You've played hard, last game got dirty. Keep your heads up, protect yourselves. Do not turn your backs. I don't want stupid injuries. Play a clean game, keep penalties down. You know they're going to try to force penalties, don't bite."

A murmur of agreement went through the room. We'd all seen it the last game—and every single one we'd played against them since I'd been traded to Nashville. The bad blood was longer running than any of us had been on the team but, like a family feud that lingered long after the reason for the argument was forgotten, it persisted.

I stood up, my turn to take the floor and give a quick speech. "This series is far from over. We've got three down, we're facing at least two more, and then there's two more rounds after this. Don't get cocky now. We've got the drive. We've got the skill. It's a mental game, a game of desire and heart. Keep that fire burning."

My glove brushed absently against my jaw. A subtle bruise had bloomed under my slight playoff beard after taking an elbow jab the last game. The bruise wasn't what I was thinking about, though. I was thinking about the kisses Daddy had given me in the hotel room afterward. Making sure I was snuggled in a comfortable bed, he kissed every bruise and sore spot on my body before sinking his cock deep into my ass, making me forget all the aches and pains I'd been dealing with.

Brax stepped in front of me before I got back to my bench. This was the last time that any of us would look human for the next three hours. In a few minutes, we'd be drenched in sweat with our hair plastered to our heads under our helmets. We'd have red marks from padding by the end of the first period that would only grow throughout the rest of the game. But that hadn't happened yet and Brax was standing in front of me looking all kinds of sexy in his home uniform, Finn tucked under his arm.

"Ready to do this thing, linemate?"

His disbelief as Coach had called out the lines had been cute. It had also faded rapidly. He was now all smiles and sexy confidence.

"Kiss! Kiss! Kiss! Kiss!" The chant started quietly but grew in intensity until my ears were hot with embarrassment. Brax stuck his middle finger in the air as he leaned forward and captured my mouth with his.

I should have been used to it by now. This had been a tradition since we'd cinched the last playoff spot in our division. Brax had kissed me short and sweet before the game had begun. Igor had seen it happen and became all too excited to call for a kiss before the next game.

Despite losing more than a few games since, it had become a pre-puck-drop tradition that made me equal parts giddy and embarrassed. I wasn't going to turn down the opportunity to kiss Brax, but the eyes on me still made me bashful.

Or maybe my embarrassment was due to the way I inevitably hummed with pleasure each time he kissed me and I knew the entire room could hear me.

Brax's lips pulled back before I was able to stop overthinking, leaving me to chase them in hopes of getting a kiss I could remember. He laughed but humored me and I hummed predictably, drawing laughter from the team and me.

The light mood lasted until our skates hit the ice and reality sank in. We were starting game four and we were going to need to channel every last reserve of energy we'd been saving. This was the longest playoff streak the Grizzlies had ever had. We were still a long shot to win the Stanley Cup, but we were going to have fun trying.

In the third period, deep in Tampa's zone, Brax got slammed against the boards. The crash sent him to the ice and my heart racing to a different level. His body hadn't fully settled on the ice and he was scrambling up. For a split second time had stopped for me. "Go! Go!" I could hear him screaming as I caught up and flew by them, the puck on my stick but just barely. A shoulder leaned into me, pushing me off balance and the puck skittering across the ice.

"Fuck!" I heard Toby scream as he adjusted course, he and Yawney rushing back toward our zone as they chased the breakaway by Tampa.

Brax skated to the bench, Jean-Luc jumping over the boards to take his place. He joined Hämäläinen and me as we raced to catch up with the others. If I'd thought time stood still when Brax got hit, it was nothing compared to watching a breakaway barreling toward our netminder.

For all the teasing we gave the goalies, they had nerves of steel, and watching him crouch as he followed the puck side to side, tracking the movements with intense focus, was both beautiful and terrifying. He was focusing so hard on the puck, he didn't see what I could. "Move!" I bellowed a fraction of a second too late.

Tampa's player crashed into Igor, dropping his shoulder to deliver a punishing blow that sent Igor flat on his ass, a whistle blowing even before Igor's head hit the ice. Chaos once again reigned on the ice as Toby and Yawney pushed and shoved at the man who had just leveled our goalie. Brax pushed another Tampa player back who tried to pull Yawney away. Any thoughts I had of checking on Igor were gone when a player came rushing at me, pressing my back against the boards with his gloves already off.

"Don't have to worry about your boyfriend this time."

*Gatzenburg.* At least this time I had a chance to finish the fight he'd started nearly six months earlier. He landed a blow to my helmet before I'd shaken my gloves off. What he hadn't accounted for was my size. A full eleven inches shorter than him, I was more agile and able to slide out of his grip despite the punishing blow he'd landed. And I was able to take advantage of his momentary confusion as I landed a blow to his left side.

"Hell no!" He swung around to hit me again, but on open ice, he didn't get much more than a slight purchase on my helmet, sending it backward and off my head.

I landed another two blows to his ribs, harder than I normally would land a punch in a fight at the boards. "That's for the cheap shot last time." As I pulled back to hit him again, a big hand stopped me.

"Enough, LB." Brax's tone meant business. "Do not stoop to his level."

Gatzenburg spit onto the ice. "Boyfriend saves your ass again."

Skating back to the bench, chest heaving, I noticed Yuri looking paler than normal as he suited up, replacing his Grizzlies ballcap with his goalie helmet. "Igor does not look good. He has pain in his head and groin."

I'd only barely seen the fall. From what I had seen, I wouldn't be surprised if he'd pulled something in his groin. His head wasn't going to feel good for a few days either. At the very least, I knew he'd be on concussion protocol for the next few games. At worst, his season was over due to a cheap shot.

"Number twelve, Tampa, five minutes, goaltender interference!" The ref called from center ice. "Number seventeen, Tampa, unsportsmanlike conduct." He continued to list off penalties, most of which went to Tampa, but we still ended up with Yawney and Toby in the box and Igor in the training room.

We finished the last six minutes of the game on autopilot. The last-minute goal by Toby that snuck through the Tampa goaltender's legs should have been enough to have us celebrating, but we were too exhausted to do more than hug Yuri before heading off to the locker room.

Yuri came in last, cursing in Russian as he stripped his pads off in record time, hell-bent on finding out his best friend's status.

Brax looked over at me. "You okay? Gatzenfuck's a fuck."

I chuckled, leaning into my boyfriend. "I'm fine. I'll be fine. Do you think that was just talk, or do you think others know?"

He didn't answer immediately, instead thinking for a moment before he shrugged. "I honestly don't know. Would it bother you if they did find out?"

"No." My giggle surprised me more than the immediate response had. To emphasize my point, I shook my head. "No. It wouldn't bother me. I'd tell the world." I reached up on the tips of my blades and kissed Brax in the middle of the locker room, not caring who was there or if any members of the press might be milling around.

Brax wrapped his arms around me and lifted me up. "I love you, LB."

"Love you too."

"Aww, you two are so sweet," Seth said, his voice coming out as a dreamy sigh.

Maz slung an arm over his boyfriend's shoulder. "Still not coming out as boldly as Seth did."

Brax set me down to push at Maz's shoulders. "Not everyone can be as fabulous as your boyfriend. Besides, this is more fitting for us."

I looked up at the men around us. "This team is going to get some playoff complex if we keep having guys come out like this."

While everyone laughed, Brax leaned in. "Get changed fast. After post game, I have a surprise for you at home." He winked over his shoulder as he headed toward the shower, leaving me wondering what plans he had and knowing that I would spend the rest of my life excited to figure out how he was going to surprise me next.

~*~

BEFORE YOU GO: Pick up the bonus scene with Trevor's playdate with Derek here. https://readerlinks.com/l/2479267

**INSANITY IS FALLING for your best friend when you're straight...** Preorder *Scored, Nashville Grizzlies book*

2 today to be the first to read Yuri and Igor's story when it releases in August 2022! https://readerlinks.com/l/2479201

As with all my books, I'm terrible at saying goodbye to characters, so here is a list of the books whose characters were mentioned in Traded.

**Derek and Colt**: *At Home, Finding Home Book 1* It was only supposed to be one night of fun, but neither of them can shake the connection they felt. When the opportunity for a repeat presents itself, it's impossible to pass up. And in the end, a lost little might meet the Daddy he's never known he needed. Pick up *At Home* here. https://readerlinks.com/l/2479052

**Seth and Mazdon**: *Seth, Johnson Family Rules Book 3* An anonymous hookup at a party, no names exchanged, no details disclosed. No sexy, secret lingerie stashes at risk, no hearts on the line. If it were only that simple. When Mazdon discovers his mysterious Pretty is his teammate, Seth Johnson, the fallout could destroy everything they've worked to build. Pick up *Seth* here. https://readerlinks.com/l/2479051

# A NOTE FROM CARLY

Dear Reader,

Thank you so much for picking up *Traded*. Trevor and Brax's story flowed so easily and I swear I could have written another 30k words of their book without blinking an eye. While I know many of you wouldn't have complained, I also know that there are some really impatient players who want their stories told!

Hockey is a passion of mine, I have three kids who play and spend hours, days, and weeks at hockey rinks. My schedule literally is filled with hockey practices, games, or scrimmages. If I'm not carting a kid to a practice or game, I'm heading up to watch the Cleveland Monsters—our local AHL team—play! Summer is a weird time where the only things I have planned are hockey camps and sometimes go weeks between ice time. I honestly can't imagine what a professional hockey player feels like at the end of a season!

I truly hope you enjoyed reading Trevor and Brax's book as much as I enjoyed writing it. These guys are so near and dear to my heart that I know they are going to show up again and again.

Please take a few minutes to leave a review of *Traded*, as an independent author, reviews are invaluable. Even a short review can help others find my books. Thank you again for reading *Traded*. If you haven't already, make sure to download the bonus scene here.

Peace, Love, and Happy Reading,

Carly

# ABOUT THE AUTHOR

Carly Marie has had stories, characters, and plot bunnies bouncing around in her head as long as she can remember. Today, she is a USA Today Bestselling author, lover of all things romance, and avid reader.

Carly spends her days writing sweet, kinky stories about men who love each other and her nights as a wife, mother, and chauffeur. She spends far too much time reading books, in hockey rinks or driving between them, and far too little time cleaning her house.

Carly lives in Ohio with her husband, four kids, three cats, and has lost count of the number of chickens in the backyard. The numerous plot bunnies that run through her head on a daily basis ensure that she will continue to write and share her stories for years to come.

Keep up to date on all the latest by following me at:

**Mailing List**: https://www.subscribepage.com/r0o1q8

**Website**: www.authorcarlymarie.com

- instagram.com/carlymariewrites
- amazon.com/author/carlymarie
- bookbub.com/authors/carly-marie
- goodreads.com/CarlyMarieWrites